VIA Folios 175

The Tomb of the Divers

THE TOMB
OF THE DIVERS

Francine Masiello

BORDIGHERA PRESS

All rights reserved. Parts of this book may be reprinted only by written permission from the author, and may not be reproduced for publication in book, magazine, or electronic media of any kind, except in quotations for purposes of literary reviews by critics.

© 2024, Francine Masiello

Cover image: "The Tomb of the Diver," National Archaeological Museum of Paestum. Photo: Michael Johanning. Wikimedia Commons. https://commons.wikimedia.org/wiki/File:PaestumTaucher.jpg.

Library of Congress Control Number: 2024942022

Published by
BORDIGHERA PRESS
John D. Calandra Italian American Institute
25 W. 43rd Street, 17th Floor
New York, NY 10036

VIA Folios 175
ISBN 978-1-59954-223-2

Table of Contents

The Narrators — 13

I. Basilicata — 26

The Narrators — 83

II. Paterson — 89

The Narrators — 159

III. Naples–New York — 170

The Narrators — 236

IV. New York–Buenos Aires — 241

Coda — 288

Author's Note — 294
Acknowledgments — 303
About the Author — 305

For Sandro Signorelli Manoleas
And his fondness for stories

I am a man in transit.
—ROCCO SCOTELLARO

But the common error was to believe that everything could be transformed into poetry and words.
—NATALIA GINZBURG

The Narrators

Lanky, tall Max Cósimo always thought in dactyls. He began with his Italian surname, displayed as a breach of the norm. Long-short-short, long-short-short: ál-pha-bet, pó-e-try. And Cósimo! The name belonged to big shots—popes, dukes, soccer stars, even a boxer who, after he had stolen the Golden Cup, quickly rose to fame. Cósimo, stress the first /o/ that you hear. Bíbbidi-bóbbidi-bú.

"This is hot," Max said to whoever cared to listen. "Not everyone has the benefit of a name alluding to planets or the fun of nonsensical sound."

He was pleased by his range of wisdom.

"We're masters of the universe," Max laughed. At first, Max thought that he had no talent for literature and even less for poetic meter; he liked television dramas, cop shows, spy films about 007, *Star Wars* with Harrison Ford. Over the years, his self-confidence grew. He read the classics, he thought about language, and he realized he had a good ear. He picked out the notes of the most popular songs and, from this, he even made a few bucks in those weekly "Name that Tune" contests held at Lefty O'Doul's. Especially in contrast to his older sister, Max thought, he stood out as nearly a genius.

Yeah, Max had to deal with his tangled-haired, chain-smoking sibling who, by miracle of God, had been accepted to college. Worse still, she was taking a class in creative writing and had begun to call herself an author. None of her poems made much sense, he mused as he read her lines typed in blue: she didn't care about the ways your breath guided words on the page; she didn't notice the effects of sound or rhythm that made you want to jump up from your chair. She only wanted a finished poem printed with blue-inked ribbon. She called it poetry in the clouds. Blue on white, didja get it?

"God help me," Max said as he reached for the Schlitz buried in the depths of the fridge. "And now Rosanna is writing a novel." Max rolled his eyes and looked up at the fluorescent tube that flickered over the kitchen table.

His sister was nuts—no great promise as a scholar, even less as an author. But she was rebelling against their parents, who pressed Rosanna beyond her limits and made sure she didn't let up. "Be a lawyer, make some money! Get a job with the city!" Sensible recommendations to their maturing girl. By choosing to study literature, she'd found a way to brush them off.

Rosanna walked into the kitchen and grabbed a cigarette from the pack on the table. With the princess approaching, Max knew royal theater was about to start.

"A suffering, obsessive lot of complainers who never took a chance on life; everyone knew them for who they were," Rosanna said inhaling the menthol flavor of Newports. As soon as she had her brother's attention, she raised her voice. "Suspicious of the world outside, distrustful of what was vaguely different, Rosie and Donato never ventured beyond the clan; they kept their circle small."

"Maybe they were afraid of the risks." Max punctuated his observation with a beer-induced burp. Brother and sister entered each other's minds as if no membrane existed between them.

"Stop living in the past," he added.

The siblings didn't really hate their parents, they agreed, but saw them for who they were. They were especially sympathetic to their father's bad lot in life. Chumped along the way, he'd been the patsy for some wise guys who'd once taken Donato for a ride. Years ago, they'd tossed him to the police much in the way the seasoned fishermen threw their catch on the planks of a Hudson pier. A fall guy. Their father had never really recovered from the experience no matter how hard he tried.

Under the shadow of family disaster, Max had grown up without ambition. He used to tinker with machinery in the family's shoe repair store; he rewired fixtures and lamps; he knew how to use a plunger.

All this under orders of Donato, who was determined to make his son useful. Rosie was the household's efficiency manager, but her plans were often waylaid. With those thieving relatives always lurking around, asking for favors at every turn, she found it tough to impose tight order over her tiny domestic space. Lots of movement, few results, she thought. It took your breath away. So, in short, here was the picture: Rosie, Donato, Rosanna, Max, the dysfunctional American family. Brother and sister, though joined at the hip, held each other in mild contempt.

Rosanna never came to terms with her brother's wayward habits. She saw him squirming from under the thumb of their father, resisting all calls to order. He refused the conventional path, Donato had said, oozing hurt through his words. Donato wanted a son who fit in, a man who would climb the greasy social pole and claim the city as his own. Fantasies, of course, because Max never complied. He refused to study; he flatly rejected the dreams that had oiled Donato's aspirations. Max needed to be bad. True, he didn't turn to the gangs—no Fordham Baldies mix-ups, no ties to the Golden Guineas. That was Bronx stuff, and Donato had dragged his boy away from all that, having abandoned the family's Bronx two-bedroom for a safer place in Inwood. Donato, along with Rosie, clung to hopes for the family's conquest. No mob nearby, nothing crooked—simply play by the rules. Max, however, was ornery, always somewhat itchy. He was fed up with his father's moralizing and his mother's micro-control. He staged his displeasure at school. Quickly he discovered that he knew things that his classmates couldn't grasp. His reading ability surpassed that of the most talented students; he was quick in language and history, yet he refused to compete with the others and eventually failed all his subjects. Only at home did Max torture his sister with endless lectures and never miss the chance to remind her of her own limitations.

This evening, as Max blathered on, never giving up his right to lecture, Rosanna listened with half an ear. Standing by the kitchen counter, she grabbed the dented Moka Express to load its filter with three scoops of coffee. Here it comes again, she thought, Max and Rosanna in battle. They couldn't agree on a thing. She considered herself a girl moving up in the world, taking lit courses in college while he couldn't even get himself started. She set the espresso pot on the stove and considered her brother's failures. To be honest, she thought, she also had to acknowledge his talents.

It's true, Max was often found with a book in his hand. He often stole a few of her books from her pile on the kitchen table. He claimed Yeats was easy to remember; he cited the Modernist poets. Nevertheless, Rosanna reminded herself, Max was hardly a scholar. He refused to sit in a classroom. No college awaited his presence.

"That's for dullards," he told her. "Sheep, bruisers, and party clowns running amok on a campus. Better to find a more prosperous route."

Plumbing and auto repair, skills he had learned in high school shop didn't grab him. Here Rosanna remembered some key episodes in her brother's work career: when Uncle Nunzio had suggested waiting on tables downtown, Max became indignant. "No way," he'd yelled. No taking orders from uppity women, ladies whose hair swelled like straw balloons, ladies who lunched with anorexia on their minds, their toothpick legs in support hose.

"No way," he'd screamed to anyone within range. "No table treatment for the Upper East Side dames who treat me like the help. Simply not for me."

Max had tried waiting tables in the Bronx at a joint called Stella D'Oro's; Donato had found him the job. He'd quit within three weeks. Too much of that Italian stuff, Max had explained. He had no interest in ethnic nostalgia. However, when an Irish buddy lined up weekend work at the golf course, Max had leapt at the chance. The work was easy enough, driving a cart and picking up balls. To his advantage, the hours were never steady, so Max was still basically free to do as he pleased.

* * * *

Rosanna was a few years older; she'd come of age when the old neighborhood was changing from one in which nerdy schoolgirls carried tiny violins back and forth from Mrs. Gersh's studio to a barrio where a parade of beauty queens swayed their hips to the beat of merengue. After a brief stint at the School of Good Shepherd in the early grades, Rosanna had transferred to public school at her mother's insistence. Her mother had said that the price was right, and no one had to foot the tuition to hear the word of God. In an instant, Rosanna's world had changed from the solemnity of Irish caution to an ongoing Caribbean street fest combined with Jewish chutzpah. In high school, Rosanna learned Spanish.

"If she's reading, she must be Cuban," a smart aleck had remarked when he observed Rosanna with book in hand as she rode downtown on the A train.

Rosanna loved the outside world. It was gritty and exuberant in a way that her family was not. Chopping it up in two languages, on the cusp of learning a third or a fourth, Rosanna liked the tussle between people, faiths, and culture. The Jews and Irish in the postwar years took charge of the tones in the hood and, after the 1960s, the Dominicans claimed Washington Heights as their own. Donato and Rosie were sandwiched in between, not unlike their children. But if Donato and Rosie had felt like outsiders, recalling their intact lives downtown, their children, by contrast, had jumped into the mix that was becoming New York at the time. Whatever remained of their Italian identity slid quickly into the muck.

In the years that he'd lived in upper Manhattan, Max heard the language changing. At first, the elderly housewives had prayed to Jesus in Connacht accent while the retired cops and garbage collectors yacked it up in the County Cork brogue. In recent times, the men who were close to the Emerald Green went to the pubs not only for Guinness and whiskey but also to throw cash in the kitty to help Ireland out of the Troubles. Even the teenagers who wore the jackets of the Irish Knights or Manhattan Shamrocks, gangs that were really drinking clubs more than a bunch of no gooders, knew about Sinn Fein and the visit of Ruairí Ó Brádaigh to meet with Congressman Tip O'Neill. Keeping this all together, Lefty O'Doul's and Molly Bloom's taverns were buddy affairs, places to draw the strapping young men who felt the call of the Celtic Ailm.

The Irish kids went to Catholic school, directed by their working-class parents. Whole families remained in a world that once was and struggled with a promise that they had found in their Gaelic past. So if the Jewish kids were reading *Call It Sleep* at JHS 52, the Irish kids from St. Raymond's tried to make sense of *Dubliners* (often to the stern reserve of the nuns' disapproving the headmaster's literature choices). Meanwhile—and here she prided herself on her youthful independence—Rosanna claimed to have found her voice in the comic strip *Dondi*, a tale about an Italian war orphan who eventually makes good. In the lower grades, she'd used it as prima facie evidence to prove to her fellow students that Italians held a place in public not under the thumb of the mob. Little Max had laughed at her naiveté even in those years. Grown up, Max sought his pleasures through Irish poems and fiction, and tried to use his ears and eyes as a way to travel the world.

"Oh, just let me get out of the house and taste the music scene downtown," Max said to his sister when he was barely sixteen. "You know that I have phony ID to get into the Village Gate."

"Breaking the law just for the fun of it," Rosanna snipped.

Following the sounds of late-night music, Max puffed up with self-satisfaction when some of the musicians said that they admired his sense of rhythm. But his sister wouldn't understand. By day, he walked through the neighborhood blocks to find his body awash in sound: with fewer Italians, Irish, and Jews, the streets acquired a different flavor. The Dominican arroz-con-pollo joints replaced the delis. Gone as well were the Gaelic gift shops and the Jewish bakeries selling rugelach and black-and-white cookies.

Max was now in Quisqueya Heights, where his untutored Spanish was good enough to order simple food from the bodega, to call for the midnight cab service, and to speak with the super about the roaches. The sounds of cumbia, salsa, and merengue rose from the parklet nearby: Wilfrido Vargas singing off the boom box "Duarte, que tristeza olvidarte;" the barking voices blaring from Chevy pickups that advertised local check-cashing joints where they never asked for ID. "Vengan todos a la casa de cambio, bajo porcentaje pa' tí." Max added the "pa' tí" to keep the rhythm. A cumbia in formation. One two, one two, step to the side and swing around, push your partner to the left as you move right. Show off your steps in royal-blue shoes. "Sabor," Celia Cruz sang out while Max imagined her smile extending from ear to ear. Spanish was like that. "Ven-gan To-dos." Very different from English. "Come on in," a recorded voice announced in flat and even stress; "Vengan todos" was another story. Let yourself dance. Do the boogaloo. Be my salsera, baby. Uno-dos merengue. Uno-dos vallenato.

"I got it," Max said when he burst into the family's apartment after a day and night on the street. "I found the neighborhood groove."

Max kept his eye on the Trocadero, a basement dance hall that had been around since the 1940s, when the Irish, who were then the neighborhood bosses, had held grand weddings on Saturday nights. Two flights below the street, paradise opened; a ballroom of the kind you might see downtown. Elegant, polished, sparkling, a silver-mirror disco ball suspended on a swivel from the dance-floor ceiling. Now salsa bands blared as gorgeous couples dressed to the nines descended to the party downstairs. "Era una pareja plástica de ésas que veo por ahí." In either case, Irish or Dominican, the codes were deep and steady. When you arrived, you went down the stairs sober; when you left, you climbed up sloshed and wasted. Max often went to these dances, but he never had a date.

Rosanna noted that Max knew how to head off the wise guys; he knew how to stay out of trouble. Yes, Max was cautious; he had learned it from his father. After that bad experience many years ago when he'd spent a stretch in the clinker, Donato refused to let his family live life on the edge, one in which thugs came around to demand cash favors for one excuse or another.

"We don't do that," Donato repeated to Max, though he knew that the family ethic was muddled. "We keep our nose clean."

Donato closed his eyes and remembered the family signpost. "Trust no one, not even your family. And take care not to misbehave."

Donato shoved this lesson down Max's throat, and for the time his son complied.

* * * *

"Max never studied," Rosanna complained to her BF Sylvia when they both entered the literature program at City College. "Yet he still knows more than me. It's worse when he starts with his literary stuff—it really attacks my core."

Never having finished college (never starting, let's be clear), Max devoured the classics. He took pride in his knowledge of the avantgarde, he loved the syntax of modern poets, he avidly consumed the Irish bards as a summa of difficult writing. Rosanna was humbled when she shared these last thoughts with Sylvia and then, in a move to regain her composure, she noted that her brother's situation was simply irredeemably bad.

"Max is a flop," she offered, covering up her envy.

"I don't get it," Sylvia said. "If you think he's a failure, why do you mind his words? You listen to him night after night as if he held the keys to the kingdom."

Rosanna withdrew into silence. "Yeah," she mumbled under her breath. "I let his words draw me in; I let him tell me what's wrong with my thinking. I even let him edit my writing."

She admitted that Max was a better reader than she. It was her own fault that she allowed him to control each sentence she wrote. She told Sylvia about the novel she was trying to compose and how Max intervened on a regular basis to bug her.

"It's driving me crazy," Rosanna said, but she knew that Max was right when he pointed out her non sequiturs and her strings of flimsy ideas. It was a kind of suicidal surrender, she thought. At a time when all around her women were staging explosive gender wars that should have drawn her into the feminist fray, she—like an idiot—went home and asked to be punished.

* * * *

Back to the coffee, now bubbling on the stove. Here, Max told his sister that her tastes weren't the stuff of his world. He was interested in the grace of the phrase; she went toward melodrama and romance.

Always seeking the happy ending that follows any crisis, her perspective had its charms. Max had a different view.

"Let's face it," Max said as he remembered that his parents always praised his sister to the sky. "You're a product of the comics that you used to read in the tabloids."

True, as a schoolgirl, Rosanna had avidly read the stories of abandoned children picked up by American GIs on the Salerno coast. She'd loved her mother's childhood books that she'd guarded for many decades: the adventures by Salgari and the *Magical Land of Noom*. And the best, absolutely and unbiasedly the best, were the comic-strip adventures in *The Daily News* about the it-girl Brenda Starr. Her model for all aspirations, the girl she hoped to become.

"You can't launch a career from that," Max said.

Rosanna pursed her mouth. "Brenda, you will remember, was the star reporter of a Chicago paper, a sleuth and femme fatale. Brenda wasn't a wimp. She was sexy, breathless, full of adventure, a world-wide traveler. A gin-drinking gal like Rita Hayworth, she also had a brain. What's more, she had a boyfriend who usually lived in Brazil, though she couldn't win him over."

Max answered in falsetto, "The dark seductive stranger—tra la la—who held his cards close to his chest." He twirled around the room, then lowered his voice to a whisper. "A man who developed a serum for orchids that he cultivated in the Amazon basin, a man of utter control and discretion, who sported a patch on his eye."

Max turned again and noted his sibling-princess was tongue tied.

Recovering, she said, "Basil couldn't live a simple life. He needed nature, he needed expanses, and only on occasion did he confess that he needed a woman."

Max wasn't certain, but he thought he traced in his sister a steamy yet unnamed desire. Lust and heat filled the room, he thought, as his sister saw stars dancing around Brenda's bright, wide-open eyes. Alas, nothing happened.

"A crying shame," Rosanna said.

Max said it was too banal.

"The comic always concluded with Brenda's task of getting home safely; Brenda only regained peace of mind when she arrived in one piece in Chicago. Safe from men, safe from intrusion, eluding the dark world of crime. In the end, the good guys prevailed, and Brenda was secure in her bed." Only recently, when she'd taken literature courses under the brilliant Professor Fone, did Rosanna realize that her flame for melodrama had first been fanned by Brenda Starr.

* * * *

At college, Rosanna pursued a major in literature. At first, she landed in a program in Renaissance English. Then she decided to drop English from her course load and take classes in Romance Studies. Not only would she avoid the lecherous old sacks who never strayed from their notes on Milton, but she could also escape the nosy intrusions of her brother, who followed her every move. Her French wasn't very good, her Italian was barely passable, and her oral-aural Spanish needed considerable work, but here she was better than Max, she thought. In a superbly foolish stretch, she imagined that Max wouldn't spot her errors or correct the lines of her papers if she wrote in a foreign language.

However, on the sly, Max read her books and followed her courses; he even pierced through her hobbled Spanish or French without the slightest struggle.

"Nothing tasty here," he often said. "She can't break out of her rut. Worse still, with this novel she's writing, she can't find any fire."

* * * *

Tonight, Max scratched his neck, lit a cigarette, and took a swig of beer. Her novel asked its readers to be detectives, he offered. You had to put the pieces together in order to make sense of the whole. "Very elementary," he said. "The do-it-yourself novel. I think I've read that before."

Rosanna remained still, holding her anger. The espresso bubbling in its pot began to spill over. She moved toward the stove to extinguish the orange flames.

To provoke his sibling again, Max remarked that her novel continued her childhood attachments to the comic strip *Brenda Starr*. Nonetheless, Max was prepared to work on the text at their late-night kitchen meetings.

"Take out the word 'startling;' put in 'unreal.' I happen to like that word," said Max.

Rosanna snarled while her intestines curled into knots. Each time he corrected her word choice, she shriveled some more. All the same, she listened.

The siblings gathered under the fluorescent light. Espresso cups in hand, they took apart Rosanna's prose until there was nothing left of her words.

"First, you want a girlie novel. Always from the female perspective," Max said. "But stories aren't told like that. The man has to have full control."

"Where have you been, Mr. Know-it-all? Stop telling lies. And if my story starts with our great aunt Eugenia, it gives me pleasure."

* * * *

Tired of the verbal jousting, Rosanna withdrew from the table to put the empty espresso pot in the kitchen sink. She then disassembled the vessel under running water in order to tune out her brother's words. Coffee grounds splashed on the wall but, hardly noticing the mess, she continued scrubbing the pot. Leaving soap bubbles in the bottom kettle, she turned the device on its belly to dry. And then his awful voice flooded her ears.

"Housekeeping isn't your thing." Max said from his seat at the Formica table. He chuckled and recommended that she learn to reduce the disorder. "The muddle matches up with your book."

Rosanna chose to ignore the insults and pursue her task at the kitchen sink. With her back to her brother, she said, "Let's face the truth. It's been a long stretch of research and writing, and I don't need you to dismiss my project."

Max grinned as he listened to his sister's clumsy explanation. Silence reigned but for a click of Max's tongue.

"To explain the family story isn't a simple task for any beginning writer, but at least I took the chance." She looked at the spent tea bags and orange pips clogging the kitchen drain and guessed that the food disposal would never dissolve the mess.

"After all, it was more than a family story," she continued. Rosanna made no attempt to remove the slimy heap. She wanted to tell an immigrant tale without the heroic trappings. No stuff about how hard it had been when they first arrived in New York; no delusions about their honest labor and clean respect for the rules. No nostalgia, nothing sentimental. Facts only based on history. Experience in the raw. "It's a story written from the feeling of anger. An exposé of sorts. Another version of how they entered America one hundred years ago."

Max didn't appreciate the details. "Too much repetition; too many stories. You have to find a single thread."

Rosanna's eyes returned to the coffee grounds that clung to the glossy white paint. She tried to wipe the wall clean but ignored the waste in the drain. The roaches descending the heat riser at 4 am would certainly stop off for a few tasty treats, she thought, before they marched down to the baseboards where they'd get trapped in the tufts of steel wool Rosie had placed in the cracks.

Sponge in hand, she said, "That's exactly the point. It's not a single story. You can't reduce a century of actions to a single tale. It's a research project about a group of people who glide through the highpoints of history but never leave their stamp on the world."

"Look, big sis," her tyrannical sibling said. "You can't say everything. Make a choice. Find a story you like and stick to it. Forget all the research; just find the plot."

It was the usual situation: Max, the younger brother always convinced of his brilliance, was directing lessons to his sister as if to undermine her story.

Still holding the kitchen sponge, Rosanna stood somewhat indignant. "The wealth is in the tale, you dope, the wealth is in the lies. The Troiano clan was made of cheats and wise guys as far back as the late 1800s."

"And reaching down to our present day." Max then cut into his sister's story, he making sure to tell her which details wouldn't hold up in the long run. "Try to be subtle, if you know what I mean."

Rosanna wasn't happy to hear Max's directives. Once again, he was lord of the flies. "After all, it's *my* research, *my* feelings, *my* inventions, and, most of all, *my voice*." Her hope was that she might appease him. She just wanted him to give her a hand without stealing her text. But he was an impossible narcissist who wanted to claim her every thought. "No, we never knew what to believe; it wasn't clear who was right or wrong. But, as you know, their lives were interesting all the same. Sure, I needed to start with the family of old man Troiano who, in a nowhere town in the south of Italy, tried to keep his head above water. But I wanted to tell it from Eugenia's point of view." Following a weighty pause, she took a breath. "And I wanted to start at the turn of the century to show how the patterns emerged, to show how the drive to lie and deceive formed part of our family story. How it was written into our blood."

"Cheap family therapy." Max winked at his sister. "It really sounds like a way to avenge the ills of the father."

"You're crazy," Rosanna said. "Just keep your trap shut and listen."

I. Basilicata

1.

Eugenia lay awake at night listening to her father's nightmares. On the other side of a burlap curtain dividing the sleeping quarters, Raffaele Troiano twisted and turned. He huffed and puffed in the dark; he screamed out names and curses. Eugenia prayed to God that he wouldn't awaken. In the olden days, her siblings had filled all the cots on her side of the curtain. Antonio had slept with Carmelo; Maria Antonietta had shared a bed with Mariarosa; and she, Eugenia, the baby of the family, had had a sheep's wool pad all to herself. In recent years, the family changed: Antonio had been the first to cross the ocean; next, Maria Antonietta had married a grocer who moved her to Buenos Aires. Then her favorite siblings had just picked up and left—it seemed like the other day—and Eugenia felt abandoned. Carmelo, not caring much about fortune, had run off in search of his brother; and then Mariarosa, on her wedding day, had announced that she and her husband planned to sail to New York. Now alone on her side of the curtain, Eugenia fell into states of nightly dread.

Tonight in Bellanera, a village perched on a mountaintop somewhere in the far south of Italy, she was roused by the sound of her father thrashing. When he turned over and his snoring stopped, he began to shout out names and places lacking a common thread. Eugenia listened and tried to capture his random thoughts. In the first hours of the night, the old man yelled out the name of a peasant. "Go away, Gaspare," he begged as if to drive him off.

"Just three hundred more," he screamed. "Give me another week."
"Another fifty and we'll call it quits."
"Fifty!" he demanded in the darkest hours of night. "Ok, forty-five."

Eugenia assumed that the numbers referred to either the size of his debt or money that people owed him.

As she propped herself on her elbows, she heard a string of familiar names: Don Michele, the priest who lived up the road; don Ciccio, the farmer who allowed her pal Silvio to sleep in a shed with the livestock; Giovanni, the man who carried wood from the forest; Signora Gallo, the woman who brought bundles of wheat. Eugenia couldn't find a story that would link these names together. Did her father refer to his debtors? Had someone done her father wrong? Was a scandal set between traders and salesmen? Or had her father cheated his neighbors again, stealing their grain and livestock?

Eugenia, in the pitch-black night, admitted her despair. A girl of thirteen, she was sinking fast into gloom. Her mother, Rosina, was a passive person, always counting bills and coins while her father was up to no good. The neighbors said that her father had pulled the wool over the eyes of peasants. He often sold five-year-old hens to unsuspecting neighbors. He loaded sacks of grain with tiny stones to increase their weight. And his tavern—oh God, that awful barroom that he used to run with her brother Antonio long before Antonio packed up to leave—was a scene of massive deception; in truth, it gave her the creeps.

But the worst, and here she couldn't even pronounce the name of the crime, was when her father rose from his bed and crossed to her side of the curtain. There, he hovered over her cot and pressed his leathery hands on her thighs. It terrified Eugenia to hear her father's deep breathing and to feel his heavy hands. There was no tender father here, she thought; this was something else. Neither her siblings nor her classmates had prepared her for these intrusions. When her father came close to her bed at night, Eugenia tightened her eyes to pretend she was sleeping and prayed that her father would leave. Usually, he grunted some words of affection, placed his hands where he shouldn't, and returned to his bed. Then she lay awake all night, shivering from the effects of his visit. At times, she was so frightened she'd soiled her bed. On other occasions, she'd tiptoed outdoors to vomit. She always shook like a leaf. Afraid to tell her mother, she kept her fears to herself.

Eugenia knew that one day he would linger, and there'd be no way of turning him back. Of course, it had been better when her siblings were still at home. When they'd all slept together, her father had shown restraint (she hated him all the same). Yet as soon as the brothers and sisters had left, one after the other, she'd felt the household tip toward chaos. Though she had ill regard for Antonio, whom she saw as an unscrupulous character allied with her father in crime, and though she'd lost sight of Maria Antonietta, who had left so many years ago that her image now was faded, Eugenia nonetheless missed them. Most of all she longed for Carmelo, whom she saw as tender and loving, and she yearned for her sister Mariarosa, who was always of good heart and intention. Mariarosa had cuddled with her at night and had told her folktales about witches and demons. Carmelo had always admired her skill at art and reading; he'd joked that the baby of the family had become the family tutor. Without them, Eugenia felt alone.

In fact, she wished she could copy her older siblings and simply pull up and leave. For this, she'd first have to finish school and find a husband. She knew she was still too young. Girls her age couldn't run off. They needed to be accompanied by an elder and carry the blessings of God. She'd searched the town for similar tales about fathers and daughters, though she always maintained a proper image of herself, revealing no personal details. Meanwhile, the aunties told of Padre Michele, a priest who was known to pursue the young girls after the evening novenas. A few reported that Padre took his business to the nearby village, telling the townsfolk of Bellanera that he was off to expand God's mission. No one shared the details; no one said exactly what happened. A nervous Eugenia held on to her questions: Was this common in other households? Were all fathers alike? Eugenia slipped into a habitual silence. Eugenia, vibrant girl that she once was and leader in her class, was shrinking with the days, recoiling into the shadows. In truth, she trusted no one save her school chum Silvio. One day, she'd told him in secret that she'd like to see her father dead.

* * * *

This night, Eugenia found some good luck. Her father skipped his usual visit to his daughter's side of the curtain. Instead, he screamed out names in his sleep, causing Eugenia to sit up and listen.

"Macario! Zaffiro! Bandolero! Pay attention to what I command!"

Eugenia understood that he was calling out the names of horses that had been sheltered at don Ciccio's barn. Eugenia had learned the story from Silvio, who'd told her that three *trottatori* were among don Ciccio's herd. Overhearing the old man's conversations with farmhands, Silvio had figured out that the trotters belonged to a duke near the town of Venosa; they were considered pedigree stallions. The new harness tracks just outside of Naples had awakened a general fancy for studs, and the duke wanted part of the action. How they'd fallen into her father's hands was a mystery to those on the farm.

"Not a word to anyone!" Troiano had said to don Ciccio's workers when he'd shown up with the horses. "Not even a word to your wives."

Silvio, who'd heard this, had reported back to Eugenia, who'd said she wasn't surprised. Silvio had eventually told her that her father planned to sell the studs at auction, where they would bring in a handsome sum. Her father had even promised don Ciccio a nice cut of the profits. Eugenia remembered Silvio's words as she listened now to her father's sounds.

After her father called the horses, he then pounded his chest as if to excise an evil spirit. Eugenia rolled over and covered her ears with a sheet. Relieved that he hadn't come to bother her, she recalled his situation as if to trace his descent into crime.

* * * *

Raffaele Troiano began his working life among those hard-pressed souls who had chosen to work in a trade: stone masons, carpenters, and shoemakers all handy with awls and hammers. Then he linked up with the occasional merchant moving products from village to village throughout the Italian South. It wasn't easy feeding a family of seven, he used to complain. Food was scarce in Bellanera, the chickens sometimes refused to lay, and each year his sons couldn't pull more than a few boars from the once-thick forests nearby. Worse, he'd lost the clients who used to purchase his woodwork, and he rarely got a new contract.

Troiano gave his family lessons to promote honesty and understanding. He explained the nature of their land, a southern territory so deeply impoverished that no one could thrive and prosper, let alone prepare a full meal. He wanted to impress upon his wife and children the need to stay ahead of the landlords and escape the lot of the peasants. Troiano had no streak of rebellion in those years. He wasn't about to join his neighbors in plundering towns and murdering dukes. No, he explained to his wife and children: the time for revolt had passed. He wanted to play it straight and clear and raise his children well. In this way, Troiano liked to think of himself as a more modern type, a guy with a steady income who was able to provide for his clan, a man moving into the twentieth century with progress in plain sight.

In those days, Troiano's prospects looked bright. Leasing his place from a relative who had left for Chicago, he figured the fellow would never return and treated the house as his own. He replaced the sod blocks with stones; he applied lime-based mortar to wall cracks. His home, he muttered, was substantially more than the tiny twig huts that sheltered the peasants who lived in the valley. After all, he had four walls and a roof.

"This is what progress looks like," he said, lest the family forget all that he'd done.

After five years, once the stone walls were up, he installed a brand-new floor. Over the dirt, his sons laid planks of pine; they then replaced the straw pads with mattresses stuffed with sheep's wool. When he dropped a burlap curtain to divide the big room, he saw his mission as complete.

"Dammit," Troiano had said to his family. "We've really come up in the world."

Eugenia remembered the sentence since he had said it so many times.

But then the hardships began. Had he been able to send a son to the priesthood, he would have resolved his problems. A role in the church promised a decent house, a plot of land, and the assurance of life-long privilege, which made it an easy cure for any family's destitution. But no, his sons didn't have the talent. He knew they lacked the finer skills to tie a proper napkin, to sip from a glass without slurping, to hold their intestinal bloat. He knew they would neither sit at the archbishop's table nor enter in conversation with those who journeyed south from Naples or Rome. Here, Eugenia had to agree with her father: the Troianos were seen as *cafoni*—untutored, unwise, and uncouth. Especially his son Antonio, a boor if ever he saw one.

As the years went on, Troiano gave up on his dreams of progress. He no longer awaited the arrival of running water that might reach his house through a spigot; he stopped glancing at Neapolitan magazines that showed pictures of indoor plumbing; he lost hope of ever lighting his house with Mr. Edison's new invention. Instead, he spent all his time posing basic questions: Could he ask the merchant from Puglia to extend his overdue loan? Could Troiano pretend that he had never received the cartload of lumber from the peasant in nearby Ruoti? And what could he do if the traveling salesman to whom he owed so much money showed up at his door with a shotgun? Troiano, always sweaty and anxious, told his wife, Rosina, that he needed to find a solution.

Eugenia wasn't certain of all her father's activities, but she sensed something strange. Lying in bed tonight, she compared all the stories she had heard to try to make sense of her father's downward turn. As gossip swirled like wind through the village, she knew something was wrong. When his business of fruit and grain slowed down, and when his carpentry orders dried up, Troiano, everyone whispered, began to skim off a few extra *soldi* by tricks of eye and hand. He bought spoiled grapes at a discount and passed them on to the bumpkins who, seeing the perfect clusters resting on top of the crates, missed the rot below; he put his thumb on the scale; he never completed a full delivery of wood or wheat or berries. With these peccadillos along with minor fibs, old man Troiano began to depart from his honest life.

Troiano's hopes for salvation dragged over a rocky course. History had revolted against him. He beat his sons to a pulp when his contracts for woodwork dried up; he grunted when egg sales didn't reach his weekly quotas; he was livid when some neighbors found tiny flecks of sand buried in the flour he'd put up for sale; he screamed when his debtors reneged on their payments, leaving him high and dry. As luck would have it, the family had missed the recent cholera scares, but that wasn't enough to keep Troiano at peace with himself.

The worst came when his first-born son Antonio went to work for him. Together the men swept up parcels of land from those who'd left their country plots in search of better horizons; together they falsified property deeds that they filed in the municipal office. Because Antonio knew how to write and his father knew how to chisel, together they forged a medallion that resembled an official seal. Dipped in wax and stamped on paper, the raised emblem gave certifiable proof of the Troianos' illegal actions. In this way, father and son were able to claim land deeds from innocent peasants. Because these people didn't know how to read and signed with a simple "X," because they had no awareness of the powers of lettered tradition, the country folk were relieved of their barren fields for a miserable pittance. In turn, this father-son team dumped the no-good land on distant buyers eager to find a quick deal. When the prospects for land turned sour, father and son opened a basement tavern and became purveyors of wine. In the tavern, on Saturday nights, they received the village's weary working men who were happy to escape from their wives. The patrons kicked up their soles. Here, the men were fine for drink one and drink two; a good evening was had by all. With drink three came the magic moment when Troiano diluted the spirits with tinctures of tannin and watered-down citrus. By that time, the clients were too drunk to know what was going on and, to make matters worse, Antonio raided their pockets. No one suspected a thing.

Songs were written about the tavern, about the good luck of finding a drink, about the meanderings of men who had returned from America and about those who were planning to leave. Even Antonio and old man Troiano were written into a few of the tunes.

"Oh, Antonio stomped on the grapes; he stirred in spit and water. So when we went to have a sip, we told him he was out of order. Antonio to the gallows; take the man away. He'll never earn an honest coin, don't let the bastard stray."

The singers howled; they fell into belly laughs that caused them to pee; they threw out more than a couple of farts to make wind bags sail through the air. But a judge caught up with the land scams. And then the wine business failed to prosper. Eugenia cringed as she remembered the customers complaining about stones weighing down the demijohn vessels that Troiano had delivered from house to house; she trembled recalling those who had caught Troiano in flagrante tampering with the spirits. In one drunken barroom scene, a neighbor accused Antonio of theft and threw a sharp stone at his head, hitting him squarely above the right brow and following up with a knife stab. The assault opened a crescent-shaped wound dangerously close to his eye. His face was changed forever, much to his mother's dismay.

"Such a beautiful face," she lamented. "And now he looks like a monster."

With so many drunken brawls, and people aware of Antonio's deceptions, and with so many customers leaving town in search of a better life, Antonio one day threw in the towel and decided to pack his bags. The family decided on the spot that the good town was decisively bad. Antonio closed the tavern and took leave of his home. He bade farewell to his siblings and traveled by wagon to Naples. From there, he sailed alone to New York.

* * * *

Eugenia carried these stories fresh in her mind as she lay in bed. They were part of a family legend that she had learned by heart though she had to admit that actions and lessons were often in contradiction.

"Don't trust anyone," Raffaele Troiano often told his children. "Try not to speak to strangers, keep your money sewn in your shirt."

Old man Troiano's warnings were hammered like nails in his children's ears. Antonio carried these words with him when he departed in 1890. Maria Antonietta wrote down the advice in her notebook before she left for Buenos Aires. Carmelo held the words in his head as his boat sailed for New York Harbor. Mariarosa felt obliged to recite these lines to her husband as they left home for a better life. Eugenia, who remained in the village, trembled each day in fear.

"Don't tell outsiders who you are. Never reveal household secrets. Keep your business to yourself. Don't let people know where you're going. And watch out for the evil priests who are always up to no good."

Eugenia was smothered by her father's directives. His fierce and angry lessons lingered like smoke after fire. Of all the children, she was the most resistant to Troiano; she saw the power her father held and couldn't wait to escape. He followed her as she went to school; he tracked her steps as she did her chores. He listened in on her conversations. But the nighttime intrusions of his brutish hands were what made her sick to her stomach.

* * * *

As daybreak came, Eugenia rose from her bed to start her morning chores. She was still haunted by questions about her father. What's the use of watching these business deals in which her father deceived his neighbors? And how could she form any friendships if she'd been told there's no one to trust? What's the use of living in this family? Eugenia twirled a button on her night shirt. When the threads holding the button broke, she realized that she only wanted to flee.

She was considered the village beauty, and she claimed many advantages that would have allowed for a different life. She'd inherited the family's intensely blue eyes; at times they looked like glistening silver, a trademark of the Troianos from the days of the Teutonic invaders. Her smile could light up the planet, the neighbors said, adding that Eugenia also had a genial talent for enthralling those who came near. She charmed the vendors in the market. She inflamed the souls of would-be poets, and—God forbid we should say it—she even inspired the priests to follow her paces, though Troiano blocked their advances. Eugenia was always noticed and then remembered.

"Good morning, don Gigio," she would say to the notary as she curtsied before him. "May you have a lovely day. My warm wishes to your wife."

"*Buon giorno*, Zi'Annibale. My mother sends her regards. Please enjoy the nice weather."

No one could turn her away. Eugenia carried signs of a well-bred politeness, surprising in light of her crude, abrupt father and the worries that beset her.

* * * *

As the family started the day, her father sent Eugenia to market. He counted on his daughter's cordial ways to secure what the family needed. He counted on the value of her eyes. Her father had taught her that eyes were meant for begging for mercy, for borrowing a kilo of sugar, for pleading for a loan. Eyes were used for regular profit and gain, he told her, for rooting out the seeds of deception that other villagers had planted. He explained that with her deep blue eyes and her smile, she would appeal to young men of the village as well as the market vendors. Eugenia, however, had thoughts of her own.

"Seeing is believing," she said as she walked to the vegetable stalls.

For the moment, Eugenia stayed away from the tactics of old man Troiano; instead, she used her very keen eyes to spot trouble and run away. Where did she learn this? Certainly not from her parents. Perhaps she came to this through Zia Lina, who was attuned to village life and sought to reform those sinners who had lost all respect for God; perhaps she learned it from Maestra Pina, who sat the village children in a single school room and taught from a novel called *Cuore*, about the moral world that Italian children needed to see. Perhaps she learned it from her Aunt Teodora, who had taught her to show restraint, to confide in no single person, but to attend to affairs of the heart. She heard these admonitions time and again, almost like the clanging bells calling townsfolk for vespers. Eugenia knew she had to be wary. She also knew she needed a soul, and she found that in the townspeople's stories.

* * * *

Eugenia also wondered why the tales took on a life of their own. Rumors spread along secret corridors and alleys, over walls and fences, high up on the clotheslines, down low near the muddied roads. Relatives slobbering as their long, wet tongues came close to the tasty salt of a story. The buzz reminded Eugenia of the sounds of August cicadas, which grew to form a huge dark cloud in the sky. Eugenia also joined in on the gossip albeit with a certain reserve. She wondered if Padre Felicetto had found the jewels that brigands had hidden in the church walls some decades ago, if ghosts in the grottos near Lago Monticchio had swallowed up innocent girls, if Signora Masucci's baby really had been born with three extra thumbs. On the surface, Eugenia rejected these village scoops, but she nonetheless found them intriguing. And she loved the way townsfolk told them. Though she didn't know the words quite yet, she was attracted to the performance of stories.

Why, she'd asked when still a young child, did rumor carry more power than the excitement of a ride through the woods? Why did the recollection of long-winded tales help her plow through her daily chores? What with cleaning the floors at sunrise, removing the eggs from their nests, and carrying buckets of water from Zio Minguccio's well, Eugenia allowed endless stories to swirl in her mind. She liked to spin them together to form an ongoing tale of her village. In this sense, she had to admit, she was no different from the gossiping townsfolk whom she loudly reviled. Then she mused on a central point: why did we all love to fib, to transform the stories of others and eventually make them our own? Thirsty for some kind of art, she shared these stories with Silvio, her schoolmate and dearest pal.

2.

This story goes nowhere without Silvio. A ward of don Ciccio, Silvio was tasked with cleaning out stables, carrying hay to the livestock, delivering wheat to the mill. With no sign of adventure in sight, he'd resigned himself to farm-life routine. Enter Silvio's salvation: Maestra Pina. With the goal of bringing peasant children into her temple of learning, Maestra Pina would leave the hilltop village each month and scoot to the valley below. She was in search of youthful subjects who would be able to learn their numbers and write their names. On the day that she met Silvio, she hardly saw his face. He was dressed in a shredded cotton shirt and a sack half masking his head as if to protect him from the sunlight. Maestra Pina asked his name, but Silvio couldn't answer. Instead, he stammered and produced a flutter of meaningless sounds.

"Try again," Maestra Pina said with gentle voice. She refused to inhale the smell of sheep that clung to Silvio's clothing; she was blind to the holes in his gunnysack shirt; for the moment, she looked beyond his clumps of dirty, knotted hair. Maestra Pina took his hand and asked him once more for his name. Silvio prepared to run away. When the teacher gave him a candy, the conversation started over again, though not in the normal manner. Not listening to huffs and gurgles that came from his misaligned tongue, Maestra Pina gave him the chance to work with shapes and forms on paper. Here, the boy's eyes lit up like emeralds—he had a skill for puzzles—and when the teacher asked him to take pen in hand, his face turned red with delight. Maestra Pina at once got the general picture and decided to invite Silvio to join her schoolhouse, of course with don Ciccio's permission.

At school, Silvio carried tufts of matted sheep's wool stuck to the nape of his neck. He picked this up in the makeshift stall he shared with the livestock at night. In class, the students laughed at him (though in truth they all smelled equally bad—some reeked of garlic breath or rat's hair, others of pants soaked in night soil and pee). They especially laughed at his stutter. They named Silvio after the sheep: "*piccolo pecora*," little sheepy sheep. "Pec-pec" they called him for short, and they laughed so much that their sides sometimes ached as they threw themselves on the floor.

"Pec-pec," the boys cried out as Silvio approached the classroom, which in those days was a wide covered shelter with tree stumps and boards for benches.

"Pec-pec, pec-pec," they screamed, making fun of his smell and his speech. Silvio tiptoed to his place in the room, where he trembled and held back the tears.

Eugenia intervened. "Don't listen to them," she said. "Feel free to sit by my side. You don't need to say a word."

Silvio's humility intrigued Eugenia, as did his talent for drawing. Over time, Maestra Pina took note of the girl's affection for the boy and always paired them together.

In the early years, the teacher devised a plan to clear Silvio's stench. Not disturbed by it herself, Maestra Pina had to manage the jokes of the other children who held their nose as Silvio walked by. On occasion, she would send Silvio back to the fields; at other times, she sent him under Eugenia's escort to visit Zia Wanda, who then provided a washcloth and basin and helped him clean himself up. Then Zia Wanda invited both children to eat a few slices of day-old bread and tomatoes. If they weren't sated, Zia Wanda then would show them the Sunday supplements from Naples and read the weekly news aloud.

Something stirred Silvio during these visits. In truth, he was less impressed by the water and soap than by the pictures he found in the papers: hand-drawn comics and sketches, photographs of the city, advertisements selling everything from women's corsets to barber cremes and toilets. As Silvio was slow to speak, he showed his pleasure with braying and bleats. However, one word he spoke to perfection: "more." Seeing these wonderful pictures, Eugenia echoed her friend.

* * * *

It had all started years ago when Zia Wanda's brother, the priest Don Felicetto, brought home the Sunday *Fortunio*, a Neapolitan magazine carrying pictures and illustrations with tidbits of local interest. Zia Wanda had intercepted these pages with palpable joy, devouring the pictures as if they were the juicy plums of July. Now, with Silvio and Eugenia generally under her care, she gave the children the chance to share in these yummy reader's delights. The supplements told stories of kings and ladies; they revealed the latest fashions and promoted the latest devices, among them Stucchi sewing machines and porcelain fixtures for indoor plumbing. Zia Wanda read stories of opera patrons swathed in a world of elegance unknown in her village.

"Those people live in fancy mansions near Piazza Vanvitelli," Wanda told the children. "I read that they covered their dining room walls with paper designs. Can you imagine?"

"*Broccato*," Don Felicetto interrupted as she lectured the children. "It comes from the Latin, *broccus*, meaning 'projected or pointing.'"

As if her brother weren't standing next to her, she repeated this to her wards.

Zia Wanda especially liked the advertisements for Kalodent toothpaste and Vino Marsala, musical instruments, and pictures of the latest dresses and shoes. Ladies with bustled skirts and gartered stockings, dainty feet in handmade boots, and *polvere bionda,* or whitening cream, to make dark southern skin look lighter. Then the jewelry shops on Via Santa Chiara; pianos at Fratelli Curci; calfskin gloves; silk slippers. Zia Wanda wanted to go to Naples to see the fancy storefronts and sip tea at Caffé Gambrinus. And though she couldn't quite make sense of the stories by Paul Bourget and Luigi Capuana, she understood that another life existed beyond her mountain village. The children followed along.

Zia Wanda showed the youngsters stories of natural wonders; she sighed when she pointed out headlines about a brand-new aquarium in Naples, the first of its kind in Europe. She let them see the report about the Japanese koi, a gift presented by the emperor to the Italian king on his recent visit (the koi were supposed to live for at least two hundred years!). The children stared at pictures of the zoological station in the Parco Comunale; they studied the fish and crustaceans; they then looked over pictures of well-dressed children who strolled through the park on Sundays. They wished they could be there too.

Zia Wanda always skipped over news about stolen babies or the Camorra; she didn't allow her wards to read about violent mobs or corruption; and she especially passed over the pages denouncing the hoax of San Gennaro's blood. But when Zia Wanda looked away to tend to her usual *minestra* of potatoes and greens, Eugenia (whose reading skills by the end of fifth grade exceeded those of her tutor) took over the lessons and began to read the news that Zia Wanda had censored.

"What's an African adventure?" she asked. "Who's the Sultan of Zanzibar? And why so much news of Somalia?"

"Wats a Sultan? Wjere ish Zanzibar? Is Somalia far frim here?" Silvio said.

Eugenia continued, "And why do they wish the anarchists to die in Eritrea?"

"Wats Eritrea? Who are the anarchists? And why do we wont dem to die?"

Then there was the question of a "hunger insurrection" that really made little sense. And with this week's news, why so much talk about the king? Pictures, more pictures, big font letters (it read like someone screaming), the paper explained that the king had been murdered by an Italian man who hailed from New Jersey. The paper said murdering the king was a way for someone evil to avenge his losses, that the guy who pulled the trigger was yelling for workers' rights. The killer came from America? Who knew?

Eugenia said, "Perhaps my brother Carmelo could explain this to me; after all, he went to New York."

"May bee Carmelo nose the killer?" Sharp-minded Silvio spoke his most perfect sentence since Maestra Pina had introduced him to school.

"If my brother Carmelo knows who the killer is, he'll be sure to tell me when he returns."

She didn't speak much of her brother, though she still longed for his presence. Carmelo was her guide, her big brother. Carmelo knew how to take care. He protected Eugenia from her father; he listened to her complaints; he supported her studies at Maestra Pina's school even when their father had insisted that girls had no need to learn. Carmelo took pride in his sister's genial passion for study. He even let Eugenia tutor him in reading and writing.

"My little sis leads us all to a love of books," Carmelo boasted to the neighbors.

He'd encouraged Eugenia to stay in school, to take time to learn about science and letters. He hoped eventually his little sister would explain the complex scientific ideas that he couldn't grasp on his own. Yet Carmelo had gone to New York and sent only one letter. To make matters worse, Mariarosa, also in New York City, had reported no news of Carmelo.

Where could he be? Eugenia wondered. Silvio, she often mused, was now filling in for her favorite brother.

* * * *

Taking leave of Zia Wanda, Eugenia and Silvio often walked as one through the fields: they nibbled at elderberry fruits; they sucked out nectar from blossoms; they broke off twigs from the mulberry trees and later used those twigs as pencils. Silvio remembered some of the magazine images and sketched a few pictures in sand: castles near the sea, clattering horses on palm-lined streets, strange towering animals with tiny horns and spots on their torsos and legs. Sometimes just a few strokes sufficed; on other occasions, a quick repetition of curvy lines gave a sense of movement. He preferred, of course, to sketch on paper rather than draw on dirt or sand. Better still, with the pencils that Maestra Pina sometimes supplied, his drawings took on new depth. Hatching and cross-hatching, accent lines, tricks of smudges and blending, a vast work with borders and edges that pleased Eugenia no end. He loved to draw the uneven tufts of animal fur; he reproduced Eugenia's curly black hair with strokes that almost glistened. He captured the wind as it swept through the olive trees and caught flickers of afternoon light as they speckled the graceful branches.

Silvio one day decided to draw on paper the three stunning trotters who had fallen under don Ciccio's care. He showed the sketch to Eugenia and referred to the horses by name. They were Zaffiro, Bandolero, and Macario, whom he had described to Eugenia weeks before; now they appeared on paper, almost alive through Silvio's art.

"Oh my goodness," Eugenia said to Silvio. "My father's dream in pictures!"

His deliberate strokes spoke without clutter or error. Here, Eugenia had definite proof that her father's nightmares were grounded in truth. She also thought to show Silvio's artwork to Zi'Annibale, the grocer who, on the side, thought a lot about art.

3.

Tuesday, an ordinary Tuesday, not that the days of the week made much difference in a town where time moved so slowly if ever it moved at all. On Tuesday, Eugenia approached Zi'Annibale as he counted cups of lentils in the back of his store. Hesitant to refer to her father's nightmares, she instead produced Silvio's sketch of the horses to praise her buddy's talent.

Looking at the drawing, Zi'Annibale said, "The kid is a natural born artist. Why don't you bring him around?" He mentioned that he would also be happy to show Silvio his studio so that he might learn the ropes. Winking, Zi'Annibale remarked he would show them the strings that held people in place on the wall. He offered no further explanation so Eugenia couldn't respond.

When they arrived, the children saw a carnival of riches tempting mind and soul. First, Zi'Annibale showed them the Sanderson camera box that he'd recently purchased in Naples; then he pointed out the table used for unloading the films, the tray that held the liquids, the clips that were used to suspend the prints, the silver salts and gelatin, the unwieldy glass plates.

"You need to know where my photography took me," he said. "Dried peas and farro used to anchor all my thoughts, but since I bought this camera equipment, I've really changed my perspective. Gelatin paper and liquid diffusers are now my principal thing."

Silvio, asking Eugenia to translate his halting garble, wanted to know how to master a camera and find a focus. Here, Zi'Annibale stretched his arms out as if to direct a band. "Someday you'll catch pictures of horses running, children at play in the fields. You'll see photographs that capture a steaming kettle or the bubbles of boiling water. Why, you'll even be able to string images together to tell a story about men on the moon."

"Right now," he said, "I'm just a photographer of the dead. I do the surviving families a service and, in exchange for a picture of their loved ones, they give me a couple of *soldi*. I'm keeping the gains in a metal box to save up for my trip to New York."

Zi'Annibale explained his task and the scope of his work, taking care to show Silvio and Eugenia the wall where he propped up the bodies for pictures before their final descent to the graveyard below the town. The wall had hooks and belts of all sizes, metal head clamps and cast-iron poles, instruments that might've recalled medieval times, but which here were designed to hold the corpses in place as Zi'Annibale posed them.

Silvio studied pictures hanging from a clothesline in the back of the store. The stiff bodies of elders stared fearfully into the lens. "What's diss-s-s all a-about?" He noted that some of the pictures were framed by embossed cardboard, some were clipped to sheets of paper.

"Each reveals a story," Zi'Annibale told him.

But Silvio saw ghastly sorrow: Don Guglielmo, staring straight ahead, looked like a deer caught in a hunter's crosshairs; Zia Filomena, the matriarch of the Arcangelo clan, with her arms tightly clamped to her sides; little Lauretta, who had left the world in June when attacked by sudden fevers, now sitting in sharp focus between her slightly blurred living sisters. The pictures were designed to restore the dead folk to life, but, as Silvio tried to say, they looked inflated, stretched out, and starched.

"The photograph is a way to trick death," Zi'Annibale said. "And because the people of Bellanera want their loved ones to live forever, I have a service to render."

Silvio studied a portrait of the Angrisano children. He knew the youngsters because he and don Ciccio had once delivered a sack of grain to their house on the hill. In the photo, little Ignazia in death was propped up against her older sister's arms. The two looked straight at the camera, though the dead child was puffed and swollen; her expressionless eyes said nothing while the older child—still living—had eyes of fear and alarm. Finding Zi'Annibale's art of the dead lacking in artistic detail, Silvio was perturbed. "You kin draw open eyes on der picture, if you like."

"At least the boy shows an appreciation of form," Zi'Annibale said to Eugenia.

Silvio continued to study the various poses the corpses assumed and gave instructions on how to improve each image with a few strokes of colored pencil. Cosmetically, he would alter the bleached-out faces and give the dead a pretense of life. Zi'Annibale was neither shocked by the boy's advice nor offended by his proposals; instead, he drank up the boy's observations in order to improve his art. He invited Silvio to return on a different day to give him a hand in his shop.

* * * *

Silvio looked over Zi'Annibale's portfolio and suggested some touch-ups. Add a rosy curve on the cheeks, paint the forehead with a smudge of brown, and if you want to take a very big chance, let the eyes be Troiano blue. It had never occurred to Zi'Annibale to add paint to the black-and-white plates, to use color to make up for the grayness that swept through the dead and the living. Silvio persisted and bid permission to add a pink smile to a likeness, a bluish smear to an eye, rouge to flattened faces, and golden curls to jet-black hair.

Weeks passed and Zi'Annibale began to work more attentively with Silvio's ideas. What if he tried to color the pictures to give his subjects a special zest? What if his gloomy figures had lightning-blue eyes and luscious red lips? His first attempts with this technique were a miserable failure since the colored paint didn't adhere to the plate, instead tending to blotch or run. He continued to practice.

One day Silvio proposed that Zi'Annibale begin to work with the living: elders posing for family portraits that would be sent to their sons in Montevideo; couples who needed identity photos in order to leave for Brazil. Silvio liked the idea of people moving abroad and leaving pictures for their parents who never would see them again. He imagined there would be photographs altered to make people look tall (when they were actually very short), pictures that let them be muscular (when they were flabby and weak), pictures that fixed their smiles and teeth (when they were grumpy and toothless), pictures that allowed them to appear as gentlemen or erstwhile ladies (when they were ragged peasants), pictures that gave the gift of beauty (when they were grouchy and ugly). Zi'Annibale followed Silvio's suggestions and trained his eye on the living. He began by shooting his own identity photo (for that future trip to New York) and asked Silvio to help doctor the picture to let Zi'Annibale look light years younger.

Zi'Annibale announced his plan: he wanted to work with history, taking pictures of churches and century-old farms, broad landscapes of the countryside, ancient castles rising high from the hills. He wanted to photograph the animals that dotted the valleys and roadways to convey the idea of a productive farm life that might define the south.

"The south as a living form," he said, "I want a picture that lets me see the vibrations of the mountain peaks and forests."

Here Silvio persuaded Zi'Annibale to carry his camera down the hill to the valley to take pictures of the thoroughbred horses on don Ciccio's farm.

"Not a bad idea," Zi'Annibale said.

Once on the farm, Zi'Annibale allowed Silvio to train his camera's eye on the steeds: Macario, with his arched neck and muscular body; Zaffiro, the strong black stallion with white markings on his torso; Bandolero, whose chestnut legs were blotted with asymmetric blonde spots. They spent the longest time finding different perspectives on the horses; Silvio even took over the camera to catch the beasts in motion.

As Zi' Annibale's countryside portraits had gained recognition in town, Don Felicetto one day urged him to find a larger venue so more people could see his work. Zi'Annibale was hesitant, but then in a rash convergence of energy and bravura, confidence and braggadocio (bored as he was by the bags of lentils and grain in his store), he sent some pictures of hills and castles for the priest to inspect. He also included Silvio's portraits of the horses on don Ciccio's farm. Don Felicetto, who was bound for Naples on a Monday in May, was happy to show the pictures to his journalist friends. The photographs of Zi'Annibale and Silvio happened to match the newspaper's needs, as the editorial team was testing a new feature on rural life. Shortly thereafter and to Zi'Annibale's surprise, the images appeared in the Sunday pullout, a newspaper section devoted to regional culture. Although they didn't yet know it, triumph and trouble were on the horizon.

* * * *

After the publication of Zi'Annibale's pictures, Don Felicetto received a letter from the chief of the Sunday paper. A duke from Venosa had seen Zi'Annibale's photos. He was focused, the duke had explained in his letter, on the images of the horses and recognized three animals that had gone missing from his corral. Don Felicetto took the letter to Zi'Annibale and warned him of complications.

"Do these horses in fact belong to the duke? Could don Ciccio give a fair explanation?" Agitated, don Felicetto wanted to know how to respond to the newspaper boss.

Zi'Annibale set off to speak with don Ciccio. Panicked, don Ciccio refused to believe that he and Troiano might wind up in jail.

"It's time to have Troiano come clean," don Ciccio said.

Talk, of course, was cheap and, in times of emergency, no one in Bellanera had the wherewithal to concoct a proper response. Then the worst news came their way. By courier, the duke had sent a letter to officials in Bellanera in which he announced his imminent arrival in the company of a regional judge.

Don Felicetto again reached Zi'Annibale, who in turn sought out Don Ciccio.

"The duke and his entourage are expected in town any day," Zi'Annibale said. "And to make matters worse, they're traveling with the law."

Don Ciccio's face turned beet red; he began to pull at his hair. Then he ran to tell Troiano. Hearing the news, Troiano reached a new stage of madness. The veins in his forehead protruded; sweat poured down his face. He ran home, kicked the backyard watering trough, and upset the nests of the chickens. Then he beat his wife. After that, he showed her a roll of bills he'd hidden under the floorboards and, thrusting the bundle into her hands, told his wife he was leaving.

"I can't stay here, Rosina. I've reached the end of the line."

Troiano packed some provisions and fled on foot to Don Ciccio's farm, where he bridled Macario for his escape and set the other horses free. He then made his way to the hills. By the time Eugenia had grabbed wind of the story, Troiano was long gone. Donna Rosina cried about her family's sorry fate and lamented her upturned life. Eugenia, by contrast, drew a deep breath and revealed a wicked smile. Later, she hugged Silvio and declared that freedom was coming her way.

4.

Eugenia experienced Troiano's departure as an opening up, like fresh air filling her lungs. No longer would she have to worry about her father's wandering hands or listen to his nocturnal sputter. No longer would she live in fear. Relieved, Eugenia dreamed of her freedom, but had no idea of what she might do. So she continued to go to school, give a hand to her mother, and volunteer in the grain store, which, by now, Zi'Annibale and Silvio had transformed into a photography shop, developing and doctoring pictures.

"*Oh Dio*," said an embarrassed Zi'Annibale as Eugenia entered his store. "We really caused a scandal with the pictures of horses. I am so, so sorry, Eugenia, that it has come to this. Believe me, I never imagined it would drive your father away."

Determined not to expose her father, Eugenia lowered her eyes and said nothing. Meanwhile, the old gossips in town confirmed the recent news: Raffaele Troiano had been up to no good.

"And look what he did to his family, leaving his wife and child high and dry."

"And running off with the duke's horse and setting the others free."

"Not a good bone in Troiano's body. Thank God he's fled the village."

The town chorus denounced him, and Eugenia pretended not to hear, but in Zi'Annibale's store, she felt vaguely at ease knowing the art of pictures had helped her turn a corner. Her debt to her friends was huge.

Soon after Troiano's flight, Zi'Annibale said to Eugenia and Silvio, "For a next group of photographs, I want to try local people in regional dress; this promises to be safer than drawing attention to stolen goods."

The youngsters were overjoyed. "Yes, better to work with scenes of real people; show off the charms of humble life," Eugenia said.

The photographer had the idea to dress Eugenia in local outfits; she would be his model. Crimson skirt, petticoat below, full blouse, a deep yellow apron: the perfect *pacchiana* or peasant. Zi'Annibale took several pictures of Eugenia in different poses: her right arm positioned on her hip to give her the air of a young woman in power; plump and flirtatious, carrying a basket of flowers; staring straight at the camera; looking away. Silvio filled in the details: he added tiny red dots to the upper garment, blue pleats to Eugenia's skirts; he painted a brooch, a belt, and a pair of earrings in ranges of ochre meant to be taken for gold. Then he altered Eugenia's gaze to accent her sapphire eyes.

Zi'Annibale's camera work proved a labor of love, and by the time Silvio finished his lively correctives, the photos resembled paintings. Again, Don Felicetto carried the pictures off to Naples, where his friend published them in *Il Mattino*.

Zi'Annibale's reputation soon extended to neighboring towns. The elites, who dreamed of reconstructing a pure, more sanitized version of peasants—charming, *allegri*, and clean, unlike the hordes of beggars who combed the streets for crumbs—took particular note. Zi'Annibale had his fans. Eugenia, his constant subject, attracted the greatest applause.

Among the admirers was a count from Matera who on a certain Sunday was reading the news. "Hey, Annunziata, take a look at the paper," the count said to his wife as she slipped into her chair for her usual afternoon nap. "There's something that catches my eye."

A pastry chef and specialist in after-dinner favors, the count had created a particularly fragrant digestif that he hoped to send out to market. It was a sweet orange-scented liqueur with the aroma of blossoms and chocolate. And while it certainly appealed to the palate, it now needed a fancy label. "I know I can do better than those farmers who sell limoncello near Amalfi; their bottles bear the sketch of only a lemon without so much as a name. Who would want to buy that stuff?" He also mentioned the prince from nearby Ferrandina who tinkered with cherry-based drinks, but because Annunziata was so annoyed with her husband, she only thought to close off her ears.

"The prince didn't know how to sell his grog; he had no sense of style. The jerk simply put the digestifs in bottles and sealed them for future storage," he said. "By contrast, our liqueur will go out with a fancy label. We'll get dramatic results, don't you think?"

About to doze off, Annunziata didn't answer.

"Why, I bet ours will last into the twenty-first century, to be sold in faraway places like New Orleans and Japan. Just you wait and see!"

Annunziata's eyelids fluttered as her chin dropped onto her chest.

The count continued to lecture while skimming the classified supplement of the Sunday paper. This section carried advertisements for sweet chocolates and women's cosmetics and pictures of giant ocean-bound ships that promised to take you to Buenos Aires.

"Look here, Annunziata," he said. "Even Mr. Galli is selling his Vino Marsala in the pages of *Il Mattino*."

When he saw Zi'Annibale's art in the photo pullout section, he gave his wife a nudge. "Hey, Annunziata. What do you think of this picture? Could it work as my label?"

"Uh-huh." She uttered a feeble "That's nice."

The count jumped up. "But look how the colors work: a dark-blue skirt and yellow apron against the blue of the southern sky. It's certainly appealing, don't you think?"

"Can we talk about this later tonight?" she mumbled.

The count couldn't stop rambling. His wife, eager to take a nap and get her husband to stop his gabble, urged him to depart for Bellanera the very next day and pay a visit to Zi'Annibale.

"I'm happy to push you out right now just to keep you quiet," she moaned as she tried to close her eyes.

* * * *

Business was booming for Zi'Annibale when the count showed up and asked to see his pictures. Some prints displayed Eugenia in dance, raising her skirt above the knee and throwing her head back and smiling. Others captured Eugenia under an olive tree looking up at the ospreys perched in its branches. Zi'Annibale showed him other stacks of images, some pointing to a bucolic past, others suggesting a modern future. Some were in black and white; others had Silvio's touch-ups of color. Pulled between these options, the count-qua-chef found himself leaning toward the colorized photo-drawings. On the spot, he offered to buy a particular image for use in his budding business.

Soon Eugenia's likeness was stamped on paper and affixed to the count's bottles of drink; it also appeared in the classified ads of the Sunday news from Naples. Zi'Annibale was cheered by the auspicious event, and Eugenia's spirits soared. Hundreds of bottles entered the homes of the well-to-do. She was no longer the girl who washed dishes or swept the porch and fed the chickens; now she saw herself as a young lady of regional fame.

"Eugenia is a heroine, a star," she said as she smiled at herself in a mirror. She'd begun to think of the published image as a dance with her other self. "I'm just like the rich Neapolitan girls who stroll on promenades near the sea. Like the figures in Zia Wanda's papers, but now it's only me."

Eugenia's grand aspirations went far into the future. Posing with open arms, as if she were on a stage, she declaimed in a lusty voice, "This image will reach faraway places. Brooklyn, Chicago, Buenos Aires—the cities where migrants from Basilicata eventually will find a prosperous life."

Sure enough, she was right. Many years later, in a crisis of nostalgia exacerbated by drink, people in distant towns and cities would turn to Eugenia's picture and yearn intensely for home.

5.

Silvio, meanwhile, stared at her pictures. He squinted and pressed his hand to his head. Somehow Eugenia of the image was different from the girl in real life. Day to day, Eugenia wore neither a festive skirt nor a peasant's garb; rather, she donned a gunnysack frock her mother had sewn and repaired. Yet, Silvio thought, there was no faking Eugenia's gaze. Eugenia continued to dazzle him, awakening a disturbing pang in his chest whenever he looked at her picture. The girl was a subject of art, and he, Silvio, was an artist. Art and heart; the two words rhymed, he mumbled without thinking.

Months after Troiano's departure, Eugenia and her mother sat alone at a table where they ate from a common bowl. Neither had a plate of her own. They shared few words about the *pater familias* but were happy he wasn't around to get the first digs at the food. Men ate before the women according to tradition; women had the remainders. Now they had the dish to themselves, Eugenia observed as Rosina turned the conversation to Silvio.

"So, do you think you'll marry him now that his picture made you famous?"

"That topic will have to wait. I don't know if I'm ready," Eugenia said. She didn't think that her friendship with Silvio carried any traces of romance.

"Well, perhaps you're wise, *figlia mia.* The boy doesn't have a *pezza.*"

At the end of the meal, and to break the trend of her mother's ideas, Eugenia stood and cleared the table. She carried the dish to a deep basin of water standing on the front porch.

While releasing the vessel of its grease and breadcrumbs, she looked up and noticed a stranger. From his position on a horse, he cut a dashing figure. Spiffed up and oh-so-dapper, like the men who filled the Sunday papers, the stranger wore a long gray cape over his riding habit. He wasn't handsome, but he had a certain appeal. He winked at her, removed his hat, and announced that he had just come to town. Eugenia, not accustomed to this kind of gracious flirtation, quickly turned her back on him and carried the clean plate inside. The stranger waited some seconds and then proceeded up the road.

* * * *

Here is where coincidence takes over, and good luck changes a life. At the turn of the century, the Marchese Gianpietro di Cimino e Valdivia left his home in the Vomero, the neighborhood that since the 1880s had soared above Naples, and set out to ride through the rough southern lands on his father's behalf. He traveled in a covered surrey pulled by two elegant horses. He'd hitched his Murgese to the rear in case weather and time might allow him a solo ride.

His carriage drove by many gypsies lugging copper wares on their backs; their pots wrapped up in cotton sheets traveled from village to village. The coach went past merchants buying grapes from serfs and tenant farmers and men who traveled on foot and traded tools for wire fencing. Finally, it hurried by old women who sold slabs of lard in exchange for handfuls of pullets. As the surrey advanced, the young marchese and his grooms took in these roadside scenes. Unlike the vendors advancing on mule or in wagons, the travelers from Naples had another purpose as they crossed through Lucanian hillsides: the marchese had been sent to settle scores for his father and bring home his annual due.

He could've taken the train, which was a novelty back then; and indeed, the Ferrovie Meridiali, the southern line that ran from Naples with a short stop in Salerno, would've cut his trip time in half. But the marchese enjoyed seeing peasants carrying their wares to market; he liked sitting down for a meal with the few acquaintances he had in the outback, among them don Felicetto, his father's friend. He delighted in the regional dishes found only in mountain towns just as he took pleasure in chatting with townsfolk to catch up with local news. He liked to hear peasants tell of miracles and saints, and adored stories about the French armies in battle against Lucanian rebels. He was thrilled to hear about the treasures unearthed in gravesites or in chapel walls. Soon, he hoped, he could leave behind metropolitan pretense and perhaps—just perhaps—build a life in the country, far from the tumultuous crowd.

The marchese was content with simple things: the forests, birds, country winds, heavy vines in advance of the harvest. He admitted he preferred the highland air over the raucous casino and racetrack. He was at home in a plain tunic shirt, a worker's cotton pants. He was happy to eat dandelion soup and day-old bread; he delighted in the guttural speech of country folk who managed to turn the mellifluous flow of court Italian into a porridge of thickset eruptions. In this regard, the marchese might be adjudicated to the category of plebian nobles, those elites who found their pleasure in copying the commoners' speech and who often preferred to hobnob with servants, to sip wine with members of the peasant classes as part of a jolly good time. Today this might be called "slumming." But in those days, this *re lazzarone*, as Croce once described the popular King Ferdinando IV who had similar downscale habits, was equally content eating hard lard and onions or dining on a bouillabaisse stew served by a white-gloved servant.

Riding near Bellanera, the marchese called the surrey to a halt and alighted. He prepared his horse, which had been trotting behind, and mounted him for the final stretch before arriving in town. The grooms, meanwhile, kept a close eye on their ward. No one doubted the young man's control of the reins, but they feared the highway bandits, those who were quick to assault the transport vehicles that hailed from cities on either coast. For a few *soldi*, horse and rider could be knocked down at any given hour. Not just by Rinaldo Rinaldini, the most famous road thief of all, but by any simple anonymous crook who might creep up behind you. As the elder marchese had reminded his son and grooms shortly before they'd departed, a cloud of famine darkened the South, making things ripe for armed avengers. No doubt, it behooved the travelers to stay far from roaming marauders. The drivers paid attention as the marquese advanced on his horse.

Drawing a brilliant flowing cape over his diminished shoulders, the marchese cantered forward striking a pose. He thought, the costume allowed him the illusion of becoming someone else. He was on his way to Don Felicetto's house for lunch and a chat, with plans for a sportive repartee about the world's changing conditions. Both men were concerned about the fate of the South after Unification, though neither took sides with the new politicians nor agreed on a single direction. They would discuss the latest essays by Fortunato or Villari on the mass exodus from the towns. They would lament the emigration, but then they would turn jolly and cap off the chat with a nice orange liqueur. The full pleasures of rural life, the young man thought as he traveled between a canter and trot toward the priest's home.

* * * *

"No horse of mine is going to slip and fall on these jagged stones," he said as he reached the partially cobbled lane that traversed the village. Guiding the horse to avoid any treacherous pitfalls, he looked up and beheld a vision that stopped time in its tracks. Dropping her arm like a sickle, a girl was tossing a basin of water over a terrace wall. He wondered who this girl was and why he knew her gaze. He doffed his hat and winked at her. With a smile as wide as a moon, he announced that he had just arrived in the village. Stunning, he thought while coaxing his horse to proceed. An unlikely vision, especially in these parts.

But he was also confused, thinking he knew this image, that he had seen this girl before.

He found it strange in this medieval village sustained by swindlers and dim-witted cheats, where history was told through failure, and economics was a matter of what you ate, that such a splendid girl actually stood before him. Besides, didn't he know that face?

Many years before Giovanni Pastrone would make a film about Cabiria, the peasant girl who was abducted from a village near Mt. Etna, the Marchese di Cimino imagined a strip of images running forward, one advancing over the other, of a girl with her head thrown back, one arm extended as if she were reaching for stars and the other arm clasping her skirt. She lifted her heels to dance, moving but, of course, not moving at all. She issued the most stunning smile as she turned and seemed to take flight in each subsequent frame. In all of this, the blue eyes followed the marchese and produced what could only be called a delirium in slow motion. He paused his horse, forgot the mud, and dismounted at his friend's door.

"*Caspita*!" He was now indignant at his own memory lapses. "Who in the world is this girl?"

His obsession was not tied to lascivious promise. The good marchese had had enough of that in Naples, where house maids and free-for-the-taking young girls always drew near to men of means. None of this appealed to the marchese, who frankly was embarrassed by female aggressions. Although his father and uncles encouraged him, he'd shirked these vulgar encounters. Walking by the buildings of Naples in various stages of decay, the marchese had noticed there was no shortage of flesh to service a gentleman's pleasures. But it wasn't enough to stop by those wretched fiends for a moment's release; you also had to breathe the foul air and soil your shoes in the rubble. The rooms weren't easy to stomach: mattresses made of horsehair that scratched your skin, and metal poles holding up bedsteads to keep the insects at bay. Here you could pass an hour without fearing roaches, but you still suffered flies and lice. Not to mention the animals belching from doorways and chickens in the apartments. The marchese wanted none of Circe's carnival lest he himself be turned into swine.

But here, in the middle of nowhere, a girl rattled his soul. A collision of art and unspeakable feeling. Not because he imagined his member pressed into a woman's nest—in fact, this rather revulsed him—but because something else lifted his spirits. He tried to focus. It was an air, a tone, an instance of grace that allowed him to perceive the divine. The marchese had studied Italian art, and he knew too well about rapturous saintly faces peering up at the heavens; he knew of mythical youth's felicity, an inspired blend of godly and human forms. Those were works of art, not the stuff of everyday life. Now, here was the dream girl, standing right before him.

He told himself not to think of the Lady with Ermine or the Birth of Venus. He wanted only to keep his mind on the girl he'd just seen.

* * * *

Zia Wanda escorted the marquese to meet don Felicetto. The men sat down for an exquisite lunch of pasta and escarole followed by delicate slices of chicken rubbed with squash seed and garlic; a dandelion salad in garlic and oil; a wedge of *caciocavallo*; a bowl of figs. The gentlemen then retired to the parlor to extend their afternoon chat. Zia Wanda served a coffee accompanied by a subtle liqueur with hints of orange. It was an amaro from Matera, the same digestif that the marchese's sisters held in their cupboards at home. The marquese noticed the bottle's label with its red-and-yellow image of a smiling peasant girl. At once, he stood, his memory excited by the familiar picture.

"Of course, now I can place her! The girl on this label is who I saw on my way to your home."

Don Felicetto nodded as the young marchese begged to learn more about her.

"Oh, you don't know the story? It's charming, to be sure. That's Eugenia, the daughter of Raffaele Troiano, most recently a horse thief who the law chased out of town. She's better than her father, for sure.

"Along with the boy Silvio," the priest continued, "she used to visit my sister quite often. They spent their earlier years in my house reading the news together. Then she and the boy called upon Don Annibale, the bean merchant and photographer who had a shop just down the street. When Don Annibale was developing his skills with a camera, he posed Eugenia in peasant dress. I was so impressed by his pictures that I looked for a venue to place them. Then I remembered my friend in Naples, an editor at the paper. I showed him Annibale's photos, and the editor liked them."

Don Felicetto stood up to refill his glass. "Then a count from Matera saw Annibale's pictures and asked to buy Eugenia's image. His idea was to affix the picture to his bottles of liqueur." The priest moved from one edge of the room to another, still holding his drink. "His bottles are now in demand. Annibale, with some bills in his pocket, recently closed his shop and left for New York."

"I'm dumbfounded," the marchese said, tripping on his heavy tongue. "I've never seen such beauty. My goodness, I need to meet that girl!"

"Don't get yourself excited. She's poor, you know, with a brief education. And she and her mother live alone."

"I'll marry her on the spot! I know that in heart and mind."

"*Attenzione, attenzione*! Just wait a minute," the good priest said as he patted the young man's shoulder. "You may be setting yourself up for a trap. After all, what will you do with a girl of little world experience, a girl who has no idea of a city? Who will make her out for the better?"

"My sisters will be thrilled. They'll teach her what she needs to know, and they'll tell her how to act. For me, I don't care a fig; I just want to bask in that beauty."

The marchese imagined Eugenia as a girl fully given to life, not a child rooted in privilege; a girl who'd never heard of salons, who didn't know the art of flirtation for gain or advancement. Here was a girl who had an enduring passion for art. Not just to be represented, but to represent herself directly.

"If you want to take her with you," the priest said, "you'll have to speak to her mother. Since her husband ran off, she might welcome some kind of a deal. I'm sure that when she hears where you come from, the mother—greedy like her husband—will quickly give in. But who knows what's to follow?"

The priest was feeling bloated, his lunch still high in his paunch, his thighs pinching from the fabric of his ever-tightening trousers. The midday wine had left him drowsy. It was time for an afternoon nap, he thought. Rising from his armchair, the priest declared their chat had ended, and the marchese bid him farewell. Early tomorrow, he would visit the house of Troiano, the place where he'd first set eyes on the splendorous girl.

6.

The marchese took a breath and tapped on the door. Donna Rosina received him with some surprise, but when he offered to show his credentials, she quickly invited him in, guided as she was by a fear of authority as well as a curious eye.

"I wish to speak with your daughter," he ventured with cap and cloak in hand. Donna Rosina trembled as she imagined this unknown man presenting her with a bill or a tax claim. She shuffled to the back of the house to gain her composure and catch her breath.

"Oh, where is Troiano when I need him?" she asked herself. "I can't believe I have to speak on my own."

She went out to the yard to find Eugenia, who was feeding the rabbits.

"Hurry," Rosina whispered. "It looks like we have someone important who wants to meet you. A nobleman from Naples, he says, but in truth I can't follow his words."

"About what?" asked Eugenia.

"Who knows?" she said with tremulous voice. "Let's hope it remains easy and simple and has nothing to do with money. For once, let's try not to get duped, and let's hope we're not played for fools."

Eugenia needed a minute to collect her thoughts. Meanwhile, her mother returned inside to attend to her guest.

Donna Rosina looked the young man over. He had a perfect mustache and a suit of exquisite stitching. She saw a needlework style that few women in town could follow. In Bellanera, the women lacked the raw materials to produce such elegant thread and fabric. The coarse hemp of Lucanian sheep couldn't match the crimp of Merino wool. Even his polished boots were novel. His posture also seemed drawn from a different world.

Rosina couldn't peek behind the splendid image he cut, but she could see the young man was nervous.

"I came to introduce myself and present my family's credentials," he said, not without some discomfort. He knew full well that his family's coat of arms held no meaning in this village except when it came to collecting rent. Nothing about his urban life could be imagined here. Nothing of his private lessons, his physical training, his attire arranged by white-gloved butlers, his father's stable of horses (albeit now reduced in size), the multiple homes his family had once held in the city and by the coast, the gifts that three hundred years of entitlement (by now largely squandered) had bestowed upon his family. "Might I speak with your daughter?"

Donna Rosina pretended to inhabit her husband's body and voice. After a deep breath, she said with a certain huff known to the Troiano clan, "What's the goal here, young man, if you don't mind my asking?"

It was legend, after all, that the noble men took peasant girls for their pleasure and then let them go after a few nights of fun. The old traditions of first-night privilege still lingered among elites in the country. Yet no one had heard of a noble approaching the mother of an ordinary girl in quite this way. The apple cart was upset, so to speak, and Rosina was deeply confused. She invited him for a *goccia di caffè,* as was the custom in even humble homes, and promised him that Eugenia would appear in due time.

When Eugenia appeared, her eyes sparkled, her full lips were the color of roses. The marchese bowed before he spoke. "I c-came to introduce myself and to ma-make your acqu-u-u-aintance. I saw your image on the amaro b-b-b-bottle and recognized you at once. In person, you are equally splendid."

Eugenia watched the visitor with hawk eyes. She found him amusing. She thought he sounded like Silvio in his most difficult moments. Eugenia smiled and knew that she had command over this silly man. Her task, then, was to calm him down, to set him at his ease, to treat him as she had Silvio in the early days of their friendship. Eugenia spoke about her life in the town. Not the household chores, the milling of wheat, the chickens, or the markets, but the way she and Silvio had devoted themselves to art.

"We have the habit of wandering in the hills to look for interesting subjects. Silvio studies the way in which light falls on rivers and stones. After all, as I tell him, art is all about light. I also try to copy nature myself, but my hand and eye are not steady. For my own taste, I'm more interested in the objects we find buried in riverbanks and fields."

Eugenia reached for a few pieces of broken ceramic she had pulled from the valley nearby.

"Maestra Pina once told the students that these were vessels from Magna Grecia. Do you know this history?"

Eugenia's listener was pleasantly surprised. Here, in the middle of nowhere, a beautiful young girl was about to discuss the ancient Greeks who once had crossed through the region.

"My goodness," he said *sotto voce*. "I'm deliriously happy!"

The marchese spoke of antiquity, the painted urns and sculptures that he so admired. Eugenia's eyes lit up as he told her of the marvelous museums that held those treasures of long ago.

"A while ago, Zia Wanda let me read the Naples papers where I saw pictures of the museums. The city caught my eye and made me wish to know it."

The conversation followed along this line until, upon leaving, the marchese asked donna Rosina for permission to visit again.

7.

One visit followed another. Eugenia spoke of photography, of the need to embellish the image; she told him of stories she'd read at school and her interest in science and letters. Then Eugenia introduced the marchese to Silvio, and the three spoke about pictures. They took a walk in the woods, and Eugenia described in detail the plants and flowers she knew. All this left the marchese in a state of unspeakable wonder. Nature and art combined; no pretensions; no noble elites to intervene; simply a passion for beauty.

The marchese began to imagine a future: Eugenia would accompany him on walks through the sun-drenched hills. They would explore the poppy-laced fields to uncover shards of ancient vases, to find mementos that once had belonged to the Greeks traveling across the peninsula from Brindisi toward Naples. She would delight in discovering stonework dating from the Emirate of Bari or finding a star of David chiseled on granite slab at the site of Venosa's unfinished cathedral. Under his tutelage, she would never assign these objects value in the style of old antiquarian collectors; there'd be no need to accumulate these treasures and put them on display. Instead, the object would speak to beauty alone; it would be free from the rush of the buy-and-sell world.

His few encounters with Eugenia had opened his mind to new horizons. Could he escape the course that had been set for him for centuries? Could he find delight in this innocent creature who shared his passion for art and rural promise? Should he ask for Eugenia's hand even though he knew he would encounter resistance? Would his father consent to the marriage? Would his sisters support his desire? And could he envision a path for Eugenia among the nearly fallen nobles who still held onto past glories?

A week passed and in a rash moment, the marchese approached donna Rosina. "Signora," he said with nervous discomfort. "I am here to request your daughter's hand."

Silence filled the room. Rosina was mute; the visitor, still as stone.

Rosina knew that if she assented, her life would be much improved. This was a chance to trigger unknown fortune, to leave poverty behind, to give her girl the chance to rise far above her station. Skeptic that she was, she didn't believe in love at first sight, but she certainly saw the advantage of this once-in-a-lifetime "deal." Her youngest child would enter a social class that surpassed her wildest dreams. But could this in fact be managed? Who would guarantee Eugenia's safety? And who would help her cross into a world so foreign and strange? Rosina said she needed time to mull this over and speak with the priest. And, oh, by the way, she needed to speak with her daughter.

* * * *

The following afternoon, don Felicetto received Rosina warmly. Speaking for his friend the marchese, the priest observed the marriage proposal's different advantages: an invitation to send her youngest child to a life of privilege, one with tutors and teachers galore; an education in the most reputable manner, perhaps lessons in French, a training for life as a *signora*. The marchese's older sisters would escort Eugenia through their social milieu. It was all a question of decorum, which Eugenia had the spirit to learn. If Eugenia had learned to read and write beyond her fifth-grade schooling, to adapt to new conventions and show off a perfect smile, then Eugenia, donna Rosina's most precious child, would also be able to greet the elites of Naples, to give her hand to dukes and counts and, perhaps, one day meet the king.

"Let me put it another way: this is an opportunity that only comes once," don Felicetto said. "Send the girl to Naples. Let her see new worlds. Let her learn the art of nobles. Let her acquire the tastes of the rich. I don't see how you can lose."

The worried mother received these words with some hesitation; after all, she was balancing her dream for a giant rainbow of wealth against the fear of losing her child. Resolutely, however, Rosina carried the news to her daughter.

"You have to be kidding, Mamma. I'm just too young for this stuff, and this man simply won't do," Eugenia said. She wasn't thinking of escaping the prison of home in order to enter the prison of marriage.

"But you say you want to flee! So now here's your chance."

"But flight under terms that I decide. Never bowing to a man I don't know."

"Don't you think that with time you'll get to know him?"

"But who is he, Mamma? Just a rich man with a cape and a title."

"Try harder, *figlia mia*. Imagine a better life for us all."

"I'm not living in a fairy tale."

"What's your choice, Eugenia? To find a man who will take you to live in a hut and feed you lard and onions?"

Here, Eugenia shuddered.

"To marry a boy like Silvio who smells of sheep and night soil? Wake up, *figlia mia*!"

Knowing that this marriage would cure all their financial ills, Eugenia understood her mother's motives but put up a considerable fight. Here Donna Rosina prevailed and won over her daughter's objections. Almost like a sleight of hand trick, mother and child reached an agreement: Eugenia would be sent to Naples in exchange for her freedom. There was no talk of love.

Months went by before the contract was settled. Through correspondence with the marchese's family (usually via don Felicetto), Eugenia's mother consented to the marriage. The Franciscan nuns, through a year of rigorous lessons in Naples, would impart the virtues of devotional practice and the rules of decorum, preparing Eugenia for her role as a high-society wife. Above all, they would offer her shelter. In the beginning, before the convent training started, her mother would be Eugenia's protector and companion. Together, they would learn about life in the strange and unruly city. The details arranged, an agreement drawn up, Donna Rosina began to prepare the ritual dowry. Lacking any property that would pass as a marriage offer, she humbly sent cheese and dried meats as gifts for the Cimino family; the aunts offered two tablecloths of impeccably hand-stitched lace, one for the marchese's sisters and another for the headmistress of the convent where Eugenia would reside. Eugenia was in a tizzy.

"I'm not sure if I'm coming or going. I can't see anything clearly," she said to Silvio one afternoon.

"But love will save the day, d-d-don't you think?" said Silvio with nary a stammer.

"How do we know what love is?" Eugenia said. "All I know is that the marriage resolves our money problems. My mother said it was important to go, so I'll obey her. But don't ask me if I love Gianpietro. I wouldn't know if he really loves me. I think we're all trapped in a dream."

8.

The marchese arranged for the voyage to Naples. Neither the habitual Vetturini coach, shared by several travelers and pulled by three horses, nor the diligenza stage wagon that only went as far as Salerno, would suffice for Eugenia and her mother.

"No," the marchese said. "These ladies deserve the best."

The voyage took three days. As they approached Naples, they were captivated neither by the colossal volcano overlooking the bay nor by the grand roadway around the shore showing off its necklace of lights. Instead, cacophonous noise overtook them. Bewildered and somewhat frightened, they covered their ears as they entered the city. Entering from the harbor side, passing the ships and breakwaters, the horses clattering past fortresses and castles, they were disturbed by discordant screaming, harsh and endless shrieks, and the rattling of nearby carriages and braying mules at the side of the road.

"How can you keep a half million people quiet?" Eugenia asked the driver. Then she said to her mother, "And when do these people sleep?"

Eugenia had read about the mayhem of Naples in the daily press. From Zia Wanda's stash of papers, she'd followed reports on city life; she remembered the columns of Matilde Serao, who wrote about urban ruin. Unsurprisingly, the turbulence she experienced here exceeded the powers of newsprint. Nothing could give a full sense of the uproar but hearing it for yourself. The hometown pundits had given advice and warnings: "Don't forget to see the San Gennaro feast and watch his blood come alive!" "Look for the Cuccagna trees that draw people to the major piazzas." "Beware the crooks in the *bassi*!" And then the endless stories of the thieves, the lottery, and the loan sharks. Of course, the village ladies and taletellers had never visited Naples and so they depended on word of mouth to instill fear in the women travelers. Some advice dated back to the previous century; some stories flowed through regional folklore; some pictures of festivities came from newspapers and magazines. But the popular fictions surrounding Naples, instead of inspiring fear, awakened Eugenia's hunger to see the city up close and in person.

The women felt trepidation as they rode into Naples and climbed to the Vomero district. The hill strained the pace of the horses as the travelers sensed that they were leaving behind the odors of garlic and fried sweets, the smell of rancid oil, the whinnying donkeys, and the ceaseless ruckus they had heard on the streets below. Up the hill they first saw the palazzi in their new Liberty style, known elsewhere as art nouveau. Eugenia held her breath. She had never seen a building more than two stories tall. Then on to the marchese's family who lived near the Villa Floridiana, a posh quarter established in recent years. The elites and phony-balonies, liking to brag about their surroundings, explained with condescension how they avoided the hoi polloi. When later they repeated that infelicitous phrase, "Today we'll go down to Naples," Eugenia, already identifying herself with those who lived below in the flatlands, couldn't help but cringe.

Even worse, when Eugenia met the marchese's clan, she couldn't find her words. Although the family was extremely gracious, she lost her courage and stumbled. When she tried to curtsy but lost her step, her face flushed and turned beet red. When her future father-in-law offered his arm, she didn't know how to take it. "A pleasure," she said to the nice sisters, but could find nothing to say.

"We welcome you with our hearts," Gianpietro said to Eugenia.

This was strange, she thought, the way he spoke to her using the royal "we." Perhaps when they were alone, the affection that he'd first displayed would return to the conversations.

But a few days later, Gianpietro still spoke to her as a teacher. "We can take you to the Portico dei Capolavori at the museum in Naples. There's a second century Antinous that we'd like you to see. It depicts a man with a handful of grapes awaiting Hadrian's touch. In the work, Antinous showed us that there was no other life, but the beauty of man cast in stone."

Here Eugenia didn't understand a thing. He'd left her out of the conversation. Perhaps her role was to be his student and listen?

Anyway, who was Antinous?

"How can I catch up? Or am I supposed to catch up at all?" she asked.

"Don't worry," he said. "First, we'll see the museums and churches, then the seashore. We'll tell you what you need to know if you let us be your guide."

Eugenia sensed that the man she was about to marry was more of a teacher than a spouse. She told herself that she didn't mind. This was part of the adventure, and he could train her in the visual arts and make up for those histories that she and Silvio had yet to learn.

When Eugenia offered her hand at the close of an afternoon tea, Gianpietro's fingers were listless, almost cold to the touch. She nodded in silence and bit her lip. No one was there to help her, and she didn't dare confide in her mother.

After two months in the city watching over her daughter's progress, Rosina chose to return to Bellanera and leave Eugenia with the kind individuals who would take charge of her training. Astutely sensing that the marchese would not dishonor her youngest child, and knowing that the nuns would oversee her education, Rosina told herself that her work for now was done. She wanted to go home to the country to regain some peace of mind.

"Remember to behave yourself, Eugenia," her mother said as she packed her bags and tucked the marchese's gifts of large bills in the folds of her undergarment. "This will keep me for a while." Rosina patted the paper bulge near her breast. Eugenia winced as if she had eaten a lemon. She repeated what she already knew: this marriage would benefit her mother; it resolved the problem of debt; it came with social guarantees. But what about her?

"I'm part of a trade," Eugenia said. But before her bold statement awakened her mother's anger, Eugenia confessed that she had understood this as part of the deal. "Don't worry, Mamma, I'll be alright. There's lots for me to learn. A new world awaits me, and the marchese is devoted and kind."

After her mother had left, Eugenia moved to the convent where, for a year, she would learn under the guidance of nuns. The first night, she closed her bedroom door and cried until morning.

9.

Life behind the convent walls failed to diminish Eugenia's fears, though it held points of interest. The swish-swish of the nuns' brown habits created an ongoing hum as if to say that she wasn't alone. And then unnamable, useless objects rolled at her like tumble weeds in the wind: the tea service with quirky silver pieces that she didn't know how to manage; luxurious settees that were as hard on her bottom as Maestra Pina's schoolroom benches; windows framed by dark wood panels and walls papered with designs of carnations; a *calamaio* or inkstand the likes of which she'd never seen. Then, the matter of language, almost impenetrable to her ears. Eugenia needed to translate the language she had brought from home: not a *pezza*, but a *lira*; not *portogallo*, but *arancia*. Above all, she had to put the vowels back in the places where, according to the holy sisters, they were meant to stay.

The nuns taught Eugenia to peel fruit with knife and fork, to sit at the table with newspapers rolled under her arms so her hands wouldn't fly in the air. She also learned to eat tender morsels of beef. No more meals of chickpeas and spinach; *addio* to lentils and noodles, boiled greens with bits of garlic.

Her hostesses arched their brows when they heard the vocabulary of Eugenia's kitchen— *latt', 'scarol, 'u pomorol, nu chiatt' di past' e patan'*. This all had to change! Not only did they try to restore the vowels to the country girl's speech, but they also demanded that Eugenia begin to learn a fair bit of French.

"Impossible," Eugenia said. "This isn't part of the deal."

"Oh yes, it is, *signorina*. If you want to eat in high society, you'll need the sounds of the *bleu, blanc, rouge*."

So Eugenia had to submerge herself in a quick course of culinary French, whose stiff and short nasal sounds recalled the pigs snorting on Don Ciccio's farm back home.

"*Paté à choux, doigts de fée.* You need to repeat."

"Enunciate! Speak properly!"

Eugenia balked, rebelled, and then raised her voice. "It's almost like blowing your nose. Why not say things in our native ways?" It was bad enough she had to learn standard Italian in order to prove she was human. Now she had to master French in order to speak about food.

"And when do we get to eat?"

* * * *

After a year Eugenia left the convent and went to live with the family in Naples. She was uncomfortable in her new abode. The marchese was usually absent, and the household help, whom Eugenia had hoped to befriend, gave no sign of interest. Only the marchese's sisters looked after her as if to check her every move. At this time, the petty nobility was still reeling from the news that an anarchist from New Jersey had assassinated the Italian king; they couldn't put the event behind them though it had happened a while ago. And now they had the upcoming social soirée of the season in which the dead king's son, now inducted, would make an appearance in Naples. The women swooned, the gentlemen cheered, champagne and French wine flowed in abundance, and the Neapolitan elites who planned the fête covered every detail. The new king and his lady Elena were received in Naples with a glorious luncheon. In truth, the meal was in honor of the Count of Vandersee, who was returning from China, but when the Neapolitans heard that the king and his retinue were also in town, the excitement simply exploded.

The marchese's sisters thought this was the moment to introduce Eugenia. After all, she now spoke close to standard Italian, she curtsied at the appropriate moments, she understood the table rules and was able with knife and fork. They outfitted her in a perfectly fitted organza gown. The bodice was boned and tight, with a V neck cut. Eugenia was astonished when she saw her reflection in a mirror.

"Look at me in this dress! I don't even know who I am."

In public, she was entirely gracious, but her eyes grew wide as she stared at the extravagant gowns, the cravats and frock coats, the endless bows and curtseys. Eugenia took careful note. Then she eyed the menus. In French, *pas moins*, the menu card was received as a model of exquisite taste. "*Dejeuner du 22 Août*" read the card for the Neapolitan banquet, starting with *macaroni a la parisienne, oeuf poche a la Villerol* and *Cotelettes de veau aux petits pois*.

A major feast, thought Eugenia, but you still had to eat in French.

At the Cimino house, Eugenia showed no real interest in these fancy meals. Bored by the conversations, the marchese's longwinded speeches, and the cues she had to follow in order to peel a simple grape, Eugenia turned her eye to other aspects of the table. What most struck her were the food's shapes and colors: the red and gold spices, the pastas molded into wheels or spiraling corkscrews. Not just the familiar *orecchiette* from Bari, which looked like the ears of a newborn puppy, but little potato dumplings called *gnocchi*; and tiny three-tiered sandwiches stuffed with green leaves, boiled eggs, and cream. There were shrimp curled up like tiny babies in white blankets, shimmering black mussel shells that exposed their plump orange cushions, squid that carried little mops you might use to tickle your face. Who could ever imagine such outlandish forms, such oddities from nature? Eugenia kept her eyes on the food to avoid the need to talk. After all, this was the first time in her life that she enjoyed a plate of her own.

Staring at a glistening fish one night, Eugenia drifted in thought. Surely this was an advance over her earlier life, an improvement over the lot of girls who continued to live in her village. And, lest she forget—how could she ever forget? —she could live without fear of her father. Now, she resided in a house with wide bay windows, polished lamps, and hand-cut crystal glasses, and chairs upholstered in finest silk. At the table, she saw a rush of stories rising up from the dishes: blue and white plates told of fishermen knee-high in tranquil rivers while squirrels hoarded acorns at the base of giant trees; the Maiolica ceramics showed chubby babies surrounded by tiny angels. Last, the silver cutlery engraved with the Ciminos' "C" reminded her that life was Complete and that she'd best resist Complaining.

10.

Eugenia tried to approach her betrothed but found the exchanges remarkably flat. Cordial, warm, and perfunctory, but never of great substance. It's true, however, that Gianpietro spoke with her every afternoon.

"You're lovely, Geni. I hope that you enjoy your life in Naples."

"Well," Eugenia said, "I feel somewhat alone. Your sisters are magnificent, but I still worry about us as a couple."

A silence followed that cut the air.

"Do you like me, Gianpietro?" Eugenia asked.

Another pause.

"Do you enjoy yourself with me?"

"I know I'm distracted, dear Geni. That's simply the way I am, but I know that I've been graced by the most beautiful woman in these parts."

Eugenia spoke not a word.

"We can go for a ride through the city," he said.

Eugenia accepted his proposal as a chance to see something new. A day later, however, it wasn't the marchese who appeared, but his two good sisters who had decided to escort their future sister-in-law on a tour of the town.

Under Margherita and Elena's charge, Eugenia found the Riviera di Chiaia, a seafront promenade where avenues of gingkoes and stately royal palms embraced the imposing statues. On Saturday afternoons, a band played on the green, with music ranging from military marches to Rossini's lighter compositions. There were no bagpipes to be heard here; neither tambourines nor upbeat tunes encouraged festive dancing. Rather, the band's solemnity captured a degree of sadness. Perhaps it spoke of the statue's gaze or of the passersby who, as she did, felt somewhat estranged. Eugenia noticed people who didn't resemble her family back home or anyone in Naples. Humble men shuffled in silence across the green, men with black hair tied back in a braid. They carried prayer books under their arms. They were strangers, the sisters told her, who came to train for missionary work before returning to China. Eugenia had no idea about China, about a school called L'Orientale, about the possibilities of traveling the world in search of knowledge. For her, reaching Naples by carriage was more than enough. But these men seemed terribly alone.

The violins whined, the cellos moaned, spreading sorrow through the air as Eugenia walked through the park. The sisters explained that the green held a temple to Virgil, a bust of Torcuato Tasso; they pointed out Octavius's horse standing on a pedestal with one hoof raised. Though Eugenia had no idea what these statues meant, she knew there were no tributes to the Lucanian brigands, those men and women whom her cousins had praised when out of Troiano's reach. These statues all suggested contemplation; they were figures alternately sitting and thinking, sometimes resting their chins on their fists, sometimes gazing out to the sea. They were always frozen in time.

One day, the sisters led Eugenia to the aquarium at the far end of the park. She was quite excited since she remembered the stories she had read with Zia Wanda. Tales about giant fish, huge vessels holding sea life. Yet it was strange to see fish, which you would never plan to batter and fry, all locked up. Did they beg for freedom?

Her great surprise came when she found the giant koi. Eugenia remarked that she had read about the koi while she studied with Zia Wanda. "It was the Japanese emperor's gift to Naples," she told the sisters. "I was shocked to learn that koi had a lifespan of two hundred years."

As Eugenia stared at the fish, she rewrote history. From the koi, she imagined a wise old man who would outlive his captors, and when he reached his two-hundredth birthday, he would then turn into a genie bestowing the gift of flight to all the imprisoned animals and people. He would liberate the medieval princess from her cell in Muro Lucano; he would release the Austrian Queen of Naples from her palace exile in Sicily; he would free Eugenia from her castle in the Vomero hills and allow her to return to her village. So much time, she thought, for the fish to realize his eventual calling. If only he gave her the chance, she would run away too.

11.

Months later, as Eugenia settled into her new life and before plans for the wedding advanced, Silvio paid a visit. Noticing how much Silvio was suffering over the absence of his only friend, Don Felicetto, traveling to Naples to meet the bishop, decided to take him along. The two school chums knew no words. Silvio's depth of feeling overwhelmed him; Eugenia wept uncontrollably as she embraced her pal.

"It's strange here," Eugenia said when her emotions had settled down. "So much fanfare about good manners and behavior: when to bring a napkin to your lips, when to use a fork instead of a spoon, where to sit, how to cross your legs, how to speak in proper Italian. So much talk about family affairs, the endless obsession with money, the rents lost and the rents gained, the marvels of what once was. When I compare this life to the day-to-day in our village, I'm nearly driven to madness."

Silvio listened with compassion.

"*Un po' troppo*," Eugenia said adding that she found herself like a bird without a nest.

"Dont bb-be hurt. You kin leave this situashun." Silvio's stutter had returned. His heart broke when he heard his friend so crestfallen. They didn't even mention Eugenia's romance with the distant marchese, who at this stage was increasingly absent, devoted (as his sisters reported) to matters of the hunt.

Silvio took her hand. "Perhaps you should return home. It's not for you."

"This is a business," she said. "A way to help my mother; a way to get out of a life of chores. No more *past' e fagiol'*."

The relationship with her betrothed, she explained, had no viable traction. Her feelings could wait for another day. Without hesitation, refusing to look sideways or inward, Eugenia basked in the scarce hours she spent with her beloved Silvio.

When Don Felicetto went off to see the bishop, the sisters offered to take Silvio and Eugenia to a museum. Eugenia was now familiar with the route, but it fascinated Silvio no end. They rode by carriage through the garbage-strewn streets and endless human squalor: unkempt children playing in alleys, women selling secondhand wares, ladies of pleasure idling in doorways, vendors hawking barrels of snails. These visions startled Silvio; they offered another rhythm and color to the life of the poor, more raucous and more begrimed. Everywhere people bunched together outdoors as if the buildings couldn't contain them. In some cases, it looked as if everyone were living out on the street. Everything was new; he saw the city as if he were a sparrow recently hatched. He felt that he was observing a novel form of events still lacking names and voices.

As their carriage clattered forward, Silvio was most impressed with the posters lining the streets. They took on grand proportions: pictures the size of full-grown men affixed to building walls; signs pegged to windows and hanging from lamp poles; graphics that overwhelmed storefronts and gallery windows. Each image sold a product: men wearing handsome hats and neckties; beautiful women modeling gloves; medicines for children; toilets and sinks, pasta and wine; bicycles and sewing machines for ladies at home.

The sisters explained that these designs promoted merchandise throughout Naples; they shouted out to the passersby to tell them what was new in the world. They reminded Silvio that even the now famous picture of Eugenia on the aperitif label was in line with this publicity. As they rode to the museum, Silvio formed a connection between a picture of some product and your desire to own it; it made you want more than you had.

The old friends concluded that no two poster techniques were alike. Paint, pen and ink, tempera washes, and engravings. Neither Silvio nor Eugenia had the vocabulary to explain the artistic techniques they saw, but they knew they were entering a marvelous realm in which the signs appealed to the senses. Silvio wondered how the people of Naples could deal with so many pictures, so many colors that tempted the imagination and occasionally tugged at the heart. How did they manage to withstand it? The signboards almost rendered him useless; his nerves were on fire, his body about to explode. Against so much excitement, Silvio felt the need to close his eyes and rest, to shut off his lens on the world.

They finally reached the museum, and, aware of his interest in drawing, the sisters were happy to lead the young artist through the various Bourbon palazzi. Here were the repositories of the greatest collections, Margherita and Elena said, the very best in the world. Eugenia nodded (though, of course, she couldn't compare Naples to any place except her hometown). From earlier trips to the galleries, she had her favorites, but now that Silvio was with her, they could study the art together. Silvio had never before visited a museum; its labyrinthine hallways and oversized salons amazed him. One room after another left him in a state of delirium.

He was equally startled (and frightened) to behold world history through art. He saw the Virgin and child looking down at the Bay of Naples, scenes drawn from biblical legends—the miracles, the devotion, the violence. He studied the peasants of Magna Grecia; the macaroni eaters in the public square, the plagues, the beheadings, the brutal beatings of men and women while Jesus hovered nearby to express his disapproval. They came upon the work of a woman artist who had painted the mighty Judith slaying Holofernes. Both Eugenia and Silvio fell into a trance-like state.

"*Oh Dio*," Eugenia exclaimed. "Look at that woman stabbing a man. Look at the strength of her arm, her determined gaze, her fixed resolve as she plunges her sword into the dying man's neck. What's more, she had a friend to help her. There they are, holding down the bad man's head as he slips off the mattress. With his fist he pushes back against the woman in red while Judith thrusts her weapon. He has a giant arm, but the women's arms are stronger; he's crying, but the women are determined to kill him."

On every visit to the museum, Eugenia studied this painting. Artemisia's canvas awakened her passion, her anger. She maybe revealed some guarded resentment against the marchese, her rage at her father and brother Antonio, or a scene in which some village ruffian tried to press himself against her. She knew the painting told an important story about the power of women's revenge.

Silvio was given less to the story and more to the canvas's forceful colors: "Look at the r-r-red blood dripping from the bearded man's neck." He pointed out the royal-blue fabric of one woman's dress against the other's crimson gown; their golden arms exposed by an unnatural white light in contrast to the man's dark-olive hues. The soiled mattress, sheets drenched in blood; the oppressive room.

The picture was made of triangular shapes that led your eye around the canvas, Silvio tried to say. Silvio pointed to the light that fell on the women's faces; he wanted Eugenia to see how the soiled white mattress cut the painting in two. No scene could be less settled, he thought.

"This is a miracle of justice," Eugenia said, "showing the power of women. But it also makes me feel locked in." She didn't yet know the word "claustrophobic," but certainly knew the feeling.

Silvio lacked the strength of breath to answer Eugenia's assertions but felt the painting's emotions came from the light's direction, the contrasting angles and colors. He nodded to Elena and Margherita when they said that it was time to go.

The visit then came to a gentle close when the marchese's sisters presented Silvio with a reproduction of the painting that he especially liked and a box of paints with brushes and tools. Silvio was deeply grateful and promised to deliver on the trust that the fabulous gift implied.

12.

Two years had passed, and Eugenia was ready for her formal entrance into Neapolitan life. The Cimino clan was ready to bring Eugenia into the family, assured as they were by her social graces, her newly found etiquette and poise. It was time for the wedding that would tie the proverbial knot. The family opted for the Cathedral at Pompeii, a significant distance from Naples but close enough to Eugenia's clan. Neutral territory, they decided, so each party would be on equal ground. They would come for the day, exchange vows at the church. A celebration would follow, and the families would dance from dusk until dawn. The next day, the couple would begin their honeymoon on the island of Ischia. Eugenia's mother would tag along, assuring discretion and order.

Just before the wedding, Eugenia was nervous. With Silvio at her side, she looked in the mirror and wondered about her future role as a wife. To go from country bumpkin to urban *signora* with a title was enough to make her alternately giddy and glum.

"What do you think, Silvio? Should I go through with this?"

"Listen to your heart," Silvio said.

She continued looking in the mirror to see if she could erase the image of a country girl smiling from the glass.

Silvio said, "Don't be sure that you're such a bumpkin. If you look in the mirror, you'll see a picture of superlative beauty."

He was her rock, her salvation.

"And the groom?" he asked.

"Don't bother," Eugenia said. "He's in his separate world. I'll see him tonight at the wedding."

Eugenia left the mirror, gathered the train of her gown, and with her mother and several relatives began her carriage ride to the cathedral. There the bishop presided over the ceremony with Don Felicetto at his side. As Raffaele Troiano had disappeared and couldn't sign his daughter's marriage certificate, the family asked don Ciccio to give Eugenia his formal blessing. Solemn rites, a nervous couple, families beaming with joy. The couple kissed and left the church in preparation for the wedding party.

The event was held at a palace, the largest Eugenia had ever seen. Eugenia was used to weddings in the woods close to Bellanera. Three or four musicians, usually uncles and cousins, played; the women brought food from home. Here, by contrast, the wedding was shaped with exquisite care, a formal event for elites. When Eugenia, in her splendid beauty, entered, all eyes turned her way.

She wore an incomparable lace gown sewn by the finest seamstresses from Via Chiaia. Nonetheless, her nervousness showed through her veil. The public took it as a sign of love and smiled; Silvio knew that her twitching was a sign of Eugenia's fear.

"Oh, help me out of this, Silvio. What am I to do?" she seemed to say with her eyes.

Silvio gently pushed his friend toward a platform and made sure she stood by the marchese to receive the guests' good wishes. Here the marchese's father lifted a glass, commending the happy couple to a successful and prosperous life.

"*Cent'anni*! *Figli maschi*!" the guests cried out. "Here's to boy babies, virile and strong."

A chamber ensemble played a first waltz by Rossini and then a cautious and slow-paced version of a popular Neapolitan song. More toasts accompanied by exquisite champagne, a few words in French (which no one from home understood), and then the wedding parties were directed to separate rooms: Eugenia's relations in one salon (where musicians performed with *putipu* and *tammorra*) and the marchese's family in another (where the guests agreed to respect the rules of social etiquette as advised by Eugène Giraudet). Eugenia was confused by the dual settings, a party set in two tones, yet everyone from the Troiano side accepted it as a move up from humble table scraps to horizons of new-found glory.

The country guests presented modest gifts: a beaded pendant for the bride, sets of linens, embroidered towels. Then the traditional *corredo*, or trousseau, for a country daughter: sheets, pillowcases, coverlets, and blankets for the couple's bedroom; nightgowns and slips, leggings and sweaters, even some handsome dresses designed and sewn by the bride's aunts. Rosina would later send a chest of grain.

Happy to give the bride away, don Ciccio gifted the groom's family with two lambs from his farm. Accompanying Zia Wanda, Maestra Pina presented the couple with a bound set of Petrarch's lyrics. Even the count from Matera and his wife came to express good will and deliver a crate of amaro liqueur. Silvio presented Eugenia and the marchese with his copy of the painting that Eugenia had admired in the Naples museum. Thrilled, Eugenia promised to hang the canvas in the parlor of her new abode while the marchese expressed his admiration for the young man's talent and especially praised Silvio's eye for light and color. Silvio's "Judith and Holofernes" was as perfect as the original canvas, the marchese announced. Somewhat bashful, Silvio accepted the compliment and then, with a slight stammer, expressed his best wishes for the newlywed couple. From a distance, Silvio gazed longingly at his friend's sapphire blue eyes and hoped she would be safe from all danger. He doubted that the love would go far, especially when he observed the couple approaching a kiss; it was no more than a brush of the cheeks, a tender peck, the kind of exchange that cousins share, that old aunties give to their nieces and nephews. That said, the parties danced late into evening. A new partnership was about to be born.

The Narrators

"Wait a minute! Just wait!" Max yelled. "After all these digressions on art and life, after all these tiny stories, let's talk about this marriage. First, do you really mean to tell me that the poor peasant girl married the marchese? And no one put up a fuss? And the family in Naples accepted a girl whose father was a horse thief?"

His sister rose from her chair. She was frothing like beans in a pot.

Max said, "Aren't you dreaming, Sister-Belle? Inventing fairy tales about nobility and peasants when we all know that poor people were left in total squalor? Who's going to believe all this?"

Rosanna shuddered and promised that if Max didn't close his trap, she'd expand upon the wedding, supplying more of the details she'd gathered from reading Eugenia's letters. She had opted to withhold them but promised to put them in the text if anyone began to doubt her sources.

"I've been concise enough, to be sure. So just back off. You should be grateful for me keeping this trim and neat."

The siblings paused the theater of war, and since it was late afternoon, they moved from kitchen to living room to await the start of the evening news. "Disaster news," Max called it to underline its calamities. Rosanna seized the sofa while Max claimed the wing-back chair.

From his throne, Max said, "And then the family in Naples allows Eugenia to strike out on her own, leading an almost independent life while her husband is off with his pals? Never heard of such a thing back then."

"Right," said Rosanna. "This stuff only started last week."

Max snorted and opened his first afternoon beer while pretending not to hear her. "And at the same time, you put Silvio and Eugenia together, so exalted by each other's presence that you'd have to believe they were the primary couple. In point of fact, with their visit to the museum, you buried the marchese on the spot. You cut him out as the leading man."

"You're wrong," Rosanna said. "Don't make me see red. The marchese is necessary to keep the story going, for getting Eugenia and Silvio to Naples so that they can find success on their own."

"I think your fiction just went a step too far. This marriage simply can't happen. And I've yet to see any triumphs."

"Nobility and peasants wed all the time. You can see it in families everywhere. Anthony's grandmother left Settefrati to marry a lawyer from Naples. When they couldn't make their marriage work in the south of Italy, they both shipped off to New York. The encounter of the marchese and Eugenia isn't fiction at all. You know that. In real life, they married, stayed together, and lasted until death took them over. Whether they lived in marital bliss is food for a different table. If you wouldn't mind, let me stick to the course of events."

Rosanna had invested years of work arranging the family's history. She identified with the figures she saw in pictures; and from letters that reached her grandmother from 'the other side,' she guessed their strong points and their faults. She wrote between the lines so to speak. Sure, she changed a few details, but it was all with the goal of preserving a family line, to save them from erasure. She was spokesperson for the clan.

Max eyed his sister with suspicion. "You have me reading for a hundred pages and nothing happens. Most of all, you omit any hint of sex. What the heck's going on?"

Rosanna, flushed and enraged, said, "You have to wait and see how it ends. It comes up in part three. Just leave me alone and keep your comments to yourself."

Max disobeyed. "You're just like that guy Lampedusa. You let your characters frolic without any sex, moony-eyed and chaste. Try to get to the dirty parts and give us something to remember."

"You know as well as I do that Lampedusa deliberately cut out the sex scenes. Nothing happened in Lampedusa's novel except for a jaunt through the palace."

"Kind of like this story I'm reading."

"You always want to know too much. Remember the phrase: 'The pig who gets to eat a lot doesn't know how the story will end'."

"I'm just trying to give you a hand. Pretty soon, I'll have to finish this story for you."

Rosanna countered. "Remember Turandot? Remember how another composer finished the opera after Puccini's death? And remember when our father took us to see it at the old Met and how the crowd screamed out 'Viva Puccini' toward the end of Act III? They only liked what Puccini wrote and were indignant that Franco Alfano had the nerve to complete the opera. Plus, the ending was so nineteenth century. Once again, the repentant woman: nothing to do with the modern, self-asserting, feminist gal who was coming forth in Puccini's day. The audience couldn't stand it, so they sent Alfano to hell and back. You're trying to do the same to me. So, get lost. And do me a favor—keep your mitts off my story."

Max and Rosanna couldn't stop their bickering. To tell this tale was a matter of control, an exercise of power. Their thinking depended on how each understood the passage of time. Max refused to look at the past. He had no interest in the real-life stories fraught with banalities of love and marriage, infidelities and betrayal. He sought something else, but his sister needed to grab onto the past in order to make sense of life. Together, with heads inflamed, they competed for the prize of narration.

"Something meatier," he demanded. "Perhaps a history of horse thieves, as exemplified by old man Troiano?"

Rosanna gritted her teeth. "Forget the horses—that's just the seed of chapter one. I'm on to other details that will show how the characters grow."

Max went to the kitchen to find something to eat. His sister continued to fume. When Max returned, she said, "Eugenia wasn't any ordinary girl. She wanted to move up in life. Unlike you, dear brother, she refused to be a flop."

But Max didn't consider himself a failure. He was devoted to his readings; he was curious about the world of ideas; he liked the people he met on the street. Wasn't that what it was all about? His golf course work put him in touch with interesting big shots. "Not too long ago," he told his sister, "I caddied for a guy with ties to the publishing world. Properly attired, with a shock of faded red hair, this Mr. McCasey knew how to be at ease with his privilege. You could see it in his perfect stride, in the way he carried himself; you could hear it in his perfect voice."

One day, after the ninth hole, Max had driven his client in a motorized cart from the green to the club house. When they passed a natural pond inhabited by mallards and Canada geese, the man began reciting a poem by Yeats. "The trees are in their autumn beauty, / The woodland paths are dry, / Under the October twilight the water / Mirrors a still sky."

Max had smiled and, going against the codes that require that caddies keep their reserve, sung out a quiet response. "Upon the brimming water among the stones / Are nine-and-fifty swans."

The golfer had been taken aback. Surprised that anyone who lived in upper Manhattan or the Bronx would know how to read and write, he'd asked Max how he knew the poem.

"I've read my share of poems," Max had said. "But I prefer fiction. Joyce is my man. He's the one who quenches my thirst."

McCasey had asked Max where he'd studied. When Max explained that he was an autodidact and had no use for school, the man had forgotten about his pitiful game, instead playing out a well-known social experiment in which the rich studied the poor. "Tell me about your life, my boy. Your background, your family history."

But Max had found little to say. As the conversation ended, the man had dropped his card in Max's pocket. "Call me if you need anything, kid."

When Max had looked at McCasey's card, he saw that the man had something to do with the book world; he worked at Vanguard Press.

Golfer and caddy continued to meet at the Van Cortlandt Golf Course.

"It's a relief to spend an afternoon in the Bronx," McCasey had told Max one afternoon. "It's a rat race downtown, I don't need to say it. That's why the golf course calms me; it's my nearby *locus amoenus*."

McCasey's casual yet erudite manner worked well with his smart outfits, Max had thought. He'd imagined an old rake like Howard Hughes moving about with similar habits. Max had never encountered a man like McCasey but he didn't want to be forward. As a result, he'd neither forced the contact nor imagined future ties.

Max rejoined the conversation with his sister, but the golfer's words still lingered.

* * * *

On occasion, Max tried to remember the tips McCasey had given him during their time on the course. "Find this new book by Seamus Heaney." "Take a look at Derek Mahon." But with his sister's constant rambling, Max couldn't stay focused; even when she wasn't ranting in that dreadful sing-song voice, she raised the volume on the evening news, and Max couldn't hear anything else. Scandals and murders were her daily passion, and he had to grin and bear it. Any story could spark an emotional torrent from her. The first case he remembered had taken place when he was six and his sister was nine. The TV news had reported the death of Laika, the orphaned dog that the Russians had saved from the streets only to send her to die in Sputnik. It had been a tense moment for the viewers, and even worse for Rosanna since her fourth-grade teacher had used the story to make political hay. The newscasts had covered the tragedy for months: a dog sacrificed in outer orbit without a friend, left with no more than a few paltry meals and air for only a week.

"That's how the Russians do it," Mrs. O'Hara had told her class. "If the Russians could torture a sweet little dog, imagine what they'll do to you."

For the longest time, Rosanna had been so scared by these stories that every night she peed in her bed. Sometimes she'd even written poems that bled with canine devotion. One began with a rhyme that Max didn't like, though Rosanna had gotten to the heart of the matter: "Oh little dog of mine / Lost in space / Hero of the human race / Speak one more time." Max had been frightened as well. What if Max's parents offered his body to science and sent him off to space? What if Max recommended that his sister go in his place?

The competition between siblings ran deep. In fact, it would be a crass mistake to skip over the day Max had nearly lost an eye. One night, hanging out with his pals in Limerick's bar, Max had fallen from a ladder. Sean had sent him up to the higher shelves to bring down a case of Guinness. The ladder had faltered, and on the tumble, Max had cracked the orbital cavity of his right eye. Max had been unable to see beyond the shadows. The doctors had recommended surgery and months of repose in muted light, an eye patch. A shame, the family had thought. It wasn't supposed to be like that, although his mother had remembered the stories she'd heard about Zio Antonio, whose eye had been scarred in a barroom brawl back in Bellanera. In his disabled state, Max could've remained in the neighborhood forever, tending bar for the Irish crowd, running some jobs for the Italian guys who owned a body shop under the El, linking up with Marty in one business or another, driving a golf cart through a green in the Bronx. A young fellow with a pirate's patch. A guy trying to pass for average. A guy who, his sister said, just couldn't see beyond his reach.

For the moment, Max forgot his vision, put Eugenia's life on hold, and turned to the tale of Carmelo, the Troiano sibling who'd left for America in order to find his brother. He didn't warn his sister of the way he had altered this story's finale. Let her be surprised, he thought; I own chapter two. Meanwhile, Rosanna reminded her brother that this distant Zio Carmelo, who had disappeared from New York, had been the light of everyone's eye.

II. Paterson

1.

"Quit shoving," Carmelo said to the bald and thickset man pushing him into the crowds. From the afterdeck reserved for those in steerage, it was hard to see what was going on. Gulls squawking overhead, steamships hissing on the bay, tugboats blasting long and short, deck hands hurling curses. The thunderous, untamed noise. Still, nothing in sight. Too many people swayed in front of Carmelo, keeping him far from the guardrails.

"Dammit," he said to some men who also stretched for a glimpse of land. "We know it's there, but we still can't see it."

A tall man didn't bother to answer but bumped Carmelo's arm as if to keep him from getting ahead. At least, Carmelo thought, when all of this was finally over, when the boat was docked and they disembarked, Antonio would appear. He was the only relation who gave Carmelo hope, who told him the world was in order. He had always guided Carmelo, making sure he had mastered his chores; he had pulled him from the muck. Antonio had promised to help Carmelo stand up when he felt that his life had no meaning. Sure, Antonio was a little crooked, but he loved his younger brother. Antonio had often said that he'd found his honest faith in his sibling. Now Carmelo paused and took a very deep breath. He imagined his brother nearby.

All of a sudden, the ship took a turn, opening Carmelo's line of sight. Out there, the giant stone sentries: Carmelo knew them from pictures. Upright in rows, their panes of glass captured the sparkling sunlight and saluted those watching from sea. They clustered like bees in a hive, he thought. No, he corrected himself, their tall bodies ate up the sky.

His gaze stretched far to the right, where he spied a yawning dragon connecting land mass to land mass. He noticed that his fellow travelers were as amazed as he. Everyone had something to say.

"So strange, so modern, but its arches look like the doors of a church."

"Take a look at its spine!"

"My God, so high above water."

An educated-looking gentleman referred to "crosshatched cables on the bridge," but Carmelo, overhearing the phrase, understood nothing.

"*Bello*," Carmelo said weakly as if to announce his presence.

Eugenia had shown Carmelo pictures of this modern wonder; they had come from pages of magazines she'd clipped from Zia Wanda's reserve. She'd shared her glee with Carmelo when she set the photos before him, inciting Carmelo's enthusiasm for his voyage to New York. His baby sister was smart, alert, and agile, he thought. Nonetheless, her pictures had failed; they lacked the power of nearness, the grandeur of present time.

As the ship approached the port, Carmelo felt impatient. Three days after docking, the steerage class was still on board. Testing newcomers for contagious disease, doctors moved through the ship and left the passengers uneasy. Most had nothing to hide, but those with minor eye or ear infections hoped they wouldn't be noticed. Until 1924, you could remain in the country without documentation, but gaining admission in the first place was a matter of public health. A strong body for work, no record of crime, and proof that you and your family were not as dim-witted as most agents suspected. And, of course, a fistful of dollars. On the trip across, Carmelo had heard the stories that had prepared him for arrival. Now he waited for the next directive. He was confident that he would succeed in the exams and slide easily through the registry room. He would elude the stern-faced doctors, he prayed, and pass by the grim policemen. He would speak in a polite but manly voice just as Antonio had advised in his letters. Nonetheless, an electric shock now coursed through his body; the nervous crowd pushed against him, and a tremor of fear took over.

Carmelo passed the initial tests and was invited to move ahead, but not before an American shipping agent welcomed him to New York and checked his name against the manifest list to make sure he carried no debts. Then he and his companions, who had spent an age in the floating dungeon, were ushered by barge to an island of intake buildings. First steps, Carmelo thought, toward reaching promised ground. Men, women, and children struggled to step off the boat. Some pushed trunks down the sloping planks; others bore sacks on their shoulders. One family followed another, pressing toward the red brick structure where their fates would be decided. The immigration process began again, and now a new set of doctors assessed the entrants as they shuffled up to the second-floor rooms. The doctors looked for people who had trouble walking; they looked for signs of physical weakness; they looked for the confused and disabled. That was round one of the tests although the passengers didn't know it.

To be sure, Carmelo was a sturdy young man. Despite his father's wayward style, Carmelo was earnest and hardworking. And unlike Antonio, who lived by his cunning and wiles, Carmelo leaned on reason. He listened, he showed himself an adept learner, he had the demeanor of a youth you could trust. And he was always grateful to Eugenia, who had helped him in reading and writing. She was far more intellectually inclined than their other siblings, but she never humiliated them. Patiently, she had helped Carmelo with his schoolwork and now her lessons were paying off. Carmelo pleased the inspectors: he showed a dexterity for puzzles and numbers; he eluded the categories of infirm and deranged. This almost veterinary evaluation was the first step toward Carmelo's entry into New York.

It was a cruel scene, Carmelo thought, as he studied the many mothers weighed down by whining children, the grandmothers with sacks of kitchenware and bedding by their sides, the brides towing satin baptismal blankets and swaddling for future infants—those who would be born in the tenements of Brooklyn, in the boarding houses of Trenton, in the cold-water flats near Mulberry Bend or in nearby Long Island City. Then he saw the humiliation of tremulous men, hefty but uncertain and dressed in their Sunday best, who were asked to sign their names. Pressing their meaty fingers to a pen, trying to control their hastened breathing, most offered only two wobbly lines crossing to form an "X."

Carmelo looked around at the cowering men and women who were as anonymous on this Tuesday afternoon as they had been for centuries in their villages at home. A monotone chain of orders pursued them: respond briefly, do as we say, mind your place in line. Carmelo realized there was no place for rest on either side of the ocean.

In the customs house, Carmelo slipped into sadness. This was neither the moment to comfort others—to help them through the check points—nor the occasion to lend a hand with instructions. His goal instead was to advance in the line and, in short, to get through. Here was a breakthrough point: every fellow for himself. He heard the voice of his father.

Next came the line for the writing test, where all the newcomers waited for hours. The crowd, too tired to stand in place, moved toward some available benches. Carmelo found a seat and began to speak quietly with his neighbor, a kindly man who had lived in New York before, traveled home, and was now returning.

"Where are you from?" Carmelo asked him.

"Motta Santa Lucia," the man said. "Somewhere north of Lamezia Terme."

Carmelo nodded but had never heard of such a village. The men turned the conversation to their futures and spoke of their New York arrival.

"The first key to success," said this neighbor, "is to know just enough English in order to recognize your name, to figure out this strange new tongue so that you can respond when they call you."

Carmelo was puzzled.

"I'm Bevacqua," the man said. "But over here they call me Waters. When they said my new name for the first time, I drew a blank. After many weeks, I finally got it; I trained my ear."

The lesson panicked Carmelo. Antonio hadn't referred to this kind of problem.

The Bevacqua man continued, "Here you have to be more than smart. I remember my parents, who were so proud of their names and towns. In America, it's different. There's no way to know how they'll choose to address you or what your eventual name will be. You could say that the way they name you is part of the fee for admission. They'll tell you where you'll live, how you'll live, and they'll decide just what you are worth."

The man was sailing over Carmelo's head, but he realized that he might not understand the sound of his name when a foreign man's tongue pronounced it. He settled into place on the bench.

Maybe an hour later, his neighbor lightly tapped Carmelo's shoulder. "You're Troiano, right?" he asked with almost avuncular kindness.

Carmelo was astonished.

"As I told you, I used to live here and I know how they get it wrong. The agent just called out for Trojan-o, and, from my own experience, this name translates from Troiano. Go and see; I'll bet I'm right."

Thirsty, tired, exhausted, Carmelo stood, adjusted his shirt, and checked the rope that held up his pants. He then went to the counter.

"Trojan-o, Car-a-mel-o, is that you?" the Irish guard asked in English.

A second agent posed twenty-nine questions in Carmelo's native tongue: *Where were you born? Are you married? What is your occupation? Have you ever been convicted? How much money do you have on hand? What is your destination and how do you expect to live?* Carmelo in 1899 lacked the wherewithal to describe his goals. Worse, he had to admit to himself, he'd never known his purpose other than finding his brother.

A temporary document was issued: Carmelo Troiano, male; brown eyes, born 30 May 1883; nation, Italian South. Political affiliation, undefined; no anarchist or socialist leanings. He carried an intense anxiety to pass, before passing was a word he might know.

Luck would have it that Carmelo knew little of political causes; he vaguely remembered occasional stories of brigands. Anarchists on the rise in Naples, socialist uprisings in Milan, protests against the king, demands for a new republic: all this passed him by. No idea of revolution was folded up in his luggage. His sacks carried only benedictions: a scapula blessed by Don Felicetto; a tin medal of the Virgin of Pompeii, another of St. Francis; a paper image of San Gennaro that Eugenia had cut from a newspaper and had given him the day he departed. Carmelo touched his luggage to make sure that his possessions were there, and he patted the flimflam document that carried only a photograph with his name, his signature, and a government stamp.

Then, in an instant, the inspector—with a glance over Carmelo's sturdy, athletic frame and a quick review of Carmelo's scores on the intake exams—nodded his approval. Asking for the fifty-cent head tax required of each new arrival, the inspector pressed a green tag toward Carmelo's fingers; this was his exit card, his admission to New York City. A second life was about to begin.

2.

In sum: after encountering waves of indigestion and nausea, the nearness of acrid sweat, the rotten meats flaring the nostrils, and the stench of night soil rising, Carmelo hoped a calm would soon take over. But the raucous gulls overhead reminded him that he still needed to find a ferry to take him to New York. Getting to the station post that changed lire for U.S. dollars, he now secured a means of transit: first a shuttle boat to the mainland and then a horse-drawn cart. To the second driver, he flashed a paper bearing his brother's address. He sought the boarding house of Zia Cristina, a widow from Tricarico, who offered beds to single men working near Mulberry Bend.

On land, Carmelo caught the rumble of motors, the staccato of flashing lights, loaded wagons and pushcarts, tall buildings crowding the sky. From ship, the eye and ear couldn't take in the city's breadth. He hoped the novelty of the street scene would never come to an end. When he finally arrived at the address in lower Manhattan, what Antonio had called the "*bassa città*," Carmelo's sensual rhapsody came to a sudden halt.

Carrying his sacks to the building's third floor, Carmelo hoped to find his brother. Carmelo treasured those rare letters that had reached their little village; regularly, he had memorized Antonio's letters as a way to keep him present. In one, Antonio had advised Carmelo of Zia Cristina's boarding house. He'd told of the landlady's greed, how she rented out two-thirds of her flat, partitioning it into small compartments, four filthy cots to a quarter. He'd explained how some lucky boarders had access to a window while others had use of a single electric lamp hanging from the ceiling. The least fortunate among them lived in stinking darkness with no air or room to move. Antonio abhorred the lack of light and ventilation. It made him cough without relief.

"It's true, fifty tenants shared the two alley latrines." Antonio had written. "Cleanliness is not a feature of the tenements over here."

Carmelo looked around as he recalled his brother's words.

"You're lucky if the fever doesn't reach your flat. And the food: Zia Cristina dilutes the soup, serves day-old bread, and loads the ragú with crackling and pig bones she steals from the butcher's waste heap. If you're still hungry late in the evening, and if you have a few coins in your pocket, you can join the tramps in the stale beer dives and buy a bread and butter for just two cents. But I was told not to do it often because crooks are lurking nearby."

In another letter, Antonio had taught Carmelo his first American word. The "*bak-hous*" referred to the outdoor place you went to relieve your bowels. Antonio mostly complained of the rising stench.

The New York scene that Antonio had described was primarily grim, but he had bragged of a novel luxury that the landlady kept for herself: her own commode with indoor plumbing and no need to go outside. Antonio had caught sight of this once and couldn't erase its image. The toilet was supposed to service all the apartments on the third floor, but Zia Cristina had hit a deal with the landlord and kept the commode under lock and key.

Carmelo remembered Eugenia once reading Antonio's letter and his father leaping for joy.

"A toilet," old man Troiano had said. "I can't believe it. Antonio is the first to experience this modern ceramic invention."

Carmelo waited for Zia Cristina to appear at the door and for the chance to embrace his brother. Finally, the old lady opened up and invited him in. Grumpy, seemingly indifferent to the presence of the new arrival, Zia Cristina listened to his story but arched her brow when Carmelo spoke Antonio's name.

"Antonio's gone," she said. "He left the apartment six weeks ago and stiffed me for three months' rent. Rumor has it he quit his job as a cart man and departed the city in haste."

A boarder, listening in, added that Antonio might have left for New Jersey since he often had spoken of his friends across the river. Carmelo was perplexed. Where could his brother have gone? And why would he leave in a hurry? And why would he post a travel bond for Carmelo if he wasn't willing to meet him?

"If you want to look in Jersey," Zia Cristina said, "I can direct you to Paterson. My cousin's Aunt Assunta runs a small home where she takes in boarders who work in the factories. She's also from our neck of the woods so I'm sure she'll show you a courtesy, especially if you're well-mannered and—most important—if you pay in advance."

* * * *

Zia Cristina offered Carmelo a cot for two nights at fifty cents a sleep. She required each man to share a bed with another boarder: Carmelo would occupy the room from seven in the morning to seven at night, and then his roommate would take the night shift. And so it was. America. Two dreadful days on Zia Cristina's flea-riddled cot.

Then he took off for Paterson, accompanied by the landlady's nephew, who walked him to Cortlandt Street where he would catch the Jersey-bound ferry. On the brief walk across the town, from Mulberry Street to the westside docks, Carmelo saw men and women in different shades and shapes, not resembling the people at home. Plain folks looking for work or buying fruit at the market. No different from anyone else. He thought how they too must fear life in these new environs. He wondered how these people ate, how they worked, how they made love.

"They all look like strangers," Carmelo said to the boy who escorted him to the ferry.

"Don't worry," the boy replied. "You're seen as a stranger too."

At the ferry docks, Carmelo saw the water and sighed. He imagined a gut-wrenching path from boat to land to boat again, and then on land some more. Worse, after his life in a land-locked town, drab and dull, he was now in a sensory vortex: the crash of water on barrel-dense piers, the horses clopping on slime, the stench of urban waste, then coal and the blazing fires, blackness spewing into the air.

So much to learn, he thought as he bid farewell to the boy and boarded the ferry. Once across, he found himself at Exchange Place Station in Jersey City. Again, he sought the help of an escort to get to Passaic Avenue, to Assunta's home. With luck, he would find his brother Antonio or someone who knew his name.

3.

Kinder than Zia Cristina, Assunta took in the traveler. Big-bosomed, welcoming, a woman in charge of her business, Assunta ran a boarding house with gaiety and song. Sometimes she hummed tunes from her southern village and invited the boarders to join her. When she served a thick soup of pork rinds, greens, and corn, no one ever complained. Nevertheless, this was no jovial scene, no vaudeville for immigrant idles. But the men were more congenial than their comrades at Mulberry Street, more devoted to one another in the hope that their group might thrive. Perhaps they had more fresh air. Perhaps they had steady work. Most of the men found employment at the silk-trade factories and devoted themselves to a cause beyond their own. Even though many hailed from northern Italian cities (Biella, Prato, Vercelli, wherever these places might be), they treated Carmelo as a brother and did their best to speak a common Italian that the young man might follow with ease. After just a few hours of friendly exchange, some boarders offered to help Carmelo find work.

But Carmelo was restless. Where was Antonio?

"Does anyone know his name?" he asked. Describing him by the deep scar over his right eye—his right eye, not the left—Carmelo waited for a nod of recognition, the moment someone might match a face to Carmelo's description.

"America wasn't supposed to be like this," he said to Assunta. "I'm not sure that I can go it alone." He felt his skull pounding against his eyebrows.

"Sleep off the journey, Carmelo. You can think about Antonio tomorrow."

She led him to a room, which, unlike Zia Cristina's squalid quarters, rewarded him with comfort and safety. Assunta's lodging was neat and simple, good enough for tired men. For three dollars a week, Carmelo had a bed of his own in a room shared with two other workers. He paid two dollars up front for a week of rent and board, and promised the remaining dollar to be paid as soon as he found a job. Carmelo settled in.

That night, he dreamed of Antonio and the fun that they used to have. Antonio, who had given Carmelo his first pair of shoes when he saw the boy running barefoot.

"I lost my sandals by the river," Carmelo had reported to his sibling.

"Don't worry, little brother," Antonio had said. "Your feet are more precious than mine." He'd produced a pair of leather shoes.

Carmelo had stared in awe. "Where did you get these, Tonino?"

Antonio had merely smiled and tousled the little boy's hair.

On the following day, fresh from his dream, Carmelo began to chat with one of his roommates, a jacquard weaver who hailed from Prato, a place that Carmelo learned was in the north of Italy. Carmelo saw his roommate as an honest man concerned about the fate of the world. He had an ear for music and wanted to work with a camera; he was nimble with needle and thread.

"I'd also like to learn those skills," Carmelo said to his roommate.

It was the start of a new life here, and for the moment Carmelo's fears lifted. He noted that his newfound friend walked with a swagger. The man lifted a glass with a certain ease. He took his seat at the dinner table as if he'd always belonged. He held forth with confidence on the day's events. Carmelo thought he must be a man of social distinction.

Always with coins in his pocket, Gaetano Bresci was known as a dandy for his fine dress and style.

"I learned my style from Pietro Gori," Bresci said to Carmelo and assumed that every man in the rooming house would be familiar with that name. "He was quite a looker."

Carmelo drew a blank but didn't want to expose his lack of refinement.

"Did you leave a girl in Italy?" Carmelo asked.

"Yes and no," Bresci said. "My story is more complicated, as you'll see. I have a girl nearby."

As Carmelo discovered over the months they shared a room together, Bresci had left a wife and child in Italy. Bresci had been locked up in Lampedusa (for crimes left unspoken) and, after his release from prison, he had abandoned his country and left his family behind. After he'd arrived in America, Bresci had taken up with an Irish girl whom he'd met in Jersey City.

"She has the loveliest red hair and deep green eyes. Just thinking of her makes me swoon."

Carmelo was impressed. He'd never met a girl with red hair and wondered what that would be like.

"I'm in love, I have to tell you. *Amore* came at first sight! No common language. I fell in love through my eyes."

Carmelo laughed.

"I stumbled over my words, I lacked the proper verbs, I couldn't speak her family name. Can you imagine such a thing? And despite the strange customs that kept us apart—her cabbage and potato stew, her bowls of Irish porridge—we still made a match. Can you believe it?"

Carmelo couldn't imagine falling in love with a person who didn't speak his language. It was hard enough conversing with boarders who came from the north of Italy.

"Yes," Bresci said. "It was a shock to my system. Everything from eating dinner to making love to speaking in two tongues. I couldn't believe this romance had bloomed. Finally, I met a woman who shares my dreams and passions. She's a partner, you could say."

Partner? An unusual word for Carmelo, who recalled the bitter feuds in his family, his father beating his mother, his uncles attacking their wives, his drunken older buddies two-timing the village girls, dropping them at their doorsteps with welts on their limbs and babies in their bellies. The idea of a partner opened Carmelo's mind. A partnership as an agreement, a way to form a pact?

"Why aren't you with her?" Carmelo asked. "Why are you living in a boarding house for men when you could be with the woman you love?"

"You'll find out the details soon enough, but let's say for the moment that my girl is safer when she's at a distance from me. She knows she has my protection and, of course, my love. I see her when I can."

Through Bresci, Carmelo found work in the textile mill run by Hamil and Booth, men of patriarchal demeanor who paid six dollars a week. Carmelo started at the bottom rung as a silk-dye helper. Meanwhile Bresci, because he'd studied some English (his mother was a teacher's assistant) and because he was an expert in hard-to-manage silk, which he'd learned at the mills near Prato, received a royal fifteen dollars. Oh so debonair, Bresci was considered a prince. His image lingered for decades in the imaginations of Paterson workers. Years later, when the silk-dye immigrants—those who'd survived the police raids and prisons, the Spanish flu, and the Great Depression—went to see *Gone with the Wind*, the women swooned when they saw Clark Gable because he reminded them of Bresci. Hobbled by arthritic pain, they were giddy for the first time in ages.

* * * *

Each morning, carrying lunch pails packed by Assunta, Carmelo and Bresci walked to work. The dinners and late-night confessions had built a brotherhood between them, but the outdoor chats were best.

"Take a look at that fig tree wrapped up in canvas," Bresci said. "You can tell that Italians have settled there. They plant their fruit trees on their front lawns."

Carmelo laughed when he saw how the Italians of Paterson took care of their delicate plants, covering them in rags for winter so that they'd bloom again in spring.

"It gives proof that the immigrants eventually prosper and settle down," Carmelo said. "It even gives me hope."

Carmelo was deeply grateful for his first American pal.

One day after work, Bresci began to talk of political action. It scared Carmelo a bit, but he listened.

"If you're ready for something new," Bresci said, "I want to show you a newspaper I've been working on. It's called *La Questione Sociale*. Remember I talked about Pietro Gori, the guy with the dapper look? Well, Gori spent three months in Paterson training the silk workers to develop the paper. That's how we know him. He stayed until he saw that the weekly had a life of its own. Then he traveled coast to coast before returning to England. Next, Gori went to Buenos Aires, where he helped anarchists with their political work and ran their publications."

Anarchists? *Capdcazz*! What the heck? Carmelo was in a fog with so much new information. To cover up his ignorance, Carmelo asked, "How does that Gori guy manage to travel from place to place and still get something done?"

Bresci laughed. "Can you read?"

"So-so," Carmelo said. "At least I can read a paper."

"Then take a look at this."

Bresci unfolded an issue of *La Questione Sociale* and let Carmelo review the pages. There were notes about Italians abroad and protests in different cities; there were stories about workers in Spain and Argentina. A gigantic space was devoted to the uprisings in Milan, the war in Africa, the anti-colonial struggle in Cuba, and stories of famous anarchist women whose demands for social equality were considered part of the "struggle for life." Columns on anarchist doctrine and the need for global freedom were on page one. Then the call for an ethical stance, a challenge to capitalist order, and the paper's refusal to acknowledge private property as a basis for modern life.

"This is hard meat to chew," Carmelo said.

His vocabulary was barely extensive enough to hold on to the terms. Moreover, Carmelo had never considered the chance of rebellion.

"Private property is poison," Bresci said as he explained the newspaper's general focus. "We need to let readers know that we didn't invent these stories. Italy was destroyed by the landlords, for instance, and your family certainly paid the price. *These* are your anarchist roots."

"Us? We didn't align with any larger movement. My father couldn't even stand the rebels who stirred up trouble throughout the South."

Bresci spoke of big investors and bourgeois beliefs. "If anarchism is one thing at all, it's the proposal of freedom. In the struggle for life, everyone is equal. Do you see what I mean?"

Largely Carmelo was lost. He didn't understand new words like mass insurrection and strike. But he liked to hear how newspapers came into print. He recalled Eugenia eager to share her newspapers with him and point out all the novelties of the classified ads.

"This is our doing," Bresci said, pointing to *La Questione Sociale*. "It was born a short while ago, and now I'm directing the show. Since I get a big salary at the silk mill, I'm able to put some money toward the paper's production. We prepare it in our plant on Straight Street and send it out to readers. Sometimes we reach three thousand copies, but most of the time, we have to work in the dark, taking out packages of newsprint through the Chinese laundry next door. Ha! What passes for ironed sheets wrapped in plain brown paper is really laundered news."

"Laundered news? Smuggled stories?" Carmelo never thought that the news would get mixed up with linens or stuffed in men's pressed shirts. Nor had he imagined news as an underground affair. Smuggle a sheep? Why not? Smuggle some grapes, for sure! He'd learned this from old man Troiano. "The idea of writing from the sidelines, moving papers from place to place as if they were sacks of cloth really knocks me over," Carmelo said.

An awkward silence followed until Bresci began to speak of his hobbies. "I take pictures. I have a camera," Bresci said.

"That's funny," Carmelo said. "My sister and her pal were always interested in pictures. Since I left, I haven't heard from her, so I don't know what they've been up to."

"I like to reveal what lies hidden," Bresci said. "I want to expose aspects of daily life that the state doesn't want us to see."

As he listened, Carmelo suffered. He felt that his halting voice was garbled compared to Bresci's and, as such, he said very little.

"I'm impressed," Carmelo finally confessed. "At home, Zi'Annibale was taking pictures of the dead. By the sound of it, you're on to something different. The pictures keep ideas alive."

Bresci laughed.

Carmelo couldn't help swallowing all his end vowels; the swish and shwa of the muffled letters were always slightly plumbed. His spirits hit new lows when he understood that he'd never speak like his older friend.

4.

As their friendship grew, Bresci continued to speak of topics the weekly paper covered: freedom and human nature; the damnation of property and greed; the oppression of the workers; their need to break their chains; the chance at a happy, fulfilling life outside the bounds of the state; the right to love.

"Love as a personal freedom," he said as if teaching a class. "Not by dictate of family structures or by a lord's commands."

"Imagine that," Carmelo said.

Too much information all at once. Each conversation, a lesson in history; every proposal, bold and new. As the days advanced, Carmelo's eyes grew wider. Ideas about freedom and individual choice forced him to rethink his life until now: his punishing childhood, his father's deviance, the ways his siblings had never thought of collective needs.

"True, we had the brigands," Carmelo said. "That was way before I was born. Yet my parents hated those men and women because they sowed disorder."

Carmelo recalled his father describing how ruffians rode through the backwoods robbing rich and poor. You had to think of something modern, Carmelo remembered old man Troiano saying, and insurrection wasn't an option. Carmelo also thought of Antonio, imagining his brother with his thumb on the scale.

"In our family, there was neither concern for the folks dying of hunger in their huts down on the hill nor a plan for us to rise against the landlords," Carmelo said. "Everything was flat."

Bresci printed articles on workers in Italy and Argentina; he wrote of different anarchist conclaves in Vermont and Oklahoma. He talked about an international cohort of men and women who passionately worked for freedom and demanded a living wage. He especially tried to remind Carmelo that rebellion was in the Southerner's blood.

"Did you ever hear of Passannante, kid? He was a cook who hailed from your neck of the woods. A Mazzini man, a pity to be sure, but he decided to kill the king. He took an hour off from his pastry chef's job in order to see the king go by in a carriage. Passannante reached out to stab him right on a street in Naples!"

Carmelo nodded and remembered that don Felicetto once cursed Passannante after Sunday Mass.

"There's even a famous poem about him. 'With the cook's hat, we'll make a flag.'" Bresci smiled, reciting a line from Pascoli. "The poet had spent time in Matera and knew all your southern heroes."

Carmelo wondered if Antonio had ever heard of this famous cook.

"Passannante's fame had spread," Bresci said. "And even though he's locked in a mad house today, you should still be proud of your neighbor."

Carmelo had a thought. What if he had known these versions of history, would he have left so soon? And what if Eugenia, that delicate, inquisitive child, had had the chance to know this life? Would she have been an anarchist too? Instead, she was condemned to sprout babies and die of neglect in the village (he couldn't yet know of Eugenia's fate and her future life in Naples). What was most disturbing, Carmelo thought, were Bresci's ideas about family, especially his sense that men and women were equal.

"I'd like to find a girl who would be my equal—a partner as you say," Carmelo said. "We would earn the same. We would share responsibilities. And, as you've been suggesting, we would even have the right to leave each other if we both saw that love was failing."

To test his own proposal, he began to rehearse little dialogues with an imaginary girl who, much like Bresci's lover, had red hair and deep green eyes. Maybe she wouldn't speak his language, but they could make common cause of love. Maybe they wouldn't last as a couple forever, but they would learn reciprocity and caring. These thoughts kept Carmelo going as he listened to Bresci stress the need for a worker revolt.

* * * *

Bresci was like an uncle to Carmelo. He took the young man to the Sunday anarchist picnics that were held in a park in Brookdale, New Jersey.

"Hey, Bresci!" a worker cried as the two approached the park.

"Good to see you," shouted another.

"Glad you're here today," a boy said.

Bresci embraced each man and child he saw; he doffed his hat to the women.

A summer feast was about to begin. Signora Rossi brought a baked pasta dish; Signora Doino carried fruit. Some men carried bottles of home-made wine.

A few men brought out their mandolins; others had piccolos. Off-key, they sang Neapolitan folk songs and engaged the laughing crowd. In another corner of the park, children played catch with a baseball. No one knew the rules for this new game, but they knew it was important. They'd have to wait to learn how to bat.

A woman climbed on to a wooden platform and announced that an anarchist play was about to start.

"No more oppression. No more lousy wages. Now pay attention to our theater," she screamed.

Carmelo heard the title loud and clear: *THE BOSS WHO GETS THE BROOM.*

He focused attentively on the narrator's words, called out from the side of the stage:

"Bernardina works as a seamstress; Mr. Curtain is her boss. He asks the workers to come in on Sunday, though he never pays them for extra hours."

"Interesting," Carmelo whispered to Bresci. "I never saw a play featuring the boss."

Bernardina: "Mr. Curtain! Don't treat us like this! We have families to feed! We need our pay!"

Carmelo missed a few lines but heard the boss speaking on stage to the girl.

Mr. Curtain: "Your wages are coming, Bernardina. Please step into my office."

Bernardina: "I want my salary, Mr. Curtain."

Then Carmelo was shocked. He saw on stage what he thought was the boss's inappropriate advance toward poor Bernardina.

Mr. Curtain: "Please take my hand for a while."

Carmelo smiled when he heard the actress's reply.

Bernardina: "My body is my own! It's not for your pleasure."

Bernardina took a broom and hit the nasty boss, leading him to stumble and fall. Here, Carmelo along with the rest of the audience burst into applause.

Then the narrator stepped on to the stage: *"The moral of the story: get rid of the boss and the state; make sure to take charge of your labor! World revolution is coming soon!"*

Here the audience cheered. Then they all laughed together.

Carmelo was especially attracted to the improvised stage. He liked that the actors used a wooden platform to enact a story. He liked the movement and voices. He liked the way life came about from only two characters speaking. He liked the voices that came from the side.

He turned to Bresci. "It's really something to see how the audience reacts to the show. They're so taken by the performance that they stick around for more."

"Gori trained the actors to deliver political stories. He wanted the public to rise up and take action. Now you see how the comrades follow his directives."

"Interesting. At home, we used a wooden platform in the forest to play music at weddings." Carmelo didn't want Bresci to think he was stupid. "It wasn't that we lacked theater in our lives. At home, there were several Christmas plays and the usual processions for the Passion of Christ. One time, I was a Roman soldier while my brother Antonio played Pontius Pilate. Giannino, the boy up the street, was Jesus, and he had to lug the cross up a hill. The kids at home loved performing. Maybe we got it from our mothers and aunts who always told long-winded stories with a certain flair. Maybe we learned it in the tavern where the old men delivered their tales. They all mixed quick talk with drawn-out words; they used deep voices to evoke the devil; they sang the roles of angels."

As a boy, Carmelo had always been taken by this play of voices. From his earliest age, he'd listened to his mother's friends as they'd hauled water up from the stream. He'd snooped at the tavern door on Saturday nights to hear the men drinking and telling stories.

"All well and good," Bresci said. "But the brief skits of our comrades have no religious fables, no stories recalling feuds among neighbors, no scenes of a man's wild passions for his brother's wife. Instead, you'll see some picnickers playing the roles of workers and others playing the terrible bosses. Of course, by the end of the show, the boss is forced off the platform."

Carmelo kept the idea of theater in his head: you could act a role, be someone else, and also talk to your soul. Acting inward and speaking outward, he thought. The drama pulls you in two directions. He hoped to test it out. "Powerful stuff, this anarchist theater," Carmelo said. "Its message really hits home."

5.

Carmelo thought of writing to his family. He knew that Eugenia would read his letters aloud to his parents; he imagined his mother sobbing and his father admiring the modern features of life that Carmelo had observed in New Jersey. He pictured Eugenia's sense of wonder reading his description of the Sunday shows that the anarchists had staged in the park. But he couldn't bear to tell his parents that Antonio was nowhere in sight. Nonetheless, building his courage, he finally took pen in hand. In his letter, he explained the new words he had learned, the need for worker revolt, and equality among men and women. Here, he especially reached out to Eugenia to let her know of the various roles that young women could have in New Jersey. And then he described Bresci—his deep eyes, his moustache, his elegant clothes, his charm. He told of Bresci's courage and his devotion to the anarchist cause. He asked for Antonio's new address. And where was Mariarosa? Closing the letter, he looked up and spoke to his roommate. "I don't know how to post a letter. Do you think you can help me out?"

    Bresci agreed to send it off. Then on a Friday evening before he went to visit his girl, Bresci pulled the letter from his pocket (he still hadn't found a stamp). Just in case, he carefully opened the envelope to read its contents. As he had imagined, Carmelo in his naiveté had reported to his family the anarchist goings-on. Bresci couldn't allow it and, not thinking twice, he tore the letter in tiny pieces and burned the scraps with a match.

    You have to put limits on the news, Bresci thought. You never know who will read what you wrote, so you always have to take care.

* * * *

Carmelo was none the wiser about Bresci's role as censor. He admired Bresci's style and language; he wished he had Bresci's pizzazz. Carmelo made a list of Bresci's key words, repeating them every day as he pushed silk bolts through the factory hallways. "Insurrection," "acracy," "ruling class." Carmelo hummed the words to the rhythm of his hand cart.

"Imitation," Carmelo said, "has become my rule of life at least until I find my voice."

One day, Bresci invited Carmelo to a Wednesday night gathering to meet the bigwigs of anarchist fame. It was held in the Tivola and Zucca saloon. The famous Malatesta, recently freed from prison in Italy, was going to speak for the first time before his New Jersey comrades. The date was September 3rd, 1899. Bresci was so excited that he couldn't be contained; Carmelo copied his idol. When the two arrived at the saloon, the comrades were up in arms. All the men and women from anarchist hall spoke with wrath about last year's murders and screamed for revenge. In Milan, a general had murdered three hundred people in the name of the king.

"Revenge! Vindication!" the crowd screamed in frenzy.

"Death to the king!"

Bresci imagined scenes of blood on the street, the lifeless monarch splayed on the ground. He stood and shouted, "Yes! Death to the king!"

Carmelo was frightened. He hadn't witnessed so much fury since he'd left his father's house. Meanwhile, the comrades continued in heated discussion about the workers' revolt when Malatesta said, "When you comrades look for revenge, you betray your anarchist leanings. Now you want a free-for-all to do as you please. It simply won't work in the long run!"

The crowd quieted, but when Malatesta challenged those in New Jersey who refused to align in groups, the audience grew restless.

"Malatesta wants structure over free-floating actions, order over violence. That's what you're hearing right now," Bresci whispered to Carmelo. "Most important for us: whoever wins the debate tonight will control the editorial decisions of *La Questione Sociale*."

Carmelo was puzzled; it was still hard to see what was at stake.

Suddenly, a curse, a scream—then the roar of the crowd. A nut case named Domenico Pazzaglia, a barber from these parts, was attacking the guest of honor with a knife. "Take that, you traitor to the anarchist cause," yelled Pazzaglia, thrusting his weapon toward Malatesta's heart but only piercing his arm.

Bresci ran up to Pazzaglia and wrested the knife from his hand.

"*Maledetto!*" Pazzaglia shouted as he realized his plan had been foiled.

Malatesta's words had spurred the audience's anger, but no one wanted him harmed. Curses, confusion, and, finally, cheers when the audience felt certain of Malatesta's survival.

"*Bravo, Bresci! Viva Malatesta! Viva l'anarchismo!*"

The crowd lauded Bresci as the hero of the night and raised their glasses in joyous toast.

Malatesta returned to the podium to finish his speech. He'd refused to press charges against his assailant, arguing that a legal case would be a concession to the state. Following his example, Malatesta's male comrades also refused to press charges; the women, however, insisted on eye-for-eye justice. After the meeting, Malatesta bade farewell to his comrades, departing shortly thereafter. Bresci, his celebrity guaranteed, was renewed to direct *La Questione Sociale*.

* * * *

It was a turbulent year for Bresci. He did his job. He loved his girl (on those occasions when he saw her). He continued to apply enough pomade to freeze his shining black curls in place. He documented the times with pictures; he used his personal savings to support *La Questione Sociale.* Above all, he wanted to avenge the injustices against people back home. The Beva Baccaris shoot-out in Milan was motive to steer his course. Brooding, he paced in his room from bed to door, from door to window. He sat down and quickly stood up; then he sat down again.

Carmelo noticed the change. Their nightly chats had become icy, sometimes ending abruptly. But Bresci assured his younger friend that his turn in spirit carried little weight. He simply had a lot on his mind. He needed time to think. Meanwhile, he took care to introduce Carmelo to the Straight Street workers who produced *La Questione Sociale*. He helped Carmelo forge a friendship with Pedro Esteve, a Spaniard who wrote for the press.

"Carmelo is thirsty for lessons," Bresci said to Esteve. "Take care of my boy and teach him the ropes. You'll be happy to have him."

Carmelo wondered why Bresci was passing the baton to Esteve. His speculations came to a halt in February of the new year when Bresci disappeared. Carmelo was unnerved. He asked the men in the boarding house; he went to the political top brass; he directed himself to Esteve's office and begged for some news.

"Not even a word of farewell," Carmelo lamented.

Esteve was also concerned. Only later, when the men on Straight Street learned that Bresci had borrowed $150 for a one-way ticket to Italy (it was *his* money, Bresci had insisted in a letter that he'd left behind), the men in Jersey began to get nervous. Carmelo, who believed in his friend's loyalty, never thought Bresci would have left without a goodbye.

6.

Also disturbed by the news, but less visibly shaken, Esteve reached out to Carmelo. He believed Carmelo had talent, more than most of the silk factory men, and as such he invited Carmelo to take on those design and typeset jobs that required a steady hand.

"There's a bit of research that I also need," Esteve said. "Your job will be to find articles from other anarchist papers, then cut and paste those stories onto the print sheets of *La Questione Sociale*."

Carmelo didn't quite understand.

"It doesn't make for original writing, but we simply lack staff and money," Esteve said. "We borrow from others, but I promise you'll never be bored. Plus, if you want, you can claim the unsigned articles as your own."

Carmelo nodded and accepted Esteve's proposal. "At least, the work helps me settle down."

Day by day, things improved. Carmelo began to trust Esteve and liked the newspaper job. Then a startling update hit the Straight Street workers. King Umberto of Italy, while presiding over a sporting event, had been shot and killed. Two thousand spectators had looked on. It was July 29, 1900. An anarchist worker who'd just returned from New York was quickly apprehended. His name was Gaetano Bresci.

Carmelo thought, how could this be? When had he planned this? Had he traveled home for this purpose? Carmelo was stunned, Esteve was mute, the others puffed on Fonseca cigars and talked the talk. The news reported Bresci's arrest, as well as his final words: "I did not kill Umberto. I have killed the king."

Bresci completed the heroic act Passannante had begun, but now he paid the price. He went to prison on San Stefano Island, where he was driven to madness. After a year, he took his life, and the guards threw his body into the sea. Esteve reminded the comrades of Bresci's undaunted courage; Malatesta in his eulogy protested the state's brute force; Gori, now in Buenos Aires, mourned the loss of a passionate thinker. Carmelo, meanwhile, back in his room, slipped into bed and cried until dawn.

Weeks passed. The police placed the Paterson neighborhoods under high surveillance. Anyone who was part of Bresci's group was subject to investigation. Esteve organized public demonstrations for Bresci in Brooklyn and Manhattan (and therefore fell under the eye of police). He set up a fundraiser in Germania Hall to help Bresci's partner (the police intervened and stopped it). He published articles in Spanish in *El despertar* and in Italian in *La Questione Sociale* (the authorities shut down the papers). He encouraged Newark anarchists to fabricate metal buttons that carried Bresci's image (the police closed in on the stockpile). Carmelo tried to help him but also quaked in his boots. He feared arrest; he feared deportation; most of all, he feared losing his friends. Carmelo's composure returned when Esteve came to see him. This time the news was bad—or, at least, worse than before.

"Listen, kid, this is no joke. You'll have to leave, take some time off, hide yourself in the New York crowds. Go find a place where you can proceed without attracting too much notice. Above all, don't write home," Esteve said. "And don't live in a boarding house with other political people. The police are vigilant and will ferret you out."

Carmelo, all of a sudden, was a criminal on the edge. "Where am I supposed to go? How will I find my way?"

After a pause, Carmelo added, "If I leave Paterson, I'll have no place to stay. And no one has answered my letters from home, so I don't know the whereabouts of my brother and sister."

Turning the pages of the daily paper, Esteve was pensive. "Why don't you seek out some friend from your village who now lives in the city? You hang out there, you remain discreet, and you find a job where no one takes notice."

Carmelo's head was exploding. Even the idea of finding his hometown folk seemed beyond reach. He had to think. Who did he know in New York? Before he'd left almost a year ago, Mariarosa had been preparing to leave for America along with her husband, Orazio, but Carmelo knew neither their address nor even if they'd arrived.

Perhaps Zi'Annibale was in New York since he'd always talked of the voyage. Then there was Pio Fella, whose siblings had sent him off to America to save the fate of their family. It was a start, but he had no idea how or where to find them (or if they were here at all). And still, there was the lingering question of Antonio. In the end, he decided to return to Zia Cristina's tenement flat at Mulberry Bend.

Mannaggia l'America, he thought. Going to Zia Cristina felt like rolling backwards, a retreat from all he'd gained. He imagined the filth, the disorder, the lack of care, plus the boarders' ailing spirits. A leap into living hell. But a visit to Zia Cristina would let him discover if anyone from home had recently arrived in town.

* * * *

Esteve's idea was to send his partner, Maria, to accompany Carmelo. They would see if Zia Cristina might give them some leads regarding any friends or relations who might have passed through New York. Carmelo didn't say it, but he still hoped to find Antonio.

Once again, Carmelo lugged his sacks to Zia Cristina's third-floor apartment, but when Zia Cristina saw Maria, she gave Carmelo an icy reception. "I can't house families or couples," she said.

They made it clear they weren't a couple. Also, they wanted to know if Antonio had returned or if any new people from Carmelo's hometown had arrived at the Mulberry flat.

"No," Zia Cristina said, "we haven't had news of Antonio, nor has he sent me the rent which is now more than a year past due. Ahem. However, we just had a boarder from your town. He stayed for two months and then he found a job with old Baciagalupo. Now he lives in the back of his store. Annibale Martino."

"I can't believe it!" Carmelo said, sweating with excitement. "This is my mother's distant cousin, a friend of my sister Eugenia. Our town's photographer is here?"

Zia Cristina said, "You'll find him if you go down to 26 ½ Mulberry Street. It's one of the arms of the Four Points, but because it's still on our side of the block, it's not as nasty as you might expect."

Carmelo left his luggage under Zia Cristina's care and flew down the street with Maria.

"Zi'Annibale! Zi'Annibale!" Carmelo called with excitement. He hoped the old man would be willing to take him in.

7.

When Carmelo and Maria arrived at the Mulberry address, they entered the full spectacle of death. The funeral home was a gilded palace: ceramic cherubs close to the entrance, potted palms lining the hallways. Inside were big painted statues of San Gennaro and the Virgin of Pompeii, each taller than the tallest man, stately and protective. They looked down upon the patrons, dead and alive. Meanwhile, Louis XIV armchairs made of beechwood invited the weary guests to sit and weep for the dearly departed.

Carmelo was awed by the luxurious living that Baciagalupo had offered the dead. Maria, more sober and hardly convinced by the fanfare, whispered that anarchist rebellion would be needed to fight this privilege.

"Perhaps they might find a simpler way to die."

Carmelo, not wanting a lecture, advanced to the receptionist's desk and asked for Annibale Martino.

"Of course, just follow me," a slight woman said. "He lives in the back of our store."

A year of waiting for a familiar face dissolved in the moment; relief and joy flooded Carmelo's heart. "I am so, so happy to see you, Zi'Annibale," Carmelo said, trying to hold back his tears.

Zi'Annibale offered a tender smile that spoke legions about bonds forged at home. It awakened Carmelo's longing for all that he thought had been lost. Without a gram of doubt, Zi'Annibale felt the same.

There were stories to tell, adventures to share, recent gossip from the village. Then the news of Carmelo's family—especially Eugenia.

"I can't believe that I haven't heard from them. It really makes me sad."

"Don't worry," said Zi'Annibale. "They always kept you in mind."

The men shared stories about settling in a giant city where day-to-day events placed a singular stress on the nerves.

"Lacking familiar faces is the most difficult challenge; it's hard to remain alone," Zi'Annibale said to his young *paisan* and then embraced him warmly.

Carmelo, sworn to silence by Esteve, downplayed the anarchist meetings and the fervent political speeches. He never mentioned Bresci but instead talked of his factory friends whom he'd come to admire. "I met wonderful men in the silk mill, guys who really touched my heart. Some were experienced weavers, others knew about writing plays. I met a man who ran a newspaper at night. He taught me a few tricks of printing." All lies, Carmelo thought. He wasn't saying a word about his feelings—as if Bresci and Esteve had had no role in his life.

Then he remembered to introduce Maria to Zi'Annibale.

"The pleasure is mine," said Maria to the older man.

Zi'Annibale's eyes twinkled. He was certain the two were in a romantic relationship that neither cared to mention.

Carmelo described how he walked to work, helped Maria's husband with typeset—how he'd come to love the Sunday picnics held in the Paterson parks.

"And, Antonio? Any word of him around here? And of Mariarosa and Orazio, who by now should be in this city?"

Zi'Annibale couldn't answer for them but told his own story instead.

* * * *

"I was lucky when I reached New York," Zi'Annibale said. "You could say that I hit the jackpot. A few weeks after arriving in town, I saw a giant parade marching down Canal Street toward the Baxter Street church. There were hundreds of people carrying banners and flags, a dozen men carrying a giant statue of the Madonna of Pompeii. I imagined the creaking of wooden beams on their shoulders and the heft of the knee-breaking weight. There was a band of musicians following the parade. I heard even our old *zampogne*. I tell you: I never saw anything like it. I'll bet that you wouldn't see this in Naples even for San Gennaro's feast day." He stretched out his arms. "It was so big. The march went on forever; it looked more like a festival for a king than your usual assembly of mourners. This five-star show, as I later learned, was the work of Mr. Baciagalupo, the undertaker for Italians here. Throughout the city, everyone knew of his funeral marches, his assemblies' grandeur, even the theater-like eulogies that treated the dead like the emperor Caesar. And because everyone from Mafia bosses to the poorest of the poor wants to die like a king, they head to Baciagalupo's store. He convinces people that their loved ones deserve a regal farewell."

Zi'Annibale laughed. "Given the work I did at home, taking pictures of the dead, I figured that he might find me a job. And he was receptive to my pictures. Stillborn babies posed next to their surviving families; dead peasants dressed like gentry. I showed him the care I gave to my dearly departed so that they looked alive and living. Baciagalupo praised my theatrical flair. On the spot, he hired me at three dollars per funeral. The best part: he gave me a place to sleep. I know it sounds strange, but he let me set my cot in a storeroom for coffins and caskets. Since funerals are abundant, I have a guaranteed future: an adequate salary, no rent, and always an invitation to partake of the sumptuous meals held in the dead person's honor."

"I'm impressed by your good fortune," Carmelo said. Egged on by Maria, who showed little patience for Zi'Annibale's stories, he asked in a shaky voice, "Do you think I could get a job with you? I need to find work and a room."

This was a big step. Carmelo knew it, but at least he'd taken a chance. Like a doting aunt, Maria stood at his side as they both awaited an answer. Zi'Annibale, like a doting uncle, said he would ask his boss.

* * * *

Somewhat giddy, Carmelo was taken by the winds of self-satisfaction. He would remain with Zia Cristina until he heard again from Zi'Annibale. Assuring herself that all was well, Maria returned to New Jersey. Carmelo began life in New York for a second time.

At Baciagalupo's, Carmelo worked as a part-time assistant. At first, he helped Zi'Annibale wash the bodies, brush out their hair, corset the women, and strap down their paunches. Later, since he was able with a pen, he sketched the funeral programs. Carmelo also stood at the door to greet the large swath of mourners—mostly Italian New Yorkers, some rich and others poor. Sometimes, and if he thought the moment was right, he inquired about his brother. No one had any idea of Antonio's fate.

As the months advanced, Carmelo began to sever his emotional ties with the Silk City comrades. The anarchist cause was slipping quickly behind him. He threw himself fully into the funereal arts. Zi'Annibale taught him to set the deceased in novel poses, to hold their hair in place with shellac, to sew their lips together, to restore their complexions with powders and creams.

"And don't forget to weave a rosary through each of the fingers," Zi'Annibale added. Then there was the plastic surgery, an art unto itself. The more prominent among Mr. Baciagalupo's clients, those with the means to pay, insisted on physical alterations for men who had run into trouble. Should a face have been deformed in a fight, Baciagalupo would adjust it; should a nose have been broken or an eye freed from its socket, Baciagalupo's team knew how to fix it. Families hoped that the dearly departed would look refined when they met the Lord.

Carmelo wondered why the dead needed so much cosmetic work. He was further surprised when Baciagalupo called in a "doctor" to assist in the labor. Usually this was a barber who had worked with scalpels, needle, and thread. He was well known in the business of restoration and had earned a good deal of respect. So when this man arrived at the funeral parlor, Zi'Annibale stepped aside and became his apprentice. Carmelo also stood by, regarding the damaged faces of the recently departed as they turned into portraits of grace.

After the doctor's third appearance, Carmelo worked up his courage and asked him if he knew his brother Antonio.

"When did he die?" the frowning doctor asked.

"I'm not sure if that's even true," Carmelo said. "But since I arrived in New York, no one has told me a thing about him." He paused to take stock. "You'd know my brother if you saw him. He has a deep scar on the right side of his temple; it runs from the hair line and covers his brow. The scar's crescent shape almost looks like the moon. Antonio used to be quite handsome, but an accident took his good looks away. The last time I saw him, he looked like a man who had lost part of his face."

The doctor shook his head. "I can check with my acquaintances and see what I can find out."

8.

Weeks went by and Carmelo's melancholia deepened. No brother, no sister, no Bresci. No regular job. Loss marked his short time in New York. Perceiving Carmelo's withdrawal and his sad sapphire eyes staring into the caskets, Zi'Annibale decided to cheer Carmelo up and walk him through the city. When they strolled through Mulberry Bend, Zi'Annibale pointed out the various shops that appealed to both men's fancy. First, they greeted Mr. Gallo in his phonograph store. The man sold Edison cylinders for fifty cents apiece, but he also stocked the new Victor gramophone disks. Zi'Annibale liked them because they carried recordings of many singers from home. Feruccio Giannini singing "Questo o quella," la Patti in the role of Mimi, even recordings by Farfariello, who'd recently arrived in New York from Salerno and was now the talk of the town. When Gallo put the stylus on a disk coated with brilliant shellac, the machine began to sing. Listening was too much for Carmelo to bear. The singer could be miles away and yet now he was right in this room. An opera that could fill a stage was compressed into a plate with grooves.

"It's a brand-new experience," Carmelo observed. "A brand-new way to hear."

Mr. Gallo pointed out the songs that had been recorded in Italy. And then he showed the shoppers the disks of singing stars who now lived in New York. "When you listen to these different songs, you can't place them. Naples, Salerno, and New York are fused as one on the shiny black records."

Mr. Gallo also explained that the first recordings were not of music or singers but of old people about to die whose families wanted to keep their voices alive. Zi'Annibale perked up when he heard of another art similar to his own. He thought to speak to his boss to see if this new recording art were something Baciagalupo could use.

9.

One week, Baciagalupo staged a magnificent funeral for the Russian wife of a wealthy Italian. Carmelo dressed the body so that Zi'Annibale could pose it for pictures. Since the woman was roundly overweight, the two men thought it best to simply plop her into an armchair, her arms and shoulders tied to the backrest. Dressing her with a long veil and hairpiece (Zi'Annibale had seen the photographs of the recently deceased English queen), they did their best to make her look regal. The Russians and Italians were pleased.

"She looks so natural."

"She's so at peace."

"She's ready to be taken by God."

"It even looks like she's smiling."

"I could swear I saw her move."

At the wake, Carmelo and Zi'Annibale distributed funeral programs while they awaited the arrival of a priest to deliver final prayers; they chatted mostly in gestures and nods with members of the matriarch's clan. Baciagalupo, by this time, had taken a kindly view of Carmelo and promised to help him find more work. Now he introduced Carmelo to a well-off Russian. Mr. Joseph Schenck and his brother had planned a hotel and casino at Manhattan's northern tip and were beginning to assemble investors for a large amusement park named Paradise Park. Schenck explained how he hoped to compete with Coney Island by offering rides, casinos, vaudeville, and taverns situated on Fort George Hill overlooking the Harlem River. He'd already secured the collaboration of a trolley company that would carry travelers from lower Manhattan to the northern end of the line, where the best entertainment would await them.

"I'm working with a young theater man named Marcus Loew," Mr. Schenck said to the funeral director. "Business is about to take off."

Mr. Baciagalupo seized the opportunity to promote Carmelo's talents. Quickly, he waved Carmelo over to meet the Russian.

"What kind of work would you like to do?" Mr. Schenck asked Carmelo.

Various translators intervened at this crucial moment. Through Mr. Baciagalupo, Carmelo explained that he was good at graphic design. Zi'Annibale helped Carmelo by praising his hard work.

"I really like the idea of theater," Carmelo added.

After several minutes, Schenck said that he might hire Carmelo to attract the Italian crowd from 110th Street. Carmelo could design leaflets in Italian announcing Schenck's vaudeville theater. For the moment, the amusements at Fort George Hill were drawing mostly Russians and Germans.

"I'll be good at this," Carmelo said, not telling the gentlemen that he had designed dozens of anarchist posters.

"The point," Mr. Schenck said to Carmelo, "is to shock the viewers into paying mind and to convince them to visit the amusement park."

"*Capito*," Carmelo said. He already knew this.

"If the kid works out," Mr. Schenk later said to his partner, Mr. Loew, "we'll use him as a barker, collecting tickets for the venue and supporting our variety shows."

"Yap at them on paper," both men instructed Carmelo.

Carmelo rearranged the publicity messages a dozen times a day. At Baciagalupo's, where he was squeezing female corpses into dresses that no longer fit them, he imagined ways to draw a crowd, to post his vaudeville announcements in shop windows around the city. He printed in block letters and italics; he drew theater curtains to bracket his phrases. In his mind, he brought out giant letters and colors that would shriek for the public's attention.

ATTENTI ! GRAN CARNEVALE ! BENVENUTI TUTTI !
CIRCO
TEATRO
GRAN DIVERTIMENTO!
VARIETÁ

Carmelo advanced remarkably well, first designing cards and posters, and then inventing games at the park to appeal to Italian crowds. Guess my age for a penny. Guess the size of the clown's shoe. Guess the correct translation of your name in English and earn a lucky charm. Carmelo invented this particular game, but sometimes he couldn't deliver. Michele: Mike. Giuseppe: Joe. Vito: Willy or Bill. Then Carmelo couldn't find the right American name that went along with Filomena. Nor could he figure out how to say Pasqualina in the American tongue. The girl contestants always beat him. Their names were stuck deep in Italian mud and, no matter how hard he tried, Carmelo couldn't pry them free.

The Italians licked up these games like ice cream on a stick. They loved the idea that someone other than Russians and Germans could show them a day at Paradise Park and heaved a sigh of relief when someone spoke their language. Mr. Loew was pleased with visitor response and gave Carmelo extra work. Before the public arrived, Carmelo had to dust off the benches. He then took his place at the entrance to collect tickets.

Soon Mr. Loew asked Carmelo if he would try some Italian skits. Mr. Loew explained that a guy named Migliaccio, also called Farfariello, had caused quite a sensation downtown. With his vaudeville impersonations and his double voiced jokes in Italian and English, he always elicited laughs. Mr. Loew didn't know that the young man had already seen Farfariello and his *macchiette coloniali*, those comedy sketches that drew upon southern Italy's popular culture. Carmelo held the impersonator in very high esteem, he explained to Mr. Loew, and promised to keep his model in mind as he tried to write his own skits. By integrating anarchist lampoons that he'd heard at the Jersey picnics with the stage material from the halls near Mulberry Bend, Carmelo was shooting for laughs. He was certain that Farfariello would never know if he, Carmelo, had taken a few of his lines and used them as his own.

Carmelo borrowed some anarchist skits to fit the occasions at hand. For Loew's arena, he omitted the parts where workers rose up against big shots; instead, he made ribald jokes about the ignorant bosses. The boss who wouldn't let his workers take a pee break and soon had to pay the price; the boss who accepted food from a worker but didn't know that the dish was laced with hot Calabrian peppers. Carmelo wrote skits about coming to America and explained how no one really fit in. He played with some off-color terms to give his public a rise. *Merda*, shit, was the center of many versions of his performance. Whenever he referred to "gli a*merdi*cani"—the *shitty* Americans—he received tons of laughs.

Here's one that the audience loved.

"George Washington was crossing the Delaware with a boat full of Indians. It's February. It's cold. There are ice caps on the river. From the rear of the boat, an Indian stands up and screams out in Italian, '*Mannaggia, fa nu' cazzo di freddo.*' Dammit, it's fucking cold.

"George Washington turns around and says to the Indian, '*Guaglion!! Pure tu si italiano?*'—'Hey, fella! You're Italian too?'"

Everyone splits their sides. Some guys peed in their pants. This Carmelo was just too funny.

Carmelo looked out at the audience and exploded with pride. With each joke, his confidence grew.

"Old Peppino comes to America and can't speak a word of English. He goes to his construction job, but he never gets to eat—mainly because he doesn't know enough English to order food in a restaurant. His buddies help him out. Repeat this phrase until you get it down pat: 'Apple pie and coffee.' Peppino commits the phrase to memory and tells himself he can do this. He goes into a coffee shop and sits down at the counter. The waiter comes for his order and Peppino asks for 'Apple pie and coffee.' Two months go by and Peppino still requests apple pie and coffee. He's getting tired of this and asks his buddies to teach him something new. They have him repeat 'Meat loaf, please' until Peppino is sick to his stomach. He goes into a restaurant where he orders meat loaf. The waiter asks him if he would like potatoes or beans on the side. Peppino draws a blank, takes a long look at the waiter, and says, 'Apple pie and coffee.'"

Everyone in the audience fell over laughing because they'd had the same encounter themselves.

Carmelo loved performing these simple jokes for the public. He knew that everyone would smile when he cried out "*Sanemagogna*,"—

son of a gun. The crowds screamed when he told them about the guy who got lost on the "*sobbuè*" as he tried to get from "*morbida stretta*" to "*siti colle*." He explained to Mr. Loew that he was describing a man who took the subway from Mulberry Street to City Hall.

Then he repeated the words of his idol, copying Farfariello. "In America, people are all mixed up. No one knows a man from a woman in the English language. In Italian, '*le femmine*' are interested in '*gli uomini*.' But in English, they say that women like women because *uomini* is pronounced as *wo-men*."

Only Italians caught the joke.

"How could a woman love a woman?" he said. "No way. This made no sense!"

The audience tipped forward from so much laughter. Some men scratched their crotches. The Russian boss drew a blank and simply scratched his head.

10.

When he wasn't at the Fort George carnival under the thumb of Schenk and Loew, Carmelo spent the week with Zi'Annibale dressing up the dead. Evenings, and as a favor to Mr. Baciagalupo, he came out to shake hands with the guests and express his regrets for the dearly departed.

"A nice young man," the clients said of Carmelo. "Clean cut and always respectful."

"I hope you meet a pretty girl," they ladies said, moving in to pinch his cheeks.

After several months, Baciagalupo bought Carmelo a standard black suit.

"You look like a baron from Wall Street," one mourner observed, pretending not to notice that Carmelo's pant legs were several inches too short.

The work continued nicely until Zi'Annibale began thinking of branching out and opening his own studio. He had the idea that new immigrants would like to have pictures of themselves with their children and family albums as a remembrance for those who lived on the other side.

"Eugenia gave me the idea when she urged me to give up on the dead and start to picture the living," Zi'Annibale told Carmelo.

Carmelo was happy to be reminded of his little sister and recalled her eyes and her smile.

Zi' Annibale continued, "I might dress up the youngsters in American costumes. The boys would be soldiers and sailors standing next to their families. What do you think?"

The older man thought that he would also give the children tiny American banners to hold. The parents could rent the outfits and keep the flags as souvenirs for an extra fifteen cents. Zi'Annibale laughed.

"'*America forever'* is a slogan that brings in good money."

"Yup, that's better than dressing the dead," Carmelo said.

Zi'Annibale needed to give the concept more time, to make sure he had enough cash on hand to buy equipment and costumes, to rent a shop. Then it occurred to him: if he were to set up a business, he'd have no money to send for his wife. But this was almost an afterthought, he grinned, since he already had a sweetheart or two in *la bassa città*. Zi'Annibale's business idea began to pick up speed when Carmelo received an unannounced visitor in early May.

* * * *

In the storeroom, Carmelo and Zi'Annibale were dozing near the wooden caskets when Maria Roda knocked. Joy overtook Carmelo when he heard her voice. While he had taken to his life in New York, Carmelo still felt affection for the Jersey crowd. At twenty-eight, Maria had an air of refinement. She spoke well, had a graceful carriage, and always wore a smile. Carmelo instinctively liked her. She reminded him of Eugenia, vital and smart.

Maria extended her hand to Zi'Annibale and gave a warm hug to Carmelo. When she was alone with Carmelo, she explained her mission. "Carmelo, I need a hand. The police have finally forgotten about Bresci so it's safe to surface again and print the paper. It's hard, you know. Esteve has been short staffed since you've been gone. Now we've brought in a new editor—his name is Galleani—and we want you to help us out." She winked and touched his hand. "And besides, we've missed you terribly and long to have you near."

Carmelo entered a no-man's-land of blankness. After all, he was just getting accustomed to big city life—walks downtown, the caffé concerts, the gatherings of Italian musicians in Washington Square, his afternoons near the Garibaldi statue where he would chew the fat with other Italians and inquire after his brother and sister. He also cared about his creative work: staging, skits, and graphic designs for Mr. Loew, programs for Mr. Baciagalupo. Now Maria was asking him to give it all up.

"It's not a long stint," Maria said. "Perhaps a year or two. We need you to keep the newspaper running and help our new director. Esteve says he can line everything up so you don't have to fret over details."

Indebted to his anarchist friends, Carmelo was freighted with guilt. He asked Zi'Annibale for advice: which path should he follow?

Zi'Annibale gave Carmelo his blessing. "Look," he said, "you know I'm planning to open a studio store. It's not like I want to dress the dead for a lifetime and then be dressed for death myself. No joke, Carmelo. I need move on. And if you come back to New York, you can count on me. Also, if I hear of Antonio or Mariarosa's whereabouts, I'll find a way to let you know."

Carmelo needed time to think this over. What if Antonio showed up in Zi'Annibale's store and he wasn't there to greet him? What if some harm befell his brother and he missed the news? And what of Mariarosa? Should he abandon his quest?

Carmelo looked down Mulberry Street and saw the bustle of pushcart vendors, women haggling for bargains, and children playing at tag. Should he leave? The city was full of adventure. And now, *oh Dio*, that he was getting used to it all, Esteve asked him to give it up.

That night, Carmelo tossed and turned. He feared abandoning Zi'Annibale, the nice people at the funeral home, and the carnival at Fort George. What a loss! He was just getting good at the skits, and he loved making people laugh.

Carmelo tossed and turned some more. Because Esteve and Maria had cared for him, he knew that he owed them a favor.

* * * *

The return to Jersey was full of emotion, considerable joy, and good will. When Carmelo saw Esteve, his ambivalence lifted. The two embraced as if long-lost family members. Then they caught up on the news.

"Some of the comrades have returned. Others are still on the loose," Esteve reported. "But don't worry: when we need them, they'll show up to help."

Carmelo described his work in the Fort George carnival, his skits in the variety shows, the stage comedy that he hoped to pursue.

Esteve nodded and told of an anarchist play about the murder of King Umberto. "There are still great minds thinking of politics in terms of theater." In his rush to share these details, Esteve failed to explain how the mayor had shut down the hall, saying he'd not allow the performances to continue.

Esteve gave updates about the growing anarchist cause: the strike planned for coming months; the newspaper's status under the new director, Galleani; the good prospects for world revolution.

Carmelo felt blessed to be back with his comrades and to return to a world in which he could define himself as part of a larger movement. All the same, he was nervous.

Esteve was nervous too, but he told Carmelo there was no need to fret. After all, the police raids were over. It was safe to seek factory work and think about future strikes. "However, just in case," Esteve said, "we'd like to have you pass with a different name."

Carmelo liked the idea. "It's kind of like being part of the circus. The pleasure of wearing another name gives you a sense of adventure."

Esteve knew to be quiet.

"Here in America," Carmelo said, "you can change your name for happier times, even to start life anew. It's like sitting on a hyphen, looking forward and looking back. I have to say I like it!"

Someone would talk about this idea one day, Esteve mused. Meanwhile, Carmelo would be known as Salvatore Cuoco, but because he couldn't adjust to the name, he preferred to remain as Carmelo.

11.

No sooner had Carmelo settled into his Weehawken home, he was surrounded by loving friends. At first, he resumed his work on the paper, but then the strike at the silk factories erupted. The workers, the police, the bosses, the sticks and clubs, the First Regiment arriving from Newark to beat down the workers' protest. Nothing was easy to bear and Carmelo panicked.

Maria dragged him along to witness what was happening. Carmelo tried to hold back.

"Oh God," he said. "What will become of us? Please let me go home."

The crowd was brewing with anger, the police had their weapons drawn. Carmelo had never seen such eruptions.

"Who can help us out?" he asked Maria as they both coughed from the effects of smoke. He thought he was going to faint. "It's better to work in the carnival than to be in the midst of a riot."

Finally, Maria allowed him to pull away. "Salvatore, go rest by the sidelines," she said. But Carmelo, already having shed his made-up name, made it his business to flee.

By day, the demonstrations; by night, full time at the paper. The goal was to spread *La Questione Sociale* and keep people informed of the news. Then the crisis worsened. Hatchets and stones wrecked the mills; torches were hurled at the factory. A fire spread through the town. The mainstream press announced that a famous anarchist new to Paterson was driving all the action.

The papers reported that Luigi Galleani headed the mob. William McQueen, an English anarchist, was the other provocateur. The two worked the crowds to a frenzy, the journalists claimed. Galleani and McQueen called for a general strike; they insisted all silk workers abandon their jobs to protest unfair wages. The strike "gathered force among a babel of tongues amid a scene of confusion," wrote the *Herald Democrat* from Springfield, Colorado. They marched down Belmont Avenue and set the street on fire. Then the mayor called in the First Regiment to put down the insurrection. That night it rained bricks and pellets. The first person to be killed was a twenty-four-year-old woman from Hackensack named Lora Salvino. She only spoke Italian and worked part time at Columbia Mill, but she had developed a firebrand spirit and had pressed other silk-trade women to join her in anarchist actions.

"*Oh Madonna*," screamed Maria when she learned of Lora's murder. She fell into a chair. Then, standing up defiantly, she said, "A policeman's life will pay for Lora Salvino's death."

Carmelo went along with the cry but, alone, he felt himself quaking.

Unfortunately, one and one made two. The police knew Galleani was one leader of the strike. Late at night, he was gathering his people on the burned-up lawn of the Passaic graveyard. There, he spoke with passion and vigor to remind the workers of world revolution. Carmelo tried to listen but fear overcame him.

"The silk strike is only a first step in changing the world," Galleani shouted from a soapbox. "A universal resurrection of humankind is in progress. Paterson is just the start."

The police approached the rally and tried to intervene. Esteve instructed Carmelo to act as a decoy—to flee on horseback to foil the cops—but Carmelo panicked and passed the reins to a comrade.

"I can't. I just can't do it," Carmelo said, flustered. When no one was looking, he ran off to hide in the crowd.

Meanwhile, Galleani escaped on foot. The police chased the decoy horse and rider while Galleani, using his wit and wiles, followed an escape route that had been mapped by comrades in common cause. The police, the army, the mayor were all on Galleani's tail. Even reporters from the *New York Times* were summoned to find the anarchist leader. Two other New York dailies joined in hot pursuit. But Galleani, who knew the art of flight, having run several times before, outsmarted them all and ran to Canada, even eluding police at the border. Carmelo trembled as he watched from the sidelines. "*Oh Dio*," he said. "I'm not made for this."

The following days were worse. *La Questione Sociale* closed its office, the printer's shop was invaded, hundreds of mock-ups were torched. Esteve and Maria took rapid leave of their flat. Carmelo ran with them, not without saying his prayers. They headed toward the Delaware Water Gap where Maria's parents had settled among other Italian farmers.

* * * *

Times were tough; funds were low; the strikers had lost their bearings. Italians were especially suspect and easily hustled away. From their safe house in the tiny village on the Pennsylvania-New Jersey border, Esteve, with Carmelo's help, tried to renew *La Questione Sociale*.

"Without an organ in print," Esteve said, "the prospects for revolution are dim."

Not revealing his fears, Carmelo hoped to run back to New York. He thought that he was about to lose his shirt and didn't know what to do.

Esteve contacted a Sicilian man, Michele Caminita, who might help keep the paper running.

"This guy," Esteve explained to Carmelo, "has a good reputation for training workers in political thought and has years of experience writing. He recently fled Palermo for Canada and has settled with our comrades at a hideout in Barre, Vermont. Now he's coming to New Jersey, and you and I are going to meet him." Esteve planned to take the train in order to find this fellow.

When Caminita arrived in Paterson and looked around for the members of *La Questione Sociale,* he was, at first, dismayed. In a café known as an anarchist hangout, no one came to his side. He waited. He waited some more. Slowly, a few newspaper workers arrived to welcome the stranger: strikers who'd trained under Galleani's wing; women who'd been the couriers and bomb-makers of the revolution. Finally, Esteve and Carmelo walked in to greet him. From the start, Caminita hit it off with Esteve and, for the first time in many weeks, cracked a smile. Carmelo smiled for the first time too. These were natural affinities, the three men announced; friendship among men with a common cause wasn't to be taken lightly. As the meeting concluded, Esteve proposed that Caminita lead the paper.

"Things are taking shape," Esteve said. "And based on your work in Palermo, I know you can handle the tricks of the trade."

Caminita nodded. "I know how to publish a broadsheet. I can write and edit. In Sicily, I also knew how to organize citrus pickers and press back on the landowners' thumbs."

The men promised to meet again—perhaps a few days later. Meanwhile, Esteve and Carmelo spoke with the leadership of northern New Jersey and confirmed their idea to reopen the paper with Caminita in the editor's role.

12.

Soon after, Esteve and Maria returned to their Weehawken flat with Carmelo and Caminita, whom they'd invited to take a room in their basement. Carmelo enjoyed being part of a family and the day-to-day routines at the kitchen table. He loved the tea kettle's whistle, the rich scent of Maria's Sunday sauce bubbling on the stove. But the peaceable home was not to last. After several months, Esteve and Maria sensed danger and again prepared to move. Carmelo and Caminita left for Paterson to seek a place to live. Their new housing was austere, and Carmelo was hard put to call it home.

The men quickly sought work in the factories and Carmelo, who'd continued to remember his carnival work in New York, decided to take a job on Saturday nights at the electric park nearby. It was an amusement arena so full of lights that it rivaled Coney Island; much to Carmelo's happy surprise, it belonged to Mr. Schenck.

Carmelo was pleased to see the Russian again and expressed his admiration of the surroundings. "Where but in an amusement park could the power of light engage such a willing crowd?" Carmelo said.

"Mr. Edison sold us incandescent lamps at a discount," Mr. Schenck replied. "So it's my hope to draw more public attention to this wonderous new invention. New Jersey, in the end, will replace our work at Ft. George."

Carmelo was overjoyed to pick up this job. It was his closest idea of home.

"The amusement park is terrific," Carmelo told Caminita one evening. "It's called Palisades Park. Lights galore, Ferris wheels, penny arcades, and peep shows. My goodness, there's even a theater. When I got there, my old boss from New York welcomed me and promised to let me perform. Just think—vaudeville in an open theater, a daytime version of a *caffè concert* with lots of high jinks and special effects."

Carmelo told Caminita of the little skits that he'd written for Mr. Loew and promised to show him the pages he'd brought with him from New York. Caminita said he was no stranger to the stage; he'd written scripts in Palermo and continued to think about future work. He'd also read about popular theater on New York's Spring Street and longed to see those plays.

The two spent the evening talking about bilingual skits. Carmelo remembered his vaudeville start, telling his jokes in two tongues. He explained what he'd learned from famous comics in order to get people to laugh. In the mixed-up world of his act, he'd liked the idea of a single performer playing all the roles. He didn't say that he'd lifted some of Farfariello's lines in order to make his skits work.

Caminita and Carmelo had a routine. They worked at the factory, came home to write, and, on weekends, Carmelo directed the vaudeville reviews at Palisades Park. On occasion, the men attended anarchist meetings at Turn Hall in Paterson, where a large Italian congregation showed up. On most nights, however, the two men stayed home to talk about theater. Caminita had a greater range; he knew the art of the stage. He knew that theater depended on the way in which you configured time and space; that voice gave birth to character; and that the audience had to believe in the lines. "And if they don't believe you, they'll leave."

He began to speak way over Carmelo's head. "Be steady. And don't forget a phrase's rhythm. It leads your audience along; it pushes them ahead."

Carmelo had never thought of rhythm; he barely knew the word.

* * * *

One day at the factory, Carmelo heard that Bresci's widow had opened a restaurant in Edgewater. It was a two-mile walk from the amusement park, so Carmelo planned to drop in after work. Here, finally, was the occasion to close the circle and meet Bresci's girl face to face. Caminita laughed and egged him on. On a Saturday night after carnival work, Carmelo walked to the restaurant. He noted the girl at once: flaming red hair and deep green eyes. This was the lover Bresci had described, and he knew her as sure as his name.

Carmelo took a table against the back wall and studied Sophie Kneiland. With confidence, she chatted with clients as they walked in and winked at the men at the counter. She was tall like Bresci, svelte in a way the women at home were not; her perfect face lacked the tough sunbaked skin belonging to girls from his village. When he introduced himself, Sophie offered her hand and then gave him a hug. Carmelo felt faint. Between Sophie and Carmelo, a friendship was about to be born.

"Of course, I know your name," Sophie said. "Bresci always mentioned you with great affection. He liked to think of himself as the older uncle in charge of his favorite nephew." She chuckled. "I guess there were a few years between you."

"I'm sorry for your loss," Carmelo said, having decided that it was best to start with humility in order to mask his excitement.

"Thank you. I've tried to pull myself back together."

They chatted for a considerable time, juggling their different tongues. Off the menu, Sophie read a litany of Irish stews and a few plates of pasta with beans. At the top of the line was a pork chop, but its price was out of bounds. Although Carmelo heard the list of dishes, in reality he'd heard nothing. Just a quiet hum of a mellifluous voice and an electrical charge that buzzed through his body. Oh, Sophie, he thought. This time I'm the *sonemagogna*—I can't figure right from wrong.

Each weekend, the two met at the restaurant, but one night Carmelo came to eat with a hunger he couldn't describe. His body was starved, his head ached so much that he couldn't find his words. He could only think of her peachy cream face and those full rosy lips. This night, Sophie invited Carmelo to remain after closing. "Considering everything," she said. "It will be easier for you tomorrow to reach your carnival job from here."

Not knowing how it happened—who started what and who first touched whom, whose lips approached the other's lips—all of a sudden a burst of stars, multi-layered explosions. Colored flames! Combustion! The pyrotechnics of summer fairs! Tongues tied and then loosened, exploring the dips and hollows of flesh, the salty foam of saliva and sweat. Heated bodies entwined.

"Mo chuisle."

"Amore mio," Carmelo replied.

Pulsations, ripples, waves. Carmelo made love to Sophie. Sophie made love to Carmelo. Neither knew who was who; lines of demarcation vanished. Would the brown legs fusing with milk-soft thighs ever stand up again on their own? The two lay exhausted on Sophie's small bed; Carmelo fell asleep with Sophie beside him, his hands caressing her cascade of red hair lit with moonlight. That night Carmelo dreamed of Bresci embraced in his tender arms.

* * * *

Every weekend Carmelo traveled to Palisades Park, and after work he met Sophie. Carmelo, enthralled with the so-called partner of his so-called uncle, now saw the family doubly braided. The two carried on this family romance for what seemed to be quite a while. Each evening, Carmelo first met Sophie's friends. They were mostly women involved in different aspects of anarchist theater; several had staged one-act skits that spoke to women's rights. Among them was Ninfa Baronio, who'd lived in Paterson over the years and stood at the forefront of anarchist art. She wrote scripts for the Sunday picnics, she performed in feminist theater, she even staged a one-act play in a Bleeker Street playhouse devoted to Italian voices. With her partner Fermino Gallo—"Not my husband," Ninfa firmly insisted, "but simply the man I love"—she ran an anarchist bookstore of far-reaching renown. Carmelo was in awe.

Ninfa and Sophie laughed heartily about the plight of desperate men; they guffawed about masculine power and chuckled at the many ways in which men twisted the truth. But they didn't laugh when they spoke about the need to fight for women's freedom.

Sophie said to Carmelo, "Though Ninfa reads Kropotkin and Bakunin, she's taken by Emma Goldman and always quotes her with pride."

Sophie said that Ninfa had written a story about Emma in New Jersey, but Carmelo knew this couldn't be true; after all, Maria Roda once said that Emma had never crossed the Hudson River. Carmelo wasn't miffed; he understood that Ninfa needed to tell her truths in novel ways.

"Fiction shows what pamphlets can't tell you," Ninfa always said. "It touches your soul before it reaches your mind."

Ninfa was always engaged, but Carmelo grew impatient as the hours dragged on. Finally, when Ninfa stood up to leave for the night, Carmelo expected that *finally* he would have Sophie to himself.

But on this particular evening, after the restaurant closed and Ninfa had gone on her way, Sophie stood up: "It's time to cut this short, Carmelo. We can't go on."

Carmelo began to tremble.

"My man," Sophie said, "is due to return from Barre, Vermont. You and I are finished."

Carmelo was in shock. "And *us*?" he finally said. "The memory of Bresci? Our future lives together?"

Sophie responded with a rasping voice, like iron scraping on iron: "If there's one part of anarchist thought that I'll never discard, it's the idea of free love for women. No one gets to own me or tell me what to do. I'm not your concubine. I'm not your servant. And I'm certainly not giving into the wishes of any fellow who wants to possess me. I have more important matters to think about, more important things to do."

Sophie went on like a Victor record; Carmelo was the listening dog. But Carmelo. who tried his best, couldn't understand what had happened. Bresci had often spoken of women's rights. He had supported the idea of the partner, equal and independent; he had opposed family conventions. Now Sophie was reading him the anarchist platform as if she were transmitting the news.

"But weren't you the love of Bresci's life? Weren't you his partner?" Carmelo said.

Sophie looked out the window. "You only live in the moment. Unhooked from past and future. Didn't Bresci teach you that? Didn't you learn this from Maria Roda? Open your ears, dear boy."

Carmelo didn't know what to say. Not only was he losing his girl, but behind the scenes the relation between uncle and nephew was grinding to a terrible halt.

The following morning, Carmelo was light-headed and sick to his stomach. Instead of going to work at the amusement park, he headed to the falls that ran through Paterson's central park. Right now, he needed nature to speak its particular language, to hear water crashing on stone; he wanted the spray lifting from gorges, the ice-clear light. The crescendo reminded Carmelo of his evenings with Sophie, a groaning roar of the senses. He beheld a break and flow of the current forcing its way through the gorge; jets of vapor rising and then drifting to final exhaustion. Carmelo was attentive. In its quiet moments, the river was crawling, slinking, meandering forward; then the spray came flushing out. Pushing past the granite teeth of the falls, the water broke into a scream.

"Water carries life," Carmelo said. He saw something larger than the river—maybe that love's pain was a matter of water and movement, immersion and dissolution. Flow.

What was it with water? He thought of Bresci's body thrown to the sea, his own fear of crossing the ocean. Against this, a flow of hope. Could he learn to retain it? He imagined the same water flowing in the Bay of Naples was right before him. All times united; histories perched on the recurrent falls. Perhaps the scene announced a rise and fall, patterns of repetition. He wondered what happened to love.

13.

Carmelo stayed at the Paterson Falls through early evening. Then he walked the few blocks to his rented room. Sadness was in the air as he greeted Caminita.

"I can't believe this happened. Do you think that I deserve this? I thought love was forever."

Caminita saw that his friend was slipping into a well where nothing made any sense. There was really nothing to say. But at last he made a proposal. "It's time to heal, Carmelo. Let's try to work on our scripts. Let's go to New York to see the variety shows and learn about anarchist theater."

Carmelo was glum and tired. He only wanted to sleep. But the following weekend, Caminita persuaded Carmelo to ride with him to the city. "There's an important meeting at Everett Hall. We can see the comrades, get up to date. And then if we have a few hours free, we'll also take in some theater."

At Everett Hall, they found a lively event in which people were striving to make their ideas heard. "Rights for women workers!" shouted a woman with raised fist. "And don't forget the need for childcare at the work site," yelled another.

"Look how the women fight for the podium," Carmelo said to Caminita as he recalled the heated arguments between Ninfa and Sophie. It was exhausting but part of anarchist custom. He wondered if life was about something more than defeating the bosses. Where was room for passion? Deciding abruptly that he could bear no more lectures, no more proposals for revolution, Carmelo left the anarchist meeting and went off to look for his friends.

Carmelo walked to Mulberry Bend in search of Zi'Annibale; later, he had a date with Maria Roda near the lion house of Central Park Zoo. A day of high excitement, old bonds to be renewed. Carmelo was flushed with feeling, but when he arrived at Baciagalupo's funeral home, the receptionist explained that his friend was no longer there.

"When Mr. Baciagalupo passed his business on to his sons, Zi'Annibale decided to set up the studio of his dreams. He opened a photography shop on Sullivan and Broome."

Carmelo thanked her, took a respectable bow, and then ran up the streets for the grand encounter. This time he had luck on his side.

"It's been a long while," Zi'Annibale said when they finally embraced. "I'd lie if I said I didn't miss you. Lots of events to share. But tell me your stories first."

"Okay, the headlines," Carmelo said. "Maria and Esteve, who were living in Weehawken, let me live in their basement. Then Caminita showed up, and we formed a friendship. Before you know it, Esteve and Maria left for Brooklyn, and Caminita and I moved to Paterson. I work at a silk mill and have a spectacular weekend job doing skits and theater. Then, the grandest thing, I met a woman."

"All this in a minute." Zi'Annibale smiled.

Carmelo inhaled. "I think I fell in love, but after a while she sent me away. Silence, nothing. As if I had never existed. This has left me in the dumps. Now I take some solace in my writing. Caminita helps me. It may be a self-delusion, but I hope to think of myself as a writer."

Zi'Annibale felt some relief. At least Carmelo had found a confidant who was lending a useful hand. New Jersey couldn't be the wasteland that Carmelo had once described.

"Any word from my sister Mariarosa? Or Antonio? Do you know if they're here?"

The two men sighed.

* * * *

"Now *my* headlines," Zi'Annibale said. "I have a lot to report. To start, I've been lucky. I only opened this studio a while ago, and I've built up a thriving business. People who liked my work in the funeral home now want portraits of the living. So business is brisk. Sort of the way it happened in Italy."

Carmelo smiled as he thought of Eugenia posing for Zi'Annibale.

"I have news for you on two fronts. First, regarding Antonio. You'd better sit down to listen. This one is a doozy. So before I left Baciagalupo's, I knew everyone who was fixing up the dead. Most are barbers and shoemakers, with a few tailors thrown in; people who know the art of skin repair and are determined with needle and thread. Some also fix up the living. So one day I ran into a man who had worked for Baciagalupo. Bragging, he told me about this colossal job he'd performed on the face of a damaged man. 'This guy had a large crescent shape scar over his right eyebrow,' the man tells me. 'And the scar was so big and bulging, extending over his eyelid, that he really looked ugly-ugly.'

"Wait!!" exclaimed Carmelo.

"This man's name is Pasquale Ferrone. He tells me about the guy with the scar. The fellow worked for the Black Hand and needed to change the way he looked so that no one would chase him down. He was involved in shady business—don't ask me what, but you can imagine—and the Black Hand now wanted their due. So this guy is on the run.

"So Ferrone gets good money to remove the scar and changes the guy's bad looks."

"Just like that?" Carmelo asked. "How did he manage to do it?"

"Skin grafts from the upper arm, lots of antiseptics, and gallons of Irish whiskey. The surgeon lifts the scar off his eyelid and pulls some flesh off the temple and forehead. Don't ask me anything else. I don't know all the details. Now this guy looks different, the surgeon told me; not perfect of course, but it's impossible to recognize him if you'd known him from ten years before. The man now works as a barber."

Carmelo was sweating. Could it be possibly true? Carmelo remembered the theater, where everything is a lie.

"The surgeon made me swear to keep the secret, but of course, I'm telling you. After all, we know that all deals are off if they're made in the house of the dead. Ferrone had even more to say."

Carmelo couldn't help himself. "But are you sure this is Antonio?"

"Look, Carmelo," Zi'Annibale said, "we're never sure of anything, but this is a pretty good bet. The question is how do you find him?

Can you really go to every barbershop in the city? And what if he's left town? You can't ask the Black Hand, or you'll give Antonio away. The only thing might be to track down Ferrone. I can't imagine anything else."

Carmelo wanted to cry. What was his brother up to? Where in the world could he be? Why was he hidden even from the people who loved him? Didn't Antonio care? "And Mariarosa?" He sighed. "Any word about her?"

"While Ferrone was telling his story, he mentioned in passing that this guy with the scar was going to rest after his operation. Take a few weeks off so to speak, and find repose in his sister's home. So we know he has a sister in New York and trusts this woman enough to let her care for him for a while."

Carmelo heaved another sigh. "So, am I supposed to walk all over New York looking for them? And what if they're not in Manhattan? Plus, tomorrow afternoon I have to return to my Paterson job. Dammit."

"I can keep an eye and ear on the matter, but I don't have a lot of contacts out there. Brooklyn, the Bronx, and uptown Manhattan are for me an ocean away. My hunch is that you'll find your people. You'll have to walk the streets, ask the shop owners and men in the taverns. Which won't be easy given the person you're looking for is trying to pass as someone else. Still, I think you'll find Antonio if he's about to be found. And Mariarosa will show up too."

Carmelo felt like he was part of a rotted history. For his brother to change his face meant that something was very wrong. His lip twitched; his temples throbbed. He told himself to be calm, that this problem wasn't of his making. If Antonio didn't want to find him, it's because he had something to hide. He wondered if he should persist in the chase.

"Look," Zi'Annibale said, "let me turn the story around. You work all week and don't have time to search for your brother. Just try to forget it. After all, he's up to no good. Antonio isn't a hero, and he won't save you through love or duty. You just have to write him off. Leave well enough alone."

Carmelo sat in an armchair, digesting the story, when some customers came through Zi'Annibale's door: mother, *nonna*, and three children had come to sit for a portrait. Knowing better than to remain in the studio, Carmelo bid his friend farewell. He walked slowly through the Greenwich Village streets and headed toward the IRT train in order to keep his date with Maria.

14.

Maria was waiting in the Central Park Zoo. More precisely, on a bench near the lion cages, where she could keep an eye on her three children and also have time to talk.

Maria and Carmelo fell into each other's arms just like an old-time couple. Although they both respected Esteve, they still liked to flirt. She was happy to see her comrade, this nervous little brother who always made her smile.

Maria claimed that meeting at the zoo was safe since the police never bothered families with children: "The idea of the happy family always keeps the cops at a distance; if they see a father doting on his kids, buying balloons and cotton candy, they don't bother him at all. Let's just speak in very low tones so no one will perk up their ears."

No sooner had she said this, Carmelo melted like molasses. His words came out sticky and slow, revealing the depths of his sorrow. He told her about Sophie and shared the news about Antonio and Mariarosa.

"Give up on Antonio," Maria said. "He has no interest in you. You don't need to hunt down a man who has no regard for your well-being. And with all the friends and comrades you have, why go after this rotten figure who's clearly up to no good?"

Carmelo said, "I don't know what to do."

Maria consoled her aimless friend. Meanwhile, her children pressed on the guardrails that kept them from the lions; they threw a few peanut shells at the cage to see if the big cats would growl.

All of a sudden, sirens and bells, screams and cussing, the rush of police on foot. Four officers bearing clubs ran through the arches of the Central Park Zoo. It looked as if they were headed toward Maria and Carmelo. The two froze. Neither spoke a word. The police ran past the frightened adults, past the lion cage and the children, and headed for the monkey house where they ganged up on a stout Italian man standing close to a society lady. The police were indignant and tough.

"You wops are all the same," one cop screamed at the man. "Now you're finally under arrest and won't bother these ladies again."

The pudgy man was stunned to learn that he'd been under surveillance for at least a week.

"The man has been touching the visitors," a guard said. "Sometimes he stands behind them so that his legs rub against theirs; sometimes he lets his hand move through his overcoat pocket to squeeze the ladies' behinds."

The barrel-chested man said the monkeys were at fault for pinching the ladies' buttocks, that the cops should leave him alone. The authorities cuffed him. Then everyone heard his scream.

"*Arresta? Gesummaria!* Do you know who I am?" the burly man asked, impertinence gaining force in his lungs. "Call my boss. Call my manager. They will show you how much you're in error."

The squat man sounded like Canio. The police were greatly incensed; here was a wop defending himself as if he were king of the roost. Finally, and with no more words, they prepared to take him away. The socialite was grateful. The zoo guards were relieved. The monkeys, indifferent, scratched their armpits and laughed. The police hauled the fat man off to the city jail. Carmelo and Maria were stunned by the commotion. They knew who the guilty man was. A famous Italian tenor was under arrest at the zoo. Months later, after the verdict was read, people agreed the trial was a sham, an attempt to scare Italians and chase them out of the city. The papers later reported that the magistrate had fined Caruso ten dollars for inappropriately touching a woman. *La commedia é finita*, Maria and Carmelo said, but they no longer found the threads that wove their thoughts together.

On the train back to Paterson, Carmelo was uneasy because of Zi'Annibale's news about Antonio. Caminita, beside him, was worried about new roundups of anarchist workers. The men stared through the windows, each drinking in the scenes of Jersey corn fields sprouting on both sides of the tracks. Repetitive and sedating, the train's clip induced the men into slumber. Carmelo dreamed of a movie he'd recently seen about cowboy bandits assaulting a locomotive; they'd stolen the safe box, the mail, and the travelers' loot before they were finally caught.

15.

Despite his friends' advice, Carmelo couldn't forget his siblings. How was he going to find them? Where was the proper place to start? Pushing his Sunday work commitments aside for a while, he began to visit New York to search for his brother and sister. He started in Bay Ridge in Brooklyn; he went to Arthur Avenue far up in the Bronx. He took the train to Astoria, Queens and looked through Long Island City. He repeated this week after week, year after year. Some people in those neighborhoods began to see his face as familiar.

"Excuse me, *cumpar.*' Have you seen a barber named Antonio Troiano? He may have had surgery on his face. He's probably kind of ugly, but he has beautiful, very blue eyes."

"Forgive me today, but I'm hoping you can direct me to Antonio Troiano. I believe that he works in a barber shop and comes from Bellanera."

"*Buon giorno, signora*. Do you know of a woman named Mariarosa Scarpa? Her husband's name is Orazio, and they probably have several children."

For years, Carmelo took his single day off to go in search of his siblings. This pursuit can't last forever, he thought.

One day, Carmelo's Sunday quest was interrupted when Caminita stopped him at the door.

"They're after me," Caminita said, almost out of breath. "They want to shut the paper down and drive me out of town."

"Why now?" Carmelo wondered if he were also in danger.

"Who knows? It could be an article I wrote about revolution or my series about the cursed white race that drives American culture. Either way, I'm sunk. I need to leave town."

"Again? It's become your life story. A man always on the run."

Carmelo was despondent. First, Bresci died. Then Sophie turned him down. Then he learned about his siblings. Now Caminita was about to depart. "What's next in this American drama? All my friends come and go. Nothing stays the same. I guess I need to leave, too."

* * * *

No one knew where they had gone; all news was based on rumor. Some reported that Carmelo, following his buddy, had gone out west to work with a Mexican anarchist named Flores Magón. Trusted in their newspaper work, Carmelo and Caminita ran the Italian page of the Mexican broadsheet; it was called *Regeneración*. Then some folks reported that Carmelo had left on his own for Mexico to join the revolution.

The comrades in New Jersey heard this gossip from Ninfa Baronio's son, a man who'd joined the rebels south of the border. From Mexico, he wrote to say that he'd seen Carmelo in Cuautla, in league with Emiliano Zapata. He was running a printing press for Zapata in order to spread Mexican news. No one knew much more. Some years later, someone spotted Carmelo in the cotton fields outside Savannah; then the Jersey folks heard that Carmelo had shown up in the coal mines near Pittsburgh. It was all very confusing; the rumors didn't add up.

16.

After an absence of nearly ten long years, Carmelo had returned to New York. Having never lost hope of finding his siblings, he first went to Zi'Annibale's store, but when he found the photography studio vacant and boarded up, he began to drown in fear. "*Oh Dio*," he said, "Where can Zi'Annibale be?"

Then he flew to the funeral parlor.

"No, Zi'Annibale isn't here; he decided to return to Italy," the receptionist said. "Life was getting tough. The war, the shortage of clientele for family portraits, the ongoing closures in business. It was a double bind, to stay or go. And don't forget the legal questions. Either you quickly got your papers in order or you lived in fear of police reprisals."

The receptionist proceeded to explain the details of work in a much-transformed New York: "We're doing a booming business here in the funeral home; we can't keep up with demand. The number of deaths from the Spanish flu keeps growing every week. And the city pays us to use our storeroom as a substitute morgue. You'll hear about this a lot, Carmelo, but for now just try to be careful."

Carmelo was at a loss. After so many years away, he lost his sense of place. No brother or sister to be found, and now no Zi'Annibale. Perhaps he deserved it; after all, he had fled New York. But how could he mend his heart? Seeing no reason to stay, Carmelo picked up his bags, drew a bandanna over his nose and mouth, and headed for the New Jersey train.

* * * *

Entering Paterson again, after so many years of absence, Carmelo directed himself to familiar faces—Maria at the kitchen table along with Esteve and Ninfa Baronio. Though they lived through extreme losses—the arrests of anarchist workers, the shutdown of papers, the dispersion of comrades, and now the most dreadful flu—they pretended that nothing had changed at all when Carmelo knocked on the door.

"*Oh Dio*, here he is! Our kid is back! Where in the world have you been?"

Carmelo hemmed and hawed; his words came out in a jumble. "You can't begin to imagine," he said. "I've been all over!"

Lots of explanations although no one really believed him. Nonetheless, the reunion lasted well into the afternoon. Then, to Carmelo's great surprise, Caminita also knocked. Each man was cheered to see the other as they sat down to chat.

"Sure, each of us had to leave. You could say we were on the run. But I've been back for several years awaiting the day you'd show up." Caminita chewed on a slice of bread. "Now we can give it a second chance and see how things turn out."

"Old weeds never die," Maria said as she noted the happiness that temporarily filled her kitchen.

Caminita wanted to resume his life as a writer; Carmelo was eager to learn much more about Caminita's tools of the trade. The years in Mexico had boosted Carmelo up. He gained confidence in his skills, he lost some of his early fears. Perhaps his time had come.

"Why don't we share a room? For old times' sake?" Carmelo said.

Caminita was surprised by Carmelo's assertive voice. In the past, he hadn't been so forward. "I'd be so grateful," Caminita responded. "We're a good match, old pal."

Their rented room was modest. They resumed their newspaper work. They made plans for the future.

"Don't forget the struggle, my friend," Caminita said to Carmelo. "Keep your eye on the prize."

As usual, Carmelo cringed but didn't quake in his boots. Instead, he expressed his exasperation for a cause that he knew couldn't be won. Here, Carmelo said that he thought the New Jersey efforts were failing. No anarchist revolution was about to bear fruit.

Surprised by his deft and cutting words, Caminita confirmed his friend's impressions. "You may be right, Carmelo. There's news of a red scare in the mainstream press, and the police are all over New Jersey. Bolsheviks, communists, anarchists, socialists, the women who wanted the vote—everyone is under suspicion."

It seemed that no one was spared. After anarchist attacks on the Attorney General's home, Mr. Palmer was bent on revenge. Along with J. Edgar Hoover, he called on the General Intelligence Office to root out alien subversives. Because the Feds had closed the most recent anarchist paper (named *L'Era Nuova*), Caminita was preparing to launch another.

"I want to call it *La Jacquerie*," he said, alluding to medieval rebellions and also to the kind of silk work young Bresci had once managed in Italy. He tried to keep some sense of calm.

"We have to try to resume our lives of years ago," Caminita said. "Forget the outside dangers. Let's just continue to work on the newspaper by day and open our hearts to theater. Pretend that everything is normal, that we have decent lives."

The men continued to tell their stories. Carmelo described his time in Mexico, his admiration for Zapata, his walks through the desert, his parched throat after days in the sun. He recalled the beautiful *soldadera* women whom he had seen in the Mexican plains.

Caminita told of anarchist dramas, the passions he shared with Big Bill Haywood of the IWW; he spoke of Elizabeth Gurley Flynn, now Carlo Tresca's girlfriend. Names flew left and right. He remembered the parades of workers on the streets of New York City. "And you know what else?" Caminita said. "Bill Haywood told me that our spectacle of theater and song rivaled even the highfalutin fuss that took place at the Armory uptown. While the hoity-toity introduced Europe's most radical art to New Yorkers, *we* were stars of the city; *we* ruled the streets of New York."

Caminita figured that the performance of anarchy would be enough to inspire the people. By contrast, Carmelo was less convinced although he described the theater and dance that accompanied Zapata's troops.

Caminita pulled out his latest scripts. He had a bundle of one-act plays he wanted to share with Carmelo. Carmelo was grateful for Caminita's trust but had fewer good works to show.

"And now that we're back to subject of danger, where will we hide if we need to?"

Carmelo thought of returning to Zia Cristina's infected abode, but Caminita persuaded him that the New Jersey air was better for the heart and lungs.

"Why expose yourself to the polluted city air when you can live near the Paterson falls? Don't worry. Just stay with me." Caminita didn't say that somewhere in a distant city his erstwhile girlfriend and child were coughing themselves to death. "Have trust you'll be safe right here."

Secretly, Caminita didn't believe they'd escape or survive. Only in his wildest dreams did he imagine they both would pull through.

One day, Caminita said, "Hey, Carmelo, why don't you keep my plays among your stuff? Just for safe keeping, if you know what I mean. I wouldn't want this work to get lost."

Carmelo agreed to hide the papers under his cot.

Those months were tough. Caminita pointed out the dangers of the Anarchist Exclusion Act while A. Mitchell Palmer, Attorney General and creep, tried to deport non-citizens of any left-wing political stripe. First, those of Russian backgrounds were sent by boat to Finland. Even naturalized US citizens, as American as apple pie. Among them Emma Goldman, who had put up a considerable fuss. This Palmer guy chased everyone in a rodeo roundup, lassoing men and women who might threaten the national peace. The immigrants who'd arrived decades ago now rushed to secure their citizenship papers lest they be deported.

Carmelo, however, remained close to home, observing events from a distance while Caminita continued writing screeds on the walls and doors. "Class war is on and cannot cease but with a complete victory for the international proletariat," Caminita's recent poster declared.

Some say Caminita was behind the bomb that nearly blew up the home of silk boss, Harry Klotz, on 31st Street in Paterson. President of Susquehanna Silk and Dye, Klotz had killed a strike the year before and drew the wrath of workers. President Wilson ordered a hunt for the flamethrowers, but those responsible fled. Then came the roundup on Valentine's Day of 1920. J. Edgar Hoover, as part of his first big job, sent in some two hundred agents along with spies for the Feds. The goal was to raid Paterson and yank anarchists from their homes. The notorious collective of *L'Era Nuova* was hauled off to a New Jersey jail. They pointed a finger at Caminita as leader of the pack and also arrested Carmelo.

17.

At the Paterson police station, Caminita stood alone in a moldy gray room. The detectives entered and pushed him into a chair.

"*Merda*," shouted Caminita. "Keep your hands off me."

The detectives struck him across the neck with a stick. Then came blows to his legs and arms. Caminita fell to the floor. His guts were tied in knots. He wanted to vomit. He hadn't experienced anything like this since the police had detained him in Palermo. Blood gushed from his mouth; he reached up to check his teeth. Swelling, pain. Where were his legs? "*Porca miseria.*" English words failed him.

Caminita broke down and began to speak. His words came out in a rush. Incomprehensible. The detectives gave him a glass of water. "Speak, you piece of garbage, or else we'll beat you again."

Caminita first revealed the names of the newspaper staff and their whereabouts in New Jersey. He then explained the Italian anarchist links to IWW members and blamed them both for last year's bombing. More names, addresses, details. In exchange for this information, Caminita was not deported. Instead, the Feds sent him to the Ellis Island jail, where for three years he wrote his memoirs.

Meanwhile, Carmelo was detained in a separate cell. An agent came to confront him. When this man spoke to him in his mother tongue, Carmelo at first didn't grasp its import. Words slid into his ear and brain much in the way soft pastina with butter slides down a hungry child's throat. Carmelo looked again at the agent and saw his sapphire eyes. He stumbled, he stuttered, he thought it unreal, and then he opened his mind to a faint recognition.

"Carmelo," Antonio said, "I've been following you all these years, but my work took me into darkness, and I couldn't risk the chance to meet you. Forgive me, *frate mio*, brother mine. I know how long you've waited; I know that you've combed the city. I know that you wrote home quite often, but I told our mother not to write back, not to tell you where I was and to hide Mariarosa's location as well. It's true, you almost had me when you learned of my surgical change, but I couldn't afford to give signs of life; my work simply wouldn't allow it. I assist the antiradical unit of the General Intelligence Office. They plucked me out from the Black Hand's claws, claiming to do me a gigantic favor. They say they saved my life, but I think they've condemned me to hell on earth by depriving me of my name."

Antonio's return as a secret agent shattered Carmelo's world. Carmelo trembled and trembled some more.

Antonio gave no sign of feeling his brother's dismay. "I can do you a favor. You have to listen to me. These prisoners who were picked up with you are scheduled for Kansas or McNeil Island; others will be deported. My higher-ups have permission to reroute some people for humanitarian causes. It's an attempt to limit the number of Reds who pass through the penitentiary portals, to keep them off the records."

Carmelo shifted his weight. He couldn't shake the feeling of defeat and loss that rattled through his body. Who was the stranger speaking right now?

Antonio continued, "If they deport you to Italy, the police will detain you in Naples. They're still looking to sting the group linked to King Umberto's murder. Probably they'll send you to the island jail where your old pal Bresci spent his last days stuffed in a hole and left to rot."

Carmelo tried to hold back his tears.

"If you remain in America, your fate under Hoover will be no better. So, this is my favor to you, little brother. I'm sorry, but it's the best I can do. I've secured your safe passage to Buenos Aires, where you can link up with Maria Antonietta. I know she married a Spaniard, and they have a store on Calle Piedras. Here's an envelope in which I've supplied you with all the details you'll eventually need. They're attached to your new ID and a passport. During this voyage, you will never mention me. You'll go by the name of Errico Cellà. Your choice, kid; take it or leave it."

Carmelo wept beyond control. As he tried to speak aloud, whole words collapsed. A liquid mash of incomprehension. Once again in his life, there was too much information. His brother Antonio, his brother. Yet short of those sapphire eyes, Antonio failed to reveal a trace of the man he'd once been. He stood as some kind of ghost or phantom, a cutout of a once-living man. Carmelo tried to stand but sat once more. Nothing was to be done. Very much unreal.

Twenty years wiped out: the theater, the plays, the designs, the prints, the publication of weekly papers; his affections for Zi'Annibale, his love for Bresci; his friends, Esteve and Maria; his all too brief romance; his years assisting the grand Caminita, his labor on skits and plays. Was this what it meant to live in America? To find a better life? And what happened to human ideals?

Carmelo didn't know that he would miss the May arrest of Sacco and Vanzetti accused of the Braintree murders; he couldn't know that he'd miss the Wall Street bombings staged by Mario Buda, the good friend of Caminita; nor could he imagine that the other Italians in New York would abandon the cause of Carlo Tresca and turn their love to Il Duce. Carmelo asked Antonio to grab his belongings, which still lay under the cot of his rented Paterson room.

The Narrators

Time passes slowly when you're free all day, when you don't have a job to tie you down. You get used to the daytime crowd and run into lots of strange faces. Old ladies with shopping carts riding the bus, loafers on public assistance, tough guys who sell you scratchers at discount, women trading WICs for an afternoon beer. This is what you see on the streets if you don't work the nine to five, Max thought as he walked the few blocks to catch a bus to Fordham Road. He was going to meet his Bronx friends for an afternoon of fun.

Max had been a kid when the family had moved from the Bronx. He'd barely been old enough to talk. One day his parents had come home with bad news: the boiler in their apartment building had gone on the fritz again, and they'd have no heat through the winter months. Exasperated, fed up with the super, his mother had decided that it was time to move. The family moved to Inwood. His mother had chosen the pre-war walk-up for the trees growing tall in the alley. Deep closets and a basement laundry were also part of the deal. The apartment had heat and hot water. But the building's greatest advantage, his mother had said, was its half-block distance from the train. After high school, when his friends had dispersed, Max began to return to the Bronx. An ancient calling, Max thought, a return to the omphalos (Max liked to practice the few Greek words he'd learned while reading *Ulysses*).

A twenty-minute ride at the most, he figured. As he waited for the bus, he fished a token from his pocket. No sweat, easy-peasy. Once there, he'd meet up with Lou and his gang to order an espresso and *sfogliatella* at Egidio's bakery. He kind of liked the Italian neighborhood in the Bronx, but he wasn't nostalgic in the style of his sister.

Once at the bakery, he and Lou talked about girls. "Take the food, quit the dreaming," Max said. "Let's explore the town."

Lou laughed. "Yeah. Why bother with those girls who are all stuck in the past? It would be like going on a date with your nonna."

In the late afternoon, the fellows cruised through the zoo and then walked to Jahn's for the Kitchen Sink sundae. A full round of sweets, and then some girls showed up. Connie and Angelica, with their painted nails and big bouffant hair. Lou and Max couldn't wait to send them on their way.

"What a bust." Max laughed. "They never asked if I had a job, but they only cared that I was Italian."

Lou snorted.

"It was good to get out of the house today," Max said when he was about to leave. "Best of all, I got rid of my stupid sister, prancing around like a know-it-all, thinking she's smarter than me."

Lou really disliked Rosanna and always called her a snob. And he didn't like her meddling in Max's affairs. "She's a real piece of work. I don't envy your situation."

"It's worse than that," answered Max. "I have to teach her how to write. In fact, I have to go home right now in order to do just that."

* * * *

So here they were in the kitchen again, the siblings teamed up for evening war. Rosanna was shrieking about the conclusion of chapter two. She pounded her fists on the table.

"You didn't tell me you were changing the second chapter's ending. I thought you were simply checking my grammar."

Max, as usual, opened the fridge to hunt down a beer. This time the bottles were hidden behind the cartons of milk. Closing the door, he turned to his sister. "Your conclusion was simply inconceivable. You wanted to say that Carmelo met up with his sister in the midst of the plague. And that his sister paid for Carmelo's trip to Argentina. Impossible! The family had no money to give to a practical stranger. I can't imagine how you would think this as a probable ending. So I added my own invention."

Rosanna's face was beet red. She wanted to punch and scratch her brother. "First, I'm reading the family archives, the letters from Eugenia that our grandmother kept. My ending of chapter two is based on that correspondence. Everything I wrote is true."

Max harrumphed. Rosanna insisted that her version of events be restored and pushed her pages in front of Max.

* * * *

After leaving the Baciagalupo funeral home, Carmelo began to look for his sister. He combed the Italian neighborhoods of the Bronx and Upper Manhattan. First the streets near Arthur Avenue, then the East Harlem enclaves.

He pounded the pavement for miles. The search went on for years. He left town for a decade (no one knew where he had landed) and came back to meet a city in mourning. Everyone was lamenting lives lost to the terrible flu. Still, Carmelo returned to his search. One day, he sat down at a café on 110th Street. Here, the Italian community was big. Surely someone would know her sister's husband, a man who worked in a pharmacy who went by the name of Orazio Scarpa. Finding a barber by the name of Antonio Troiano might not be so easy. What if Antonio had changed his name?

On 112th Street and Lexington Avenue, Carmelo crossed paths with a hometown acquaintance. "Orazio and Mariarosa," the kind man said. "I think I can help you out. My cousin lives near their building. 64 West 98th Street. It shouldn't be hard to find."

Carmelo's heart skipped a beat. This was it. Twenty years in the chase. Carmelo took the bus to the corner of 96th Street and Broadway. How many times had he passed this stop and never once thought of his sister?

Carmelo exited the bus and ran like a bull toward his sister's building. He first checked with the super to make sure he had the correct address. "Careful," the super said. "There's lots of illness upstairs."

Walking up to her fourth-floor apartment, Carmelo met an uncanny silence. No children's voices in the halls, no peddlers screaming from the alley, more than a few apartment doors chalked with Xs, vacant hallways with burned-out lights. Ruins among faded sunlight. A surfeit of quiet.

It was as if a thousand years had passed when Carmelo reached Mariarosa's door. He knocked and waited until a haggard, diminished woman answered. She opened the door a crack and coughed. Then she coughed some more. Mariarosa appeared to be at least sixty although she was barely thirty-five. When Carmelo's eyes adjusted to the limited light, he saw that she had potato slices tied with cloth to her wrists; she also had a net of camphor balls held by string to her waist; in her hand, she clutched a rumpled handkerchief. A woman in decay, Carmelo thought, aged far beyond her years. Carmelo took a deep breath and moved to embrace her. But Mariarosa urged him to keep his distance and remain in the hallway. Weeping quietly as she took stock of her brother after so many years, she coughed again.

"In the midst of catastrophe, you come to call at my home. I can't tell if it's a miracle or the devil's curse."

The two began to describe their histories: their arrival in the daunting city, their search for a place to live, their hope of finding work. They also lamented their missed opportunities for meeting each other, the anguish each suffered by leaving the homeland, the fear of never returning. Then there were her children. She hacked. Not a word about Antonio.

"We thought you went out West." Mariarosa wheezed as she spoke. "Back home, we received only one letter, and we figured—on a positive note—that you had left New York for better pastures. Someone from Muro Lucano had traveled to Colorado to work in the mines, so in our heads, we thought you had also set up a new life out there. But your silence weighed upon us like stones on the back of a mule." Mariarosa's lungs issued a harsh vibrating whistle. "When we arrived here, we inquired, we passed the word, we asked in Italian Harlem, we left messages in the bars and churches. Even in the stables. We asked the iceman since he traveled from house to house and knew the people in each apartment."

Mariarosa looked at a puzzled Carmelo. "It didn't occur to us to speak to Baciagalupo because we wanted to believe that you were still alive. But how could we have overlooked Mulberry Bend? I feel drained and diminished right now," she said, her cough reprising.

Carmelo reached for her hand, but Mariarosa withdrew it. "And here you show up for the flu, which is why I don't invite you in."

La grippe had infected the home of Mariarosa and Orazio. "We tried everything. We slept with the windows closed so the virus wouldn't enter; we put potatoes next to our bodies to reduce any chills and fever; we said prayers to the Virgin and even called in the witches to break the *malocchio* spell. But it was just our misfortune. The children were hit hard. And I'm stuck with this airway obstruction that makes me sputter.

"Officials came by and insisted that the children go to school. Orazio and I wanted to keep them home to avoid any danger. Our newspaper, in our language, confirmed that it was safe. 'We should trust them,' Orazio said, though I cried to keep them with me.

"So we walked Rosie to elementary school, and Joey went on his own to high school. Now Rosie is hard of breath and the flu has affected her hearing; fever attacked Joey, though he's better. Dora, thank God, never left the house so she's safe with me. But you cheer me up, Carmelo," she added with a timid smile.

A shy three-year-old peeked out from her mother's skirts and introduced herself as Dora. Carmelo picked her up and gave her a hug and asked her to call him uncle.

"That's right," Mariarosa said. "This man is your uncle, and we've waited for him for years."

"And Antonio?" Carmelo asked, not sure if the moment was right.

"At first, we saw him every so often. He would come here to eat and leave a few dollars to help us through the month. Then his visits became less frequent. He disappeared." Mariarosa coughed. "One day, after many years had passed, he surprised us by asking permission to live in our home. He'd had an operation and needed a place to recover. After we got over our initial shock—if you saw him, you wouldn't know him—we took him in. He lived with us for months, and then the months turned to years."

"Zi'Annibale told me about Antonio's operation," Carmelo said. "It was the first time I knew that he was alive."

Mariarosa took a deep breath. She was surprised Antonio's news had spread through the city. "At first things were acceptable. No questions asked. Dora and Rose gave up the cot they shared to their uncle. Later, he worked in a barbershop a few blocks away. Then he became more aloof. We thought he was involved in shady business, but we couldn't figure it out. Finally, a year ago, he told us he was striking out on his own. It was very perplexing. Of course, Orazio, straight arrow that he is, was scared. And now you show up to replace Antonio!"

Carmelo tried to embrace his sister. Mariarosa pushed him back.

"I don't want to lose you, Carmelo, but I can't risk having you near. If you stay with us, you're sure to catch *la grippe*."

The disease of proximity, Carmelo thought. He was too embarrassed to explain that Zi'Annibale had been his only downtown friend. He didn't dare mention his Paterson years and the commotion of anarchist strikes. Nothing about Bresci, of course; nothing about Esteve and Maria; no mention of Caminita. Easy, he thought. He shouldn't give her a nail that eventually would poke through her shoe. Erase twenty years with a swipe. Carmelo knew his sister had other worries. And he carried a sketchy past. So Carmelo stood back.

Meanwhile, Mariarosa discussed the issues weighing the family down. "At first, we rented in the Little Italy of East 104th Street, but the police surveillance was constant; we never found peace. So, at the suggestion of Dr. Masucci, our sponsor, we moved over to the West Side. For a while, things were bearable. Then, with anarchist raids all over the city, the authorities arrived at our door. Orazio quaked in his boots.

"When the war started, the president came after Italians with lots of arrests and deportations. They said they were worried about the communist element. Cops here give you the evil eye. Now they blame us for *la grippe*. Sometimes they make us cross the street just to stay out of their way. And they say that we spread *la grippe* because we kiss our children; Orazio read this today in *Il Progresso*. It said one should avoid kissing children as much as possible. Imagine that. If I don't kiss my children, who will?"

Mariarosa continued coughing though less than before. "Orazio is scared. After all, three kids and—*oimé*, I forgot to tell you—another one on the way. We don't know if we should go or remain. If we stay, should we just tremble in place? Waiting for the police to arrest us and give notice that we'll soon be deported?

"Orazio thought we might apply for our naturalization. After all, we've been here long enough. Dr. Stella, who attends our family, is willing to speak on our behalf. And Orazio has another friend, Dr. Sacco; he's an eye doctor in Jersey City who will also put in a good word. And then there's our sponsor, Mr. Masucci, who welcomed us at port."

Mariarosa was weary from so much talk. Carmelo was weary too.

"You shouldn't stay any longer, Carmelo. They say that men your age are prime targets for *la grippe*."

Carmelo hesitated to leave his sister, but her exhaustion was clear. She coughed so much and doubled over in pain such that words couldn't rise from her throat. Perhaps she wanted to tell him about her life in New York: Sunday gatherings in Central Park, train rides to Coney Island, neighbors sitting on the stoop at night to escape the unbearable heat. And he also wanted to share stories of his time with Caminita and his work with the anarchist press. But this would have to wait for another day. Carmelo promised to visit again. He was still hoping Mariarosa would tell him more about Antonio, and he wanted to know about her other children.

One Thursday afternoon a few weeks later, he took the train to 96th Street station and walked to Mariarosa's building. When he arrived, he heard a commotion. The health inspectors had come by and found Dora fairly ill.

"Dora came down with the fever a few days ago," Mariarosa told Carmelo. "Her temperature had been so high that she fell into a state of delusion. Cold compresses don't seem to work. And in the past few hours, she doesn't hear me call her name."

Carmelo issued a desperate sigh.

"All the neighbors and paisans have come to help. Each brings a special remedy—infusions of garlic, cups of beaten egg and vermouth, pots of steamed wine and water that Dora is supposed to inhale. Mr. Bacci wanted to apply burning hot cups to her chest, but I said I was too afraid. Today the city inspectors told me these cures were hogwash, another superstition that had to be stopped. I started to cry. They sternly told me to call Dr. Stella, who now is on his way.

When Dr. Stella arrived, he was grim. "Dora appears to have suffered an occlusion," he said. "You'll have to keep an eye on her and see how she develops."

He told Mariarosa to be careful. Then he went to speak with Carmelo, who was waiting outside the apartment, leaning against the winter-cold hallway where he'd decided to light up a smoke.

"So many children have died in the building," Dr. Stella said. "The local undertaker has buried the babies en masse. But let's hope we can save this one. Your sister told me that you were away for the epidemic's early days. Consider yourself lucky. Entire families wiped out; apartments marked by a funereal X. No one would even clean out the premises and discard the furniture of those who'd died; no one would take care of the remaining food and clothing, the pestilent sheets and towels. It took the city almost a year to acknowledge this illness. I came in because the city administration wanted to blame the Italians. I've been challenging them tooth and nail. Believe me, it hasn't been easy."

Through puffs of smoke, the two men remarked on the putrid air the tenants had to inhale.

"I'm afraid that I might have contaminated Dora," Carmelo said. "I was here three weeks ago and gave the child a hug and a kiss."

"Don't feel guilty. Everyone who survives thinks he's responsible for spreading the virus. It doesn't work that way. You're not the *monatto* who comes to the door of the nearly dead; you don't shovel bodies for a living or take them to a common grave. The girl will recover; have faith."

Carmelo nodded. But he was still filled with remorse.

"I want to tell you a story that brings this home," the good doctor went on. "It's not my story, mind you, but it was written by a man I met while I was at medical school in Italy. His name was Pirandello. He was finishing his degree in Bonn. When returning to Sicily to write, he spent one night in Naples. He was reading drafts of his stories and enjoying the evening with friends. This one stuck in my head since it was about a medical problem.

"A long time ago, in times of plague that ran through the whole of Italy, there once was a man who thought that he had spread the virus himself. He was thinking that because of his breath, the others near him suffered. At first, he met four people and, shortly later, all of them died; then he saw that the larger community around him was dying day by day. He thought it was all his fault. So time goes by, and the guy goes out on the street again to see if his breath really spreads a mortal disease. Then guess what? A second round of the plague returns and kills more people than before. He of course bears the burden of guilt, but there's a moral question here. Did the man really spread the illness or was this the work of the narrator who had invented the problem in the first place?

"Do you follow me?" asked the Doctor.

"I'm not much for abstractions," Carmelo confessed.

"There's no need to feel responsible for something caused by higher design," the good doctor said. "God, the mayor, and the public inspectors all have roles in the spread of disease. It's not the fault of one person alone. Do you see what I mean?"

Carmelo looked curiously at the doctor. An anarchist could have delivered this talk. Dr. Stella sounded like Esteve and Maria, he remembered with a pang of longing. Carmelo remained silent, fearing that any comment would put Mariarosa and Orazio in danger. Pay attention, Carmelo thought. Pay attention to Dora's fate.

Dr. Stella said, "Dora is the fourth child in the building to fall sick in the last few days. You can't have infected them all."

Still, Carmelo was swaddled in sadness. His sister's family was in danger, and he had nothing to give. In fact, he was burden. He promised to stay in touch.

Carmelo crossed the river to resume life with his anarchist friends. It promised to be a difficult year. He continued to visit his sister, which allowed the siblings to build up trust. Mariarosa shared stories about her migraines, her shortness of breath; Carmelo discussed his love of theater, his work with Zi'Annibale. But he never revealed details about his New Jersey life. Nor did Mariarosa confess that she'd been receiving monthly checks from Eugenia. Eugenia wrote on a regular basis to keep her sister informed of life at home and to tell of her life in

Naples, where she'd been for many years. She also inquired about her brothers. By return mail, Mariarosa reported on her children's health, her family's struggles in *l'America,* and her insufferable migraines. She gave details of life on 98th Street and Orazio's work in the drugstore. Never a word about Antonio, who had insisted that Mariarosa never speak of his presence. And until Carmelo showed up at her doorstep, never a word about him, because for twenty years he'd been missing as if he had ceased to exist.

Eugenia surmised that her sister was living a difficult life. Few extra dollars to spare, and now *la grippe.* Without any consultation, Eugenia began to wire cash to her sister as often as she could. They were acts of joyous fulfillment, Eugenia explained in one of her letters. She wanted to help her favorite sibling. Life in Naples afforded Eugenia this privilege, and she hoped that Mariarosa would accept her gifts and never speak ill of her gestures. This was a secret among sisters that Eugenia hoped would endure.

The relationship between Carmelo and Mariarosa continued to flourish until the dreadful events of 1920 when Carmelo was arrested. Thrown out on the streets, with only some papers retrieved from his Paterson room, Carmelo traveled to Mariarosa's house.

"Sister, dear, I've not been honest with you," Carmelo explained one afternoon. "I've not explained my past life in New Jersey."

Mariarosa, to channel her nervousness, began to fidget with the sack of camphor balls she'd strung around her waist.

"Recently, I was arrested as part of a raid on Paterson workers. The police threw me into an Ellis Island cell and called for my deportation. I'm now under surveillance and can't figure out what to do."

Mariarosa trembled at the news. Another piece of bad luck. She couldn't bear the tragedy of her newly found sibling. "What can I do for you, my little brother?" she asked as tears ran down her face.

"The authorities tell me I have to quit the United States. I'm only allowed a few days here to gather my things, and then I'll have to depart."

"Do they know where you are?"

"The officials accompanied me to my apartment to get my stuff, and now they've escorted me to your doorstep. After I visit with you,

I am to return to the authorities tonight. I need proof that I will soon leave the country or I'll be sentenced to prison or sure deportation to Italy." By now, Carmelo was crying and felt like a fool for his lack of control.

"Why can't you return to Italy?"

Carmelo, uneasily moving from foot to foot, told her that if he returned to Italy, he would face instant reprisal since he'd been linked to Bresci.

Mariarosa was aghast. "You can't go home ever again? *Oh Dio*, don't tell me. That's too much to bear. Listen, brother, I think I can help, but if I tell you the story, you'll have to keep this to yourself. Forever."

Carmelo nodded. His puffy eyes were grateful.

"I told you that for twenty years Eugenia has been my steady correspondent, so she understood the desolation that has defined our lives in New York. Several years ago, she began to wire small sums of money to keep us going. In truth, I was so embarrassed that I've never told Orazio. It would wound his pride as husband and family provider. So I've kept Eugenia's transfers in a metal box hidden in the bedroom closet. I always thought that if I needed to help the children, Eugenia's gift would come in handy. So far I haven't touched it. Perhaps we could use it to buy you a passage from here to another place."

Carmelo was at a loss. He couldn't take his sister's money. Given her situation, it would be akin to theft.

Mariarosa proposed that Carmelo go live with their sister in Argentina. After all, Maria Antonietta had lived there for many years. Surely, she'd take in her brother.

A shocking thought, sun breaking through the rain. If his sister would only receive him, he could depart within short order.

The siblings struggled with their grief. Carmelo wept with gratitude, Mariarosa wept for her brother's fate. They cried in each other arms.

In the days that followed, Carmelo booked his passage abroad, paying for the ticket with Eugenia's money. Leading her brother to port, Mariarosa sent him to Buenos Aires.

She then wrote to Eugenia to let her know where her money had gone.

III. Naples–New York

1.

Eugenia straightened her skirt and took a seat in front of the fish tank. The koi's eyes, on top on his head, peered through the marine-tank glass. Reciprocating, she stared at the koi and *sotto voce* explained, "It made sense, more than twenty years ago, for me to send Mariarosa some money on a regular basis. Don't tell me that I was wrong. New York hasn't been very good for my sister, so at least I gave her a hand. But things change. Finally, she sounds upbeat. She tells me that her son-in-law Donato is coming to see me in Naples."

The koi turned his back to her; Eugenia saw only a tail fin swishing from side to side.

"I can't wait for that magic hour. It will be good to have a face-to-face conversation with Donato after so many years. He was just a boy when he left for New York. Who can imagine who he's become? He's married to Mariarosa's daughter, Rosie, and, for me, that's all that counts."

The fish turned to the left and circled around. His fins and tail seemed to twitch.

"But first, I'm saddled with that visit Gianpietro has arranged for me in late afternoon."

No response from the fish.

"I can't believe I'm in this business of selling Silvio's art to a parade of dealers. Just one more encounter, and I quit. Gianpietro thinks it's profitable work, but I don't like what this does to Silvio. His art is reduced to a business, and I'm his agent in crime. It's slimy. But, you know, I'm actually good at it. Gianpietro says I can sell sandcastles at the beach."

Eugenia returned to thoughts of her sister: she was sorry for Mariarosa's physical ills—migraines and ghastly arthritis. Worse, the rathole where she lived.

"Mariarosa says their apartment is infested with mice and roaches. Sounds like the *bassi* of Naples. And I can't get over my brothers. First Antonio mooched off her, and then Carmelo. What a nightmare!" She loved Carmelo, but he lacked for direction. Even in New York, he depended on Mariarosa. Aloud, she continued, "Imagine, she paid for his ticket to Argentina to keep him out of trouble. It was *my* money, you know. In one moment of madness, she spent it all on Carmelo."

Eugenia told the koi that she wouldn't allow her melancholia to reach Donato's ears. No longer the reserved and reticent girl of Bellanera, she now thrust her stories of woe upon any *paisan'* who would listen. When relatives occasionally stopped in to visit, she returned to same topics—her misplaced life in Naples, Gianpietro's business direction, her desire to stay in touch with her siblings, all of whom lived far away.

"Be positive, be discreet," Eugenia warned herself as she left the aquarium to take care of business.

In the city, Eugenia had matured from a country girl to a splendorous middle-aged woman. No one in Naples saw her sadness; instead, they encountered a high-spirited woman, well dressed with a few extra pounds, still jaunty in gait and appearance.

Once home, Eugenia changed into a full skirt in boho style and put on the chandelier earrings that were all the rage. Wearing great stone rings, she fancied herself a nonconformist amidst the city's upper crust. Eugenia, under Gianpietro's instructions, had trained as an afternoon salonnière, receiving guests in her parlor. And she always set out late-day sweets and prepared to talk about art. This was one indication of Eugenia's adjustment to Neapolitan life. She sometimes betrayed her Lucanian trill, but by and large, her tongue was properly groomed in the cadences of high-born Naples. Now, her sentences glided like swans on water. In short, Eugenia, after more than thirty years in Naples, had successfully transitioned from small-town girl to charming hostess, the shining wife to the aging marchese whose family had lost its luster. At this cordial visit held in the first week of May, Eugenia was to preside as hostess over a standard afternoon tea. Her visitor was a Mr. Kälin.

2.

The directors of the Capodimonte Museum had invited a number of connoisseurs to tour the art collections. The marchese, always interested in these events, attended a four-star dinner to welcome the travelers, among them Bernard Berenson, a Harvard-bred intellectual who lived in Florence's Villa i Tatti. Berenson devoted his life to Renaissance art and was a distinguished and wealthy consultant. Until the start of race laws in Italy somewhat later in 1938, you could say that he had lived a privileged life. Berenson was often seen with his friend and confidante the Marchese Serlupi Crescenzi, a protector of Tuscan paintings. On this occasion, the two had traveled to Naples with a Swiss gallerist of no notable fame, Franz Kälin from Zurich, who was known to have journeyed the length of the peninsula in search of available art. Amidst a club of connoisseurs, Kälin was testing Neapolitan waters to determine which works could be brought to the surface and wrangled from southern hands.

At the dinner, Kälin introduced himself to the Marchese di Cimino. He had learned that the Ciminos held a remarkable number of Renaissance reproductions. The paintings were so precise in stroke and palette, he had heard, that discerning the real from the copy was hard. Kälin was hungry to know these works and, following nearly an hour of silk-smooth conversation, he secured an invitation to tea at the Cimino apartment. The marchese then advised Eugenia to receive him on Friday, promptly at eighteen o'clock.

At first, Franz Kälin hit it off with Eugenia; he seemed taken by her earthy beauty and southern charm. He'd come to view the imitations of late *cinquecento* art and was surprised to find Eugenia a master of Renaissance lessons. But this might have been a façade, Kälin thought as the chatter proceeded.

Eugenia, meanwhile, studied her guest and thought him affected and false. When he asked her how she'd come to painting, she answered coyly. She didn't let on that Silvio had been her tutor, that over the years Silvio had traveled to Naples to learn the museum collections and, with each successive visit, the boy—now a man close to fifty—had trained her eye for brushstroke and color, for line and composition. Eugenia had been his principal student, fully devouring his lessons. Now she was his representative—in vulgar terms, his agent.

Over time, Silvio's theories of painting had grown. He understood Renaissance pigment; he found the center of gravity in any work; he knew the tricks of working with light and dark. From Silvio, Eugenia had learned to appreciate the Neapolitan school in its majestic detail. She understood the naturalism that inhabited Mattia Preti's dramas; she delivered herself to Ribera's theatrical light. Now, in this conversation with Kälin, Eugenia echoed her pal. She offered opinions on azurite and ultramarine; she found emotion in lead-tin yellow. Ignoring Franz Kälin's condescension, she rambled on about the reddish tones in the *jaune d'antinomie*.

At first, the meeting was lovely. The baked-fruit tartlets engaged the visitor's palate; the petit fours were perfect. Then Kälin got down to business. "I heard that you possess a rare and distinguished collection of imitations—not exactly reproductions—taken from a canon that includes the Caravaggio-school tenebrists."

Eugenia nodded and offered to show him some of Silvio's works, which graced her Vomero home. As they went to the dining room, Kälin was shocked to see the framed painting of Judith and Holofernes.

"Oh my." He sighed, taking two steps back as his eyes swallowed Artemisia's work. He knew that the original still hung in the Naples museum but was nonetheless taken by the paint's texture, the colors' movement, the perfection of brushstrokes, the drama of shadow and light. "My goodness! Beyond all imagination. Simply magnificent."

Eugenia suspected, from the visitor's excessive praise, that Kälin was about to pounce for a sale. He told her the canvas allowed him to hear the muscular man's cries as he was about to suffer his beheading. The lines, the depth, the able flesh, the plush bodies drowned in shadow, the linen's wrinkled texture exposed by thistles of light.

"I gather that you're as taken by this painting as much as I am," Eugenia said.

"Had I not seen this work in the museum, I would have ascribed it to Artemisia Gentileschi. Its surface is exuberant, impressive beyond any words. Is it for sale?"

Eugenia knew to hide her annoyance. "I thought I'd explained: I count this as my most precious holding."

"And who, may I ask, is the artist?"

"Silvio, a man who lives in the countryside southeast of Naples, has painted for over thirty-five years. He started in his youth with the Gentileschi painting you see right here.

"Yes, his art is exceptional, and it's only getting better. Some of my husband's acquaintances have blushed at the sight of his works. As his representative in Naples, I can show you others."

"Yes!" Kälin's voice had turned ravenous and hungry. Eugenia noted the change in tone and found herself on alert. Exercising caution, she showed him a few of the canvases.

"Most of his copies are based on the Neapolitan school, though he often changes focus and style. When we lived through the Spanish flu, for instance, he took up the work of Micco Spadaro, who had painted the piazza filled with Neapolitan masses about to succumb to the plague. Silvio was so obsessed with the topic, because of personal losses, that he made several copies of this painting and traded one to the Marchese Ruggi d'Aragona. It wasn't destined for Ruggi's parlor wall—it's hard to look at day and night—but for a hospital building at the University of Salerno. The marchese took the painting in exchange for a favor—to treat Silvio's family members during the flu years. It was perhaps Silvio's most successful early venture."

Eugenia took a breath. She always recited this introductory speech to whet the clients' appetites. "But Silvio is in love with his work. As a boy, he suffered from a serious stutter. For many years, his only expression was not through speech but on canvas.

"When melancholia invaded his soul, he began to paint the forlorn boys who belonged to Botticelli's studio." Eugenia headed toward the wall where one of those copies hung. "The original belongs to the Filangieri Museum. It's Silvio's experiment with tempera on wood. For a while, Silvio held it in high esteem. He identified with the young man whom Sandro had taken into his fold." She described the sadness of the painted figure, his timid and dejected regard.

"I think Silvio saw himself in this man; there's vulnerability combined with fear. Then Silvio tried something new and experimented with the verso—the sealing wax, the enumeration, the autographs of different owners—as if to make the copy more 'real,' whatever real might mean. He left the work with me because he claimed that he'd lost all interest. I think he saw himself in the portrait and it scared him half to death. He now makes the work available to interested parties."

Kälin dismissed Eugenia's story. He knew, because Silvio had paid attention to the verso, that the young man was attentive to market resale—fake or otherwise. Any dealer would look behind the painting to check for its provenance, its record. Seals, dates, and numbers count as much as the painting itself when it comes to matters of transfer. From the looks of it, Kälin thought, this artist had all the skills of an excellent forger and had announced that this was his business. His plan was to go larger. But first he would buy the works from this woman for the lowest possible price.

Much to her guest's irritation, Eugenia continued. "Silvio's choices weren't arbitrary. Indeed, as the years advanced, he worked to reproduce the paintings he viewed and to inhabit the master artists' lives. He found an affinity with them and wanted to share their intimate space. Salvator Rosa was a case in point. Silvio saw him an underdog, a man who'd lost all hope. Rosa's 'The Death of Empodocles' is in my husband's study. Silvio copied the dark figure to a tee. Now he's painting portraits of slaves and soldiers because he's thinking of the Abyssinian war. He says it's his turn with Carracci."

Kälin fixed his gaze on the paintings. It's extraordinary, he thought. They were perfect reproductions. He bet she didn't realize what a treasure she had on her hands. The two walked toward Midaro's vast painting, with its scene of dying masses. Kälin again sighed for the painting's minute detail, the exact replica of Midaro's brushstrokes.

He thought this would carry an astounding resale value among foreign buyers. It would surely pass the assessments. Why, this fellow's work could be in museums and galleries, and no one would be wiser. "Might I be introduced to the artist?"

Silence sliced the air while a late-afternoon haze scarred the parquet floors.

Eugenia thought this guy was here to clean out Naples and took her for a fool. He wanted her out of the way.

"I'm sorry, but my artist is incommunicado right now." Eugenia was lying. "He lives like the monks at Monte Cassino Abbey, far removed from the world. As I told you, I'm responsible for any transactions regarding his work."

"No, no," Kälin said. "I really must see him directly. Does he have a vault of canvases?"

Eugenia told Kälin in most explicit terms that Silvio was not available. "But if you are really interested, I can arrange a transfer of the Midaro."

"Of course, the Midaro, but if you're willing to part with the Gentileschi or the Botticelli, please let me know." Kälin then explained that there was a considerable market in copies. He never used the word "forgery" for its sordid associations with crime. "Foreigners from the north always revere Renaissance art as the center of our civilization. They will cherish any of Silvio's reproductions and preserve them with impeccable care."

Eugenia understood the codes and was not about to let Silvio's work find a place in the Chancellery halls in Berlin (everyone knew of Hitler's appetites for this sort of thing; the papers told of his upcoming visit to the Uffizi in order to look around). She took a deep breath to clear her mind. Then she negotiated a proper price for the Midaro, spoke of delivery dates and transfer, and congratulated Kälin for his refined sensibilities. "Nevertheless, a visit with Silvio will have to wait for another time."

Kälin, understanding that the petty nobility in Naples was about to fall into ruin, spoke with the elegance of a confident man. "I'm happy to wrap this up. You'll advise me when the canvas is ready. Later, we'll speak of other collaborations that might benefit all parties."

His cordiality was superficial, but Kälin knew that he had to soften Eugenia. By the looks of things, she was a model of southern thinking, which meant, he thought, that she'd succumb to sentimentality despite all her claims to reason. So he insisted on making himself available to her every need, a temptation she couldn't refuse. He thought of her extended connections in Naples, her circulation among collectors, and the sluggish pace of the meridional world in which no one took stock of their assets and often gave away the store.

3.

In New York, Donato dealt with the harsh residuals of Shinola and 3-in-1 oil. He had to rub his hands with Gresolvent each night to soften his clumsy fingers, thick as October turnips. He tried to forget those deadly machine wheels that rounded off heels and soles. So at the end of the day, when he closed his shoe-repair shop, he heaved a sigh of relief. His stupid job was below his rank, he thought, although he always loved the chit chat that his customers brought to his counter.

"Have you walked across the George Washington Bridge?"

"Have you seen the museum under construction? It's going to focus on medieval art."

"They're even planning afternoon concerts," Mr. Zager had said earlier that day. This newfound luck had left the neighbors entranced. For a while, at least, it had made up for the lousy news: subway strikes and broken sidewalks, a shortage of good meat and fish, wilted vegetables turning black that avid housewives scooped up all the same.

"And don't talk to me about the Hooverville camps," Mr. Katz had added.

"So much for the heroic men of the trenches," Donato had said. "Hoovervilles all around us, even though Hoover is gone."

Mrs. Baar had expressed her dismay. "A new one appeared overnight on the eastern edge of 207th Street, by the Harlem River Canal. This time they housed men in boxcars."

Mr. Yost had heard that the social services came by with tanks of Mulligan stew. And if the handouts failed to quash their hunger, the men filched a few potatoes from the nearby vegetable wagons. These rumors had spread like weeds.

That night, when he returned home from work, Donato learned of his father's death. He knew he had to return to see his mother and sisters. They had to mourn as a family and Donato needed to be at their side. Quickly, he booked passage on the Rex, the most fashionable ship of its day. He'd read that the boat was elegant, with modern design and décor. It had a gilded staircase, glistening floors, a dining room and theater. "It rivals the Titanic," Donato had boasted to his wife Rosie. Most important, the Rex lacked a steerage hold. Refusing to trade in penniless travelers, the ship's owners preferred a smoother voyage, carrying passengers in only two classes. Donato wanted no reminder of the below-deck immigrant space that once had transported him to New York.

Before he departed for Naples, his anxieties ran high.

"Discretion," his mother-in-law Mariarosa urged. "Watch what you say to the family. You know they're a bunch of snoops."

"And don't tell them about Dora's illness; don't mention the Spanish flu."

"Keep quiet about the Depression. They don't need to see our affairs." Rosie added.

Donato listened with half an ear as he gathered up the presents: fabric, yarn, packaged nylon stockings; for Eugenia, an Evening in Paris perfume Rosie had bought on sale at Woolworth's (Rosie had wanted to send a Shalimar, but the price was out of bounds); and Loft's chocolates, caramel filled, boxed in fancy wrapping.

At last, Donato closed up the shoe-repair shop and bid farewell to Rosie; he'd picked up his heavy valises. This would be his first return to Italy since 1922. He would see the port of Naples by the end of the first week in May. His hopes and emotions rose.

After a week-long voyage, the Rex pulled into harbor. As the engines were cut and the boat settled in port, the adjacent piers became cacophonous. Rumor had it that Mussolini and the King were about to welcome Hitler. For miles around, people heard the pomp and circumstance of their arrival. An unbearable din of planes. Nearly two hundred naval ships dressed in bunting. *So it's real*, Donato thought. *No way to avoid these monsters.*

As he waited his turn to disembark, he could breathe the air of the bay; he tasted the city's salty-fried flavors; he felt the nearness of his village. He pressed his weight on the deck rails. The bay rocked him with tender feelings for the city: turn-of-the-century buildings cropping up on the shoreline; the Aragonese castle still standing guard; the hills aglitter from springtime sun. It was as if time hadn't passed at all. To the north, derricks and cranes populating the shipyards, to the east the majestic volcano. Almost home, he thought as he walked past a mirror and stopped to adjust his necktie and raise the pocket square of his jacket. Carrying his springtime coat—it had once belonged to Cousin Emma's dead husband—Donato headed toward the egress. When another mirror greeted him, he gave himself a wink. "I look fine," he smiled as he pulled his luggage toward the ships's gangway. But before he could take the train to his village, first he had to stop in Naples and visit Eugenia; he had promised to deliver the many gifts that his wife's family had sent. By cable, Eugenia had asked him to visit at six in the afternoon.

* * * *

Donato's knock at Eugenia's door cut short Franz Kälin's stay. The three spoke briefly in the parlor, exchanging cordial remarks about the world's conditions—FDR, the state of affairs in Europe, the threat of war. Donato discussed modern life in New York, the economic depression, and the move to build up the city. Then his post card reminders of Rockefeller Center, the Chrysler Building, the Empire State, Fred Astaire with top hat. Kälin smiled though it wasn't clear if he regarded Donato as country bumpkin, part of the vast immigration to America that filthied its urban streets, or if he concurred with Donato in admiring the powerful metropolis.

Because he wanted to keep in Eugenia's good graces, Kälin as he was about to leave promised to put Donato in touch with his brother Günther who lived in New York.

"I'll send Günther a letter at once," he said to Donato. "Better still, let me leave a small package for him—a token of my affection."

Kälin considered it an investment. Donato promised to deliver both gift and message. When he saw Günther's New York address, Donato realized that they were neighbors.

* * * *

"That was quite a visit," Eugenia said. She sounded exhausted, but her eyes bespoke affection for Donato. "I think he was up to no good." She described Kälin's visit and his hungry regard for the paintings. "Perhaps I erred in speaking too much. But at least I didn't reveal the name of our town. He'll have to search every village between Naples and Catania in order to find Silvio. Thank God I kept my calm."

Donato put Eugenia at her ease: "As long as you don't put him in touch with Silvio, you really have nothing to fear."

But Eugenia explained the number of art thefts throughout Europe and the dealers always on the lookout for forgers who could supply a growing demand for Renaissance art. "Not only that," Eugenia added. "Looting has become the norm. These characters send in crooks to the best museums and substitute a fake work for the real one. It's complicated, but it happens often enough that I need to be careful. All the dark world wants Silvio's work. That said, Silvio's art keeps all of us in the money."

Donato rolled his eyes as he thought of Eugenia on the edge of major swindles. She was a good person; she wouldn't get into trouble, nor would she ever dream of putting the hometown folk in danger.

The two started to discuss life in the village.

"So sorry for the death of your father," Eugenia said.

They exchanged stories of death and loss, the way memories slide away. They laughed to consider that in their traditions all times were one; past, present, and future were always combined. As they left the topic of mourning, Eugenia expressed her relief to have Donato in the family, to hear that her sister's clan had a good man to protect them. She was also glad to learn that Antonio was no longer in the picture. "Poor people don't have the luxury of always being good," she remarked as she thought of her older brother and his trail of crooked dealings. "But he was a bad egg from the start. A *stronzo*, if you know what I mean."

Eugenia liked and trusted Donato. After all, he was from her village and spoke her native language. Plus she'd taken a special confidence in him because he'd married her sister's eldest daughter.

"Tell me about your years in Naples," Donato said. "By the looks of it, you've had the most exciting life of anyone from our clan." He studied the silk brocade stamped on the parlor walls. He wanted to stand up and touch it but knew to mind his place.

"Look," she said, "it's a long story, some of which you know. I married the marchese before you were born. I figured he was a meal card. But the move to Naples required a lot of adjustment. Legions of pretentious people wearing their histories like medals were constantly reminding me of who they were—as if to say that I had come from nothing. Yet the marchese's sisters took care of me, probably because they also knew the limits of this petty, decadent life.

"The marchese is odd; we're not exactly husband and wife, you know. I quickly came to understand that. It was extremely painful at first. The marchese was rarely around; he left me in his sisters' care. When I looked to him for conversation, even to hold my hand, I felt a certain numbness. He was always aloof; his heart was somewhere else. As a young bride, I was of course confused; later, when I saw this as my liberation, I won a certain freedom. Do you follow me?"

Donato continued to study an inlaid table that showed St. George slaying the dragon.

"While he was off with his friends, riding horses, taking care of his business, I would explore the city and learn about the arts. I acquainted myself with the markets, the crafts, the people.

"Meanwhile the marchese's sisters loved me. They showered me with gifts; they taught me the ropes, so to speak. In return I had to appear when needed as a wifely appendage: I was there for the dinners, for entertainment, for the larger family's events; I attended horse races, the opera, even a luncheon one time with the King. A precious life in a gilded cage."

Donato noticed a dining table that could accommodate twenty, Louis XV chairs carved in balloon-back style, needlepoint carpets, flocked wallpaper, cut-velvet drapes, crystal chandeliers. He kept thinking that Eugenia had hit the jackpot. And, by extension, so had all of her clan. Certainly a switch from the lifestyle of those who went to America to look for streets paved with gold.

Eugenia rose to go see about the evening *aperitivo*, returning with two glasses of limoncello and a plate of *taralli* and chocolates. Getting by with just a few sweets on hand, Eugenia began anew to describe her life with the distant marchese. She cast all discretion to the wind.

4.

"Everything was subdued between the Marchese and me. Although we dined together, shared jokes—he has the sharpest wit—often he seemed lacking in spirit. I knew that he really envied my youth, but the rest was an enigma. Then, three decades ago, he began to vacation on Capri.

"The sea, the sea, the sea! Life on the Mediterranean, the marchese told me as he flipped through a poet's pages, was always full of tragic potential; we were always on the edge of loss, he said."

"I don't know if I follow," said Donato.

"My husband is melancholic, moody; so it made sense even back then he would drink up words of woe to explain the sea."

"Maybe Gianpietro only wanted to spend time at the beach."

Victoria laughed along with her guest, but then she turned serious.

Donato listened to her story as if it were a radio drama. He expected a pop or a whistle, some sound effect to go with the tale.

"A few years after we married, probably around 1908, Gianpietro reserved a suite for us at the Villa Blaesus, one of the island's nicer resorts. We arrived in April and, at first, we were charmed; we had carriage rides, we followed the winding paths down to the grottoes; we took breakfast on the hotel terrace to admire the turquoise sea. This was also the hotel of the Russian Gorky; apparently, he'd moved to Capri to escape the conflicts in Russia. The concierge told me that Gorky was a permanent fixture there; later, more Russians appeared. 'Keep an eye on Bogdanov,' the concierge told me. 'He's a strange duck who was supposed to be teaching the art of revolution.' By the looks of it, the guy was committed to esoterica that no one understood."

Donato was perplexed but fearful of asking questions.

"Apparently the hotel was a training school for revolution; the God Finders, they called these guests. I was fascinated by these weirdos. All quite unfriendly, let me add. They really were *training* students; a handful of Russian men arrived every couple of weeks. They went for walks, sat cross-legged in the gardens, lifting their hands to the skies. And guess what? Suddenly, Lenin showed up!"

"Oh wow!" exclaimed Donato. "How did you know him?"

"The concierge let me know that he was a real big shot from Russia, there to raise money. But he only seemed to play chess in the afternoon. More Russians appeared. Sometimes it looked like an academy; at other times, it was just men going for hikes in the woods. There were two women among them who at first tried to draw me in.

"I spoke in hand signals to one woman who introduced herself as Bogdanov's wife. She invited me to play chess.

"'*Scacchi, scacchi,*' she urged me, leading me to a small table.

"I smiled; although I didn't know how to play. Then, raising her eyebrows as if to say 'southern scum,' she left, probably to speak badly about all Italians. On the side, when no one was looking, I stole a few photos from the concierge. If you'd like one, carry it home."

Donato chuckled at the thought of showing Lenin's picture to his customers at the store.

"As I said, the Marchese and I started the day in the friendliest manner. We took tea on the terrace and admired the cobalt sea below. The geraniums in garden boxes gave a marvelous rush of color while the white cliffs below captured the brilliant sunlight. We took carriage rides to the villa of Tiberius and the gardens of Augustus. Then we'd return to the hotel and hear the Russians in heated debate. I must say we were amused, but soon we tried to skirt them.

"Then one night, everything changed. Gianpietro told me he was going to walk along the shore. This became a regular event. He wouldn't return for hours. I was barely twenty. Meanwhile, my husband was becoming more sullen, itchy, annoyed. His eyes wouldn't meet mine. He had little to say. Something had cracked between us. I began to plead with him to tell me the truth.

"We returned the following spring and for many more summers after that. The Russians remained at the Blaesus, though the cast of characters had changed and their energy had dwindled.

"Sometimes when we took carriage tours, Gianpietro gave me lessons. He pointed out a road where his friend had a home. Beyond was a French poet who built a palazzo. We drove to see the building. Expansive, graceful, a strange combination of Roman-villa style and art nouveau. Villa Lysis, they called it. It promised to be the new center of social life for this group of friends. Gianpietro described balustrades in marble, gold inlay on the arches, graceful sculptures one thought only stood in museums.

"Then Gianpietro said he imagined the gentlemen on the island might be interested in buying art and decided to move us to the Quisisana hotel. A better class of people, he said; it's more suited to our taste and for the business I have in mind. The men at this hotel were exceptionally beautiful, I thought—well dressed, always refined. Many foreigners among them. Not all of them were hotel guests, but it was a convenient reunion place for my husband and these men.

"Strange things began to happen. Sometimes the marchese would disappear for a night and a day and would offer few excuses. Or, he would claim the need to walk down Krupp Road for a late afternoon dip in the sea. I begged to go with him; he pushed me back.

"'The walk is too strenuous, Geni. You'd best rebuild your forces at Marina Piccola beach. Besides, I'm making art deals for us, and I'm trying to sell Silvio's art.'

"I left him alone, but when I lingered at the hotel, I overheard a conversation. Some vacationers said groups of men were drawn to the indigo waves.

"'They're part of a pink congress,' a woman told me one day, inviting me to join her as we both lounged on the terrace. She and I were alone as our men had left for a walk.

"'They gathered close to the Blue Grotto and had a wild time well into the night,' she said. 'My boyfriend says the Blue Grotto looked like a vivarium of frenzied fish. He denounced those guys as sissies.'

"This obnoxious woman said she'd stolen the line from her boyfriend Marinetti who was writing about life on the island. She then told of love between men, narrating their follies in detail. I was flummoxed. This woman continued to assault me with these perverse ideas that she'd cribbed from her boyfriend's novel. Finally, I cut short the conversation and went off to walk in the hotel gardens.

"Eventually, our trips to Capri came to an end. The marchese became increasingly restless and dissatisfied with the island retreat. I assumed he had a woman, and I demanded that he tell me. I half expected that this was the end of our marriage and began to plan to return to the village.

"'No, no,' Gianpietro said. 'I swear on my life there is no woman nor will there ever be. You're my love, Geni. You're the treasure of my life.' I accepted his words. Nothing more was said until he suggested again that I try to sell some of Silvio's art. He had proposed this idea when we first were married, and, once again, I took offense. First, I didn't know if I wanted to be Silvio's go-between. And second, I had never sold anything more than eggs and grain.

"Here's where my life changed. Gianpietro taught me tricks of sale, the proper countenance for dealing with clients. I learned to read papers that detailed art's value and the process of transfer. He told the hotel guests I was open for business after the island vacation.

"For the first time, I took charge. When I returned from Capri, I consulted Silvio, and we decided to start a business, which continues to this day."

Donato was confused, "And what happened to those handsome men?"

"Can't you figure it out, Donato? What I gained from art, I lost in love."

* * * *

"Donato, am I telling you too much?"

Donato encouraged her to continue. They came from a village where no one held secrets for long.

"I gave a lot of thought to this second life, to the business that kept me close to Gianpietro. I thought of my mother, my aunts, and cousins. I thought of the lire I had to send home each month, and the gifts that made my mother's life easy. And I thought selfishly of my privilege: my days in the city streets, the shops, and local brio. Naples was now more of a home to me than my childhood village. So here I am, stretched between two worlds. Do you ever feel that way too?

Do you call New York your home?"

"Don't ask me that," Donato said. "If I begin on this topic, I'll lose my mind. In New York, I live between two stripes of gray. You remember home as the sweet fruit in August but forget the winter chill; you remember the touch of your mother's hand but forget the family feuds. Home is like a heavenly star; it drinks up whatever brightness fills the sky."

Eugenia nodded. Of course she understood this although she hadn't crossed an ocean.

Eugenia was grateful for Donato, a companion to hear her stories, to receive her painful secrets. She followed his eyes as he looked intently at the paintings on the walls.

"These are Silvio's works. By and large, I've done a good job with his paintings. I always take caution. If I sniff out an aggressive buyer who wants to intrude on Silvio's life, I quickly cut off the trade."

After they completed the fruit dessert and coffee, Donato asked, "Did Silvio ever want to turn away from imitations and find his own subjects? Did he ever discuss how copying affected his heart and soul?" Donato had begun to think that he also lived in the realm of the copy. In New York, he had taken someone else's culture and made it his own. It was my choice, he thought. I'd left the real thing behind.

The following day, he needed to take a train to the village.

Before she escorted Donato to the station, Eugenia said, "Be aware of changing times, Donato. Be alert to the 'rules.' Learn to read between the lines. Our fate is in a madman's hands, and no one knows how this chapter will end."

Donato nodded. He wasn't naïve.

With that, a final exchange of gifts. Eugenia also sent along some paints for Silvio. Just as Donato was about to leave Eugenia's house, a package arrived addressed to him. Franz Kälin had sent a gift for his brother.

5.

Sixteen years away, Donato mused as he boarded the train. Donato's father was gone; his sisters were ill; his brother was off to Eritrea. The family was in disarray. And with war on the horizon, who knew how things might unfold? As the train passed through the mountains, Donato observed the tiny villages and farms. He imagined the taste of goat milk and rounds of freshly baked bread; he hoped to hear the clopping of hooves on stone, a rhythm he'd nearly forgotten.

"It will be nice to awaken to whinnying mules," Donato said to traveler seated beside him.

"Yes," the man replied. "But don't forget that life down here is fragile and people speak in two tones: one for public revelations and one for maintaining their secrets. Still, you're right, it's always nice to go home."

Little had changed since Donato had left, but he still knew things were different. He listened to his companion.

"A few vehicles here and there. Some families with radio sets and sewing machines—Il Duce's gift to those women who had increased the population. In the shops, a couple of typewriter services if you need to dictate a letter. Now, the compulsory Fascist Saturdays and banners hanging from all the windows to sing the leader's name." The traveler had filled Donato's head with these stories as the train rumbled ahead, but when he arrived at the station, all talk of politics changed to love.

His sisters met him with deep emotion. Following the embraces, the sobbing, and the many delirious fingers caressing his ears and eyes, his sisters at last led their brother to the family home where they sat down at the giant table that his father had built decades ago. Though he had missed his father's death, Donato received all the details of his funeral: who attended the wake, the words of the priests, the slow walk downhill to the graveyard, which lay on the outskirts of town. And then the updates since Donato's departure for 'the other side.' Emilia, with an eye for copying the latest fashion she'd seen in the Sunday papers, was now known as the finest seamstress south of Naples. She laughed when she said that her bias-cut dresses put Elsa Schiaparelli to shame. When she wasn't reading the history of saints or short novels of science fiction, Peppinella worked in her husband's dry goods store and took care of her brood. Rita was a midwife. The fascist regime had regaled her with gifts for having increased the national birth rate. She had also relieved many a womb of their swelling burdens, helping women too poor to bring another child into the world. Caterina, the eldest, had moved to the countryside. She and her children worked in the fields. And Donato's only brother, Mimmo, had joined the army in Eritrea and was now rising in rank.

Everyone chatted with great animation. They cried for the death of their father; they lamented those who had left for the army. They praised the farmhands who had slipped them a cured pork hind in exchange for a bundle of tools. They spoke of the miracles of Padre Pio and the feast of Monte Viggiano. A step away from poverty themselves, they hoped their daughters would marry well in the style of Eugenia Troiano.

As dinner began, Peppinella marched out her two daughters dressed as *massaie rurali*. Following Mussolini's dress codes for women, they pretended to be peasants. The style was supposed to recall the days harvesting wheat with scythe and sickle. No manly girls, no women dressed in pants. Instead, the young women wore dirndl skirts and embroidered blouses with billowing sleeves, their breasts covered by bodices laced with black and red cord. They reminded Donato of Eugenia's image on the liqueur bottle. Perhaps with this peasant garb, these girls could also nab a noble. Laughing, Donato reminded them that some women worked in the fields, not remembering how they dressed, while others dressed up in peasant garb, not remembering how to work. Upon hearing this, Emilia stood up, Rita jumped, Caterina raised her voice, and Peppinella hammered away at her brother.

"How dare you bring your American ideas to poison our peaceful lives? I dress the girls like peasants precisely to help them avoid a life in the fields. This is the art of acting that sooner or later bears fruit."

His sister then gave him a photograph to take home to New York. It was a picture taken by Zi' Annibale who continued his work as a photographer when he returned to Bellanera.

The siblings spent a long evening in conversation. The quarreled, they cursed, they bit each other's hands, they made signs to drive off the evil eye. Donato's chest expanded, tears of joy streaked his face. At last, for a while, he was home. After several days of family renewal, Donato wandered out to meet old friends, to visit the Troianos, and, fulfilling Eugenia's wish, to check up on Silvio.

* * * *

The artist, by now nearly middle-aged, received Donato with a warm embrace. After Silvio had accepted the paints Eugenia had sent, the two men sat down to gab. First they recalled the olden days, then the crush of modern times. Silvio told of his family, Donato spoke of his. Pondering the dilemmas of fascist life, Silvio explained a new taxation law that seemed written just for him.

"Unmarried men are now expected to pay for the state's child-welfare programs," Silvio said. "As Mussolini wants us all to wed and have children, those of us still alone now have to pick up the tab. It's hogwash." Silvio sighed. "At least, I have this business with Eugenia that allows me to get by."

Donato laughed. It was the same all over. He noticed on an easel a canvas of an African woman who looked seductive and coy. "What's this about?"

"This one is *not* going to Naples," Silvio said. "But if I ever sell it, it will be for my friend in Addis Ababa."

Silvio described Giulio Vetromile, a local who'd left for Abyssinia in 1935 and never returned. "After Eugenia, Giulio was my confidante, my most trusted friend. I relied on him to explain the truth of my heart, to let my dreams take voice. He spoke for me when I couldn't find the words; he mended my broken tongue. Then Giulio, somewhat younger than me, was recruited for the army. And I, too old for service, had to wave goodbye and pray. The government propaganda enticed poor men from these parts. Africa was a land of possibilities, they were told, better than New York. So Giulio sailed off to war. He survived the Field Marshal's reckless orders; but then he fell in love with an Ethiopian woman and decided to remain abroad."

Donato asked, "Why would he stay in Ethiopia?"

"Good question," answered Silvio. "He couldn't bring his wife to Italy. The state no longer allows it. I became obsessed with his family because I don't even have a photo of them. I don't know what they look like. So I started to scourge the museums for images of Africans painted in Italy. A clerk at the Museo Nazionale showed me paintings of slaves and servants, always subservient people. When I thought of Ife, Giulio's wife, I became indignant. I wanted to see pictures of free Africans, people who weren't regarded as strange or exotic.

"Then I found a Carracci portrait of a marvelous African woman. I like her because she's holding a golden clock; and she's coy, not dressed like a servant. Her eyes are trained straight on me. With no humility, she lets me know that she's sensible, competent. In any case, I made several copies of this image, but like this one the best. I felt as if it brought me closer to Giulio and Ife."

Silvio escorted Donato to the easel.

"Painting gives you a kind of secondhand life, huh?"

"Right," said Silvio. "Sometimes it scares me, but at other times, it shows me an unparalleled beauty."

Over the weeks, Donato studied Silvio's paintings and admired his remarkable skill. Silvio's work was a miracle set against time, Donato thought, a way to reverse the order of life. More than representation, the art played between now and then. It was the tension between what existed right now and what might've been in another moment.

* * * *

One afternoon, right before Donato's time in Bellanera came to an end, Silvio timidly approached his friend. "I'm worried if war breaks out, we won't be safe in our homes. And we won't have enough to survive." After a lengthy pause, he continued, "C-c-could I ask you a favor?"

Donato knew this was coming. Someone always asked for something at the end of the day.

"Could you take my African portrait to New York? It's probably safer in America than here. And if you ever decide to sell it, I hope you'll send part of the profits to Giulio and Ife."

Silvio described his fears: the connoisseurs who were eager to reach him, the bullies and marchands not far behind. They were unsavory types who lurked in the shadows of art. And Eugenia was playing too close to the edge. "Then there's even the greedy regime, trying to build its coffers. No one knows what might happen if the Germans nose into our business."

Silvio said he had confidence in Donato. He'd know how to protect the painting. If needed, he'd find a dealer. After all, New York was the center for these transactions.

Donato pushed back. "You know I don't have these connections in New York. I'm liable to make mistakes. And why just this single painting? What about the others?"

"That's easy," Silvio said. "Eugenia has plans for the other works, but I'd like to launch the Carracci on a path of its own. It's really for Giulio's children. If you agree, I'll prepare the canvas so it fits in your luggage."

Donato was hesitant to accept. He wasn't up for smuggling artwork through U.S. customs. But in the end, Donato said he'd do it. It's what you did for a friend.

When Donato left the village, he took the canvas with him and traveled up to Naples where he again met with Eugenia before he embarked for New York. Now it was Eugenia who also asked for a favor. Since Silvio had given Donato a painting to hold, could Donato also carry a few other items—*only a few,* she promised—and a small sum of cash?

"Cash? With the customs agents hanging near every gate? Do you want to get me in trouble?"

"Four thousand dollars in cash and an equivalent sum in drawings."

Donato began to swoon. "Not even Rockefeller keeps that kind of money on hand. That's a mighty big favor."

"Look, Donato, things are very dangerous now, and no one has a future. You see that war is close to us. Over the years, I managed to accrue a large sum of money through art—not only through Silvio's works—and now it's time to protect it, something we can't do here."

Donato was flustered. "Carrying bills out of the country? *Oimé!*"

"But this is really our only chance. The banks won't move large sums. When you get there, you can transfer the cash to dollars and hold the bills as you choose. As for the drawings, I'll only send a few charcoal sketches that will bring an eventual fortune. I know how to wrap them for travel and will pack the materials safely."

Eugenia paused and saw the fear in Donato's eyes.

"When you get to New York, I'll direct you to the appropriate gallerists and to the few collectors I know. And, of course, there's a cut for you."

"But Eugenia," cried Donato. "This isn't my world. I wouldn't know how to begin. Don't you think this is too much to ask me? I'm simply a working man."

"You're precisely the right man because you'll pass unnoticed. You'll never raise anyone's eyebrows, and you'll be safe. I promise."

"My God. When Silvio asked me to carry his Carracci wrapped in a towel, I agreed because his request had to do with love. But this is something else. You're making me an accomplice."

"You're doing a favor not just for me but for Mariarosa and the family. Just imagine, had I not sent Mariarosa some money years ago, she would never have been able to pay for Carmelo's ticket to Argentina. Consider this endeavor as part of a newer, more modern mission. And, for your information, there's nothing dishonest at play."

In the end, Donato not only consented to Eugenia's request but also agreed to carry the cash through customs. He figured that if he opened a hole in the heels of his shoes, he could slip in the bills and seal them. After all, why work in shoe repair if you don't know how to do this? With a taper point knife and some carpenter's glue, Donato cut and secured the leather. Testing his work, he tapped his feet as if to dance.

"Not for nothing they call me twinkle toes when I step out onto the ballroom floor. Now my feet are twinkling money." He flexed his shoes again and laughed.

Donato traveled to New York, his mind and feet both weighed down. He carried wedding gifts for Rosie, a bracelet for Mariarosa, silverware, and embroidered runners, even a *soprasatta* and a wormy round of cheese. He also carried Silvio's African woman packed in flour sack towels, a roll of drawings, and enough cash in his shoes to buy a kingdom. As the Rex sailed from Naples for the New York harbor, Donato felt sea water causing waves in his head.

6.

Donato regaled the New York family with stories. He described Eugenia's sunny apartment as almost a castle. He discussed progress in Bellanera—electricity, running water, and cars. He spoke at length of the relatives, their expressions of sorrow and joy. He also unpacked Silvio's Carracci painting and propped it on Rosie's favorite table, displacing a vase of white-silk flowers and a squared-off art deco lamp. Then he unrolled Eugenia's bundle, flattened out the sketches, and stored them in a bedroom closet. He gave Eugenia's cash to Rosie, whose eyes opened wide with surprise.

"Oh boy," Rosie said. "You're on the path to crime. Until you figure out how to unload this stuff, we're like fish in those amusement park games waiting to be plucked from the water."

Despite her vehement protests, she made a point lickety-split to transfer the lire to dollars at a downtown bank. Donato, meanwhile, had decided to get in touch with Franz Kälin's brother.

On a Sunday morning, Donato met Günther Kälin. They'd agreed on a commonly recognized place, by a mulberry tree close to the Hudson River. This was Donato's favorite spot. Günther also knew it well. Like Donato, Günther was a Sunday stroller and, during the warmer months, usually parked himself on a bench under the shade of trees.

Günther enjoyed the Hudson River; its splendor held firm in his mind. Sometimes he took his sketchbook. Today, Günther explained that instead of apprehending the Hudson, he saw the Sihl River that flowed through his Alpine village. In his drawings, the George Washington Bridge became a covered walkway; Swiss peasants dotted the shores; New York men fishing eel and porgy became prim gentlemen in frock coats. These transformations fascinated Donato; he understood from his sketches that Günther longed for home.

Günther was more genial than his brother, not stuffy though always proper. He seemed less obsessive, less anxious. Günther followed art as a hobby. From his job as an upholsterer, he earnestly knew his colors, devoting himself to the mastery of tones and hues, the perfection of the weave. Against the general move toward modern art, which Günther said he abhorred, he cultivated pastorals of farms and running rivers, simple scenes of rural life.

"The more traditional, the better," Günther said, attempting to describe his tastes to his new acquaintance.

Günther also had his opinions regarding the changes in Europe. "What can I say?" Günther asked with his Romansh accent. "There's a werewolf upon us and we need to beware. I'm glad that my brother, if he remains in Zurich, will avoid the Wehrmacht."

Günther and Donato continued to meet. Günther even encouraged Donato to take his turn at drawing. Günther could offer basic instructions and help him with technique.

The confidence between the two men grew. Then, one blistering Sunday in summer, Donato became dizzy from heat. He had to brace himself by the mulberry tree and hold his head in his hands. Günther, fearing for his friend, proposed that he accompany Donato to his home.

Donato at first objected. Günther, in his proper style, replied that he felt no inconvenience; Donato's apartment was quite close to his. At his building's doorstep, Donato thanked Günther and invited him upstairs to meet his wife. In the city, it was unusual to invite a person outside the family to enter one's apartment. But Günther had just offered Donato an enormous favor; in return, he deserved the attention normally reserved for close relations. Günther, who also knew the rules, hesitated, then agreed.

Rosie, somewhat flustered, greeted them at the door. However, with courtesy, she invited Günther into the living room and offered him a glass of iced tea. Inevitable, hapless mistake. On the table where the silk roses had once stood was Silvio's reproduction of Carracci's African woman. Günther gazed at the canvas. "I'm stunned," he said. "Here's a perfect Carracci."

He persuaded Donato to tell him the story behind the painting. Donato recited Silvio's lectures. Then Donato asked Günther to wait while he retrieved the charcoal drawings that he kept in a bedroom closet. An art show was about to begin, but Rosie stopped her husband cold.

"The bedroom is a mess," she said. "Leave that for another day."

Donato and Günther, however, surrendered to the bliss of art. They carried on for at least an hour about the merits of art and the copy. They talked about Renaissance painting and Silvio's projects. On and on, almost every secret disclosed, while Rosie tried to talk about other subjects. Had Donato really been about to faint down by the river? Could he stand to drink more water? Could they believe this weather? So dreadfully hot and muggy.

She moved uncomfortably in her chair as if to adjust her garters. Her husband once again was hoodwinked by his own irresistible voice. He was throwing away all their secrets!

Eventually Günther stood up to leave, thanking his hostess and Donato.

As soon as he left, Rosie rolled her eyes and bit her lower lip. "If you care at all for Eugenia, you won't give away the store. These artworks are supposed to be held in secret until Eugenia sends you instructions." Annoyed, she went to the kitchen to attend to the simmering tomatoes that were the center of her Sunday ragú.

* * * *

Donato and Günther continued the Sunday meetings even as the war began and young men marched off to service. Rosie's brother Bill joined the Italian front and would soon land at Salerno under General Clark. Her brother Joe sailed to China. Donato and Günther weren't drafted owing to their age. The friendship between these men deepened as they continued to share their feelings. Both longed for their European towns. Günther dreamed of the Sihlsee shores and hikes up Mount Etzel. Donato dreamed of the southern mountains. Donato, meanwhile, became upset when the war effort forbade all letters to the Axis countries. One day, Günther proposed an idea: a letter could reach Donato's family in Italy if brokered through Günther's brother in Zurich; the Swiss always escaped censors.

Donato understood and jumped at the suggestion. "Oh, I'm immensely grateful," he said with joy.

A family meeting was held to discuss Günther's offer.

Rosie raised her voice, "And what if Franz Kälin reads our correspondence? Do you really trust him?" She remembered that Eugenia's earlier letters—those written before the war—had described Kälin as an aggressive man with a dishonest agenda.

Pushing Rosie's reservations aside, the family clamored for Günther's proposal. To play it safe, Rosie assumed the task of scribe and censor and, in her letters, she offered news devoid of substance or depth. She wrote of their health, the shortages of coffee and tea, the limited eggs and the ration books, the rising cost of meat, although never a word about the blackouts the civil guard enforced.

* * * *

Usually, the letters from Italy were stitched with well-worn threads: lack of food, spreading typhus, terror among the children; the names of those who had left for northern climes and were now returning to escape the war. Among the writers, Donato's sister Peppinella had a literary flair.

"She has the best imagination," Rosie said, "because she likes to suffer. I think she learned it from the penny dreadfuls and from reading the Sunday news."

Peppinella conveyed the histories of saints in Zia Wanda's style. She told of Santa Rita's wounds and San Rocco's dogs, but when she wrote about San Gennaro, her prose acquired emotion and power.

She always began her letters, "Oh my God, you'll never believe this."

Stories about Father Bartolo Longo's satanic cult and Santa Gemma's penance knocked Rosie on the floor. While the rest of the New York family members searched for information about the good health of those in the village, Rosie imagined a florid conversation with Peppinella about blood and torture. Rosie wanted to know about countryside miracles; she hoped to read about the Black Madonna, about adulterer priests and loose girls on the run, about the young seminarians practicing black magic in nearby Matera.

There must be a story in here, Rosie thought as she read aloud the most recent letter, adding details to give the tales more force.

One day a letter arrived from Eugenia. The missive, addressed to Donato, was neatly typed on decent bond.

"How strange. We haven't heard from Eugenia for a long time, and now she shows she can't write by hand."

> *Cara sorella, cari cugini*, especially my dearest Donato:
> It's been a while since I've written to you but that doesn't diminish my affection. When I look out over the ~~river~~ bay, I hold you dear to my heart. My own fate is less secure; you might say that life has crumbled. Nonetheless, the marchese and I are happy, and continue to bask in our blissful romance.
>
> It is time to ask a favor. Donato carried to America one of Silvio's paintings, Carracci's image of an African woman. Now Silvio needs the money from that work, and I beg you to sell it well. Perhaps Franz's brother will know how to manage the trade; he knows Kälin's associates in New York, and they will give you a hand. Trust Günther to make the transaction. From there, we can determine the rest.
>
> Your loving sister and aunt, Eugenia

Mariarosa was overjoyed to hear her sister's news. Donato was less attentive, somewhat lost in thought.

Rosie broke the silence with a resounding "Noooooooo!" She bit her lower lip; she stomped her feet. "This can't be real. First, we don't hear from her for an age. Then she sends a typed letter telling us about her marital joy when we all know what's going on. Franz Kälin wrote this. I'd bet my bottom dollar."

The family members were confused; Donato was annoyed.

"Wake up, Donato," Rosie said. "I knew it was a bad sign when Günther set his eyes on our painting; of course, he wrote to his brother. This hooligan is about to steal Silvio's art."

* * * *

Donato was crushed. He felt defeated. Had Günther betrayed his confidence in order to collude with Franz? Or maybe Eugenia really did believe Günther was the best one to sell a painting?

Rosie decided that the family would stop sending letters via the Kälins. Instead, she prevailed on her brother Bill, now under Fifth Army command, to transfer correspondence between New York and Salerno. In this way, the New Yorkers saluted those in Bellanera while those in Bellanera sent their warmest regards to New York. The US Army Service guided these conversations.

* * * *

What they couldn't know in New York was that Eugenia, still in Naples, continued to plumb the art world to sustain the collectors' interests. She learned about German art connoisseurs and dealers who, despite the darkness of war, traversed the southern city to see what they could buy or steal. She'd heard, for example, that Hermann Göring directed the looting of art museums and that his agents Angerer and Hofer were always hunting for new collections. Eugenia, like the many avid brokers who traded in one-to-one deals (take this Luca Giordano in return for your best Monet; I'll give you this Botticelli for three Manets and two Renoirs), now forgot her lofty declarations against the Reich (spoken before the war) and jumped in on the business. Money was rarely exchanged. They instead traded in art.

But trading began to get risky. Some nasty collectors wanted her out. And, with Gianpietro's prestige in decline, few were willing to lend her a hand. What if the Germans entered her house and examined Silvio's works? Would they know the works were only copies? Or, thinking the art original, would they cart the paintings away? And if Göring's men came around, the marchand from Zurich would follow.

7.

By winter, Eugenia and Gianpietro knew it was time to leave. The unbearable air raids by Panzers and Warhawks—it really didn't matter which side they were on—were now routine. The couple tried to contact Berenson, the art historian from Florence whose reputation was beyond reproach, to see if he knew of a safe house to hold Silvio's remaining paintings. They never received a response; they couldn't know that the Germans, by winter of '42, had placed Berenson on their most wanted list and forced him into hiding. So they decided to roll up Silvio's paintings and take them back to the country village.

Migrants now, Eugenia and the Marchese di Cimino traveled south into the mountains. Far from Benevento or Battipaglia, cities now reduced to heaps of rocks, they pressed toward their little town, which they heard had avoided the bombings. En route, they passed people walking like snails, their homes on their backs. Bed frames, dressers, broken valises, and cardboard boxes loaded with dishes advanced on the sides of roadways along with packs of dogs. A man and his children pulled a tall cart that carried an elderly woman plopped on a bed.

Eugenia was relieved when they finally reached Bellanera. Still out of sorts from the journey, the couple told each other that at least they'd arrived in one piece. Despite the crisp mountain air, the poppy and broom fields, and arching eucalyptus, the couple remained on edge. The marchese looked over the daily papers for stories about the bombings: a major ocean liner exploded in port; dozens of churches collapsed; as the Germans wandered freely, everyone trembled and looked away. While he read *Il Mattino* aloud, Eugenia listened. She then relayed the stories to others, adding her own opinions as if to correct the news.

"Eugenia wants to rewrite history," Rosie said. "To show herself in a starring role."

"Not unlike everyone else," Donato and Mariarosa said as they listened to Rosie telling stories that surely she had invented.

* * * *

In another letter, Eugenia reported on the dust that filled the air. Eugenia was fed up with her weekly sponge baths using water boiled in a cauldron. She wanted water to fall from a high-up nozzle, spraying the top of her head. One day, in a moment of courage, she asked the marchese to flag a coach that would take them to Potenza, the county seat not far away that housed some public baths. Eugenia was momentarily happy; she frolicked as drops of clear fresh water dangled from the tips of her hair. While lathering herself many times over, each time with relief and joy, Eugenia was interrupted by a female clerk who reported that Eugenia's time in the shower was about to expire.

Eugenia said, "Strange, I thought I heard German in the adjacent stalls. Could the Nazi army be here?"

"No," the smiling clerk said. "No Germans have arrived. The bathers are Austrian Jews who have found protection in Potenza. They were first detained in the north and then sent into confinement, but here, instead of tragedy, they have found a warm and sturdy welcome."

The clerk explained that they had the freedom to work and wander on their own. "The women are really quite nice," she said, "and have formed part of the life of the town."

Eugenia didn't understand this conversation. As she prepared to leave the bathhouse, she looked to the marchese, but he was also lost. This was nothing like the German *razzias,* in which the occupying army picked Jews from the streets of Naples (she once had seen her neighbor detained at night and never forgot the sight). No, something else was going on—as if the refugees enjoyed official protection. In her letter, she then described the late-afternoon journey back to the village. The coach's advances over unpaved roads caused the country dust to rise. Once again, Eugenia was covered in grime as if she had never left home.

* * * *

Rosie's feelings lay in the shadow of words. It wasn't only her perceptions of the exchanges of joy or despair that sailed from letter to letter but her sense of a history brewing, a story yet to come. Perhaps for that reason she focused on Italy. In New York, the experience of war was too immediate, too raw. She never mentioned the blackout curtains that locked the family in darkness; she never spoke of the chard and tomatoes she grew in pots on the window's ledge; she refused to remember hunting down coupons for pasta, shoes, or even an aspirin. She put her migraine headaches aside. Rather, she focused on the letters that arrived from Bellanera. Eugenia's letters enthralled her. Less about bullets and bombings, Eugenia's version of the war was full of private complaints about her living far from home.

8.

Eugenia and the marchese remained in the little town through the end of the war. They focused on life in Bellanera to drive away their nightmares of bombings in Naples. In the village, Eugenia continued in dialogue with Silvio and saw him every day. They spoke of art, the lack of materials, the crises of their families. She helped him hide his paintings in a chapel vault. "Protect your art," Eugenia told him as they carried his many canvases to a hidden space below the altar. Eugenia checked to make sure that the artwork was secure though, of course, it didn't matter now since the promise of sales had vanished. Silvio tried to guide his friend through the lighter topics and proposed that they walk through the fields as they once had done as children. These loving conversations continued each afternoon. But then, by the summer of '43, Eugenia had competition. A rival acquaintance had begun to slice into Silvio's time: Rolf Zwilling had arrived in town. First sent to Potenza in special confinement, he was among the two-hundred Jewish families dispersed to the southern hamlets. The hill town's residents reached out with good intention—who had a room to let, who needed an extra hand—and the government's promise of stipends also helped open doors. In Bellanera, a group of Austrian Jewish families arrived on July 25th.

The refugees settled in local homes; the priests eased the transition. Padre Michele thought to introduce Rolf to Silvio. Rolf had come from a Viennese family of dressmakers and painters. He knew about the arts; he had studied architecture and cities. He accumulated languages the way a skinny dog draws mites and fleas. He liked to chew the fat well into the night and enjoy a good glass of wine. Silvio told Rolf about his devotion to Renaissance painting, his despair over the Nazi lootings, the ruin of the Naples museums.

The men talked for the sake of talking. Silvio discovered such comfort in Rolf that in the following weeks Silvio showed him his paintings. A man for all times and seasons, Rolf reciprocated with his passions for art.

One evening, and in a somewhat stilted Italian, Rolf said, "You are indeed a man of quality, a man of humanist interests. Your words are found in your canvas's color and nuance. I can hear every tone I see. It reminds me that the rhythm of painting can express what the voice fails to say."

Silvio, of course, was flattered. On impulse, he decided to show Zwilling his greater collection and led his friend through the nearby church in order to reach the hidden cellars.

* * * *

Silvio wrote to Donato. Eugenia wrote to Mariarosa. Rosie read all the letters. Each had described the same events though neither mentioned Silvio's emotions nor Rolf's growing feelings for his artist friend. Rosie came to the rescue by adding several details to fill out the gaps in the story.

Through part of 1943 and into the following year, the men joined the local priests at night and listened to the BBC. Rolf studied English. He figured this would improve his chances for employment with the US Army. Rolf found a copy of *A Farewell to Arms* nestled in a bookcase; it belonged to a young man who'd left the village to study law. Rolf memorized a few of Hemingway's phrases, practicing them aloud, and imagined himself in conversation with the famous General Clark. Silvio, who didn't know a word of English, noted that Hemingway's sentences held a certain allure.

Rolf soon found work with the US Army. Hearing of his language skills, the Allies called upon Rolf to translate documents and ease the post-war transition. He did this in service of reconstruction on the southern front. Within months, his job was to assist the Army's top brass, to communicate with locals, and restore a sense of peace. First in Salerno and later in Naples, Rolf shuttled between Italian and English. His halting Italian had much improved. He brought up

Hemingway's sentences whenever he thought they were needed (he loved the author's masculine force in writing; he was taken by the authors' crisp descriptions of the countryside and its people) and, although he had little interest in driving an ambulance through the war-torn hills, he hoped that his quick and efficient phrases would persuade the Allies of his language skills in war-torn situations. Soon, Rolf accompanied the US leadership though cities and little towns.

Silvio reported this story to Eugenia, who then passed it on to Rosie. "The best," Silvio added, "was Rolf's access to food. Working for General Clark gave him free PX passes. There, he picked out surplus tidbits, and brought them back to me."

* * * *

It was well into 1944 when Eugenia and her husband figured it was time to return to Naples. Despite the German retreat, neither Eugenia nor the marchese felt relieved. Their house had been bombed, then the earthquake had followed. A thousand calamities had erupted. The marchese worried about the disasters he'd see while Eugenia feared she'd be left in the rubble. At this thought, the couple invited Silvio to join them; he would help calm Eugenia's nerves, and he would get to visit Rolf, who by this time held a guaranteed post in Naples as a translator for the US Army.

As their car approached the city, Silvio observed that history had been flattened. Ancient Pompeii and Naples shared a surface of ash. Eugenia winced at the thought.

Never at a loss for words, the marquese couldn't resist a comment, "Perhaps it was Pliny's revenge."

No one understood what he meant.

As the marchese strummed his fingers on the window, Eugenia bit her lower lip and Silvio grimaced. They recalled the Naples of so many decades ago, a metropolis alive with billboards flashing novel ideas. In 1902, it had been an urban wonder. By contrast, in this post-war scene, the city unfurled its shrouds. Not Dante's hell, but something worse. Toppled buildings, twisted convoys; boats once afloat in water now split in two. Docks splintered, steel girders with broken spines. The stench of ruptured sewers, typhoid fever making the rounds. Eugenia wondered if the aquarium and zoo had survived.

* * * *

Massive domestic collapse greeted Eugenia and the marchese. The roof of their home was gone. Glass was shattered, books soaked by rain and soot, beds drowned in cat pee, cupboards and closets gnawed by rodents, overstuffed chairs torn up by munching crows, zero supply of tapers to help them in the dark. Some acquaintances unspooled the news: deportation, labor camps, death in burned-down buildings. Others described the Montecassino bombings that had started in January and lasted well into May.

"These weren't just any bombings," a few neighbors said. "Not just any battle."

"And don't get so hot for the Allies," others added. "At Cassino, they really blew it."

Silvio sent word to Rolf to let him know that he had arrived. The marquese's sisters had refused to return to the mess and continued to live in their compound near Lecce.

* * * *

One afternoon, as they settled in (Eugenia wrote that it was like camping), Signor Borrello stopped by to visit. A former official at the National Museum, he lived in the apartment next door and was Gianpietro's longtime friend. Beyond explaining the lack of food and the absence of sterile water, Borrello was eager to tell his friends about the art world's ruin.

"It started when Göring's agents came to plunder our collections. Their plan was to purchase some art; in other cases, to steal. As you know, our government gave few protections, and even cut the legal strings to allow the artwork to leave. Here's where we could've used Silvio's paintings to stand in for the grandest Renaissance art. But since Silvio was missing, we had to invent audacious plans. Last September, when the Germans set fire to the Filangieri collection at Nola, we began in haste to peel the paintings from our museum's walls. We packed what we could in straw; we wrapped sculptures as if they were babies.

"We sent anything of value out of Naples; in fact, we sent 187 crates to Montecassino Abbey. Nothing could be safer, we said, but we weren't as smart as we thought. By late September, the Nazis had beaten us at our game. Respecting the Reichsmarschall's wishes, the Germans had gone to Montecassino early on. They told the abbey monks about the future bombings and recommended moving all the art to the Vatican's vaults. The art then got mysteriously lost in transport. In January, the Allies decided to bomb the abbey, but the Germans, under Kesselring's orders, knew to stay away.

"We still don't know where the lost material is," Signor Borrello said. "The only reminders are in Silvio's hands. His copies are our record of some of what we lost."

Silence reigned; Eugenia looked down. Silvio issued a humbled 'thank you.'

Everyone sighed. The marchese looked at Silvio, Silvio glanced at Eugenia; Eugenia sent a knowing look back to the marchese. Rolf, who by this time had arrived back at the apartment after his day's work, raised his hand to shield his eyes.

As if this weren't bad enough, Signor Borrello had more unwelcomed news: Franz Kälin had been in Naples.

"Last July, shortly after Mussolini stepped down, Kälin showed his face. Under German protection—free entrance and egress—he searched for Eugenia. He said that he hoped to buy her paintings, but everyone explained that Eugenia had left. A few days later, people found him snooping around, looking through the windows. Kälin came up empty handed but promised to return."

Signor Borrello revealed Kälin's motives: he and a crew of sinister types—certainly underworld ghoulies—had planned to invite Silvio to Switzerland and offer him a chance to paint.

"It sounds like they want to kidnap Silvio and hold him hostage to his art," Rolf said as he shuddered.

"Kälin was really up to no good," Eugenia said. She summarized his plan: in Zurich he would demand that Silvio copy famous artworks.

Kälin would then pass them to unsuspecting clients. No telling what would happen to Silvio.

"Oh, come on, Geni. A little less theater," the marchese begged.

"Shocking but not usual," Signor Borrello said. "In this current age of cruelty, why not hold a painter hostage in exchange for a slice of bread?"

No one liked the joke.

* * * *

After Signor Borrello left, Rolf said, "If you'll permit me, I think you're all too nervous. Let's take stock: Silvio's work is safely hidden in the village church. And no one knows the town's name or Silvio's present location."

Everyone reached for a cigarette though there were none to be had. Suppressing his Viennese background of grumpiness and gloom (these were Eugenia's words), Rolf ignited a strange route of analysis still unknown to most Italians of those years.

"You're reacting too strongly," Rolf told them. "You need to find your center."

Then he added with great authority, "Right now, our priority should be to protect Silvio so no one will take him away."

Rolf pressed his hand on Silvio's arm. Not since his days with Giulio had Silvio been so awakened. He began to cough, but it sounded as if he were gasping for air.

* * * *

Rolf brought the Ciminos back to earth and gave them a bit of hope. He calmed Silvio with gentle words and guaranteed his protection. He aided the marquese and Eugenia with some of their household repairs. Later he produced two cartons of Lucky Strikes to cheer up his friends.

"The PX sends you a present," he chuckled.

Everyone was relieved.

One day Rolf arranged for a dinner to be held at the US Army compound in the Parker's Hotel, a once sumptuous locale that used to house the Germans. Some American officials thought it wise to strengthen local contacts and favored Rolf's proposal of inviting Neapolitan friends. The gesture was seen as post-war rebuilding.

"Reach out to the city's high-toned figures and build a conversation," one lieutenant said.

"And apologize for the air raids that left the city in ruins," another volunteered.

The top command agreed that they needed to bolster social ties.

"Next Saturday night at eight?"

Eugenia and Silvio eagerly jumped up; the marchese nodded. The promise of a decent meal was on their minds.

Though the dinner was sparse—much to the guests' surprise—the conversation was lively. Rolf introduced his friends to various military figures, among them Major Gardner, a man from Somerville, Massachusetts, who in the States had run several galleries and was passionate about Renaissance art. Then there was a captain, a historian trained at Yale, as devoted to painting as Silvio and with many passions to share. Amidst puffs of smoke and cheap whiskey, the conversation turned to the Nazi's raids of the Naples museums. The officers lamented the Germans' skills, their expertise in painting, their cunning approach to the monks and priests who'd stood guard at the various abbeys that had sheltered works of art.

"They were brilliant," Major Gardner admitted. "We inspected convoys, we blocked trucking routes, and made sure to stop the trains. Most often, however, we were late to the scene, as was the case at Nola. Montecassino was even worse."

There were tiny tea sandwiches made of Army pre-sliced bread, a chard soup, early tomatoes brought from a farm near Avellino. There was a fish wheeled into the dining hall by a fellow named Giuseppe. Finally, for lack of an Italian pastry chef, there was a dessert of two-colored Jell-O (some cups in red and green, others in red and blue)—a binational salute to the Army's creative kitchen. Some of the guests didn't stay around to taste it, but for the moment, let's rewind to the fish.

The marchese sat next to Eugenia, who sat beside Silvio. Rolf mediated between his Italian guests and the American brass. Everyone was cordial; some were even jolly. The Army fellows raised their glasses to toast to the end of the war. Some imbibed too much. All smoked between courses. The visitors tried to control themselves and not look excessively famished.

The party ran smoothly with pressed-out remarks in which each man exposed his finest manners in a men's club sort of way. The waiters set down a giant fish on the master table. The meter-long fish was roasted whole, caressed by tiny shallots and rosemary twigs, and coated in pungent wine sauce. After presenting it, the waiters wheeled the fish to a sideboard, where they took the art of filleting to its highest form. With robust knives and agile hands, much like expert surgeons, they swept in upon the piscatorial body and began their task. Skimming their blades across the fish's spine to separate flesh from bone, they prepared exquisite fillets and dusted them with pepper, adding a spoonful of herb and wine sauce scooped from the platter.

"My goodness, where did you fellows find this splendid gift from the sea?" Rolf inquired.

"Don't think it comes from the Bay of Naples," a burly cook replied. "Tonight we have a specialty from the aquarium tank of the Parco Comunale."

A wide-eyed Eugenia quickly understood and began to swoon. Her eyes rolled in their sockets, her cheeks turned violet. She pushed back from the table, her head weakly balanced on her chair's backrest. Not accounting for the disorder that would soon ensue, the waiters continued to slice through the fish much the way we would handle the pages of a book that told an interesting story.

This was her friend of forty years, she thought, the giant koi who had listened to her thoughts, the koi who had stood by in her moments of deep abandon; the koi who had heard her laments and offered consolation. The koi as priest confessor. As all these thoughts raced through her mind, Eugenia's body weakened and, fish-like and limp, reclined.

The marchese asked that they be excused; he offered her an arm, but in her delusion, she took his fin. The pair withdrew to the terrace.

"I'm sorry, Geni. I know how much you loved him. Trust me, I understand." The marchese tried to explain the cook's gesture: because of the dangers, current law in Naples prevented fishing from the bay.

"But the koi?" stammered Eugenia. "A fish that lives quietly in his tank for over half a century now fills the paunches of craven men?" Beads of sweat grew large on her brow.

"Calm, Geni; calm. This aquarium stock was a last resort to relieve the city's hunger."

She heard his words as liquid babble but soon Eugenia composed herself. It was time to go. Rolf remained with Silvio, devouring every morsel.

9.

The Ciminos had a brutal few weeks. At once, they had too much to do and were too depressed to move. Eugenia spent her days on a tattered divan thinking about her koi while the marchese oversaw house repairs. As he was helpless to hold a hammer, he resigned himself to a spectator's role, watching as workers cleaned debris and patched the roof's holes. Finally fed up with post-war life in a broken city, Eugenia proposed that they return to the village, far safer than life in Naples.

"At least in the little town, they don't kill pets for dinner," she said, forgetting the many chickens and sheep that had lived and died by her father's hand.

The marchese sullenly agreed, but first he had a plan. After all, they were there by the bay. And, *carpe diem,* he should take advantage of the glorious afternoon. He announced that he would soon depart for several nights on the isle of Capri.

* * * *

Regular postal service had resumed, and Eugenia wrote to her American family; she made sure to say she thought that Gianpietro's idea was absurd. The Germans had mined the harbors while the Allies had hammered away at the shores, she wrote. She'd lost her temper with the not-so-good marchese.

Rosie frowned as she read aloud Eugenia's words.

"He failed to recognize the peril. He wasn't even disturbed when he learned that the German high command had previously ordered evacuation of buildings within a thousand feet of port. It was further proof that the Germans saw the sea as a source of danger."

Eugenia in her letters was distraught. Rosie was distraught too.

* * * *

At home, Eugenia sat up straight on the couch, straightened her nightgown and robe, and with her face still pale, she raised her voice to Gianpietro. "Why would you do this to me? Don't you know that the bay is still unprotected from German mines?"

The marchese was quickly dismissive, explaining in great detail how the Allies had swept the bay. "The water is safe again. Certainly it's fine for boating."

"Don't delude yourself, Gianpietro. Not even the most able fishermen have permission to sail those waters."

"But Clark was in Capri, and the Germans before him. Everyone has frequented the island, even in times of war."

Eugenia continued to lambast the project, deriding her husband's frolics. At last, the marchese conceded: instead of sailing from Naples, he would depart from the port of Sorrento, which offered a shorter route.

In the marchese's absence, Eugenia decided to spend her days discarding furniture, lamps, and books the leaky roof had ruined. She closed the kitchen but because she rarely used it, she felt no loss. The shortage of tasty nibbles, the marchese's absence, the crummy food that Cristina now served killed all thoughts of dining at home. Since the lure of black-market provisions had swallowed all her funds, she relied on tins of sardines and boxes of crackers that Rolf had secured at the Army PX.

Then the news arrived: returning from Capri, Gianpietro's vessel had exploded; a German naval mine had eluded the Allied sweeps. The travelers hadn't stood a chance, the radio newscasters reported. The boat had gone down in an instant. The captain, two deck hands, and thirty-five travelers had shared their final breaths. The coast guard announced that no body was found intact.

The news numbed Eugenia. Her torso was suddenly icy. Her migraines flashed like glaring white beams on the evening sea. "How could he do this to me?" she screamed though, of course, she knew the answer. "How can this possibly be?"

The few family members who had returned to the city came to express their sorrow. Silvio told Eugenia that Gianpietro had at last found his voice in the sea; the waves defined his song. "This wasn't a defeat; he was taking charge." Silvio trembled as he spoke.

"He was Parthenope," Rolf added. "Perhaps he'd really thrown himself into the sea after he'd failed to find his Ulysses."

* * * *

The allusions puzzled Rosie, and she asked for Donato's assistance. "These men turned to mythology to explain an itch on your nose."

Then she continued reading Eugenia's letter. Eugenia assumed her widow's weeds and prepared to live as a woman alone. Her sorrow seemed to suit her, Rosie opined. After all, Eugenia was used to the marchese's absence, and she had her own routine. As Eugenia had grown older, her grief changed in color and tone.

"He was my friend, my supporter, my confidant," Eugenia wrote regarding her husband. "I didn't need much more."

By her third letter to Mariarosa and Rosie, Eugenia had peeled off her mourning clothes and prepared for a different existence. After that, Eugenia rarely spoke of Gianpietro again unless it concerned her business.

* * * *

Silvio and Rolf, who'd remained in Naples, had developed a relationship that exceeded mere friendship. Nevertheless, they kept Eugenia nearby, and Eugenia was always grateful. In their presence, she felt like Isa Miranda, star of stage and screen. Still stunned by her loss, she relied on her men for comfort but she also felt her role as a queen bee protecting her drones.

There were knowing glances, moments in which one man's fingertips grazed the other's arm or scenes in which one man's napkin dropped to the floor and the other man retrieved it with grace. There were smiles, nods, lowered eyes, the slightest movement of one man's boot inching toward the other man's shoe. Eugenia watched from the sidelines. An irony, she wrote to Mariarosa: in all her years of marriage, she never came close to the ardor and trust these men shared. Wistfully, she wondered if Gianpietro had ever found a similar love.

After the war, Eugenia was urged on to business. No food, no money, no cultural life: she had to get out of her widow's rut. One day, Eugenia proposed to Silvio that they once more traffic in art. She extended her soft and well-lotioned hand to reach his delicate fingers.

"Listen, Silvio. I have an idea. Everyone knows that the museums were cleared out. No one knows for sure if the hidden paintings are safe. What do you think about reconstructing some of the works that once hung in the Capodimonte? Taking your art from the Bellanera vaults and putting them up for sale?"

In the past, selling Silvio's fakes had been a fairly tame endeavor. A rising bourgeoisie wanted copies of the masters to hang on their living room walls. And everyone admired Silvio's talent. His reputation had spread from Naples to Rome. Eugenia, through her late husband's contacts, had sustained a lively trade.

"As the museums assess their losses, the time is ripe to revisit the curators," she continued. "We can help them out of a tight spot so that they can reopen their doors to the public."

Eugenia's proposal seemed straightforward. The museum directors already knew Silvio's work; now they'd have the opportunity to display his canvasses until the real works reappeared. They'd be placeholders, as Signor Borrello liked to say.

Here Rolf intervened, "But don't you think this will open to fraud?"

Rolf's comment annoyed Eugenia. She wanted to ask him to leave, to have a private moment with Silvio, but she knew both men would receive this badly. Instead, she repeated her point: Silvio's work in the post-war moment would be a temporary solution. It would bring in a little money and satisfy the curators as they tried to restore their galleries.

"I'm afraid you woud be opening yourself to a lot of trouble," Rolf said. "Even if you run an honest shop, the art thieves, once they hear that you and Silvio are back as a team, will press you for nasty favors. Don't do it, Eugenia. Please."

Eugenia retired for the evening, and the men returned to their quarters. She continued to mull over her new idea, dismissing Rolf's warnings. Silvio, susceptible to doubt, began to fear the return of people like Kälin.

* * * *

One day, Eugenia offered Signor Borrello Silvio's complete run of Salvator Rosa's paintings. Borrello reminded her that the museum was still short of funding, but he could put her in contact with individuals hoping to renew their business in art. When they learned of this, Silvio and Rolf told Eugenia that they feared Borrello's contacts. This wasn't part of the original plan.

Rolf said, "Even the most honest men in the art world have notebooks filled with the names of people who live in the darkest shadows. Don't do it, Eugenia; just keep it simple. You don't know who knows whom nor where the paintings will eventually land."

Silvio asked if there couldn't be a reasonable solution.

"You can always sign your name, Silvio," Rolf said. "That would dispel the myth of false provenance, and we'd be done with the problem."

But Silvio insisted that his artwork be an exact copy. Adding a twentieth-century "S" would disrupt a fixed moment in time.

Rolf was sure that Silvio was on the level, but he lacked faith in Eugenia's plans. "I'm afraid she'll get you in trouble."

Silvio pushed his lover away. "I can't have you doubt my friend whom I've had for a thousand years. She means too much too me."

After this, Rolf became withdrawn and began to distance himself from Silvio. Meanwhile, he began to close down his work as translator for the US Army bigwigs. These men respected Rolf and always took to him kindly. Then one day they offered him passage to New York when his work was done. The proposal left Rolf breathless. After much ambivalence, sustained by nights of insomnia and an excess of cheap Army whiskey, Rolf for the first time began to think of life without Silvio.

10.

Eugenia, unaware of the pain that her good friends suffered, began to build an agenda. Each day she met Gianpietro's friends to see if they were interested in Silvio's art.

"Not today, Eugenia," one man told her. "We've hit the bottom. It'll be years until we can again devote ourselves to beauty."

"Maybe at some later point. But right now, it's out of the question," said another.

"I'm always inclined to favor requests that come from the marchese's widow, but at present we have no funds."

Door after door, the same responses. Eugenia sank into financial despair. She looked for help. The Cimino sisters had returned to Naples without a lira, the family fortunes squandered. No one among the Neapolitan elites could promise Eugenia a gift or a loan. She returned to Signor Borrello to see if he could help her. This time she wasn't inquiring about museum acquisitions. She hoped that Signor Borrello might dip into his underworld contacts. Sure enough, one day she received a visit from a marchand, a middle-aged man eager to rebuild his business. He had heard of Silvio's art, he said. Eugenia at first shuddered. Then her fear for her friend quickly dissolved in the humid air of profits.

"I think these paintings will do well in London," the broker said. "Especially the Botticelli, which seems to have disappeared from the Cassino vaults."

Eugenia knew that she was passing through portals that opened to chambers of danger and was taking Silvio with her. With each new proposal, she pressed Silvio to remove another canvas from his Bellanera storage.

"A post-war reconstruction plan," she said. "Isn't that the point?"

The going was getting too tough for Silvio. What fate would await him? What kinds of demons would be awakened? There was also the continued rumor about Kälin, who they said was traveling through Italy, always looking out for Silvio in order to make him a slave of art.

"Kälin hasn't yet found us, and you're still safe and sound," Eugenia said, trying to comfort her friend. What she didn't say was that Signor Borrello had announced Kälin's imminent arrival in Naples. This time—only this once—Eugenia planned to meet him.

Silvio retreated into silence. Rolf had warned him to stay out of trouble and to avoid the risks. As a substitute for the business at hand, he'd encouraged Silvio to launch a training school for painters, "to teach them the craft of the trade."

"Never; it's too much of a challenge." Silvio said. "I have so many problems with language that I simply can't fathom that role." He concluded that his destiny was to remain as Eugenia's partner in trade.

Rolf, fed up with it all, decided to leave for New York. He realized that Eugenia's clutch on Silvio was too strong for him to break. Their breakup wasn't explosive but mired in darkness. Silvio was afraid to leave Eugenia; Rolf needed to clear the air. Silvio had no imagination for life in the English language yet Rolf insisted upon New York.

"Please stay, *amore*," Silvio said. "I need you by my side."

"I'm superfluous," the other replied. "You have a clear object of love, and it's not me."

The conversation between lovers came to an end. Packing his goods after so much time with the US Army, Rolf prepared his departure. Silvio was despondent as Eugenia sharpened her knife.

"Please stay in touch," Eugenia said to Rolf. "Once in New York, write to me and let me know where you are."

All this for a "just in case" moment that Eugenia hadn't yet imagined, a plan that awaited design.

* * * *

As the months advanced, Eugenia's control increased and Silvio's suffering grew. His stutter returned, his muscles ached, his neck was cramped from nervous tension. Eugenia continued to drum up business, hatching plans that excluded Silvio's opinions but always demanded his art. Her clientele became increasingly shady, less proper than before. Then came the day when Signor Borrello arrived at her house with Kälin.

"*Mia cara,*" Kälin gushed with unnatural charm. "It's been so many years since we met. My condolences for your husband and for the war's unspeakable effects on your city. Signor Borrello tells me of your great success in selling Silvio's works. I promise that I'll no longer bother you for an introduction as I did many years ago. It's clear that he's under your wing and enjoys your devoted protection."

"And what can I do for you, Mr. Kälin?" Eugenia said.

"Just coming to reestablish our friendship and let you know that I might leave for New York. I traveled the length of Italy before and after the war. But the scene isn't as prosperous as I'd hoped. It's time to visit my brother."

Eugenia was careful not to say too much except to note that Rolf was also en route to America with plans to start life anew. Casually, she added that Donato had carried a few of Silvio's artworks in the years before the war.

"Perhaps we can talk of sales at a later time," she said.

Kälin promised to stay in touch. "*Tante belle cose*," he added. "I'm sure we'll meet again."

* * * *

Eugenia was perseverant. A social butterfly of post-war years, she expanded her list of clients. By and large, business was picking up while Silvio was slipping day by day. Finally, Silvio gathered his courage and announced his plan to leave the country. "I can't do it any longer," he said. "I need to go."

Silvio thought it best to focus on love and leave aside the way Eugenia had betrayed him. "I'm upset at having lost Rolf. And I need to try something else, Eugenia. Another country. Not the United States since Rolf said that he wanted to travel there alone. But perhaps South America: Argentina wouldn't be out of the question. My brother lives in Luján. I have a few contacts in Rosario. And your sister, Maria

Antonietta, has a cheese store in Buenos Aires." He remembered that Carmelo was there as well. "My family in Argentina has promised to help me. Rolf said I should start a school for drawing. 'You're a copyist, not a forger,' he told me time and again. He thought I should move to a city where I might make my talents known. In Buenos Aires, I imagine, I'll hit my stride."

Eugenia collapsed in a chair. It was just a matter of time, she thought, until everyone she knew will have died or crossed the ocean. "You can't do this to me, Silvio."

"But I need to find myself, to do things on my own. And I need to be in a business in which I can sign my name."

11.

Throughout the war years, Donato had always looked forward to hearing the letters that came from abroad. Rosie delivered the news with a theatrical flair. She knew how to pause at the exciting moments. She read as if she had lived through the dramas unfolding in Eugenia's prose. Rosie loved when her family sighed over the ongoing adventures; how they laughed, then quibbled, then disputed the truths that Eugenia relayed.

They wondered how any of this could be possible, if Eugenia had made this stuff up. They doubted Eugenia's confidence; they put her hyperbole in question; they laughed at her skittishness as she wrote stories of impossible love. Rosie turned Eugenia's letters into works of art, but Mariarosa didn't share all of Eugenia's letters with her daughter. She kept the best for herself.

Privately, Mariarosa took inspiration from the courage her sister had shown. Eugenia had a flair for business that no one else in the family had. She was elegant and well spoken; she had confidence in her work. From her years in Naples, Eugenia had gained wealth, charm, and prestige. Eugenia's letters also revealed that she was capable of feeding her darker impulses, suggesting the ends of sales and profit justified the steps along the way. Mariarosa kept the letters describing Eugenia's shady affairs from the rest of her family; she feared they would look down upon Eugenia for her less than scrupulous projects. She guarded Eugenia's most intimate letters by hiding them in a suitcase meant to hold winter coats. Rosie wouldn't find and read these letters until years after Mariarosa's death.

* * * *

As the years advanced, the correspondence lessened. Eugenia rarely wrote, save for a perfunctory card now and then. Rosie thought that her aunt had fallen into depression as her beauty declined. Peppinella's correspondence also dwindled, revived only when she chose to deliver news about the state of her ailing kidneys, her life as a widow, the unpleasantries of aging. Then Peppinella sent a telegram: Eugenia had drowned at the seashore, somewhere near Positano. The family was in shock and at first refused to believe it.

Tears came to Donato's eyes. Mariarosa kneeled before a crucifix and commended her sister to God. Rosie was quick to suspect malfeasance but her arguments took her nowhere.

An era had passed, they said. Antonio and Carmelo were gone, and now Eugenia drowned at sea.

Donato, surrounded by disconsolate women, said, "Let it go. Time will heal all sorrows." He thought, too, with relief, that the family would now escape art's burdens.

As time went on, Rosie felt the absence of Eugenia's letters. After all, without her auntie's stories, she had to find another voice. Her subject was no longer the family news from abroad, but reenactments of Broadway shows that she had seen downtown. Everything from "Oklahoma!" to "South Pacific" (starring Ezio Pinza) came under Rosie's gaze. She then told the family about details of costume along with tuneful renditions of songs. It was her way of bringing the news of Times Square straight into the home. But she also went to the Italian movies to see on the giant screen the stories that Eugenia and Silvio had once described with such inimitable flair. She saw Anna Magnani shot dead in the streets of Rome; she saw the American soldiers in Naples befriending young boys with candy. She drank up the films about American travelers falling for foreign girls. Were these movies as real as the stories that Eugenia used to tell in her letters? Did her brother Bill, during his stay in Salerno, have the same experience as the army private who walked the *lungomare* in Rossellini's film? How much do we need to be real? Or is the movie a documentary form of something that we already feel and think? Can this all be true?

* * * *

In the post-war years, Rosie and Donato received a double blessing: the birth of their two children. Max and Rosanna entered the world to considerable joy and fanfare. Largely under Rosie's watch, the babies were assigned to Donato for Sunday morning strolls. "Perambulator," Donato said as he pushed the carriage to the river park. He was delighted with the sound of the word, easier to pronounce than "pram," which was at once too sharp for his tongue and too abrupt to be understood. Donato pushed the perambulator to the pristine path by the pretty park. And how many pecks of pickled peppers did Peter Piper pick? Donato laughed because he could never pronounce this phrase no matter how hard he tried. As in the past, he headed toward the mulberry tree.

One Sunday he ran into Günther after not having seen him for several years. "Where have you been, Günther? I hadn't heard from you since the war was over. I figured that you'd moved to another part of the city."

"Yes, I'm on Long Island. Sorry I forgot to leave a forwarding address. Lots of anguish: my wife was ill, and my children wanted to move. So now we're near Hempstead, and I continue my business."

"And your wife's health?" Donato inquired. "I hope she's fully recovered."

"Thanks for asking," Günther said. "Don't worry, she's on the mend."

Donato perceived an initial stiffness, like creaking floorboards needing repair, but the two men slowly regained their old rhythms. They spoke of war, the changing neighborhood, the city's unparalleled growth, the loss of LaGuardia and FDR, the rise of Robert Moses. And Günther lavished praise on Donato's children, though it was against his style to gush.

"So what brings you back to the neighborhood, Günther?"

"I came to deliver an upholstered armchair to Mrs. Katz on 204th Street. I still repair her furniture whenever she gives me a call. Meanwhile, I'm very happy to see you. I hope we can stay in touch."

Not a word about his brother Franz, Renaissance paintings, or Silvio's African woman. Of course, Donato thought, with Eugenia gone, the art world was now behind them.

When they were about to take leave of each other, and almost as a shy afterthought, Günther mentioned that he'd not heard from Franz for many years. "I doubt that he's alive any longer. The last time I heard from him was before the war ended. Franz wrote to say that he was traveling to the south of Italy to visit the little hill towns."

Donato sat up. He felt chilled.

"I guessed from the newsreels that his train had never arrived," Günther hastened to add. "This was in March 1944, the time of the Balvano train crash, a disaster. I always wondered if my brother had been aboard that train."

"A gas explosion," Donato said. "Certainly, I remember. All the passengers died on the spot."

Günther shook his head. "Since most of the travelers were train hoppers, riding the cars for free, the authorities threw the dead in a common grave and tried to seal the case shut. We never had a full list of survivors. I'm not sure that Franz was on that train, but I can't find another explanation to justify his silence."

Donato expressed regret for Günther's loss. Privately, though, he was relieved to know that the no-good marchand had come to his end.

A tepid friendship between Günther and Donato ensued, never reaching the high temperatures of their exchanges from years ago.

* * * *

One morning, beneath the mulberry tree, Günther asked a favor. He wanted to see the Carracci painting again (after so many years). Donato's blood pressure rose on the spot. True, Donato had never tried to sell the portrait. And as Silvio no longer wrote to him, Donato wasn't worried at all. He still had the canvas on a living room table and kept the other art in his bedroom closet. Donato and Rosie had slipped into the comfort of doing nothing. Silvio's art work was part of their living room decorations, and no one gave it another thought. Moreover, since Eugenia's death, it had slipped from all conversation.

"What?" Donato asked. "After so much time?" He tried to temper his nerves. After all, Günther was gracious, friendly. There was nothing to fear.

Günther repeated his gentle proposal. He wanted to bask once again in the Carracci's beauty. Since he infrequently traveled to Upper Manhattan, he didn't want to pass up the chance.

Donato pushed aside his doubts, regained his psychic balance, and invited Günther to visit the following week.

* * * *

As she had many years before, Rosie greeted Günther at the door. Her eyes said it all. What were Günther's motives? Did Günther need to revisit this painting? What could that possibly mean? For a moment, she guessed that Günther was taking cues from his brother.

She wasn't wrong. Another week had passed, and Günther met Donato again. This time, with a new favor to ask. "I'm setting up a local art presentation in Hempstead, Long Island. Would you be willing to loan us the Carracci to feature in our show? It would be a terrific surprise."

Although Donato was uneasy, he agreed to the loan. After all, Günther was a friend and the painting was only a copy. Günther carried off the Carracci much to Rosie's chagrin.

"*Citrullo!*" Rosie shouted, meaning that Donato was a jerk.

Günther visited one more time. "There's a chance of turning this into a Renaissance fair, and I'm trying to assemble the pieces." He asked permission to see the closeted artwork Donato had mentioned years ago.

Donato was very surprised that Günther even remembered.

Günther looked over Silvio's sketches and made a quick decision. "I'll use the Carracci painting for my show and perhaps call for the drawings at a later date, if that's okay with you."

Donato quietly assented. not knowing that Silvio's Carracci would be used for a major art heist, a "substitute and steal." In fact, Franz hadn't been killed in a train wreck. He'd crossed the ocean to set up business with his sibling. The two had established themselves in restoration and sales, slinking through New York's art underworld in which Franz staged the show and Günther played the straight man.

Kälin wanted to acquire forgeries one by one and place them in different museums. His team would remove the original paintings and sell them to underworld traders. By moving slowly, one by one, his idea was not to call public attention. He planned for this endeavor to run over many years.

"It still needs some fine tuning," Franz had said. "But I have a scheme that works."

The assault on the Metropolitan Museum of Art was to have been Franz's crowning achievement. Twenty years in hiding, moving art through dealers here and there, Franz Kälin from the time he had arrived in New York knew he would one day hit the jackpot. He had spent years collecting forgeries at bargain basement prices, he knew the sharks from the minnows. There was no particular limit when it came to making a buck. And after he confirmed that Donato was still alive in New York, still guarding Silvio's art, he knew he could score a win.

"The jerk will come in useful," Franz had said to Günther. "I saw it in his face when I met him that time in Naples."

Franz had sent Günther to retrieve the Carracci and see what else he could find. Franz had remembered that Eugenia once spoke about some Renaissance sketches that Donato had carried from Italy before the war. The brothers had wondered where the drawings had landed. Had they been sold? Or were they still in Donato's apartment? And if the latter case were true, could Günther convince the bumbling jackass to agree to a short-term loan? Günther had tried to see them on his first visit, years ago, but Donato's witchy wife had blocked the door. Now on his second round of visits, and after weeks of chit chat, Günther came again to ask Donato to retrieve Silvio's sketches.

"They're practice sheets, don't you think?" Donato had asked, referring to the drawings. "Not worth much to my eye."

Without responding, Günther again had asked that the sketches be left in Donato's closet, thinking to keep them safe. The time would come when they'd see the light; for the moment, the brothers had other plans. With Silvio's Carracci in play, the Kälin men had sensed their rise in fortunes. They believed they'd be the stars of stage and screen, heroes among men of big finance with all their highfalutin ways.

They then contacted Rolf, who, by now, was living in Lower Manhattan with a gallerist of some repute. Many years ago, when Eugenia had revealed to Franz that Donato was still holding on to her trove, she'd also told him that Rolf had set up shop in New York.

"It's just a matter of time," Franz said to his brother. "Now's our moment in heaven."

At first, the Kälins had wanted little to do with Silvio's ex-lover, but when they saw his name, his associations, the prestige that he'd acquired (all reported in the Sunday social columns of the *New York Herald Tribune*), they realized that Rolf Zwilling could open certain doors.

"It's icing on the cake," Franz said. "Let's make our introductions."

Rolf had formed part of a well-known gallerists' circle that controlled New York art. He also was a friend of museum's director and attended various charity soirées. The brothers imagined with a little buttering-up, along with sentimental reminders for old times' sake—the war, Eugenia, Italian art—that Rolf would fall in their hands like a cream puff. Then they'd use his contacts to gain access to the staff of the Metropolitan Museum.

"Zwilling will us secure a pass," the brothers said with confident affirmation.

When they met, Franz did most of the talking to warm up Rolf Zwilling's heart. Their plot took form: Rolf would introduce the Kälins to the Met's administrative team; in turn, these people would let the Kälins take a peek at the surroundings—delivery doors, walkway maps, access routes, guards' schedules. After several conversations with staff, the brothers would produce an effective rendering of the space.

The brothers set out their final plan. At night, Günther would enter the museum with the fake Carracci and remove the original art. Franz would wait for his brother on 83rd Street across from the museum.

On the designated night, Günther entered the property along with two assistants. One worker disarmed what he thought was the only camera and remained by a door as a lookout; another advanced with Günther to Galley 214 with the plan of removing the Carracci to replace it with Silvio's art. Barely a sound of flickering light bulbs, no movement in the halls; Günther's team had advanced to the second floor. Then, the unexpected.

Sirens on the street, commotion at the entrance. Uniforms, sticks, and weapons running past on foot. Alarms and a general brouhaha. A new security system had apprehended one of the men on camera. Günther had been visible as he walked in, his pals not far behind. Meanwhile, a guard had caught sight of Franz's getaway truck across the street. When flashlights had cast their beams on him, Franz knew he was surrounded. The gig was up.

The thieves hadn't resisted arrest. According to Walter Cronkite, the intervention had been quick and nimble.

No one mentioned Rolf; his name never made the news. But early on, Rolf had smelled a fish and had advised the Met's director.

"I don't trust this guy," Rolf said to the museum's top brass. "From stories I had heard about him in Italy, I knew he was a cad."

Rolf and the museum staff kept quiet until the day of the heist. They had called the police, secured extra help, and saved the museum from theft. It was a carefully executed counter-plot in order to ensnare the thugs.

In the arraignment, Franz pointed a finger at Donato in the hope of getting a deal. After all, he said, without the Carracci that Donato had carried from Naples, they could never have planned the heist. He added that Donato had hidden the Carracci and other works of art for nearly thirty years.

"It was deliberate," Franz's lawyer said. "The accused knew to protect the works. He was sure of their market value, and he brought them to the Kälins. The Carracci trade was only one of many planned."

The authorities, with evidence of probable cause, secured a warrant to enter Donato's abode. Donato spent the days in jail.

"When we searched the premises, we found eight verified Renaissance drawings in a bedroom closet," read the text that members of the Asset Recovery Unit had prepared.

The brothers' lawyer accused Donato as being their ringmaster.

"It really wasn't our fault," the brothers said; "after all, we were working for this man."

In court, Donato was charged as leader of the pack. The FBI said he had supplied material for the crime. They used phrases like "custody and concealment," "efforts to defraud." "Objects of cultural heritage," they said, referring to the Carracci painting and drawings.

"It is a violation of federal law to transport or receive stolen goods valued at more than $5,000 through foreign or interstate commerce," the lawyers for the FBI declared in the downtown courthouse.

"This is part of an international crime ring that has been going on for decades," the court said.

The FBI collaborated with the Italian Carabinieri's office in charge of cultural heritage. These authorities had never located the stolen works lost during the war, but now with Donato's cache, their search was beginning to open wide. The original canvas and sketches had been stored in an apartment in Upper Manhattan, the papers reported. No doubt about their authenticity, this indeed was the "very real thing." There were probably many more, the authorities suggested.

"The provenance is stated in each work," the lawyers maintained. "The records match. But more important, the artwork is expert, leaving no doubt as regards authentication."

"For thirty years," one lawyer said, "this conniving thief kept Renaissance art in his apartment. Not only did he help the Kälins in their plan to defraud the Met, but he also had a history of transporting art from Naples."

From under her bed, Rosie retrieved Eugenia's money, which she had kept in a shoe box. She was glad she had transferred the lire to dollars years ago. At least they still held some worth.

She used the money to hire two attorneys to represent Donato in court. But they couldn't get Donato a fair deal. The DA's office then took over the case, but these lawyers also failed to defend him. For the time, Donato's case was doomed. Here, enters Rolf Zwilling in order to save the day.

"This man is innocent," Rolf declared before judge and attorneys. "I heard of him while I lived in Naples. He was duped by Eugenia, but his record was basically clean."

"Why are you telling us this? What's your motivation?" asked the judge.

Rolf's words were persuasive. "He has no trace of dishonor. Ignorant of the art world, he kept these artworks in his home as a favor both to Silvio and to his less meritorious agent in Naples."

Only because of Rolf's testimony and because Donato had had no prior convictions, the judge let Donato go free. "We have an innocent man," the judge declared, much to Donato and Rosie's relief. But when *The Daily News* published the story, Donato wanted to crawl in his shell and die.

12.

In the late 1960s, Donato still carried memories of his legal ordeal. He didn't serve a sentence—just a couple of nights in jail—but he suffered irreparable harm. As Rosie observed many times over, Donato emerged a broken man. "We were painting partners," he repeated dumbfounded referring to Günther. "We met at the river and inhaled the same air. We shared ideas about art and life. Then he betrayed me."

Donato repeated himself like a Victrola whose stylus bounces over a record's grooves. For a time after the art heist, he rehearsed the scenes of Günther's visits. The children were bored to hear the story for the umpteenth time. But now, many years after the crisis, Rosie shot up a new detail.

"Well, now I have a story that hasn't made the evening news," Rosie said.

Last night, she said, she found her mother's stash of letters hidden in an old suitcase Rosie had planned to discard. The letters had been folded in the sleeves of winter coats that reeked of years-old camphor. Rosie withdrew a few envelopes bearing stamps from Naples. "Both sisters may be gone, but their words have a life of their own." She waved Eugenia's letters before her husband and children. "I just discovered these documents. I wish I had had them at time of the trial."

"Years ago, Eugenia had colluded with Franz Kälin. She didn't tip him off just once. Rather, over the years she had advised him in detail about ways to profit from Silvio's art in New York—not only those works that Donato had carried, but also many pieces that had been transported by other friendly travelers. It seems Eugenia cleaned out the Bellanera church vaults where Silvio had hidden his paintings. And Silvio didn't know a thing. Later, in correspondence with the Kälins, she also gave them ideas about where they could sell Silvio's paintings.

It was she who suggested the substitution game at the Met and gave Franz Kälin a forceful nudge. Here, read for yourselves."

But no one cared to read.

"The crooks had no research to do; Eugenia set up the cards and helped them lay their treacherous plans. Of course, they didn't enact the heist until well after Eugenia's death."

"And she wrote this to Mariarosa?" Donato asked.

"She was begging forgiveness. Guilt plagued her," Rosie said. "She thought death was upon her. And, in fact, it was."

Donato said, "I have no patience for Eugenia's confessions. She's no better than her father."

Here Rosie closed the chapter: "The apple doesn't fall far from the tree."

The Narrators

"Look," Rosanna said to Max. "Before you continue any longer, you need to know what I'm up to. I won scholarship money to go to Buenos Aires. And I'm going to leave this summer."

A deep pause. A pause bloated and full like the moment when gas pinches down on your belly. A pause like when the projector breaks in the movie house, and you have to wait in the dark. A pause like when the IRT stops between stations in summer, and you think that you'll die for lack of air. Max finally spoke.

"So, the princess is leaving the palace?" He was now well into his third beer. "Yeah, like when you were going to Italy in high school and then chickened out at the final moment?"

An additional gratuitous dig.

Silence, this time on Rosanna's part. She swelled not from food, but from rage.

"I'm the chicken? Like the brainy guy who can't channel himself toward anything useful? Who can't even leave the neighborhood to go to community college? Who's the real chicken here, little brother? Reading *Ulysses* alone under the sheets at night because no teacher knows more than you? I'm going. I'm leaving. Talked it over with the parents this morning, and I have their blessings. You think you're going to stop me? Good luck, buddy." More silence, then *agita* followed by electric shocks to the nerves. Rosanna felt a light-tapping buzz fill the room.

"Look, big girl, I'm not saying that you should stay home. What's more important, it seems to me, is that you finish what you've been writing."

Rosanna's ears were exploding. The novel she'd been working on for three years was a family saga. Her book was the road between past and present, and the whole family was waiting to read it, but all too often her manuscript was a heap of crumbling stones. "This is my story, and I will tell it at my own pace. I have the tools and the know-how to write it, here or in Argentina."

"Right," Max said. "But you'll be lost without me."

He walked out of the room in search of another beer.

* * * *

It was her sentence, she thought, to listen to her brother's babble. Max, after all, did have an eye for literature; he had a quick mind for detail. In the long term, he had claimed the roles of scholar and scribe. It was time for her to flee.

He walked off to the kitchen to look for something to drink.

Awaiting his return, Rosanna looked for a place of comfort. She imagined steam expanding in her head. Steaming, she felt her temperature rising. Steaming, she resented her brother's clarity especially when he was three sheets to the wind.

Sitting on the edge of the sofa, Rosanna ran her hand over her mother's Duncan Phyfe table, her fingers opening a one-way street through the dust shading a once-perfect veneer. Not that the house was filthy, but her mother was getting tired, less attentive than before, which probably explained why she put doilies on the tables: not only to protect the furniture from Max's beer cans, still wet from Frigidaire frost, but also to cover the ashes that had dulled the mahogany varnish.

"It used to be," her mother would say time and again, "when you bought nice furniture, the repair man came once a year to touch up the stains and scratches. That's all in the past, of course. But I still remember who did what: your brother left a beer can here, and Zi' Mike burned the table when his cigarette slipped from the ashtray. Over there, your father dragged a cuff link across the mahogany surface. It's like writing, don't you think? They all signed their names on my tables."

Rosanna didn't want to think about mahogany anymore. Worse, she didn't want to believe that her mother was using tropes of lit. crit. while referring to household stains. Rosie and her brother Max were always invading her sphere. Signing? Oh, give-me-a-break!

When Max returned, she listened to him with half an ear as she sifted through the end-table drawers' contents. Each compartment held folders of family photos. In the first packet, dated 1900-1920, she found her great-grandfather holding a flask of wine. Then a studio portrait of her grandmother Mariarosa who was holding her baby Rosie while her young son Joe stood at her side. Following, an undated photo of Farfariello on stage (why was his picture here at all? Perhaps her grandparents had seen him in a show? No telling). In another envelope marked "1938," she saw souvenirs that her father had gathered on his trip to Italy: the family wishing Donato a bon voyage; a shot from a deck on the Rex; a sketch of Mussolini and Hitler on the cover of *Il Mattino*; a picture of Lenin at Capri; a photo of Donato's nieces Maria and Raffaella dressed as peasants; Zi'Annibale and family at the dinner table. Then there were heaps of photos in a folder marked "Rosie": Donato and Rosie posing in a park; Rosie and Dora; Bill in his army khakis; a birthday party with the New York family.

Rosanna was thinking that each time you opened a folder of photographs, strange characters bounced into action: some people were distracted or feeling sad, others were laughing. You never knew what was really going on in each picture and you had to invent a story. On the verso of some of the older pictures, she saw a postcard's structure. Under the words "*cartolina postale*" was a lined block for an addressee and an empty block for a greeting. Rosanna liked those relatives from long ago who sent their image across the sea. They were proud to be seen, she thought; their pictures had something to say. Remember me; I'm thinking of you; don't forget my face. Probably the elders on the other side never saw their children again.

"Don't get so pensive," Max said. "Family photography was a pastime. No deep thinking required."

"Don't dismiss it. In those days, no one had a telephone. Just an occasional letter or picture." It was odd, she thought, that there were no photos of Eugenia. The family beauty, the person most concerned with image, Eugenia had never sent a photo of herself; only a trove of letters. Perhaps her image on the bottle of bitters had been enough to define her presence. Perhaps she was embarrassed by so much self-promotion.

"It was her history, not yours," Max said.

Rosanna scratched her toe. "But it's my job to put it together." She tried to remember her brother's Oscar Wilde quote, something about our duty to rewrite history. But history in this instance was just a person with a smile or a knitted brow dressed in a particular outfit. Behind it, a truckload of secrets.

"You're too focused on finding a story," Max said.

"But isn't that the point of photography? To let people see an image and, from that, to invent a past?"

"More sentimentality, sister. Perhaps it's time to grow up?"

No wonder all the women in the family suffered from migraines, Rosanna thought. Her head was about to explode. This man was driving her crazy. Making fun of her research. It was really just too much.

Max began speaking about Joyce (as if Rosanna cared). While his friends read stories from *Dubliners,* Max took a turn with *Ulysses.* The novel bowled him over, he said. He liked the way it sounded; he liked the first character to appear in the book. "A man of my heart, Buck Mulligan. You could rewrite the opening line of *Ulysses* as 'Lanky, tall Max Cósimo.'" He laughed at his own cleverness.

"It's my brother passing as Buck." She groaned and pretended to look away. "Another way to put me down."

Rosanna didn't want to hear any more about language tricks, the ways in which Joyce managed time. She really had no interest, especially now as she prepared for her trip.

* * * *

She remembered something one of her Spanish professors had said. "You can't study literature by watching television." Professor Genio had been imposing his grand authority on her diminished sense of self.

"Okay, okay. Perhaps you're right."

Rosanna's professor had helped her line up contacts in libraries and bookstores in Buenos Aires.

"But I want to study women writers," she'd told him.

"Forget the women. Look up Roberto Arlt," Professor Genio had said. "He recorded the violence of the lower classes, the fight for survival that defines those on the edge. Very powerful stuff."

Everyone giving advice, Rosanna thought: Max at home and this guy on campus. To study the lower classes, she had only to look at her family. Besides, in the age of Betty Friedan, it was time to speak about women. The personal was political, she kept repeating as if riding the feminist wave. Of course, she wouldn't say it aloud for fear of her professor's reprisals.

"Forget Professor Genio's mandate. Forget my brother," she said in a quiet voice as she descended the stairs from the family apartment in order to reach the street. "It's time to travel out."

The weeks passed and Rosanna made a copy of her novel to stuff in her luggage. She left the original text with her brother and asked him to keep it wrapped in foil in the freezer for long-term protection.

Max had never heard anything quite so stupid but promised to stand guard by the fridge.

IV. New York–Buenos Aires

1.

On the flight to Argentina, Rosanna imagined meeting writers who would treat her like a queen. She would visit Borges at his café in Recoleta (she hoped he was still alive). She thought about Julio Cortázar (forgetting he lived in Paris). She thought she would visit the tango haunts. She'd learn to sip tea from a gourd. She'd have pizzas and ziti with Sunday sauce in the neighborhoods south of the city. Maybe she'd learn about soccer.

"The pictorial kitsch of travel," Rosanna said to the man seated beside her as both watched a travel video showing Iguazú Falls. He nodded.

"*Buena estadía, señorita*," he said as the plane rolled to a halt on the tarmac.

Rosanna followed the typed-out instructions that Professor Genio had thrust in her hand. Taxi from airport to city, money-changing stores, the address of a lady who had promised to rent her a room. She took a deep breath and started this new adventure, all the while trying to push aside her father's admonitions. "It's a dangerous time over there," she remembered he had told her. "Secret police and nasty leaders." Max had corrected his father by saying that difficult times had passed. The dirty war against citizens no longer mattered. "It's safe now, Pop. It's 1985 and the bad guys have been defeated. So don't worry; she'll be fine." And though Rosanna tried to cling to Max's sunny version of the news, she still heard Donato's warning, "You'd better stay out of trouble. Watch your every word."

In Buenos Aires, she moved into a señora's apartment on Callao and Santa Fe. A comfortable place, centrally located, with good heat in the June–July winters, the home was maintained by a savvy old woman who knew the lay of the land. She introduced Rosanna to her neighbor Eduardo, saying he would answer all her questions. Rosanna panicked. What to ask him? What to share? How to figure out the topics that would make her look good? She didn't understand much of the culture, but the smoking awed her.

"So easy, here—no restraints. No one stigmatized for their habits. You can smoke in bars and restaurants, even at the movies." Rosanna added that she liked to buy packs of cigarettes that came without a Surgeon General's warning. "People here must live forever," she said to her new acquaintance.

Eduardo grimaced but kept his cool. This unknown woman rambled on about nothing and showed no political interest in the current state of affairs. To pass the time, he reminded her of a tango Sara Montiel made famous: "Smoking is a pleasure, genial and sensual. Smoking is my Eden as I wait for the man I love!"

Exhaling smoke, Rosanna smiled thinking of Max, who might like this city's freedom. She tried to explain this idea to Eduardo who laughed.

Rosanna was puzzled by his response. She didn't know that he thought her a fool but was relieved when the meeting was over. The next day, she headed out to meet the Troiano family, whose story she had planned to pair with her own.

* * * *

When Rosanna knocked on the apartment door and asked for Maria Antonietta Troiano, the young woman who answered was clearly taken aback. "Why, Maria Antonietta died many years ago. Her daughter, Costanza, survives her and lives here with her adult children and me."

Rosanna received this with shock. No one had bothered to alert the New York branch of the clan of their aunt's death in Buenos Aires. Now it was Costanza, Maria Antonietta's widowed daughter, who tried to run the family compound, but as she was often immersed in a sea of forgetfulness, she kept Paula there as a caretaker to lend a hand. After the initial introductions, Paula escorted Rosanna to the living room sofa and went off to prepare the afternoon tea. As she waited, Rosanna noticed a resemblance to her parents' apartment. Modest layout, noisy pipes, a kitchen without too much light, a sofa covered in plastic, stains on the parquet floors. The TV console acted as display case for the many souvenirs that her grandmother Mariarosa must've sent to her Argentine sister: a cup with a stenciled image of the 1939 World's Fair, an Empire State Building in a snow globe, a reproduction of an olive-green Statue of Liberty perched on a shiny white cube. Perhaps as the family watched Sunday soccer games, they imagined the opportunities that life might have brought them had they chosen to land at a Mulberry Street flophouse instead of the Buenos Aires Immigrants Hotel.

After Rosanna had met Costanza and her children, she saw that the new relations were truly happy to meet her. This was the first time someone had come to visit from New York. They embraced her warmly and served tea and pastries as part of a late-afternoon Argentine ritual.

Trying to sound informed, Rosanna referred to the topics Eduardo had recently mentioned: inflation, police corruption, disappeared workers dragged from their homes in the quiet of night, the scary presence of unmarked police cars that roamed the streets looking for trouble. But Costanza and her family expressed no particular interest.

"We're beyond these questions," Costanza's children remarked. "We're trying to straddle normal and normal."

When Rosanna asked about the protests of the Mothers in the Plaza (amply covered in the US news), Costanza's children said that those were Yankee rumors designed to humble the nation. "Forget the nonsense Jimmy Carter told you," they said. "Here, we're human and we're right!"

The family then turned the conversation to soccer, but Rosanna was too distracted to listen.

Sensing Rosanna's discomfort, Paula changed the topic, "My grandmother Lelé had been Maria Antonietta's best friend and was regarded as part of the family. On Sunday afternoons, after they'd washed the luncheon dishes and their husbands had settled down for their naps, the ladies devoted themselves to card games of '*casita robada*' and sipped on Fernet-Branca. Maria Antonietta told me that as neighbors they shared a special love."

"How did you come into this household?" Rosanna asked.

"Tragedy always takes over. When I was a child, my mother and grandmother were in a dreadful accident. They were hit by a truck that overturned on the sidewalk, and I lost them. Maria Antonietta raised me as one of her own. Can you imagine the debt that I hold? So now I stay on to help with the household chores."

Paula had studied literature but because of the local circumstances, she rarely found work as a teacher. "When the economy is tough, as it always is in this country, you have to seek a job as caretaker or cook. And giving a hand to the family is better than teaching at a crummy high school in faraway Santos Lugares. I still have time to read novels and, if the whim so moves me, to write a story or two. This is far better than nothing."

Paula, it was clear, was the family's ears and eyes. From what Rosanna could tell, she was the household's most lucid person. Rosanna inquired about Carmelo.

"This requires a little background," Paula said. She began to explain Troiano family history as if it were her own. Costanza, who was hard of hearing, did her best to listen in. The other adults were bored and simply left the room.

2.

"Maria Antonietta traveled to Buenos Aires at the turn of the century. She and her husband then set up a cheese store in Barracas and rented an apartment nearby. Within weeks of her arrival, María Antonietta had learned enough Spanish to make herself understood. 'The transition between tongues was easy,' Maria Antonietta always said to her family."

With a certain twinkle in her eye, Paula added, "I have to agree. More than anything else, the difference between Italian and Spanish is only a matter of stress and a couple of verbs. Soon Maria Antonietta left the Italian tongue behind, reserving it for the funerals and weddings her countrymen often attended. By the time her children had come of age, she only conversed in Spanish and made sure to tell them how she kept politics out of her life.

"'I always kept my nose clean,' she used to say. I think Maria Antonietta carried that rule from her hometown in Italy."

"That's funny," Rosanna said. "The relatives from Italy weren't exactly honest."

"You're right. Later I heard about Maria Antonietta's father and Antonio, her crooked brother. But as years went on, Maria Antonietta forgot about family crime over there. She used to tell me that life in Argentina gave her license to start clean." Paula smiled and looked around, making sure none of the family was within earshot. "Everything was running smoothly, the cheese store was turning a profit, the kids were thriving. Life was good. Then—all of a sudden—Maria Antonietta received the shock of her life. In October, 1920 she received a letter from Mariarosa saying that Carmelo was on his way to Buenos Aires."

* * * *

"'*Oh Dio*! After more than twenty years, my baby brother will be at my door,' she said. Then in anticipation of his arrival, she prepared various plates of southern Italian treats to remind Carmelo of home. She gave me all the details, but now they slip my mind.

"When she saw him entering the apartment, Maria Antonietta said that she had taken Carmelo's hand, squeezed his cheeks, and kissed his eyelids. She had wept like never before.

"'This is too good to be true,' María Antonietta had said.

"Carmelo arrived tired by all of his losses. He described how twenty years prior, he'd stood at Zia Cristina's door waiting to embrace his brother. But Antonio wasn't there. He described the aching loneliness of living in New York, his years searching for his brother and sister, and his repeated disappointments.

"Maria Antonietta told me that Carmelo standing in her doorway had appeared as a large and awkward man who had wanted to keep to himself. He was unlike the little brother whom she'd left behind in Bellanera. He was morose, she told me. She thought that he couldn't find his heart, which made her feel helpless.

"She asked him how Mariarosa was, and Carmelo rushed through his answer, disregarding Maria Antonietta's emotion. He said that he hadn't had much contact with their New York sister and had only met her briefly during his final year in New York.

"He also had little to say about his big brother Antonio. 'Carmelo's lips seemed oddly sealed.'

"'I knew more about the New Yorkers than he did,' Maria Antonietta told me.

"Within weeks after settling him in, Maria Antonietta's children began to notice that Carmelo was strange. He barely spoke.

"'What's with this guy?' they asked. 'He spends his days reading magazines, his anger flares, and then he goes silent.'

"Carmelo had no appreciation of the household's goings-on, Maria Antonietta said. So she didn't feel that she needed to dote on him. Her habit was to play cards with the lady next door. That was a certain Señora Brava. Maria Antonietta said she would complain about her brother while Señora Brava talked about her son, a kid who was a neighborhood thief and had a big reputation. He duped the butchers at the market, stealing sides of beef and pork. Then he sliced them up and sold steak and ribs to the neighbors.

"In hush-hush tones in the kitchen, the women talked money day and night.

'Wouldn't you like to swim in a tub of centavos that pressed against your body?'

'I'd rather wade in the ocean and touch the silver that bobs on the surface.'

'Coins twinkling in sunlight, imagine that.'

'It makes me think of diamonds rubbing on my body.'

"Carmelo listened to the women's chatter as they played cards in the kitchen, but he began to feel excluded. He even told Maria Antonietta that he'd been left out of a private joke.

"Maria Antonietta and her husband put Carmelo to work at their cheese store. But in the store, Carmelo was also snooping, always with his ear to the ground. Maria Antonietta thought that her brother was putting his nose in her affairs. As she explained the situation, she had to maintain her household, which involved what today we'd call a black-market money exchange. But Maria Antonietta thought of it in simpler terms, and Señora Brava offered to help her.

"One afternoon, Carmelo accused his sister of being tricky. The customers would give a large bill to pay for an order of provolone and soprasatta. She would retreat to the back room for a while and then she'd emerge with bright new bills to complete the sale. The customers took what was due them, smiled, and went on their way.

"Maria Antonietta regarded this transaction as a little fib. She'd bought the bills from Señora Brava, who had sold them to her at a discount.

"Then, a few days later, at home, Carmelo overheard Señora Brava quarreling with his sister. Señora Brava was asking her to pay more for the counterfeit bills by saying the rates had increased: now it would be sixty centavos for every peso. Maria Antonietta protested, claiming that this new exchange would cut into her profits.

"Carmelo accused her of dealing in counterfeit trade, of behaving like their father.

"Things got worse."

* * * *

"When Maria Antonietta expected a shipment of rice and polenta, she called Señora Brava to deliver her 'weekly gift.' Soon the neighbor came into Maria Antonietta's kitchen with a stack of bills concealed in folded paper. The following day, in the store, Maria Antonietta opened the same brown wrapper and withdrew a bunch of cash to pay the delivery man. When the dairy man came with cheese and milk, Maria Antonietta reached into the kitty she kept hidden in the back of her store and produced a handful of starched new bills. The gestures were repeated; usually they occurred on the day after Maria Antonietta had met with Señora Brava.

"Carmelo was troubled, Maria Antonietta had said. He'd traveled to Argentina to escape the police, yet here he found his sister and neighbor in the business of making jack. His sister's habits annoyed him; he had said that they raised suspicions. By then, everything bothered Carmelo. His sister's household décor also drove him up the wall: the ornamentation, the calendars of saints hanging on doors, the artificial flowers dipped in hardware paint. It reminded him of Baciagalupo's funeral home, he told his sister. But that really wasn't the issue.

"Carmelo didn't like it one bit that his sister was trafficking in phony bills. She said that she always pushed back. Lots of bickering and so forth until one day, in a fit of anger, Carmelo complained about the magazines that Maria Antonietta had left on the kitchen table.

"'Look at this!' He held up a copy of *La patria degli italiani*, 'The magazine is a hoax! It pretends to serve Italians in Argentina, but it doesn't give a damn about workers. I'm not reading this stuff anymore. In this country, no one wants Italians from Italy, people who work with their hands. Instead, they want a Marconi or a musician like Toscanini. These stories make me ill.' Then Maria Antonietta said he had cleared them from the table with a single swipe of his hand.

"Maria Antonietta told me she was afraid. She could see that fire had filled his body. To calm him she had tried to explain the value of the magazines. She said, to give an example, that the women's section always gave good household hints. 'There are tips for cleaning rugs and polishing the silver, not to mention a focus on women's style and ads for good shops in the city,' she had told him. 'Which shoes to select at Harrod's, which outfits to see at Gath and Chaves, how to spruce up last year's dresses by applying Colibri dye.' She told me that she remembered that her voice had sounded like a radio announcement pitched to ladies on Saturday nights. But Carmelo didn't buy it.

"Carmelo was disgusted, she told me. Screaming, Carmelo said that the last thing we needed were instructions on how to shop and buy ridiculous things.

"Maria Antonietta feared his roar. To please him, she brought in new material for reading. How-to-fix-it magazines, weekly publications on political topics, penny dreadfuls bought for ten cents apiece at the newspaper kiosk downstairs.

"Carmelo seemed to calm down. He began to read what his sister brought home. He took a liking to *Caras y Caretas* and largely looked at the pictures of human curiosities the magazine always carried. Maria Antonietta was surprised that Carmelo would spend his time reading about Argentine weirdos. There were stories about men who dressed like women, about Indians who lived far away in the mountains. He liked to share the stories with his sister and with his nieces and nephews. 'There's nothing like this in Italy,' he said to Maria Antonietta. 'Not even in New York.'

"He clipped magazine stories about Mapuche chieftains; he became interested in the dinosaur tracks that someone had uncovered in the Andes mountains; he followed the story of Ceferino Namuncurá, an Indian from the pampas who had traveled to Italy to study religion.

"'Ceferino's classmates were awful. They bullied him at first and then tried to drive him away. All in the name of God,' he told his sister's children over a dinner of *past' e fagiol'*. Some of the kids thought Carmelo was trying to pry the family away from the church; others protested Carmelo's moral voice. He didn't like them to make fun of the Indians. But what was the big deal? What was it to them?

"'Everyone slurped their soup and looked suspiciously at their uncle,' Maria Antonietta said.

"Carmelo droned on. She remembered him telling the plot of a story: 'Feeling awful, Ceferino asked the archbishop for a transfer. He wanted to study in Turin, and his request was quickly approved. In Italy, Ceferino was a trophy; the priests put him on display much like the Indians who had been taken to Europe by Christopher Columbus. When Ceferino reached Turin, he fell ill and died. They sent his bones back to Argentina where people hoped to enshrine them."

"'Everyone knows this stuff, Tío Carmelo,' one child said. 'Pass me a piece of bread.'

"In private, the children complained about their uncle. 'Ma, I can't take it anymore. Dinner time is Tío's story time.'

"'Let him talk,' Maria Antonietta said. 'It's the only thing that calms him.'

"But each time Carmelo told a different story about Ceferino, the children made faces and pouted.

"One night when Carmelo went out, Maria Antonietta gave her children a stern lesson. 'Look, Carmelo sees himself in Ceferino. He thinks of himself as a martyr. Just let him go on, give him some space. And everybody, *zitti*. Shut up!'

"Carmelo was disgusted with Buenos Aires. No friends, no allies, no family to trust. 'These people are like strangers,' he said to his sister. 'I should have stayed in jail with Caminita.' Shortly thereafter, he quit working in his sister's store and explained that he'd gotten a print job in nearby San Telmo.

"His sister was surprised, though, in fact, she was somewhat relieved to get rid of her dead-cow brother. He also told her that he'd started acting classes in a nearby studio.

"No one knew what to believe. How could a drip like Carmelo be an actor?

"Carmelo then explained that in his years in New York he'd learned something about scripts and performance. 'I really enjoyed it then and now I'd like to resume my training,' he said.

"Maria Antonietta was surprised to hear the upbeat comments.

"One night, Carmelo announced that he was leaving. He told the family that he was going to work as an actor and planned to travel south. Maria Antonietta was happy to let him go.

"Carmelo was hush-hush about his travels. Only later did the family learn that he'd been involved in something that Maria Antonietta could never abide. Carmelo had gone to the Patagonian sheep farms to help the rural workers. These men—some came from Spain and Ireland, others from Germany and Italy—had planned an uprising against their bosses to demand fair wages and safety. Luck would have it that Carmelo wasn't around the day the Army arrived at the ranches of Santa Cruz province. The Argentine generals moved in and shot nearly six hundred workers and ordered many others to prison. Carmelo escaped because he'd been sent to Río Gallegos to search for replacement parts for the printing press. He then returned to his family.

"Carmelo found himself depressed, and the only thing that revived him was the Firpo-Dempsey fight he heard on Radio Cultura.

"'Firpo, *el Toro de las pampas*,' he moaned, 'was betrayed by the capitalist state. The triumph of the rich over the poor once again.'

"'What do you mean, Carmelo? After all, it's only a sport,' Maria Antonietta said. 'So why make such a big deal?'

"Despite her commanding words, his sister lacked the slightest insight about Carmelo's goings-on. Carmelo wasn't a macho man, he lacked all interest in sports, and he really cared less when one of his nephews became a star of Argentine soccer. But this Firpo fight really roiled him; it heated up his blood.

"'The refs threw the game to Dempsey by giving him extra seconds.' Carmelo was reading the paper to his sister and turned Sunday-sauce red.

"Maria Antonietta saw the throbbing veins in his temples. To calm the situation, she tried to distract Carmelo by playing the radio theater station.

"'There are so many radio programs that warm the heart,' she said. 'Stories of gauchos riding through the night or playing folk songs on their guitars, tales about treasures hidden in the cordillera or buried under ice in Tierra del Fuego.'

"She wanted Carmelo to find himself, to lose his moody ways, to put his wrath aside, but she knew he was a loner and there wasn't much to be done. Carmelo became somber and secretive; he usually kept to himself. Maria Antonietta couldn't figure out a thing. First, he was a dead head, then he studied acting, after that he traveled south. Then he returned to Buenos Aires and made a fuss about a boxing match because he said it showed signs of unfairness. 'Sounds *pazzo*,' she told me.

"For her, the stable lines of truth began to blur and fly. Like sheets on a clothesline on a windy fall day, questions fluttered in the air. Where had Carmelo gone when he'd left for the south? Was he really involved in a theater group? When he'd returned to Buenos Aires, where had he spent his evenings? Maybe Carmelo had a girlfriend, but his gloomy late-night pacing in his sister's home left little room for romantic ideas. Was he an artist? A man of political conviction? Or simply a loner? For Maria Antonietta, it was hard to tell.

"While his sister studied his bad behavior, Carmelo gave in to his sadness. 'After all is said and done,' he had written in a diary that his sister later read, 'the only family that has given me help, that has lifted my spirits, are comrades of the anarchist enclaves.'"

3.

In the present time of Rosanna's visit, Carmelo is simply a rumor. It's difficult to discover the truth, Rosanna thought, but she wanted to know more. She returned to her rented room and typed like mad. This new string of anecdotes certainly added to her novel, but now she struggled to get the syntax right since so many voices and times had overlapped in Paula's tale. After a few days' absence, Rosanna returned to the Troiano house to hear more from Paula whose fondness for the American traveler was growing day by day. A bite to eat, a round of yerba mates, and many late afternoon smokes. Paula, now called Paulina, continued her tale.

"So Carmelo returned from Patagonia. For a while, he was somewhat blue; he rarely had much to say. Then one day, Carmelo came home with some news. 'Hey, I got a typesetting job at a publishing house. A man named Zamora took me on. I told him of my work up north and he seemed to be impressed.'

"'*Fatti onore,*' Maria Antonietta said in praise of her brother. Nevertheless, as soon as he reported that he was going to work for a big-time press called *Claridad,* her face went pickle-puss sour. Maria Antonietta thought it was communist stuff and wanted nothing to do with it.

"'You'd better not bring any of that political stuff home,' Maria Antonietta said to Carmelo. 'I don't want to see a thing with that *Claridad* stamp. They're reds, you know. I saw it in the Sunday news.'

"Carmelo ignored his sister. And even though she despised *Claridad,* Maria Antonietta always leafed through her brother's papers. She was thrilled when she found *Claridad*'s sex manuals—how-to-do-it books, so to speak. Stories about sexual perversions, how to live with venereal illness, how to punish a wayward lover, different positions for making love. When Carmelo left the little books in the bathroom, she removed them and read them too. Maria Antonietta never discussed their contents—no one seems to remember—but years later the family found some of the books stuffed in her drawer.

"The dog-eared quality of the pages might prove that Maria Antonietta was an avid reader," Paulina noted and showed a few copies to Rosanna.

"Don't you think it was Carmelo who read this stuff in detail?" Rosanna asked.

"Nope. It had to be María Antonietta because she wrote notes in the margins. We all recognized her hand."

* * * *

Carmelo became increasingly involved with *Claridad* and began to associate with a group of artists who were its offshoot.

"Hey, the guy knows how to do layout and he knows typesetting to a tee," Vigo said to Riganelli. "You're hot stuff, Carmelo. Where did you learn how to do this?"

Carmelo began to trust these pals who reminded him of the New Jersey crowd. Slowly, he unfolded some of his Paterson stories when they went to a bar in the evenings.

"Oh wow," Bellocq said as he sipped a late-night whiskey. "You were really in the thick of it. You met Bresci and Malatesta?"

But Carmelo really wanted to discuss his interest in theater. "I used to work at an amusement park where I wrote and performed a few skits. Then under Caminita's tutelage, I began to improve my writing."

Riganelli offered to give Carmelo a hand. "Maybe we can help you, Carmelo. There are lots of theater venues here, especially in the south of the city."

Carmelo explained that he'd carried some of his work from New York. He had playbills, scripts, and newspaper clippings about the theater he liked. "I even have my one-liner jokes and some ideas for vaudeville performance."

"We can take a look if you like," Vigo said.

"It's better if we introduce you to some people who work in theater," offered Tuñón.

While Carmelo worked in the press by day, he developed theatrical sketches by night. He enjoyed Buenos Aires immigrant theater, particularly the work of two brothers who wrote skits about Italians who'd settled in Argentina. These plays had lots of humor and raw jokes about immigrants' struggles. Carmelo told Riganelli that they reminded him of the one-act plays that he'd seen at the picnics in New Jersey.

After a lot of hesitation, Carmelo finally announced that he'd completed a play. He was hoping to produce it if a small venue would accept him.

"Let's take a look, Carmelo," his buddies said. Carmelo was shy but his friends encouraged him.

"The play is called *Sonata Elegiaca*. It's about a rich man named Parson who, although married, is in love with a red-haired woman named Lillian Owen. The play takes place in an industrial city. I tried to set it in Rosario, but when I wrote the first draft, I placed the action in New York."

"So let's hear the plot."

"Parson proves himself to be a card-carrying member of the industrial bourgeoisie and, prompted by his wife, he turns his back on Lillian and calls the police to arrest her. The cops take Lillian and her comrades away, and she later dies in prison. It's a story with lots of bitter laughter about those who blindly trust the bosses. It's a story about betrayal. What do you think?"

"So far so good."

Carmelo went home to practice his play and even shared his ideas with his sister.

"It sounds interesting," she said. "Is the leading lady supposed to be the Irish girlfriend you told me about?"

Carmelo was frustrated that his sister was after the same old topic: when was he going to find a girl? It was a waste of time to talk about anything else with her.

The men at work introduced him to some guys who ran a tiny theater in La Boca, a neighborhood south of the city. They used volunteer actors and worked late at night. After a few months, the performance was ready. Carmelo became excited. He even invited his family. The play was a success.

"Bravo, bravo," the audience roared. Carmelo came out to take a bow. Tears came to his eyes. Vigo and Bellocq embraced him, and Barletta—the theater director—grinned from ear to ear. After the show, the audience waited in the lobby to shake Carmelo's hand. For the first time since his carnival days, Carmelo glowed in self-satisfaction.

Then one night, Carmelo came home drenched in a tub of sadness. "A man from the United States—probably part of the international brigades or a disciple of Malatesta—saw my play."

Maria Antonietta was shocked. This was the first she'd heard of Carmelo's ties to this political world. "*Oime*, dear brother, what are you saying? You're scaring me half to death."

Carmelo was annoyed, "I haven't even begun to tell you." After a pause, he went on. "A guy recalled having seen the same production in a New York theater. He denounced me as a thief."

Maria Antonietta was appalled as Carmelo continued the story.

"Hey, fellow," the man had addressed him.

"*Piacere. Un gusto.*"

Carmelo stood up to greet the stranger.

"Do I know you?" asked Carmelo.

"No, but I know your play."

The man spoke in a mash-up of Spanish, Italian, and English: '*Sono da Niu York*, I used to *pasear por la calle catorce*.' He said he was also involved in anarchist theater and was a big fan of the shows—he used to see all the plays they staged at the Olympic theater. 'That's where I saw Caminita's show so I know what's going on. If you ask me, your play sounds a lot like Caminita's.'

"Yes, Caminita was my roommate. We worked on this show together."

"Oh yeah?" the man said in a broken español-italo-english. "If so, where's his *nome* on the *programma*?"

It was very warm in the theater. Carmelo began to sweat and couldn't breathe. He coughed and reached for his air. Then he coughed some more.

"You know, Caminita is a comrade, and he's also well known in the theater. Wadda you gotta say about that?"

Carmelo looked around, hoping that one of his buddies would come to help him out. He realized he was alone.

"I'm sorry, comrade. There must be some mistake. Caminita gave me permission. In fact, he told me that my work was so good that he'd use it when he had the chance. Maybe Caminita took the script from me."

The story seemed to be changing now. Did Caminita steal from Carmelo? The man in the audience was puzzled for a moment but went back to his original theory that Carmelo had been the thief.

"The man gave his story to the anarchist paper called *La Protesta*, and now my name is splashed all over the news," Carmelo told his sister. "He said I had made up a tale about having lived with Caminita. But the play performed here in Buenos Aires was Caminita's work, he insisted. He said he had seen it performed in the Olympic Theater in Lower Manhattan."

Here, Paulina interrupted the story and turned to Rosanna to ask a question, "Have you ever heard of the Olympic Theater?" Rosanna drew a blank. She needed to go home and write up these details that she never had heard before. All this information about Carmelo as a thief put him in league with his brother Antonio, Rosanna mused; she would have to figure out how to explain this in her novel. Meanwhile, Paulina was eager to continue her story and didn't allow Rosanna to complete her thoughts.

4.

"I really didn't think it was stealing. I thought I was honoring my pal Caminita. Putting his ideas on display, so to speak." After a pause, Carmelo added an extra detail: "And I did all the revisions, so it seemed like it was my own work."

Carmelo was being called a thief of ideas; the artistic community had turned against him. A kind of delirium took over, and Carmelo lost sense of reason. He smoked, he fretted, he paced, his heart pumped so hard that he couldn't think.

"I'll never recover," Carmelo said to his sister. "I want to die."

Maria Antonietta tried to calm him down, "We love you all the same, Carmelo. I'm sure these accusations are false. Relax, take a nap. This too will pass."

Maria Antonietta became obsessed with finding out the truth. She looked through the daily papers for news about the play. Then, she went to the Biblioteca Juan B. Justo—a socialist library for workers in the Caballito neighborhood—and found among the Italian collections Caminita's original play! She slipped the book in her purse and later dumped it in the trash.

"Never make waves, if you can avoid it," she said. "And always cover your tracks."

After taking stock of the terrible news, Maria Antonietta suffered in silence. Then she came up with a different interpretation of facts in order to settle her nerves. And, after all, she loved her little brother so much; he really wasn't bad.

"What's the difference," she asked, "if you present someone else's work without using that person's name? You tinkered with it. You gave it shape. And you gave the original guy the chance to show his stuff in a distant land."

Her words gave Carmelo little comfort. Maria Antonietta had never managed to grasp the worldwide reach of the anarchist project, but she was beginning to see that New York, Buenos Aires, and Italy were barely a breath apart.

Carmelo tried to explain that his life in Buenos Aires was finished. "It's all my fault," he cried.

"No, little brother," she said. "Just keep doing your work." Maria Antonietta told him not to worry; if the play had any bad parts, that was Caminita's fault.

* * * *

Paulina explained the background: "In those years, the playwrights in Argentina had no patience for this mess. In fact, if you look in these folders that Carmelo had assembled over time, you'll see that a woman playwright sent Carmelo to hell and back. Her name was Alfonsina Storni. In the newspapers, this woman exposed the nature of weak and wobbly men who tried to rule the world by robbing the works of women. She wrote that the world of letters had always been dense with thieves, dishonest writers who were especially cavalier when it came to lifting the work of others. She didn't mention Carmelo by name, but she was furious at men in general and the length they'd go to cover the truth. She was incensed by masculine "cowardice" and exposed the "cruelty" of men's behavior. Carmelo thought she was referring to him and then, according to Maria Antonietta, he collapsed in pieces."

Heated by excitement, Rosanna leaned forward in her chair. Right up her alley, she thought. Here was a famous woman writer attacking her uncle Carmelo.

"I can't believe it, *no lo puedo creer,*" Rosanna exclaimed forgetting for the moment about the family romance. "Alfonsina is one of the writers who form part of my dissertation."

Paulina looked puzzled. A woman journalist was no big deal; no one would raise an eyebrow.

"Just another writer from the 1920 and 30s," Paulina said to clear up the mystery.

But Rosanna was giddy. Quickly she explained to Paulina the research project she had at hand, and how her trip to Buenos Aires had been shaped by women writers.

"Is it possible that Carmelo had crossed this woman?"

"Well," Paulina replied, "he was in Buenos Aires for a very long time and had dipped his toes in the arts. No telling. Everything is possible here. Just stay around for a while and watch."

After several hours of conversation, served with tea and little pastries called *masas*, Rosanna noted that her host was tired and thought it best to leave. She promised to return on another day to hear the rest of the story. For now, she needed to go back to her apartment and write up this part of the tale.

5.

Carmelo remained depressed in those years. Embarrassed, he withdrew from the theater world and began to work full time at the press. He secured a job with the Artistas del Pueblo, a group of left-wing artists who ran a weekly publication. Some men in this group refused outright to accept the story of Carmelo's crime. They claimed that all invention of art found its birth in another vessel.

"Originality isn't the point," one said. "Rather, it's how you reach the people, inspiring them to rebel."

Carmelo felt a safe for a time, but he wasn't really happy.

In these years, Carmelo met Del Vecchio, a writer who was part of leftist literary circles. Del Vecchio first began as an anarchist and then became a supporter of Russia. He was always a fly in the political ointment and opposed the conservative regime.

In 1935, Del Vecchio invited Carmelo to travel to Russia to attend a Congress of the Comintern.

"No, I'd rather not do that," Carmelo said. "It's really not my role to stick my nose in this communist business."

Still, their affection for each other prevailed despite the differences between them. Del Vecchio treated Carmelo like family, which meant the earth and the sky to Carmelo. Del Vecchio reminded him of Bresci: he thought he'd found a loving uncle. But this also meant Carmelo had to endure Del Vecchio's speeches.

His buddy's long-winded lectures often involved the history of landowning oligarchs who had defined Argentina through the late-nineteenth century when the immigrants began to arrive. The man was so encyclopedic in scope that Carmelo began to keep notes. Then he would go home and recite everything he'd learned on a given day.

"Hey, Maria Antonietta," Carmelo said. "What was Buenos Aires like when you arrived at the Hotel de Inmigrantes?"

Her brother's question surprised Maria Antonietta. He'd never bothered to ask about her past. He'd simply seemed to take it for granted that his sister had lived in Buenos Aires since the beginning of time. "Why do you want to know?"

"Del Vecchio told me about the city life some forty years ago. Truth is, I've never heard you speak of those times when you first arrived in the city."

Maria Antonietta didn't want to discourage her brother, but she had no patience for empty questions. In the depths of it all, she had really assumed that Carmelo carried no curiosity about her family's life in Argentina. Besides, she didn't want to remember the days when she and husband had been poor and empty-handed. "We're happy to live in the present," she said.

By contrast, Del Vecchio, with his endless speeches, wanted to make sure that Carmelo knew history. Carmelo, to show his own credentials, vaunted his New Jersey triumphs. He told in detail of the anarchist journals, his work with Bresci, and the time that he'd met Malatesta. A flow of names ran through the conversations, but he never discussed Antonio. Nor did he explain his whereabouts the day the Army invaded the Patagonian ranches. Carmelo tried to hold up his protective screen, not letting Del Vecchio pierce his heart. And, as luck would have it, Del Vecchio never bothered to ask for details.

Del Vecchio would let Carmelo read his creative stories, his essays and plays, and in return, Carmelo described the skits that he'd written while he lived in New Jersey.

"How did you get involved in theater?" Del Vecchio asked.

"I had a number of skits that an enterprising theater man thought were worthwhile. He began to produce my work in a theater on the Lower East Side."

Del Vecchio knew that his pal was lying: Carmelo's answers lacked depth.

Carmelo lied when he said he'd staged several plays. He lied when he described his family's heroic deeds in Italy. He said they'd supported brigands and that Carmine Crocco, the brigand leader, was a friend of the family. Carmelo's father, a simple and honest man, had helped plan the king's death. From his years in New Jersey, Carmelo also talked about befriending Pietro Gori, publicly defending Malatesta, supporting Bartolomeo Vanzetti despite the leadership's voice against it. Del Vecchio knew these stories weren't entirely true because Carmelo would slip up on the places and dates. But Del Vecchio figured that Carmelo was an artist and writer, and forgave him his errors.

When he came home, Carmelo would review the day's events with his sister.

"You should be happy," Maria Antonietta said. "Del Vecchio trusts you."

"But he's the only one who wants to listen. Other than that, I'm a failure," Carmelo said. "Everyone else has lost faith in me and doesn't give me the time of day."

"But I'm here. Del Vecchio is here. Life will get better—just wait."

Carmelo brooded and, as had often occurred in New Jersey, he felt as if he were losing his anchor.

Del Vecchio even helped Carmelo line up a few jobs after his recent assignments had fizzled. Then some news people hired Carmelo to write notes on the labor movements: workers in factories, men in the fields, women in public assemblies. He had achieved the role of reporter and artist; still, he was always moody.

"Hey, buddy," Del Vecchio said. "You need to take charge of your life."

6.

The decades passed. In the late-1940s, Carmelo was still plodding along until one day he heard a knock at the door. Silvio had just arrived from Italy and come to visit Maria Antonietta.

"Oh my God, I can't believe it," Silvio said as he embraced his childhood friend. He was thrilled to see his hometown acquaintance and thanked the heavens for their encounter.

"This is a grand moment of luck," Silvio said with high enthusiasm. Carmelo was unimpressed.

"Carmelo, tell me about your life in the United States. Was it exciting? And your life in Buenos Aires?"

"Not great." Carmelo went on to explain some of his losses. He hesitated to trust Silvio, fearful that his old friend might see him as a man condemned to failure.

Silvio said, "But you're here, my pal. We'll have great adventures. Our friendship means so much."

Carmelo thought Silvio exaggerated their connection. After all, Silvio was Eugenia's friend; Carmelo was almost a decade older. In his deepest thoughts, Carmelo saw Silvio as intrusive, perhaps a bit too emotional over nothing.

"How was your trip to Buenos Aires?" Carmelo asked.

"Like every immigrant's voyage, full of fear for what lay ahead."

"Are you starting anew as an artist?"

"I'm not sure. I've brought some canvases with me. I left others in a chapel vault at home. When Donato came to visit before the war, I even gave him my favorite painting to store or sell in New York. I suppose you could say I'm all over the place."

Both men laughed. Carmelo explained that he'd never seen Donato in New York since he'd left in 1920. Donato hadn't arrived until 1922.

Silvio put his arm around Carmelo's shoulder. They walked through the street like brothers. Carmelo's façade of ice and snow slowly began to crack and dissolve.

Silvio told of his losses: his love of Rolf and, before him, Giulio. He spent hours telling Carmelo how much Eugenia's actions had hurt him.

"I don't want to say she betrayed me, but she shook the air from my lungs. You won't believe it, but after I announced my departure from Eugenia's business, my stutter returned. I couldn't get past it until just now, when I reached Buenos Aires."

Carmelo was disturbed to hear that his little sister had fallen from grace. He began to express his disdain, surprised that she would betray her best friend.

"No, please don't be so harsh, Carmelo," Silvio said. "She was trying to survive. Naples after the war wasn't a happy place. She had faith in me as her accomplice and partner, but in fact I acted more like a coward. I couldn't rise to the occasion. I was never very brave."

Carmelo tried to reimagine the scenes between Silvio and Eugenia. Had she turned into a vicious art peddler? Was she simply trying to earn some change? And why was Silvio so syrupy good, so kind in his regard for his sister?

"Look, she was my childhood friend. She helped me set up as an artist. If I have any paintings to show, it's owing to her."

"That's a big debt, I suppose," said Carmelo.

"My biggest fear, and I have to admit it, had to do with the marchands in the art world. A man named Franz Kälin turned the tables for me. At first, he just wanted to buy my work. But then he wanted to take me to Switzerland to be his private painter. He pursued me for years. It sounded like a planned abduction. He wanted to keep me on his estate to make forgeries for a black-market business. The idea was to swap out the reproductions with originals that hung in museums. And, I don't have to tell you, Europe is filled with these shady transactions." Silvio paused. "Maybe nothing would've come of it, but I was scared to death."

Carmelo thought that Silvio had delivered quite a mouthful. A whole life driven by fear. In that sense, they'd led similar lives. It was bad enough to nestle yourself in the anarchist world, Carmelo thought, but international art theft was out of his range.

Silvio wanted to speak of Zwilling.

"My love at the time, Rolf Zwilling, was fed up with the intrigue. He had no patience for Eugenia. And now, in retrospect, I see that he had no patience for me. For my timidity, I mean. So we parted, and I was miserable. Once I was alone, Eugenia upped the ante—selling my reproductions to crooked marchands. I couldn't handle it, and I didn't know how to tell her. But I loved her, perhaps more than I loved Rolf. In so many ways, she was my light and life."

Carmelo was humbled by Silvio's faith in his sister. To change the topic, Carmelo spoke of his days in New York. "My brother's absence still haunts me."

"We need to see this in a different way," Silvio said. "Perhaps through the lens of art. You found art in your theater, in the skits you wrote in New Jersey. Now in Buenos Aires, you have an older comrade to guide you. Don't take all this for granted."

Carmelo nodded. Silvio sounded like a priest. He had the calm of a pastor, Carmelo thought. For all that he'd suffered, he still found joy in his work. "I wish I could be more like you." Carmelo looked Silvio in the eye.

"We're all different, old pal. Just find your peace."

Silvio and Carmelo spoke of art and theater, the state of the world.

"Tell me about your fears, Carmelo. Certainly, I'll tell you mine. You must know that travel makes me nervous and this trip to Buenos Aires ate at my bones."

Carmelo felt the same. However, he couldn't speak of his anguish or losses even though he spoke often about Antonio. Silvio's openness impressed him, his acknowledgement of pain.

"You're trusting and open," Carmelo said. "I apologize if I'm less so. Ever since I left New York, I've lost my confidence in the people around me."

Over time and with patience, Silvio tried to draw out Carmelo.

"Are you religious, Silvio?" Carmelo asked one day as they walked through a city park.

"Not really, but I find a spirit in my work. God is hidden in beauty, and it's my calling to draw him out."

"What do you think about the stories I've told you of Antonio? Do you think my brother is a rat?" Carmelo asked.

"No more of a rat than anyone else. He needed to survive. Learn to forgive and forget." Silvio put his arm around his friend.

They walked through the municipal zoo to see the strange animals of the Southern Hemisphere. Silvio focused on the capybaras that trotted through the park.

"Friendly rodents with square faces. You'd never link them to rats; they're more akin to dogs. I'm inclined to take out a pencil and draw them."

"You like animals? I only went one time to the Central Park Zoo with my good friend Maria. The fact is that I didn't pay attention to the animals. I was completely distracted by the events of the day and my need to speak with Maria."

"The animals give you hope, Carmelo. They teach us the breadth of our being human. The next time we come to the zoo, I'll give you a lesson about these creatures: it's not just the majestic condors, but the little fellows who seek your blessing."

"Saint Francis, eh?" responded Carmelo, somewhat smiling but still in his doldrums. He touched the metal image of the saint that his mother had given him years ago and that he still wore close to his breast.

In time, their roles reversed and Carmelo, losing his inhibitions, came to be Silvio's protector. Carmelo showed Silvio around Buenos Aires and pointed out the highlights. He treated Silvio to modest meals and taught him to sip tea from a gourd.

"I hope you'll like your new home, Silvio. Count on me for all that you need."

And Silvio, bashful, embarrassed, confessed to Carmelo that he hoped to find a job.

It didn't take a great deal of coercion for Carmelo to play the cards in hand. At once, Carmelo took Silvio to meet Del Vecchio and his artist friends and asked them about employment. When the men saw Silvio's portfolio, they scooped him up on the spot. Silvio was adamant that he wanted no political connections. In this sense, he was similar to Maria Antonietta. That said, Del Vecchio saw that Silvio was truly a master artist and should be put to work in the most distinguished venues, politics aside. He agreed not to corner Silvio in any untoward way.

Silvio explained his conversations with the artists whose work he had copied. He described his imitations as acting in sympathy with those artists. "I don't know if you're familiar with the work of Salvator Rosa. He was dreamy and delirious. Many thought he was mad. Well, I found in him a soulmate who had explained to me the meaning of demonic times. I wanted to copy him to perfection because he told me how to experience our dread of the current moment."

Del Vecchio nodded in approval and urged Silvio to continue.

"I don't know if you follow, but the paintings allowed me a kind of communion through form. My artwork allowed me to put myself in another's place," Silvio said. "It let me feel replenished."

Del Vecchio welcomed Silvio to the club of artists and found him a job as a print designer for a local press.

"It's just a start," Del Vecchio said. "We'll find better work for you as soon as something shows up. Carmelo will keep you informed."

Silvio was humbly grateful.

More and more, Carmelo placed his trust in Silvio, whose gentle and unassuming presence was balm for the heart. Soon after their first meetings, Carmelo left Maria Antonietta's house to live with Silvio. Their friendship was based on their hometown connections of course but also on their common sensibilities for art and life. Carmelo, for the first time in years, felt that he could breathe freely. He said he'd found in Silvio the love of his missing brother. As long as no one spoke of politics, Carmelo felt relief. Silvio felt the same.

After María Antonietta hadn't heard from Carmelo in some time, she wondered if he and Silvio were involved in artist collectives or if her brother was safe in town. Then, one night, Maria Antonietta received a phone call from the police. Carmelo and Silvio had been at a men's spa in a hotel on Avenida de Mayo.

"I have to leave," Silvio had said to his friend. "I need to finish a sketch."

Carmelo had chosen to remain at the spa, a luxury for a modest man who was working his way up through the city. Carmelo was overwhelmed by the intense heat and the vapors. He'd stayed in the sauna long after Silvio had gone. Perhaps the coals were too hot, the boiling mist too intense: Carmelo had had a stroke and drowned in a cloud of steam. The Hotel Castelar's management had called the police right away.

"Oh, no," Maria Antonietta screamed when an officer delivered the news. "I can't lose my little brother."

She tried to accuse the hotel of the death, though in truth she had other suspicions. She then blamed Silvio for having left Carmelo alone in the sauna. Silvio, she said, was responsible for Carmelo's demise. Silvio found out she was angry and never saw Maria Antonietta again. He saw himself as a failure.

7.

Rosanna returned to her apartment to process the stories that she had heard about Carmelo and Silvio. She compared these new anecdotes to the material she had gathered about Silvio as a younger person. Silvio now appeared to be a man of wisdom. He was avuncular, even protective of Carmelo, and seemed to have found his way. She worked these notes into her novel along with the event of Carmelo's demise. Her manuscript was nearly at its end. Amen. She just needed to learn the final details about Silvio. Rosanna's excitement was clear.

"Just a few more points," she said eagerly as she closed her notebook and prepared for bed. Tomorrow she would visit Paulina again to expand her story. Meanwhile, she kept the figure of Silvio alive in her mind.

The winter chill of Buenos Aires in July seeped into Rosanna's bones. She had never felt anything like it, she thought as she dressed to leave her abode. Traveling with only a heavy sweater, gloves, and a woolen scarf, she felt exposed as she rode the number 152 bus to Paulina's house.

"And what about Silvio?" Rosanna demanded of Paulina after warming up with a cup of tea. "I hope he's still alive. We have to figure out a way to find him."

"Don't ask me too much," Paulina answered. "Remember that all of this happened before I was born."

Paulina saw Rosanna's distress. "Sorry I'm in the dark, Rosanna, but I think if we have to find Silvio, first we need to find Del Vecchio."

Paulina proposed a little detective work. She knew Del Vecchio was still alive from what she'd read in the papers; to find him, she planned to visit the Argentine Writers' Society, which received guests on Wednesday evenings. Surely some of the octogenarians would remember Del Vecchio.

"Yes," an old writer told Paulina when she inquired. "Del Vecchio lives in Liniers, on the city's outskirts. It'll take you all day to get there, but you'll surely find him."

"An hour on the bus, God save us," Rosanna said when she heard Paulina's good news. "Let's hope this trip is worth it."

The bumpy ride to Liniers had both women in a pickle, but when a friendly man answered the door, they left their complaints behind.

Del Vecchio was kind, though somewhat diminished in strength. After offering the women some whiskey (he figured that the American tourist had the habit of drinking Scotch), he quickly got to the point. No, he hadn't seen Silvio for many years, but he knew of a young artist who'd been Silvio's companion.

On the way back to Buenos Aires, Paulina said, "Well, you have to admit that Del Vecchio was gracious; and he gave us useful information. Not bad for a guy who's almost ninety years old. I think we've hit the jackpot."

But Rosanna wasn't hopeful.

"Everyone in this country says that we're all relations twice removed," Paulina continued. "If we ever locate Del Vecchio's contact, this will prove once more to be true."

Several days went by before Rosanna and Paulina checked out Del Vecchio's lead. They were searching for an artist named Cati who lived and worked in the Tigre Delta, an outpost up the river, about an hour from Buenos Aires. Half tropical forest, half muddy swamp, the delta was the mouth of the Paraná River.

"The locals call it *la isla*," Paulina said as the two women boarded the number 60 bus that would take them out of the city. "The area has lots of interconnected waterways running through marshy land. After we leave the bus, we'll have to take a boat."

Rosanna hesitated when she heard they'd be traveling by water but decided to veil her fears.

"Someone told me that Nazis settled here after the second World War. You can see a bunch of Tyrolian structures that they built along the river," Paulina said as a motorized vessel carried them upriver.

"It reminds you of Heidi in the Alps or Julie Andrews in *The Sound of Music*," said Rosanna, not certain that her friend would get her joke.

After a bus, a boat, and a walk in the muck, Paulina and Rosanna reached Cati's house. Cati explained that her property had been a rundown barn she'd restored as a living quarter and studio for painting. Like Silvio, she entertained herself with imitations of classic artists; unlike Silvio, she felt no embarrassment by saying she painted for money. Cati had been copying Latin American masters for a while, she told her guests. Her focus was the avant-garde of the 1930s—lots of Torres García and Xul Solar—and the Brazilian concretes who, by the late 1950s, were all the rage in Buenos Aires.

Seeing that Rosanna was interested, Cati directed her to the Museo de Bellas Artes to see some of her work.

"Some of *your* work?" Rosanna asked with surprise, wondering if she meant for them to see her forgeries hung on museum walls.

"In this world, there's a problem with possessive pronouns," Cati added when she saw Rosanna's distress. "*My* work, *their* work. It's hard to know how to say it."

Silence filled the air. Cati winked at her new acquaintants.

"So tell us about Silvio," Rosanna and Paulina asked.

Cati had built a friendship with Silvio over the years. Much younger than Silvio, Cati had met Silvio at an art fair many decades ago.

"The day I met him, Silvio looked overwhelmed. He didn't know a soul. He was shaking. Later, he apologized and explained that first encounters made him nervous. He'd just lost his best friend Carmelo and was trying to find his place in the city. I put him at his ease and promised to give him a hand. Camaraderie in times of trouble, let's say. Our friendship began that night.

"After the art fair, we agreed to meet again, and Silvio opened up slowly. First, he spoke of his friendships, which mattered more than anything else. He told me about his relationship with Rolf Zwilling, a man whom he'd met in his village during the years of war and who'd left him brokenhearted. He also described an earlier lover who also had left him. Giulio remained in Ethiopia and never returned to Italy. He spoke at length about Giulio's children whom Silvio had hoped to sponsor.

"When Silvio reached Buenos Aires, he knew that he had to make provisions for the children's care. He had a special painting, a copy of a Carracci, whose profits—when it was sold—would be directed to Silvio's kids. The painting was in New York."

Here, Rosanna sat at attention. She'd never expected to hear this. Timidly, she said, "I can add to this story."

But Cati kept talking. "One day—it must have been in the 1960s—Silvio was reading *La Nación* and came across an article that left him shaking. I remember the scene as if it were yesterday. He was reading about an attempted art heist at the Metropolitan Museum in New York. 'Oh my goodness, this is all about me! Franz and Günther Kälin were caught in the act! They were moving my Carracci into the museum!'

"Silvio explained the details of his painting, how before the war he had pestered Donato to carry his canvas to New York, how he'd lived in fear of Franz Kälin and other art dealers in Italy. His pain was thick, slow, and heavy. He couldn't escape the weight of his words.

"'But to see this in print—unimaginable!' he said.

"I also read the article and realized there was a third figure in the scene," Cati said. "A man who'd brought the false Carracci from Europe and helped the Kälins enact their plan. I told Silvio this, and he grabbed the newspaper from me.".

"'No, this can't be Donato's fault,' I remember Silvio saying. 'He was a good and honest man. I trusted him like a brother. Franz Kälin must've tricked him.'"

* * * *

Rosanna couldn't bear to listen to this. "You two know that Donato is my father?"

Cati looked at her in amazement. Rosanna's face turned red.

"My dad is a good guy, if somewhat naïve. He told us over and over again about distrusting Franz Kälin's brother. And then when the art heist happened, he truly fell apart. It was clear that the episode had scarred my father's life."

"It happens in the best of families," Paulina said.

Rosanna lowered her head and began to cry. She'd never expected the family's humiliation to reach Argentina.

"Don't worry," Cati said. "Silvio knew it wasn't Donato's fault. As soon as he read Kälin's name in the news, he understood the plot and intrigue.

"*'Yerba mala nunca muere,'*" I told him at the time. "Bad weeds never die.""

Rosanna rushed home to write up her notes. The new discovery in Buenos Aires added a significant detail to her novel. She typed in her room until dawn.

* * * *

On the next trip to the Delta, Paulina said, "I don't know where she's going with this stuff, but she certainly likes to gab."

"As long as she doesn't tell me more about my father, I'm okay with her stories."

Both agreed that they shouldn't push Cati in any direction and simply let her talk.

When they reached her cottage, Cati once again discussed Silvio's humble stance.

"Silvio wasn't the typical artist. He didn't think of celebrity or financial gain. Nor did he carry the usual anguish of artists who suffered for art."

Rosanna remarked that she'd heard this same story from her father.

"Instead of talking about his accomplishments and goals, he usually discussed the biographies of artists he'd copied. He also spent a good deal of time talking about technique."

Rosanna said again, "This description is familiar."

Cati continued. "We often disagreed, but the exchanges were always refreshing. I paint only for money. I'm not interested in knowing the life of the artist. I don't expect our souls to meet. I just want to keep up with my monthly bills—the light, the gas, the rent. For this, I'll paint anything. I'll copy any master."

Cati poured them all another round of *mate* tea. "But Silvio had other ideas: he invested himself in the painter. He wanted to experience the world as a sixteenth-century artist and absorb the details of that painterly life. He wanted to put his hands in the same paints and minerals that had belonged to Carracci, to use the hog bristles that Midaro would've chosen, or to reinvent Gentileschi's scarlet and olive pigments.

"For him, the canvas was a mirror that let each artist grasp the other's life, inhaling it, tasting its bitterness, delighting in its texture.

"Who knows? Maybe Silvio was right. You could say it was also a way of stopping time and finding a perfect voice. 'If you confuse historical periods,' he used to say, 'you can even beat death.'

"He was describing an art of survival: finding lasting connections with the past, reaching the souls of long-gone artists, hearing a common language. Quite a remarkable man, that Silvio. He never thought about shortcuts or the profits he surely would've gained had he consistently sold his work.

"And, my goodness, oh so humble," she repeated.

Seeing that the hour was late, Paulina and Rosanna took proper leave and returned to the city.

8.

The rush of traffic at the corner of Callao and Santa Fe, the full aroma of *café cortado* at the bars, the dampness of winter evenings. Sensations overwhelmed Rosanna, disturbing her line of thought. Yesterday, Cati had given her a loaf of bread to carry back to her room on Avenida Callao. When she'd left, the scent of slightly sweetened yeast still wafted through her apartment. Rosanna began to name pleasures that she never had sensed at home. Time was about to change. Her sensory impressions helped her think another way about life—not just by the printed word.

This Thursday afternoon, she and Paulina waited with nervous expectation for the number 60 bus. They were returning to the Delta.

When they arrived at Cati's home, they sensed the slowness of hours. Cati seemed depressed. Lethargic. After some conversation, a little weed, and almost two packs of Jockey Suaves, Cati announced that her tale was ending. She slurred her words and looked down at the floor. Something was very wrong.

"I'm afraid Silvio took the fall for me and for other artists," she confessed. "But I want you to hear it in detail."

Rosanna and Paulina were puzzled.

"One day several years ago, during one of Argentina's darkest moments, an artist called to arrange a visit. He said he had a proposal for me and Silvio. He and a few others were aligned with a poet-journalist of certain fame. They were involved in an oppositional group that wanted to enter the private homes of top-ranking military brass under the pretext of art. They'd win the military brass's trust by offering them great masters at bargain-basement prices. They wanted to recruit Silvio and me to produce a number of convincing forgeries to allow these friends to present as samples of great art for sale. To whet the generals' appetites, they first would show them recent art catalogues and magazines. They would amuse the army brass with stories from *Artforum*; they'd talk about the delicious photo spreads that appeared in *Aperture*; they would recount the various art shows taking place in New York and Paris. Together art dealers and military men (the *crème de la crème*, they told us) were supposed to drool over the glory of renaissance and modern art. Then they would show some paintings immediately available for purchase (our work, of course). Meanwhile, once in the generals' apartments, the friends would map out the living spaces, counting the windows and balconies, the escape doors, and attics; they would assess the household staff on call. The friends assured me that Silvio and I would simply be the behind-the-scenes artists, and no one would discover our names."

Cati paused for what seemed like an eternity. "What happened is far beyond words," she added. "At first, I wasn't nervous. I trusted my friend. I told him that I had no trouble helping the cause, but securing Silvio's complicity was bread from another basket. I knew he wanted nothing to do with any political hanky-panky. To persuade him to see the light. I built up our endeavor's integrity: the artist's mission, social commitment, the role of art in securing freedom. Not a word about the fate of the forgeries that we were asked to supply. I worked on him some more. For weeks, I spoke about the history of artistic copies in political deals; I talked to him—incessantly—about famous fakes in history."

"I don't follow," said Rosanna.

Cati explained that she'd had to make the case that sometimes floating a copy or forgery carried positive social impact. Cati had presented the idea to Silvio, but she hadn't convinced him yet.

* * * *

In order to persuade Silvio, Cati started with the story of Rolf Van Meegeren and the fake Vermeers.

"I know this story by heart," Silvio had said. "I heard it while I was in Naples."

Cati wouldn't stop despite Silvio's protests.

"Van Meegeren gave the Nazis a sock in the nose," she said. "By selling fakes to Göring, Van Meegeren was clearly depleting the Reich's resources. It was sabotage, so to speak, in the name of art."

"No," Silvio said. "It's bad logic. The world doesn't work that way. Eugenia tried to tell me similar stories, but I don't ever want to be involved in something like this again."

"Selling forgeries to the generals would be a heroic gesture; you'd be defying the presence of evil."

Silvio raised his brow.

"*Imitatio* as the highest honor you can bestow on an artist. And, in this instance, imitation is also a way to retaliate against the military junta."

Silvio didn't buy it, so Cati pressed on. Her goal was to show Silvio that piracy would be the key to upend the state. "I even went in a different direction," Cati told her guests. "And tried to explain that the art of the copy even allowed for celebrity and fame. Silvio had no interest."

"I drilled Silvio hard with examples. I even started with the story of Michelangelo passing off his own sculpture of 'Sleeping Eros' as a work from classical Rome. He doctored it up, made the sculpture look old, and sold it to a famous cardinal. Even after the cardinal found out he'd been duped, he admired the young sculptor's talents so much that he offered to be Michelangelo's patron. The sculpture then made the rounds and was sold time and again. Dukes, cardinals, even the king of England were willing to invest in the falsified work."

Cati pursued the theme, still trying to convince Silvio, "Imagine that—Michelangelo started his career as a forger and, from that first step, he found his name."

Silvio shook his head in despair. He was retreating from Cati's lecture.

"Please, Silvio," Cati begged. "Try to think from today's perspective. What would be the difference if you had a sculpture by Michelangelo's hand or by an unknown artist from the age of antiquity? It really doesn't much matter."

Silvio wasn't convinced, and Cati again pushed back, "Michelangelo was still the artist so it wasn't an act of fraud."

Cati said they were in a zone of evolving moralities. Thugs were in the government, in the army and schools. Working with the copy to defeat them wasn't an ignoble task.

Silvio called Cati a "cultural terrorist." He longed for the good old days when he could tell Cati about his heart's affairs. He especially thought of his disappointments with Eugenia, who had taken advantage of his good will.

Cati took him to an arthouse theater that was showing a film by Orson Welles. It was called *F Is for Fake*.

* * * *

Cati spoke to Paulina and Rosanna in somber tones, "Silvio finally agreed to help out the resistance group. For several months, he and I painted up a storm in the name of an unnamed struggle. I worked on a painting of Xul Solar; Silvio worked on a Caravaggio. Silvio even produced a few extra paintings and then donated several canvases that he'd carried from Italy.

"In short, we assembled a respectable collection to send in the name of 'war.' The poet-journalist's comrades were grateful. We took a deep breath and felt relief at having reached closure. Then promising each other that we'd never mention the topic again, we opened a good Malbec."

Rosanna and Paulina were bothered by so much talk. Giving each other knowing glances, they hoped that Cati would trim down her story.

"This story doesn't end well," Cati said with downcast eyes. "Something must have gone wrong. We never knew how it came to be."

Cati got up and walked around the room several times before again taking her seat, one leg tucked under her thigh.

"Silvio disappeared," she said, checking to make sure that Rosanna knew what this phrase meant in modern Argentine life.

Rosanna nodded.

"One day, the police went looking for me at my apartment in Villa Crespo," Cati said. "No one knew of my whereabouts out here in *la isla*. This was my saving grace. But my address in Buenos Aires was more or less common knowledge. In any case, I was off visiting my cousin when Silvio, who was staying at my apartment, answered a knock at the door. The police were looking for me since, for better or worse, I had an aggrandized reputation in the world of copies and fakes. Silvio probably protected my name. God knows what else he said, but the police ransacked my apartment and then took Silvio away. We never saw him again.

"I'm still awash in grief," she said after a pause. "Imagine the police taking a man of his age. God knows what they did. I don't want to believe that they killed him by dropping him into the sea, but their cruelty knows no limits. He was so very fragile."

Paulina and Rosanna heard the leaves rustling on the trees, the rush of the delta's water, the howling wind. This was not the moment to speak.

"It wasn't supposed to end this way," Rosanna finally said.

Rosanna was weeping quietly while Paulina clutched her arm.

Cati interrupted, "If I'd had any doubts about the unnatural workings of a country where rule of law has been suspended, in that moment I came face to face with its emotional truth, the bare bones of living."

Rosanna and Paulina took deep breaths.

"Is silence the only response? Not to say what cannot be mentioned? Some friends went to find the police, but they had no records of Silvio. This was the commissaries' usual answer, and you had to be careful not to respond with indignation. You learned to control your anger, or you too would be considered suspect."

Paulina and Rosanna held hands and looked down. They wished they knew what had happened to Silvio. No one had learned a feather of truth regarding Silvio's fate.

At one point, Paulina embraced Rosanna, who responded in turn. The women lingered in silence, a downpour of sadness drenching their minds and senses. Cati had already gone through the process of mourning her many lost friends. As an outsider, Rosanna was new to this kind of grief and Paulina, although she had lived in Argentina through the hard years of military rule and should have known better, was as inept as her friend from New York.

"History wasn't on Silvio's side," Cati said.

9.

Through their visits to *la isla*, Paulina and Rosanna had found a special bond. They mourned Carmelo and Silvio's deaths and acknowledged that most questions about Rosanna's Italian clan had been answered. Rosanna had learned everyone's secrets, their whereabouts, their endings. She had more than enough material in order to finish her work.

When Rosanna confided her nightly struggles to form her story, Paulina offered simple advice. "There's no need to carry these histories around to find a link between parents and children—or to extend the webs of contact among aunts and uncles and cousins. It doesn't repair the damage; it doesn't improve your life."

 Paulina nodded in agreement and smiled.

By now, Rosanna and Paulina were bonded, each offered a calming embrace to the other. Subtle, of course, nothing obvious; a hazy aura surrounding them as their conversations advanced. They trusted each other, they found a comfort in nearness, a quiet discovery that gave solace. Both were aware of the growing interdependence that gave each woman her separate voice.

Rosanna confided to Paula that usually she was indifferent to others. She kept her distance—perhaps because of the closed quarters she'd shared with Donato and Rosie and the ever-intrusive Max. She had needed this aloofness. But here in Buenos Aires, she liked to feel Paulina's arm next to hers. Here, the quibbling family receded; only friendship remained.

At Paulina's suggestion, they prepared to travel to Mar del Plata. "It's a needed break from the *la isla*, from the muddy waters of Cati's story."

At Retiro station, they boarded the overnight Cóndor Estrella bus that would travel through eastern pasture lands in order to reach the sea. They reserved semi-reclining seats in the hope of catching some winks, but the chairs were stuck in upright positions. They had no choice but to stay awake, to munch on provisions, and chat the night away. To kill time, they nibbled on packaged biscuits until not one remained.

"Yum," one of the travelers said. "Chocolate Terrabusis!"

"I don't like the chocolates; the best are made with *dulce de leche*," said the other.

It would be a long time before they would fall into slumber; meanwhile, they looked out at the flat Argentine darkness and told each other stories about dreams that would never come true. Plans for escape or running away. Growing apples in Rio Negro, raising sheep in Patagonia, husking corn from the New Jersey crops that had matured in the bleached August heat. The joy of sucking on milky-white kernels.

"This farmland extends forever," Rosanna said. She imagined Hereford cows stained caramel and white as they meandered through the pampas. "Plains of repetition." She saw it as a movie.

Rosanna thought of the landscape as a continuation of the grazing lands she knew from the northeastern seaboard, a long stretch of dairy farms that lined the I-95 corridor from Wilmington to Bayonne. South is everywhere as the poets have said; for persons who claim to respect the land, there is in fact no North.

Who knows what South looks like in daylight? Perhaps the women were riding past acres of grasslands, perhaps they were passing tomato farms or thousands of blueberry bushes. Pear and peach trees along the highway? Or high grasses that waved in the wind, evidence of nature's lithe and supple arm? She imagined the pampas moving, never standing still.

By three in the morning, the travelers had run out of things to say. They'd also eaten their remaining treats. The biscuits and apples were long gone; the envelopes of blond *alfajores* sat among a heap of discarded wrappings. No *dulce de leche* left in the tin, no *mate* tea in the thermos. The travelers rested arm in arm for what was left of their five-hour journey. It was the first time, Rosanna thought as she fell into slumber, that the two had been alone in the dark. Despite little sleep, Rosanna awakened rested. Paulina's head was still on her shoulder.

They arrived in early morning to take in the icy gray sea, then dropped their bags at a two-star hotel that they found on Avenida Colón. Walking toward the beach, they first passed by a casino.

"Give me your lucky number." Rosanna laughed. "We can play it at the tables."

She thought of her mother choosing lotto cards based on the locations of cemetery plots that the family maintained in the Westchester suburbs. Area number, section, and grave: mix up the numbers to try your luck!

But Paulina stayed Rosanna's hand. "I'd rather bet on the ocean."

They decided to go to La Perla Beach and see the statue of Alfonsina, the poet who threw herself to the sea.

It was a tourist trap laid out with boardwalk objects—balloons and taffy, swim equipment, flippers, and rubber rafts—but Rosanna was taken off guard when she saw the ocean. The past clawed at her like so many waves beating on the shore. The rush of water that Silvio might've met had the regime hurled his corpse to sea. The ocean crossing from the other side. Rosanna had hoped to write about this with an unpretentious hand. But instead she spouted cliché, gargling declarations of anger, tremulous sounds spilling over the boundaries of speech and writing. She was stuck, Rosanna thought, as she imagined a blood-filled ocean. Max had been right when he'd said that this story would never hold. She lacked the talent to protect its meaning. Her sentimental bouts with age-old themes often left her voiceless.

"I surrender to its power," she told Paulina as they both looked out at the sea. "It marks a line between life and death. In the end, it swallows us up."

"Diamonds of imperceptible foam: Paul Valéry," Paulina answered with a smile.

Rosanna thought of the waves as phantoms extending eerie fingers. They left pebbles on the beach; they threw out rusted words. The remains of life tossed on the shore? Rosanna heard the laments of ghost ships. Could she speak to the present without the luggage of so much past?

Paulina and Rosanna went to a souvenir store on the boardwalk, and Paulina bought a dark-purple mood ring; when she placed it on Rosanna's finger, the ring's color was nearly black. The vendor had claimed that the ring changed colors based on the wearer's temperament.

"You can see the results at twilight," he said. "Even in the dark."

"We'll wait to try it out," the women responded.

"It's a placeholder," Paulina said to Rosanna as they walked away from the shop. Rosanna offered that it would oblige her to acknowledge her feelings.

Once back at the two-star hotel, each woman holding her thoughts in silence, they reclined on the newly starched linen that carried scents of lime and orange to cover the *lavandina*. Paulina spoke gently to Rosanna as she held her in her arms. Rosanna felt Paulina's breath on her shoulder as the coolness of sea air at night. Everything was alive in a minor chord: a slow rhythm amidst fading evening shadows. Paulina began to tell stories, this time not about families but about the way a family structure was in constant evolution and change. When two became one; when one counted as two; when the sum was a constellation.

"Numbers aren't awful," Paulina said. "If you can elude the accountant's habits, numbers give you a lively chance to rearrange all the parts."

As if the women lived on an island, their world was this room. They stretched out in the winter darkness, lingering as one, nothing misaligned. They checked the mood ring on Rosanna's finger: embers twinkling beneath the coals.

"It's a strange concept," Rosanna said. "The ring knows more about me than I do."

The women spoke in muted tones, a confluence of streams. Both preferred the idea of fluid time and space.

"This actual moment is better," Paulina said, "than so many stories about copies and repetitions, endless mirrors to explain the past."

"Maybe it's like a helix spiraling to something new?" Rosanna answered. Here, she was thinking of Silvio's reach for the artists he loved.

"Less appropriation than promise," Paulina said. "And now take a look at us. One and one can be the same, but each affirms a difference."

A silence, a comfortable silence in which their voices blended.

Rosanna felt the sea in Paulina's hands. The undulation, its rhythms, its differences aligned, the pull of a winter moon. These were Paulina's lessons, a promise that embraced a future without the draw of a sad return.

"If you always go back to beginnings," she said. "You get stuck in the deadness of loss."

A fluid sweetness overcame Rosanna. Paulina kissed her on the lips, a closeness not before considered. Of course, thought Rosanna, it should be this exactly.

A current of refracted light coursed from body to body.

"*Mi vida*," murmured one.

"My heart," said the other.

A dive in the shallows, whispers of waves through liquid words. Muted tones emergent. An intensity rising from a clearwater spring, unclouded, expansive. In softened breath, with hours passed, the women lingered on a question: "Can we free ourselves of history if only for a while?"

10.

The kitchen door looking out to the garden was always open. Rosanna had a new apartment that she shared with Paulina in Villa Ortúzar. They had returned from Mar del Plata and closed off the outside world. For months, Rosanna lived in pure contentment, in contraband, against the rule. Adjacent to their apartment, a patio with space for planting. The concierge allowed them to put in some squash and tomatoes, a few clusters of herbs. Here, in Buenos Aires, Rosanna no longer thought that she was the *contadina* of Eugenia's famous picture. With a smile, she recalled her great-aunt posed in regional dress. Here Rosanna was just a weekend gardener, pulling weeds and softening the earth with a hoe, drawing pleasure from the loamy soil.

"No peasant outfits, not too much kitsch." Paulina teased Rosanna with great affection. "But, if you like, I'll dance the tarantella to scare away the fevers."

The women laughed and understood that this no longer mattered. Rosanna had finished her manuscript and felt a certain relief.

At Paulina's prompting, Rosanna had stopped writing to Max. After telling him about Carmelo and Silvio, she decided to break the connection.

Paulina said, "You'll feel better for this, I promise."

The break was a liberation, a freedom for Rosanna's mind. Her brother would never know that she'd finished her dissertation, that her work in the national library had proven fruitful and delicious. The archive had yielded countless texts that continued to excite her spirit. And now she'd completed her novel, and he would never know. This was her story, and she was proud of it, and no longer needed Max's approval. And he wouldn't know of her current engagements, her budding love.

She saw life through a different lens. She was always thirsty, her senses on alert. She explored her feelings and desires. On occasion, she mused that her birth language had failed her. English: too masculine, too precise, excessive confidence in the act of naming. At other times, she thought that no great redemption was due her from writing; no victory assured over history and people. Hardly a way to avenge a loss. Language held few guarantees to describe this new situation.

Maybe, Rosanna thought, the idea was to grasp pleasure in the moment, a chance for a rare kind of freedom. In this respect, the creative inspirations she had found in the city left her happily bewildered. She'd never given herself permission to stretch, to think outside of routine, to experience sight and sound, to touch and inhale the world. Here was something new.

"But there's something else," Rosanna said to Paulina. "I once envisioned a two-tone world of surface truths and hidden stories. Clawing through those darkened spaces, I had hoped to learn it all."

"And what's the secret you had sought to unlock?" Paulina asked.

Smiling, Rosanna stepped outdoors to tend to her summer garden.

Coda

Max was not prepared for her absence, even less for her silence. He found himself helpless. The curtains had been drawn between countries; no light entered his room. He told himself that he lacked the experience to synchronize the details; he couldn't match up the stories. Even worse, in the absence of her letters, he lived in the realm of the post. Post-data, post-mortem, post-poning a moment of truth. Max found himself in an icy tomb, his emotions frozen. The metaphors were chilling.

Rosanna had chosen to remain abroad. Max looked again at the letters alluding to her defection. With a single twitching Cyclopean eye (the other eye still suffering the fracture that had come from a serious fall), he reread Rosanna's last letter: she was enthralled with Buenos Aires. At last, she'd found her way. She referred to a strange companionship that filled her with infinite pleasure and which gave her inspiration to think and write. She quoted her friend Paulina. "Practice your own fiction," Paulina had advised Rosanna. "Don't dwell too much on facts. Just find your voice, and you'll see that the story will fall in line."

"Smart chick, this Paulina," Max said as he read.

He looked for Rosanna's letters every afternoon. To no avail.

This time, she's really fled the coop, Max thought as the weeks grew longer.

One late summer afternoon, he lay down on the couch to escape the unbearable heat. He wished he could avoid his parents.

They were resigned to their daughter's departure. Wistfully, his mother said that her daughter would now achieve what she'd wanted in her youthful dreams: a new life, an adventure, a foray into freedom.

"Time to let her fly."

His father, in his dotage and plied with regret and sadness, was less enthusiastic. He was anxious about the distance that kept his child far from home. "The few relatives residing in Buenos Aires are not enough to help her; she doesn't know how to live on her own, she's never done it." He paused. "We didn't train her well."

"That's not the issue now," Max said from the sofa. A towel covered his eye. Coolly, he told his father that he was off base about his daughter. "You don't know a thing about her."

"I relent," his father said with some irritation. "And I repent. If it makes you happy, forget that I opened my trap."

"No one was supposed to leave home without destiny or purpose," Max said, guessing his father's thoughts.

"Nonetheless, they all chose to migrate one hundred years ago," his father said. "Now no one remembers the crossing, and the young ones just make up tales. The voyage to America wasn't easy; it wasn't an adventure. Just hard work in the name of duty, and obligations to family and home. Now that we're all Americans, there's nothing more to say."

Max sat up. He thought again of his sister's last letter that had arrived some weeks ago. Her prose had gained a forcefulness that he'd never read before. Rosanna surprised him; she had proven him wrong. She was on to something new. Humor, levity, a crisp syntax lacking the flutters of ornamentation, sans the usual clunky adjectives and the awful weighty pomp. There was a great deal of wit. For the first time, she was clever.

Someone must've been helping her, Max thought, looking up at the living room ceiling. "But she'll never finish her dissertation, and I'll bet she abandoned her novel. Too bad."

"She really had no talent," he continued, raising himself from the couch. Thinking he was outside of his father's range of hearing (after all, the old man was nearly deaf), Max said, "Rosanna is a good for nothing,"

But, surprising Max, his father gave a clear endorsement. "After all, she lacks a steady job and a wedding ring to show us."

"Let's see how long she lasts," Max said. He hoped for her failure.

When Max had recovered from the pulsing sensations that had attacked his head, he went to the refrigerator and opened the freezer door, withdrawing the frosty parcel that contained his sister's novel. She'd left it there for safekeeping among the Eggo waffles and Birds Eye peas. Taking the gelid bundle in hand, Max breathed deeply.

"I am master of the universe if only for a day. She is the sister who cannot perform; I am the brother who is smarter."

He removed the tinfoil and peeled back the plastic wrap. The manuscript was cold and humid to the touch. *The Tomb of the Divers* in its full pretensions. He'd never liked the title; no one knew its full allusion, but he of course had researched it.

Who was she fooling? Max had asked after he'd read about the Magna Grecia frescoes painted on limestone slabs. An archaeologist had found them near Paestum in 1968. One panel showed a young boy diving into the sea; others showed the boy at a symposium graced by older men. A scene that linked pedagogy with eros, the boy and his teachers. Scenes of water and queer desire; the thought revolted Max.

He had warned her she was in over her head in advance of her travels. He had warned her, but what was the point? In late evening, Max sat down to review the pages in detail; by now, they had lost their initial chill. He reached for an aspirin and a Schaefer to calm his throbbing head. He remembered all the late-night editing that had taken place at the kitchen table.

Max felt the dampness of each page. Or did he confuse humidity with cold? He liked the way it read at first. After all, it had been his hand that had steadied his sister's pen. For all its problems, the novel had given Rosanna a language. He'd then tightened up her thoughts. She wasn't hip, Max thought, smirking. She still lingered in romance.

His parents shuffled back and forth in the kitchen as they waited for a kettle to boil. Reaching for a tea bag, his mother said that Max had been reading too long. "Why not take a break?"

For some reason, the elders spoke of life in New York in 1923 shortly after Donato's arrival. Donato remembered the Dempsey-Firpo fight and nothing else. He thought he had won special tickets to the Polo Grounds arena; Rosie here reminded him that he had heard the fight on radio WJZ.

His parents distracted him. Max decided he'd return to the manuscript late at night after his parents were fast asleep.

Chapter two was even better than the first. That's where he'd put in the most work. Small wonder it was so good. He scratched his leg and continued reading. It was a man's world described in full, a world that needed no women.

Unable to rest in bed, his father came into the kitchen and looked over Max's shoulders.

"Are you reading about Carmelo?" he asked. "He was a gentleman as I recall. We played Scopa in the evening; sometimes we walked through Central Park."

Max reminded his father that he'd lost track of his dates: "Uncle Carmelo had left the country way before you arrived in New York."

Silence and humiliation. Max had won this round; he declared his father the loser by knockout.

Max moved onto chapter three but cringed when he read (once again) that Donato had been taken for a fool. He didn't want to be reminded.

His father then inquired about the plot. How had his daughter arrived at her scenes? Had she invented them? Had she taken notes from family scrapbooks? With a flash of illumination, his father then whispered, "Do you know about the men who wanted to send me off to jail? Do you think it's fair that my name showed up in the news?"

Max was quickly annoyed. "How the hell can I think about them if you're peering over my shoulder?"

His father left the kitchen. Max returned to his sister's text.

Then his mother, also restless from insomnia, heard the babble in the kitchen and came into the room to talk. Knowing that Max was meddling in his sister's affairs as he corrected her novel, she sternly warned him: "If you say anything that makes her look bad, if you change her words to make her look stupid, then trust me, I'm on alert. I'll rip up your story with my teeth; I won't let her name be tarnished."

Max was annoyed. In no uncertain terms, his mother always protected her girl. Worse, both were willing to stretch the truth when any need arose. Max thought that they lacked the style of digging deep; they offered just knee-jerk reactions. They had no claims on storytelling; they simply rambled on, as gabby women often did. Now his mother wanted to save Rosanna from the consequences of her writing. Why doesn't she go back to bed?

Weeks of headaches, numbness in his legs and arms, an ongoing vision problem. Max felt his health declining. At the end of this stretch, he once again picked up a pen to correct his sister's text. Max edited his sister's infelicitous phrases; he flattened her tendentious excess; he diluted her characters' pomp; he tried to make them real. He knew he was really attempting to display his power over his stunted sister.

Not bad, he thought, when he'd nearly finished editing. It was a crucifixion. He laughed, imagining his sister with a book in hand, dangling high from a cross.

It was time to sell the novel, to put it out there fair and square. "Célebrate, célebrate," he announced, recalling his passion for dactyls.

He called upon his old pals Liam and Tom. He turned to Marty and Lou. No one seemed to know. They were blind to a writer's work. They didn't know about agents. They had no idea about how you might send your finished novel to press. Max didn't know how publishing worked; he admitted his one-eyed blindness. Waiting for inspiration, he recalled Mr. McCasey, the golfer from many years ago who had recited Yeats with him while crossing the Van Cortlandt green. McCasey had worked for a publishing firm. Perhaps by now he was even the boss.

Max scrambled through his dresser drawers. He plucked McCasey's calling card from the mess; after years, it hadn't moved from the heap of notes and song books, from the stash of Yankee ticket stubs that he'd kept since he was seven, from the pile of cardboard coasters that he'd swiped from local bars, from the dozens of unmatched socks. No, he couldn't push through the rubble that failed to add up to a whole, but yes, he found McCasey's card and decided to take a chance.

Max made the call. He felt awkward as he remembered McCasey's dapper image; the man came from a different world. The book man (an editor? a publisher? Max found it hard to place him) sounded happy to hear his voice.

"You're about to retire, Mr. McCasey? Then I'm very glad that I caught you. Thank you, sir."

. . . .

"Thank you, sir. I've tried to keep up with my reading. Now I have a novel that I'd like you to see."

. . . .

"Yes, I'd be honored if you were to take a peek."

. . . .

"A meeting? Why, of course."

McCasey had proposed a drink at the Squash Racquets Club close to Central Park.

Max thought it sounded like a gym but realized it was a rich man's hangout. He was going to be out of his league.

Max gulped. He agreed to meet McCasey but asked for a few more days. He needed to tie loose ends.

Max edited and corrected. He added and rearranged. He supplemented the text with details that had eluded his sister's grasp. He would show the world his range of knowledge. He tinkered with the sentences and invented new conversations. He eliminated his sister's half-ripe romance and projected his own control.

He wanted to show that no story was simple. To support this, he alluded to truths and lies that perpetually slipped away. He thought of stories that would never be written and those that we wouldn't remember. He considered the faulty memories of his parents and all his clan. He especially loathed his sister for her lack of craft and grace.

"Less girly lit, more he-man tales," he insisted. "Give it heft" (he repeated the word several times in order to give it hell).

Heft, Heist, Hoist. Hell. Max made the story what it was, a book of lies and crimes, a fiction about dishonest men. He pushed his sister's voice aside. This would not be a family romance. He would change the title, his final show of force. Not the THE TOMB OF THE DIVERS, as his sister had proposed, but a title that would speak to other worlds both sinister and oblique. His title now carried an endless truth: THE TOMB OF LIARS. The book now stood corrected. Fatigued, Max called McCasey and awaited the next step.

Author's Note

Historical fiction is exactly this: history and fiction combined. For the first chapter of this novel, I took inspiration from the long history of the Italian *mezzogiorno* in literature and political thought. For a general overview on the South, see Benedetto Croce, *History of the Kingdom of Naples* (1925; English translation, 1970). Of greater impact, see Antonio Gramsci's foundational essay, *The Southern Question* (1925; Engl. trans. 1995); for its critical repercussions, Jane Schneider, ed., *Italy's 'Southern Question': Orientalism in One Country* (2020) and Nelson Moe, *The View from Vesuvius: Italian Culture and the Southern Question* (2002). For an impassioned defense of the *mezzogiorno*, see Pino Aprile, *Terroni* (2010; Engl. trans. 2011).

Poverty, hunger, and deprivation have described the South to the point of exhaustion. Among the canonical essays, see John Dickie, *Darkest Italy: The Nation and Stereotypes of the Mezzogiorno, 1860-1900* (1999); Tommaso Astarita, *Salt Water and Holy Water. A History of Southern Italy* (2005); Edward C. Banfield, *The Moral Basis of a Backward Society* (1958); Ernesto de Martino, *Magic: A Theory from the South* (1959; Engl. trans. 2015) and the literary memoir of Carlo Levi, *Christ Stopped at Eboli* (1945; Engl. trans. 1947). I confess that I had little interest in tracing paths of abjection but wanted to signal the creativity of southern craftsman who, despite the conditions in which they lived, prevailed as inventors and artists. At the same time, I explored the power of the popular press over the rural imagination. Even among barely literate populations, the newspapers from Rome to Naples encouraged consumer desire. From the ads that they saw in *Il Mattino* and *Fortunio* (two papers I read with zeal), Zi'Annibale awakened to the art of photography, Silvio filled his head with pictures, Zia Wanda dreamed of beauty cremes and elegant Neapolitan caffés, and the chef from Matera imagined new ways to launch his product to a wider Italian market (the southern aperitif Amaro Lucano also inspired this part of my story). And characters marveled at film culture from beginning to end.

As I moved the story to Naples, I was helped by the writings of Matilde Serao (see *The Land of Cockayne*, 1891*;* Engl. trans. 1901) and selected English translations by Jon R. Snyder in "On Naples, 1878-1884: Six Translations. Matilde Serao," in *California Italian Studies*, 2012). Walter Benjamin's "Naples" in *One Way Street* (1925; Engl. trans. 1979) and Georg Simmel's "The Metropolis and Mental Life" (1903) were indispensable for this first chapter.

The debate over modernity took place at the Neapolitan dining room table. For their banquets, the characters preferred *haute cuisine* and insisted that Eugenia learn some French. This is inscribed in a wider discussion about forming a national palate. Pellegrino Artusi, for example, wrote a cookbook to reeducate the tastes of Italian elites and the middle classes. He thus imposed a Darwinian plan to alter the country's cookhouse with healthy local foods and, as such, claimed to save his people from the French-fried table. See Pellegrino Artusi, *Science in the Kitchen* (1891; Engl. trans. 2003). The King of Savoy took more extreme measures. In 1907, he issued an edict preventing noble households from printing menus in French and mandated that culinary choices be written only in standard Italian.

Chapter one closed with reference to Artemisia Gentileschi's famous painting of Judith and Holofernes, frequently praised by contemporary feminists as an art of angry resistance (see Sheila Barker's recent *Artemisia Gentileschi*, 2022; Mieke Bal, *The Artemisia Files: Artemisia Gentileschi for Feminists and Other Thinking People*, 2005; and the wonderful novel by Anna Banti, *Artemisia,* 1953; Engl. trans. 1988). Finally, the marriage of rich and poor, positioned centrally in chapter one, built on a repeated trope in European literature. See, for example, in the nineteenth century, Alessandro Manzoni's *The Betrothed* (1827; Engl. trans. 2022) and, in the twentieth century, Giuseppe Tomasi di Lampedusa's *The Leopard* (1958; Engl. trans. 1960). Max makes fun of this second novel in "Narrators, 2."

Chapter two opened with Carmelo's arrival as an immigrant to New York at the turn of the century. Fundamental for learning about Italian immigration experience through literature is Martino Marazzi, Ed., *Voices of Italian America: A History of Early Italian American Literature with a Critical Anthology* (2001; Engl. trans. 2004), and Francesco Durante, R. Viscusi, A. J. Tamburri, J. J. Periconi, Eds., *Italoamericana: The Literature of the Great Migration, 1880-1943* (2005; Engl. Transl. 2014). While exhaustively covering Italian American memoir, theater, fiction and poetry, Durante also dedicates a considerable section of his book to Italian American anarchist literature of the era.

Bresci, Malatesta, Galleani—major figures in the anarchist movement—all had cameo roles in the novel as did the feminist pioneers of Italian American anarchism, Ninfa Baronio and Maria Roda. Most important, Ludovico Caminita—journalist, playwright, and mediator between different anarchist cultures—took stage center as the novel advanced. Caminita wrote a notable memoir and in 1921 published his play, *Sonata Elegiaca,* which Carmelo later claimed as his own. Caminita's articles also pointed to a formidable race consciousness during the first decades of the twentieth century. On this, see Salvatore Salerno, "I Delitti della Razza Bianca (Crimes of the White Race). Italian Anarchists' Racial Discourse as Crime" in Jennifer Guglielmo and Salvatore Salerno, *Are Italians White? How Race Is Made in America* (2003: 111-123). Worth noting also is Caminita's collaboration with Ricardo Flores Magón, whom I mentioned in the novel only in passing. Directing the newspaper *Regeneración,* the famous Mexican anarchist gave Caminita a front-page column and allowed him to write in Italian. For a deeper assessment of Italian American anarchism, see Nunzio Pernicone and Fraser Otanelli, *Assassins against the Old Order: Italian Anarchist Violence in* fin de siglo *Europe* (2018); Marcela Bencivenni, *Italian Immigrant Radical Culture in America* (2011); Philip Cannistraro and Gerald Meyers, Eds., *The Lost World of Italian American Anarchism: Politics, Labor, Culture* (2003); Michael Kemp, *Bombs, Bullets, and Bread. The Politics of Anarchist Terrorism Worldwide, 1866-1926* (2018).

I was attracted to the stage culture of immigrants since, after all, it kept me on track regarding performance and representation. Richard

Migliaccio kindly allowed me access to images of his grandfather Farfariello, a vaudeville star of early twentieth-century New York. See the website http://www.farfariello.com/ that includes extensive information about early Italian-American theater. Emelise Aleandri's book is required reading. See her *Italian-American Immigrant Theatre of New York City, 1746-1899* (2006). And for carnival culture of the early twentieth century, and particularly the enterprises of Joseph Schenck and Marcus Loew, see Barbara and Wesley Gottlock, *Lost Amusement Parks of New York City: Beyond Coney Island* (2013).

A few details on the tropes that kept this novel going. Readers will note, from the title forward, the importance of water. The sea in Italian studies also commands a considerable bibliography. Among recent books, see Iain Chambers, *Mediterranean Crossings: the Politics of an Interrupted Modernity* (2008); Franco Cassano, *Southern Thought and Other Essays on the Mediterranean* (2012); and Claudio Fogú, *The Fishing Net and the Spider Web: Mediterranean Imaginaries and the Making of Italians* (2020). When Carmelo stood at the Paterson falls and observed its power, I couldn't help but take direction from the poetry of William Carlos Williams (*Paterson*, 1946-1958). I leave it to Max in the Coda to explain the significance of the novel's aquatic title.

Carmelo often alluded to his uncertain life, neither here nor there; in one instance, Esteve remarked that someone, someday, would write about the condition of sitting on the hyphen. See Anthony Tamburri, *To Hyphenate or not to Hyphenate: the Italian/American writer, an other American* (1991), whose essay pushed me in that direction. The chapter closed with allusion to the Spanish flu of 1918 and the Palmer Raids on Italian communities especially in New Jersey. On the flu, see Sandra Opdycke, *The Flu Epidemic of 1918: America's Experience in the Global Health Crisis* (2015); and Laura Spinney, *Pale Rider, The Spanish flu of 1918, and How it Changed the World* (2017). Spinney narrates in detail the anti-immigrant sentiment in times of pandemic and the interventions of Dr. Antonio Stella who tried to protect his infirm patients from anti-Italian attacks. In the novel, I had Dr. Stella refer to a short story by Luigi Pirandello, "The Breath" (composed early in the century, but published in Italian in 1931; Engl. trans. in *Stories for a Year*, www.pirandellointranslation.org, 2021). For a touching and earnest representation of these years of transition from Italy to America, see Giuseppe Fuccella, *Memorie di Giuseppe Fuccella / Memories of Giuseppe Fuccella* (2018).

In chapter three, with Donato's arrival in Naples, I homed in on the fateful gap between family members who had left for America and those who had remained in Italy. Eugenia and Donato lamented their distance from home; other characters expressed the contradictions of a multicultural south. This is seen not simply through Silvio's desire to help his Ethiopian friends, and Eugenia's horror as she learned of Jewish deportations in wartime Naples, but also through Rolf Zwilling's confinement in Bellanera. I composed his story from a cluster of testimonies given by Jewish refugees who had found protection in southern Italian hamlets during the years of Nazi occupation. On this, see Fortunoff Video Archive for Holocaust Testimonies, Yale University Library, oral history Ilse W. (HVT-2177) and from the U.S. Holocaust Memorial Museum Collection, the oral history interview with Hans Heiman: https://collections.ushmm.org/search/catalog/irn504585/.

On the war years in Naples, see Norman Lewis, *Naples 44* (1978); Rick Atkinson, *The Day of Battle: The War in Sicily and Italy, 1943-1944*, Vol. 2 (2007); Aubrey Menen, *Four Days of Naples* (1979); Tim Keogh, *Occupied Naples and the Politics of Food in World War II* (vol. 6 of *War and the City*, 2019), and for an overarching survey, John Santore, *Modern Naples: A Documentary History, 1799-1999* (2001).

Curzio Malaparte's *The Skin* (1949; Engl. trans. 2013), a barbed account of the American presence in Naples, hilariously describes a dinner for American military elites at which a sea siren pulled from the national aquarium is cooked and served on a platter. I am certainly in his debt for my account of Eugenia's koi, but there's also a long tradition of stories of this kind. Far before Malaparte's example, nineteenth-century famines led Parisians to steal animals from Les Jardins des Plantes and prepare them for human consumption. See also Filippo Tommaso Marinetti's *Mafarka il futurista* (1910; Engl. trans. 1998) where a cooked human penis (almost forty feet long) is served as a meal.

I couldn't help but dwell on the celebrities whom Eugenia met on Capri. Lenin retreated to the island resort to train revolutionary squadrons while notables such as Oscar Wilde and Nathalie Barney also frequented Capri more for sexual adventure than for any political mission. Their safety was guaranteed by the 1889 Zanardelli Code, which prohibited all punishments against consensual homosexual relations. Nonetheless, homophobia was in the air: Edoardo Scarfoglio, husband of Matilde Serao and director of *Il Mattino*, denounced the gay soirees held on Capri by armaments producer Friedrich Krupp (see his "Capri-Sodoma," *La Propaganda,* 10-15-1902); F. T. Marinetti wrote an aggressive denunciation of queer Capri in his book, *L'isola dei baci* (*The Island of Kisses,* 1918), coauthored with Bruno Corra. Later, the fascist regime called an end to queer freedoms in Italy and sent homosexuals to prison.

Art theft and forgery during and after World War II have a large bibliography. Most useful to me is the now-famous study of the Monuments Men: Robert M. Edsel, *Saving Italy. The Race to Rescue a Nation's Treasures from the Nazis* (2013); also Ilaria Dagnini Brey, *The Venus Fixers: The Remarkable Story of the Allied Soldiers who Saved Italy's Art during World War II* (2009). Forgery is another intriguing topic that enjoys an extensive bibliography. See, for example, Noah Charney, *The Art of Forgery: The Minds, Motives, and Methods of Master Forgers* (2015); Saskia Hufnagel and Duncan Chappell, eds., *The Palgrave Handbook on Art* Crime (2019); Thierry Lenain, *Art Forgery: The History of a Modern Obsession* (2011); William Casement, *The Many Faces of Art Forgery: From the Dark Side to Shades of Gray,* (2022); Denis Dutton, Ed. *The Forger's Art: Forgery and the Philosophy of Art* (1983); and Orson Wells, Dir. "F is For Fake" (1973).

When Carmelo, at the start of chapter four, made an appearance in Buenos Aires, we were introduced to an important moment in Argentine history: the period of high immigration. By 1914, more than 312,000 Italians lived in the city of Buenos Aires (comparably, 370,000 Italians lived in New York City at the same time). On this, See Samuel L. Baily, *Immigrants in the Lands of Promise: Italians in Buenos Aires and New York City, 1870 - 1914* (1974; 2016); José Moya, *Atlantic Crossroads: Webs of Migration, Culture and Politics between Europe, Africa and the Americas, 1800-2020* (2021); James Scobie, *Buenos Aires: Plaza to Suburb, 1870-1910* (1974); Carl E. Solberg,

"Mass Migration in Argentina, 1870-1970," in McNeill and Adams, eds., *Human Migration* (1978: 146-70). And in Spanish without English translation, the studies by Fernando Devoto, Tulio Halperin Donghi, Gino Germani, José Luis Romero, and Diego Armus.

Within the same time frame, Italian and Spanish immigrant workers staged important labor actions. In this context, Carmelo headed south to participate in the anarchist cause in Patagonia of the early 1920s. There, mostly Spanish and Chilean workers tending the ranches had initiated a strike for better wages. In response, the army entered the province and, according to many records, shot and killed close to 1500 men. It is remembered as the "Tragic Patagonia" or "Patagonia Rebelde," one of the bloodiest events in early twentieth-century Argentina. See Osvaldo Bayer, *Anarchism and Violence: 1923-1931* (1985) and Ronaldo Munck, et. al., *Argentina: From Anarchism to Peronism. Workers, Unions, and Politics, 1855-1985* (1987).

Throughout the first half of chapter four, Carmelo interacted with Argentine magazines of wide circulation. He read the popular *Caras y caretas* and *La patria degli italiani,* an Italian language paper, but most important, he found employment with the socialist periodical *Claridad.* Here he met with writers and printmakers of convincing left-wing persuasion. In real life, some of the *Claridad* contributors met as the "Artistas del Pueblo," a collaborative effort in which sculptors, engravers, and writers shared their work. See Patrick Frank, *Los Artistas del pueblo: Prints and Workers' Culture in Buenos Aires, 1917-1935* (2006); also, Juan Suriano, *Paradoxes of Utopia: Anarchist Culture and Politics in Buenos Aires, 1890-1910* (2010). On a multi-political front (communist, socialist, anarchist, and independent thinkers), the most significant writer of this wide coterie was novelist and playwright Roberto Arlt. Immigrant theater was also a specialty of this diverse left-wing cadre. Because of the depiction of the harsh life of marginal sectors—most often Italian immigrants in the city of Buenos Aires—this dramatic form was often described as a "theater of the grotesque."

Later in the chapter, as Rosanna learned about Argentina, she was obliged to think of the brutal military dictatorship of 1976-83. In those years, the authoritarian government conducted what has become known as Argentina's "dirty war" in which the secret police "disappeared" nearly 30,000 persons (mostly students and workers), often dumping them from airplanes into the Atlantic Ocean. Those bodies were never found. On this, see Marguerite Feitlowitz, *A Lexicon of Terror: Argentina and the Legacies of Torture* (1998); Juan Grigera and Luciana Zorzoli, *The Argentinian Dictatorship and its Legacy: Rethinking the* Proceso (2019); and Federico Finchelstein, *The Ideological Origins of the Dirty War: Fascism, Populism, and Dictatorship in Twentieth-Century Argentina* (2014). For a general overview of Argentine history, David Rock, *Argentina, 1516-1987: From Spanish Colonialism to the Falklands War* (1987).

* * * *

CITATIONS IN THE TEXT

Marinetti, Filippo Tomasso and Bruno Corra. *L'isola dei baci. Romanzo Erotico-Sociale.* Milano, Facci, 1918: 80. My translation.

Valery, Paul. *Le cimetière marin.* Paris: Emile Paul frères, 1920. My translation.

Yeats, William Butler. *The Wild Swans at Coole.* New York: The Macmillan Company, 1919.

Acknowledgments

There's an Italian phrase, "It's not true, but I believe it" (*Non è vero, ma ci credo*), which might signal the way I absorbed family histories when I heard them as a youngster. In New York, my parents Rose and Peppe Masiello and my cousin Frances Fuccella Sapere carried until their final moments tales about the "other side" and immigrant life over here. I abandoned any questions about what might have been true or false and listened simply for pleasure. In present time, I thank Theresa Gerardi who, in a language few remember, continues in New York to narrate these family fables from long ago. In Italy, Alfonso and Pina Izzi opened their hearts as well as their library to nourish my interest in Italian history while the generous Tarantinos—Giuseppe, Anna, and Maria—fused stories of their land and its people with verve and imagination; and Enzo Sansone, consummate scholar of the southern past, supplied me with more than a few points of entry to keep this novel going. My debt to them is huge.

For the many friends and readers, my deep appreciation. In the front line, and lending unfailing support and attention, the incomparable Maryann Wolfe. She buoyed this endeavor when I thought of backing out and always kept the faith. Along with her, Teresa Stojkov, Gwen Kirkpatrick, Alison McDonald, Vicki Silkiss, and Sherry Keith read drafts of this project and offered keen observations. They surely deserve a badge of honor for their devotion to this cause. My gratitude to Marian Zager, Nancy Katz, and Susan Yost, my New York homies, who read for neighborhood details and laughed at my maps of the city. A giant thank you to those who gave wise and thoughtful suggestions along the way: Florencia Abbate, Marco Bianchi, Anna Deeny Morales, Ivonne del Valle,

Rob Kaufman, Bill Lordi, Peter Manoleas, Mercedes Roffé, and Lelé Santilli. And when time was running out, Louise George Clubb took the time to read this story. Her generosity exceeds all bounds.

Finally, an *abbraccio* to Anthony Tamburri both for decades of friendship and for giving this book a home. And thanks to Nicholas Grosso for his expert editorial eye as he shaped this project into final form for Bordighera Press.

About the Author

FRANCINE MASIELLO is a writer and critic who has taught at the University of California at Berkeley where she holds the Ancker Distinguished Professorship in the Humanities (Emerita). With a long career as a Latin Americanist, she published on topics ranging from nineteenth-century literature to avant-garde movements of the 1920s. In recent years, she has turned to the representation of the senses under neoliberal order and now writes about the Global South. She has lived in New York, Italy, and Argentina, and has published fiction in English and Spanish. *The Tomb of the Divers* is her first novel.

VIA Folios

A refereed book series dedicated to the culture of Italians and Italian Americans.

PIETRO DI DONATO. *Collected Stories.* Vol 174.
RACHEL GUIDO DEVRIES. *The Birthday Years.* Vol 173.
MATTHEW MEDURI. Collegiate Gothic. Vol 172.
THOMAS RUGGIO. *Finding Dandini.* Vol 171.
GARDAPHÈ, GIORDANO, TAMBURRI. *From the Margin.* Vol 170.
ANNA MONARDO. *After Italy.* Vol. 169. Memoir.
JOEY NICOLETTI. *Extinction Wednesday.* Vol. 168. Memoir.
MARIA FAMÀ. *Trigger.* Vol. 167. Poetry.
WILLI Q MINN. *What? Nothing.* Vol. 166. Poetry.
RICHARD VETERE. *She's Not There.* Vol. 165. Literature.
FRANK GIOIA. *Mercury Man.* Vol. 164. Literature.
LUISA M. GIULIANETTI. *Agrodolce.* Vol. 163. Literature.
ANGELO ZEOLLA. *The Bronx Unbound ovvero i versi bronxesi.* Vol. 162. Poetry.
NICHOLAS A. DiCHARIO. *Giovanni's Tree.* Vol. 161. Literature.
ADELE ANNESI. *What She Takes Away.* Vol. 160. Novel.
ANNIE RACHELE LANZILLOTTO. *Whaddyacall the Wind?.* Vol. 159. Memoir.
JULIA LISELLA. *Our Lively Kingdom.* Vol. 158. Poetry.
MARK CIABATTARI. *When the Mask Slips.* Vol. 157. Novel.
JENNIFER MARTELLI. *The Queen of Queens.* Vol. 156. Poetry.
TONY TADDEI. *The Sons of the Santorelli.* Vol. 155. Literature.
FRANCO RICCI. *Preston Street • Corso Italias.* Vol. 154. History.
MIKE FIORITO. *The Hated Ones.* Vol. 153. Literature.
PATRICIA DUNN. *Last Stop on the 6.* Vol. 152. Novel.
WILLIAM BOELHOWER. *Immigrant Autobiography.* Vol. 151. Literary Criticism.
MARC DIPAOLO. *Fake Italian.* Vol. 150. Literature.
GAIL REITANO. *Italian Love Cake.* Vol. 149. Novel.
VINCENT PANELLA. *Sicilian Dreams.* Vol. 148. Novel.
MARK CIABATTARI. *The Literal Truth: Rizzoli Dreams of Eating the Apple of Earthly Delights.* Vol. 147. Novel.
MARK CIABATTARI. *Dreams of An Imaginary New Yorker Named Rizzoli.* Vol. 146. Novel.
LAURETTE FOLK. *The End of Aphrodite.* Vol. 145. Novel.
ANNA CITRINO. *A Space Between.* Vol. 144. Poetry
MARIA FAMÀ. *The Good for the Good.* Vol. 143. Poetry.
ROSEMARY CAPPELLO. *Wonderful Disaster.* Vol. 142. Poetry.
B. AMORE. *Journeys on the Wheel.* Vol. 141. Poetry.
ALDO PALAZZESCHI. *The Manifestos of Aldo Palazzeschi.* Vol 140. Literature.
ROSS TALARICO. *The Reckoning.* Vol 139. Poetry.
MICHELLE REALE. *Season of Subtraction.* Vol 138. Poetry.

MARISA FRASCA. *Wild Fennel.* Vol 137. Poetry.
RITA ESPOSITO WATSON. *Italian Kisses.* Vol. 136. Memoir.
SARA FRUNER. *Bitter Bites from Sugar Hills.* Vol. 135. Poetry.
KATHY CURTO. *Not for Nothing.* Vol. 134. Memoir.
JENNIFER MARTELLI. *My Tarantella.* Vol. 133. Poetry.
MARIA TERRONE. *At Home in the New World.* Vol. 132. Essays.
GIL FAGIANI. *Missing Madonnas.* Vol. 131. Poetry.
LEWIS TURCO. *The Sonnetarium.* Vol. 130. Poetry.
JOE AMATO. *Samuel Taylor's Hollywood Adventure.* Vol. 129. Novel.
BEA TUSIANI. *Con Amore.* Vol. 128. Memoir.
MARIA GIURA. *What My Father Taught Me.* Vol. 127. Poetry.
STANISLAO PUGLIESE. *A Century of Sinatra.* Vol. 126. Popular Culture.
TONY ARDIZZONE. *The Arab's Ox.* Vol. 125. Novel.
PHYLLIS CAPELLO. *Packs Small Plays Big.* Vol. 124. Literature.
FRED GARDAPHÉ. *Read 'em and Reap.* Vol. 123. Criticism.
JOSEPH A. AMATO. *Diagnostics.* Vol 122. Literature.
DENNIS BARONE. *Second Thoughts.* Vol 121. Poetry.
OLIVIA K. CERRONE. *The Hunger Saint.* Vol 120. Novella.
GARIBLADI M. LAPOLLA. *Miss Rollins in Love.* Vol 119. Novel.
JOSEPH TUSIANI. *A Clarion Call.* Vol 118. Poetry.
JOSEPH A. AMATO. *My Three Sicilies.* Vol 117. Poetry & Prose.
MARGHERITA COSTA. *Voice of a Virtuosa and Coutesan.* Vol 116. Poetry.
NICOLE SANTALUCIA. *Because I Did Not Die.* Vol 115. Poetry.
MARK CIABATTARI. *Preludes to History.* Vol 114. Poetry.
HELEN BAROLINI. *Visits.* Vol 113. Novel.
ERNESTO LIVORNI. *The Fathers' America.* Vol 112. Poetry.
MARIO B. MIGNONE. *The Story of My People.* Vol 111. Non-fiction.
GEORGE GUIDA. *The Sleeping Gulf.* Vol 110. Poetry.
JOEY NICOLETTI. *Reverse Graffiti.* Vol 109. Poetry.
GIOSE RIMANELLI. *Il mestiere del furbo.* Vol 108. Criticism.
LEWIS TURCO. *The Hero Enkidu.* Vol 107. Poetry.
AL TACCONELLI. *Perhaps Fly.* Vol 106. Poetry.
RACHEL GUIDO DEVRIES. *A Woman Unknown in Her Bones.* Vol 105. Poetry.
BERNARD BRUNO. *A Tear and a Tear in My Heart.* Vol 104. Non-fiction.
FELIX STEFANILE. *Songs of the Sparrow.* Vol 103. Poetry.
FRANK POLIZZI. *A New Life with Bianca.* Vol 102. Poetry.
GIL FAGIANI. *Stone Walls.* Vol 101. Poetry.
LOUISE DESALVO. *Casting Off.* Vol 100. Fiction.
MARY JO BONA. *I Stop Waiting for You.* Vol 99. Poetry.
RACHEL GUIDO DEVRIES. *Stati zitt, Josie.* Vol 98. Children's Literature. $8
GRACE CAVALIERI. *The Mandate of Heaven.* Vol 97. Poetry.
MARISA FRASCA. *Via incanto.* Vol 96. Poetry.

DOUGLAS GLADSTONE. *Carving a Niche for Himself.* Vol 95. History.
MARIA TERRONE. *Eye to Eye.* Vol 94. Poetry.
CONSTANCE SANCETTA. *Here in Cerchio.* Vol 93. Local History.
MARIA MAZZIOTTI GILLAN. *Ancestors' Song.* Vol 92. Poetry.
MICHAEL PARENTI. *Waiting for Yesterday: Pages from a Street Kid's Life.* Vol 90. Memoir.
ANNIE LANZILLOTTO. *Schistsong.* Vol 89. Poetry.
EMANUEL DI PASQUALE. *Love Lines.* Vol 88. Poetry.
CAROSONE & LOGIUDICE. *Our Naked Lives.* Vol 87. Essays.
JAMES PERICONI. *Strangers in a Strange Land: A Survey of Italian-Language American Books.* Vol 86. Book History.
DANIELA GIOSEFFI. *Escaping La Vita Della Cucina.* Vol 85. Essays.
MARIA FAMÀ. *Mystics in the Family.* Vol 84. Poetry.
ROSSANA DEL ZIO. *From Bread and Tomatoes to Zuppa di Pesce "Ciambotto".* Vol. 83. Memoir.
LORENZO DELBOCA. *Polentoni.* Vol 82. Italian Studies.
SAMUEL GHELLI. *A Reference Grammar.* Vol 81. Italian Language.
ROSS TALARICO. *Sled Run.* Vol 80. Fiction.
FRED MISURELLA. *Only Sons.* Vol 79. Fiction.
FRANK LENTRICCHIA. *The Portable Lentricchia.* Vol 78. Fiction.
RICHARD VETERE. *The Other Colors in a Snow Storm.* Vol 77. Poetry.
GARIBALDI LAPOLLA. *Fire in the Flesh.* Vol 76 Fiction & Criticism.
GEORGE GUIDA. *The Pope Stories.* Vol 75 Prose.
ROBERT VISCUSI. *Ellis Island.* Vol 74. Poetry.
ELENA GIANINI BELOTTI. *The Bitter Taste of Strangers Bread.* Vol 73. Fiction.
PINO APRILE. *Terroni.* Vol 72. Italian Studies.
EMANUEL DI PASQUALE. *Harvest.* Vol 71. Poetry.
ROBERT ZWEIG. *Return to Naples.* Vol 70. Memoir.
AIROS & CAPPELLI. *Guido.* Vol 69. Italian/American Studies.
FRED GARDAPHÉ. *Moustache Pete is Dead! Long Live Moustache Pete!.* Vol 67. Literature/Oral History.
PAOLO RUFFILLI. *Dark Room/Camera oscura.* Vol 66. Poetry.
HELEN BAROLINI. *Crossing the Alps.* Vol 65. Fiction.
COSMO FERRARA. *Profiles of Italian Americans.* Vol 64. Italian Americana.
GIL FAGIANI. *Chianti in Connecticut.* Vol 63. Poetry.
BASSETTI & D'ACQUINO. *Italic Lessons.* Vol 62. Italian/American Studies.
CAVALIERI & PASCARELLI, Eds. *The Poet's Cookbook.* Vol 61. Poetry/Recipes.
EMANUEL DI PASQUALE. *Siciliana.* Vol 60. Poetry.
NATALIA COSTA, Ed. *Bufalini.* Vol 59. Poetry.
RICHARD VETERE. *Baroque.* Vol 58. Fiction.
LEWIS TURCO. *La Famiglia/The Family.* Vol 57. Memoir.
NICK JAMES MILETI. *The Unscrupulous.* Vol 56. Humanities.

BASSETTI. ACCOLLA. D'AQUINO. *Italici: An Encounter with Piero Bassetti.*
   Vol 55. Italian Studies.
GIOSE RIMANELLI. *The Three-legged One.* Vol 54. Fiction.
CHARLES KLOPP. *Bele Antiche Stòrie.* Vol 53. Criticism.
JOSEPH RICAPITO. *Second Wave.* Vol 52. Poetry.
GARY MORMINO. *Italians in Florida.* Vol 51. History.
GIANFRANCO ANGELUCCI. *Federico F.* Vol 50. Fiction.
ANTHONY VALERIO. *The Little Sailor.* Vol 49. Memoir.
ROSS TALARICO. *The Reptilian Interludes.* Vol 48. Poetry.
RACHEL GUIDO DE VRIES. *Teeny Tiny Tino's Fishing Story.*
   Vol 47. Children's Literature.
EMANUEL DI PASQUALE. *Writing Anew.* Vol 46. Poetry.
MARIA FAMÀ. *Looking For Cover.* Vol 45. Poetry.
ANTHONY VALERIO. *Toni Cade Bambara's One Sicilian Night.* Vol 44. Poetry.
EMANUEL CARNEVALI. *Furnished Rooms.* Vol 43. Poetry.
BRENT ADKINS. et al., Ed. *Shifting Borders. Negotiating Places.*
   Vol 42. Conference.
GEORGE GUIDA. *Low Italian.* Vol 41. Poetry.
GARDAPHÈ, GIORDANO, TAMBURRI. *Introducing Italian Americana.*
   Vol 40. Italian/American Studies.
DANIELA GIOSEFFI. *Blood Autumn/Autunno di sangue.* Vol 39. Poetry.
FRED MISURELLA. *Lies to Live By.* Vol 38. Stories.
STEVEN BELLUSCIO. *Constructing a Bibliography.* Vol 37. Italian Americana.
ANTHONY JULIAN TAMBURRI, Ed. *Italian Cultural Studies 2002.*
   Vol 36. Essays.
BEA TUSIANI. *con amore.* Vol 35. Memoir.
FLAVIA BRIZIO-SKOV, Ed. *Reconstructing Societies in the Aftermath of War.*
   Vol 34. History.
TAMBURRI. et al., Eds. *Italian Cultural Studies 2001.* Vol 33. Essays.
ELIZABETH G. MESSINA, Ed. *In Our Own Voices.*
   Vol 32. Italian/American Studies.
STANISLAO G. PUGLIESE. *Desperate Inscriptions.* Vol 31. History.
HOSTERT & TAMBURRI, Eds. *Screening Ethnicity.*
   Vol 30. Italian/American Culture.
G. PARATI & B. LAWTON, Eds. *Italian Cultural Studies.* Vol 29. Essays.
HELEN BAROLINI. *More Italian Hours.* Vol 28. Fiction.
FRANCO NASI, Ed. *Intorno alla Via Emilia.* Vol 27. Culture.
ARTHUR L. CLEMENTS. *The Book of Madness & Love.* Vol 26. Poetry.
JOHN CASEY, et al. *Imagining Humanity.* Vol 25. Interdisciplinary Studies.
ROBERT LIMA. *Sardinia/Sardegna.* Vol 24. Poetry.
DANIELA GIOSEFFI. *Going On.* Vol 23. Poetry.
ROSS TALARICO. *The Journey Home.* Vol 22. Poetry.

EMANUEL DI PASQUALE. *The Silver Lake Love Poems*. Vol 21. Poetry.
JOSEPH TUSIANI. *Ethnicity*. Vol 20. Poetry.
JENNIFER LAGIER. *Second Class Citizen*. Vol 19. Poetry.
FELIX STEFANILE. *The Country of Absence*. Vol 18. Poetry.
PHILIP CANNISTRARO. *Blackshirts*. Vol 17. History.
LUIGI RUSTICHELLI, Ed. *Seminario sul racconto*. Vol 16. Narrative.
LEWIS TURCO. *Shaking the Family Tree*. Vol 15. Memoirs.
LUIGI RUSTICHELLI, Ed. *Seminario sulla drammaturgia*.
    Vol 14. Theater/Essays.
FRED GARDAPHÈ. *Moustache Pete is Dead! Long Live Moustache Pete!*.
    Vol 13. Oral Literature.
JONE GAILLARD CORSI. *Il libretto d'autore. 1860 - 1930*. Vol 12. Criticism.
HELEN BAROLINI. *Chiaroscuro: Essays of Identity*. Vol 11. Essays.
PICARAZZI & FEINSTEIN, Eds. *An African Harlequin in Milan*.
    Vol 10. Theater/Essays.
JOSEPH RICAPITO. *Florentine Streets & Other Poems*. Vol 9. Poetry.
FRED MISURELLA. *Short Time*. Vol 8. Novella.
NED CONDINI. *Quartettsatz*. Vol 7. Poetry.
ANTHONY JULIAN TAMBURRI, Ed. *Fuori: Essays by Italian/American
    Lesbiansand Gays*. Vol 6. Essays.
ANTONIO GRAMSCI. P. Verdicchio. Trans. & Intro. *The Southern Question*.
    Vol 5. Social Criticism.
DANIELA GIOSEFFI. *Word Wounds & Water Flowers*. Vol 4. Poetry. $8
WILEY FEINSTEIN. *Humility's Deceit: Calvino Reading Ariosto Reading Calvino*.
    Vol 3. Criticism.
PAOLO A. GIORDANO, Ed. *Joseph Tusiani: Poet. Translator. Humanist*.
    Vol 2. Criticism.
ROBERT VISCUSI. *Oration Upon the Most Recent Death of Christopher Columbus*.
    Vol 1. Poetry.